TWO ACTION-PACKED ADVENTURE NOVELS IN ONE LOW-COST VOLUME!

VAMPIRE STRIKE

Blade could see the Vampire's glassy eyes widening in consternation. He raised the M-16 to his right shoulder, sighted, and fired. His initial rounds smacked into the lead Vampire's head, catapulting the ghoul backwards.

Sergeant Havoc, Boone, and Thunder took their cue from the Warrior. Each cut loose with skilled precision.

Caught in the open in a withering spray of automatic gunfire, the Vampires were decimated. Six dropped in half as many seconds, their bodies riddled with holes. Two foolishly tried to reach the bus and were cut to ribbons. Only one was left alive; he wheeled and attempted to flee.

PIPELINE STRIKE

Blade squeezed the trigger on the big M-60, the machine gun bucking in his arms, the thunderous blasts music to his ears as the heavy slugs smacked into the charging shrew and stopped the mutant in its tracks. Geysers of blood erupted from its body as it thrashed and convulsed, shrieking like a banshee. He stalked forward, unrelenting in his determination to exterminate the ravenous brute and prevent it from ever killing again.

The shrew, its body riddled with gaping holes, toppled from the cabinets, out of sight.

Had he finished it?

The *Blade Double* Series:
FIRST STRIKE/OUTLANDS STRIKE

BLADE
DOUBLE

VAMPIRE STRIKE/
PIPELINE STRIKE
DAVID ROBBINS

LEISURE BOOKS **NEW YORK CITY**

A LEISURE BOOK®

August 1992

Published by

Dorchester Publishing Co., Inc.
276 Fifth Avenue
New York, NY 10001

VAMPIRE STRIKE Copyright © MCMLXXXIX by David Robbins
PIPELINE STRIKE Copyright © MCMLXXXIX by David Robbins

Printed in the United States of America.

VAMPIRE STRIKE

Dedicated to...
Judy & Joshua & Shane.
And to Bram Stoker,
who started the ball rolling,
and Jeff Rice and Anne Rice
for superbly upholding the tradition.

PRELUDE

But first on earth, as Vampyre sent,
Thy corpse shall from its tomb be rent;
Then ghastly haunt thy native place,
And suck the blood of all thy race;
There from thy daughter, sister, wife,
At midnight drain the stream of life;
Yet loathe the banquet, which perforce
Must feed thy livid living corse.
Thy victims, ere they yet expire,
Shall know the demon for their sire;
As cursing thee, thou cursing them,
Thy flowers are withered on the stem.

Lord Byron
The Giaour
1813

PROLOGUE

The Vampires were aboard.

Ethan Hogue felt his skin tingle as he gazed at the forest bordering the asphalt road. On both sides the dense walls of murky vegetation reared toward the inky sky and the canopy of stars. He heard a rustling noise to his left and raised the lantern in his right hand overhead to increase the radius of its illumination.

"Did you hear something, Ethan?" his sister asked nervously.

"No," Ethan lied. "No, Greta, I didn't."

Greta glanced at the lantern, then at the trees to the left. She knew he was lying, but she refrained from reprimanding him. He was trying to quell her anxiety, and she loved him the more for his concern. "How far are we from Aguanga?"

Ethan stared down the roadway. "A mile. Maybe less."

"We should hurry," Greta urged. She brushed at her blonde bangs.

"Fine by me," Ethan said with a forced nonchalance.

They increased their pace.

Ethan placed his left hand on the Astra Model 357, snug in its brown leather holster on his left hip. The feel of the checkered walnut stocks reassured him and served to calm his jittery nerves. Perhaps he was wrong, he told himself. Perhaps the rustling he'd been hearing for the past five minutes was nothing more than the breeze stirring the nearby foliage. Or perhaps the cause was a harmless nocturnal animal. He shook his head to clear his mind of a vague premonition of doom. What a dope! He was letting his worry get the better of him! A few lousy noises and he was ready to crap his pants! The Vampires had not been reported in the vicinity of Aguanga in over a year.

So why was he getting all bent out of shape?

Ethan grinned at his idiocy, his brown eyes twinkling.

"What's so funny?" Greta asked.

"Look at us," Ethan said. "We're acting like six-year-olds instead of mature adults!"

"A person can never be too careful at night," Greta commented.

"Traveling at night isn't as dangerous as it once was," Ethan remarked. "The Raiders haven't operated in this area for more than a decade, according to Dad, and the Army wiped out most of the mutants. The worst we can bump into is a hungry rabbit."

"I hope you're right," Greta said.

"I know I'm right," Ethan assured her.

"I guess we shouldn't have stayed so late at Aunt Harriet's," Greta mentioned.

"Why not?" Ethan responded. "Aunt Harriet and Uncle Brice are fun to be around. We owe them a visit every now and then."

"I still can't understand the reason they live so far out of town," Greta said.

"What's to understand?" Ethan queried. "They like their privacy."

Greta frowned. "Maybe so. But I know I would never live two miles from the nearest village or city. I like the security of having others close at hand."

"The trouble with you, sis," Ethan observed, "is that you have a postwar mentality."

"What's that supposed to mean?" Greta demanded.

"World War Three took place over a century ago," Ethan noted. "Yet you, and a lot of other people, act like the war ended recently. You seem to think that California is sitll crawling with muties and Raiders, when it isn't. Oh, there are some, but they're confined mainly to the mountains and the uninhabited stretches. The area around Aguanga is relatively safe. There's no reason in the world a person can't live outside of town.''

''You're forgetting the Vampires,'' Greta said.

''I'm not forgetting them,'' Ethan stated. ''But a Vampire hasn't been seen around here in a long time.''

''They'll show up again,'' Greta declared.

''You don't know it for sure,'' Ethan disagreed. ''They may never come back.''

''They'll be back,'' Greta insisted. ''They know there are hundreds of women living in or near Aguanga.''

''How would they know that?'' Ethan inquired.

''They have their ways,'' Greta said.

Ethan snickered. ''You've been listening to the old-timers. They believe the Vampires are endowed with supernatural powers.''

''Don't you?'' Greta questioned.

''Hell, no,'' Ethan said. ''There must be a logical explanation for the Vampires and their activities.''

''Like what?'' Greta queried.

''If I knew the answer,'' Ethan said, ''I'd be famous. I'd lead an expedition to the Dead Zone and wipe them out.''

''No one has ever gone into the San Diego Dead Zone and lived to tell about it,'' Greta remarked. ''No one in their right mind would enter a Dead Zone.''

''The Vampires live in the Dead Zone,'' Ethan said. ''And the only way to destroy them is to find their base and exterminate them.''

''Maybe the Vampires live in the Dead Zone,'' Greta mentioned. ''Maybe they don't. All we have to go on is rumor.''

''Where else could they live?'' Ethan questioned. ''They must have a base somewhere.''

There was a sharp retort to their right, the distinct snapping of a branch.

Both halted.

''What was that?'' Greta asked apprehensively, her green eyes wide.

Ethan scanned the forest, his left hand tightening on his revolver. He debated whether to extinguish the lantern. Without the light, Greta and he would be harder to spot. Both were wearing dark clothing; he wore brown pants and a black shirt, while his sister was wearing green slacks and a cinnamon-colored blouse. But whatever was lurking in the woods might possess better night vision. If he turned out the lantern, they would have the advantage. He decided to leave the lantern on.

"Let's keep going," Greta advised.

Brother and sister hastened onward. The night seemed exceptionally still and silent. Not so much as a cricket chirped.

Once Ethan thought he detected a glimmer of white to his right. He surveyed the vegetation, but he could see nothing out of the ordinary.

"Look!" Greta exclaimed happily after several minutes.

A cluster of lights were visible ahead.

"Aguanga!" Ethan declared, intensely relieved. He ran his left hand through his brown hair.

"I can't wait to get home," Greta said.

They pressed forward until the first residence was discernible, outlined against the backdrop of the ebony heavens by a bright porch light. The interior lights were all out.

"McCallister's," Ethan commented.

"I hear they got a new dog," Greta said.

"Yeah," Ethan confirmed. "I saw it yesterday. A big, mean mongrel. If anyone comes within ten feet of their fence, the mutt barks like crazy." He paused. "I also saw Bob yesterday. He says he's thinking of asking you to the dance."

"What?" Greta responded in surprise. "I didn't know Bob likes me."

"He's seventeen, you know," Ethan said.

"So? I'm twenty, and I don't date boys," Greta stated stiffly.

"I wouldn't call Bob a boy," Ethan said. "And since when did you become so fussy about the guys you date? You keep this up, and you'll be an old maid."

"You wouldn't understand," Greta said.

"What's to understand? My sis is stuck up," Ethan declared.

"I am not!" Greta responded.

Ethan stared at the McCallister house as they stepped onto

the sidewalk next to the wooden fence. The front porch was ten yards away.

"That's odd," Greta commented.

"What is?" Ethan inquired.

"Where's their dog?" Greta asked. "I thought you said it barks at anyone who comes near their fence."

"Maybe they took it inside for the night," Ethan suggested. "Bob was taking a liking to the mutt."

Greta scrutinized the McCallister home, wondering if there was any significance to the dog's absence. She took another step, then abruptly stopped, her eyes narrowing.

Ethan halted. "What's the matter?"

"Their front door is open," Greta said.

Ethan gazed at the house. The front door was indeed open a hands-breadth. "So?"

"Why would they leave their front door open?" Greta queried.

"Give me a break!" Ethan replied. "They're probably letting some fresh air in. What's the big deal?"

"Go check," Greta said.

"What?" Ethan responded. "You're nuts. I'm not about to make a fool of myself."

Greta looked at her brother with a pleading expression. "Please, Ethan. For me?"

Ethan sighed. "What am I supposed to say when one of them comes to the door?"

"You'll think of something," Greta assured him. "Please do it. I have a bad feeling about this."

"Over a stupid door being open?" Ethan said testily.

"Please," Greta insisted.

Ethan gave in. He never could refuse his sister. "Okay. I'll go check. I just hope their dog doesn't attack me." He extended his right arm. "Here. Take the lantern."

Greta took the lantern and lifted it above her head.

"I'm going to look like a dope," Ethan mumbled as he gripped the top of the gate, a slatted affair painted white like the rest of the picket fence.

"Be careful," Greta said.

"Nothing will happen," Ethan asserted flatly, then pushed

on the waist-high gate. Normally the gate would swing inward on well-oiled hinges, but not this time.

The thing wouldn't budge.

Perplexed, Ethan tried to open the gate again with the same result. It moved a fraction, then stopped. He knew the McCallisters had not bothered to install a lock on the gate.

So why wouldn't it move?

Ethan leaned over the top of the gate and spied the vague form sprawled at its base. He froze, his eyes registering the distinctive black and white markings he'd seen on the McCallister's new dog. The mongrel was lying flat on its side.

"What is it?" Greta inquired.

Ethan leaned over the gate, striving to recall the dog's name. Homer. Bob had told him the mutt was named Homer. "Homer! Remember me!"

Homer remained motionless.

"What is it?" Greta repeated, taking a step toward her brother.

"I don't know," Ethan said, reaching down to pat the dog. Was the mutt asleep? His right hand patted the dog's head and started to stroke its neck. A sticky substance caked his fingers. He straightened, horrified, insight dawning. Of *course* the dog wasn't asleep!

The mongrel was dead!

"Ethan?" Greta said, touching his right shoulder.

Ethan raised his right hand into the lantern light. He gaped at the crimson coating, dazed. Fear flooded over him as he realized the truth; his earlier premonition had been correct. He'd managed to convince himself everything was okay, but now he knew better. He should have heeded his presentiment.

The Vampires were in Aguanga!

Greta spotted the blood on his hand and gasped.

"We're heading home," Ethan declared. He wiped the blood off on his pants leg.

"The McCallisters . . ." Greta said, staring at the house.

"Forget them," Ethan stated, drawing his revolver. "We need to worry about Mom and Dad."

"You don't think something has happened to them?" Greta questioned in alarm.

"Let's find out," Ethan said grimly.

They raced to the north through an unusually quiet town. Except for the streetlights and a few porch lights, Aguanga was dark and eerie.

Ethan gazed at an unlit house to the right. Not everyone would be asleep at this time of night. There should be homes with their inside lights on. But there weren't any.

They reached an intersection and took a left.

"Look!" Greta exclaimed. "They have their lights on!"

Frame houses lined both sides of the street, four on each side, and all of the homes were amply lit except for the first residence on the left. But even as they watched, the second house on the left went totally dark.

"Mom and Dad!" Ethan cried, racing along the sidewalk toward the last home on the left. His home.

Greta sprinted alongside her brother, the lantern bobbing and swaying in her hand.

They were abreast of the third home when all the inner lights flicked out.

"Damn!" Ethan snapped in mounting frustration. His black boots pounded on the sidewalk.

"Please!" Greta said in despair. "Please!"

They came to the edge of the Hogue property, an acre of land with the house situated 20 yards from the street, and angled across the front lawn.

Ethan took the lead, dashing for the front porch. He was 25 feet from the cement steps leading to the porch before he perceived the front door was wide open. "No!" he shouted, cocking the Astra on the run.

From within the Hogue residence arose a terrified screech.

"Mom!" Ethan cried. He reached the steps and darted onto the porch. Ignoring his own safety, he plunged into the house.

Every light was simultaneously turned off.

Ethan stopped in the center of the pitch-black living room. Someone must have killed the current to the house! But how? He squinted, waiting for his eyes to adjust, and listened. "Dad? Mom?"

There was no answer.

Ethan cautiously moved toward the rear of the house, toward

the kitchen. He leveled the Astra, his finger caressing the trigger.

A sibilant titter sounded upstairs.

"Dad? Mom?" Ethan called, turning and heading for the stairs. He knew the house like the back of his hand, and he could navigate in the dark with ease. Skirting the couch and a rocking chair, he arrived at the base of the stairway and paused.

Someone tittered again.

His gun arm steady, he advanced up the stairs. He was three steps from the top when he halted. In his haste and anxiety over his parents, he'd completely forgotten about his sister! Where was she? Waiting outside? He couldn't see the glow of the lantern anywhere below.

What if something had happened to her!

"Greta?" Ethan yelled.

A foul stench suddenly assailed his nostrils.

Ethan faced the top of the stairs, his breath catching in his throat at the sight of the pale, scarecrow-like figure perched above him wearing only a black loincloth. Glassy eyes glared at him.

A Vampire!

Ethan squeezed the trigger as the Vampire swung its right arm. Excruciating agony rocked his jaw and his head was lashed backwards. His ears ringing from the deafening boom of the Astra, stunned by the Vampire's blow, he tottered on the brink of the step.

The Vampire snarled and struck a second time, a hard fist to the midriff.

Ethan lost his balance and tumbled down the stairs. He landed on his back at the bottom, bruised and battered and stunned. Shaking his head to clear his sluggish mind, he rose onto his elbows.

With a hiss like an enraged cat the Vampire began to descend the stairway.

Frantic, overcome by abject fright, Ethan heaved to his feet and spun. He ran out the front door to the yard.

"Ethan! Help me!" Greta screeched from off to the left.

Ethan peered into the night, catching sight of four white shapes loping to the south. One of them appeared to be carrying a burden draped over its left shoulder.

"Ethan! Help!"

The burden was Greta!

Ethan raced in pursuit of the four Vampires and his sister. The creatures seemed to flow over the ground, avoiding obstacles with consummate ease.

"Help!" Greta wailed.

Gritting his teeth in determination, Ethan poured on the speed. He was one of the fastest young men in Aguanga, but his speed was inconsequential compared to the unearthly swiftness of the Vampires.

"Ethan!" Greta cried in despair, her voice growing fainter.

Ethan refused to acknowledge defeat. He kept after them, covering five hundred yards, then a mile.

The Vampires were barely visible.

For over two miles Ethan chased the vile creatures. Twice he tripped and almost fell. Once he banged his shins on a small boulder. He crossed a field, a stretch of forest, and another field.

Where were they?

The Vampires had vanished in a thick stand of trees.

An acute pain was developing in Ethan's right side. His breathing was ragged, and his legs were ready to buckle at any moment. He reached the stand of trees and halted, leaning on a trunk for support.

He'd lost them!

And lost his sister!

Ethan sagged to his knees, misery engulfing him. No one had ever been rescued from the clutches of the Vampires. He would never see his sister again! Tears welled in his eyes, but he suppressed the impulse to cry. Instead he rose unsteadily and shuffled toward Aguanga. His parents were still in the town, and although the possibility of their being alive was remote, he could not simply abandon his folks. The Vampires specialized in abducting young women; a middle-aged couple would not appeal to them in the least except as victims of their renowned blood lust.

A stiff wind from the west stirred his brown hair.

He needed a plan. Ascertaining whether his parents were alive was the first step. Should he go from house to house afterward searching for survivors of the raid? Or should he locate a telephone? Phones were a rare luxury in Aguanga. The Upshaws owned one, and hopefully they had already used it to call for help. Unfortunately the phone lines in rural areas were beset by problems and service was deplorable. World War Three had totally disrupted all utilities and forms of mass communication, and while some semblance of order had been restored, conditions were a far cry from their former efficient estate.

A twig cracked behind him.

Ethan turned, his reflexes sluggish. He caught only a glimpse of a pale figure holding an object in its hands, and then that object crashed into his forehead and the world abruptly tilted on its axis. Cimmerian darkness engulfed him, and with a groan Ethan pitched into oblivion.

CHAPTER ONE

The pair of thundering jets swooped out of the northwest, dropping to treetop level in seconds and roaring toward Highway 79. They streaked over a large clearing adjacent to the highway and banked in a tight loop, their speed rapidly decreasing. Both jets slowed to a complete stop above the clearing and hovered for 30 seconds, then sank to the grass accompanied by a muted whine.

A small door located just under the center portion of the canopy on the jet nearest the road opened and a green rope ladder unfurled to the ground. The first occupant appeared, a veritable giant of a man squeezed through the doorway and clambered down the ladder. He turned and stared at the two jeeps parked alongside the highway. The giant stood seven feet in height, and his awesome physique was powerfully muscled. His eyes were gray, his hair dark with a comma hanging over his brows. A black leather vest and green fatigue pants served to clothe his massive form. A Bowie knife was in a leather sheath on each hip. In his left hand was a Commando Arms Carbine. A camouflage backpack rested between his shoulder blades. He moved several feet from the jet, then raised his right fist overhead and pumped it three times.

Both jets disgorged other figures.

The second man down was a lean six-footer attired in buckskins. His shoulder-length hair was brown, as were his keen eyes. A matched pair of Hombre revolvers were strapped around his lean waist. He carried an M-16, and like the giant he toted a backpack.

Next came a full-blooded Indian wearing a fringed buckskin shirt, pants, and moccasins. Black hair fell past his broad shoulders. His brown eyes scanned the nearby vegetation as he adjusted his backpack with his left hand while cradling an M-16 in his right arm.

From the second jet came three more. A slim woman climbed to the ground. She wore fatigues, combat boots, and a backpack. An M-16 was held in her left hand. Fine brown hair draped almost to the small of her back. Her face was exceptionally attractive, hightlighted by her alert brown eyes, her high, prominent cheekbones, and thin lips.

Next down was a man who radiated an air of supreme confidence. He stood six feet tall and weighed close to 200 pounds, and every square inch was solid muscle. He was wearing a brown T-shirt, fatigue pants, and black combat boots. His backpack was snug against his back. An M-16 was slung over his right shoulder, and like the Indian and the woman he was armed with a pair of Colt Stainless Steel Officers Model 45's in holsters on each hip. His blue eyes gazed at the jeeps.

The last to appear was decidedly different from the others. Unlike the rest, the only clothing he wore was a black loincloth. Unlike the others, his sole weapon in evidence was an M-16. And unlike his companions, his five-foot-eight frame was covered with a coat of short, light brown fur from head to toe. His face resembled that of a bear; he had a receding brow, deep, dark eyes, circular ears, concave cheeks, and a pointed chin. His elongated nostrils flared as he sniffed the air, and his lips curled upwards to display a mouthful of tapered teeth. Both his upper arms and shoulders were especially dense and rippling with layers of muscle.

The giant waved his right arm toward the jeeps, and the others keyed on his signal and formed a single file behind him as he advanced to the side of Highway 79. The morning sun was warm, the air humid.

A portly, balding man dressed in beige pants and a brown shirt was seated at the wheel of the closest jeep. He smiled as he slid out and extended his right hand. "Hello. I'm Cyrus Upshaw. You must be Blade."

The giant nodded as he shook Upshaw's hand. "Yes. Thank you for meeting us."

Upshaw was impressed by the giant's steely grip. He released Blade's hand and motioned at the jeep. "Thank you for coming. Why don't we get in and I'll explain everything on the way to Aguanga?"

"Good," Blade said. He glanced over his right shoulder at his unit. "Grizzly and Athena with me. Boone, Thunder, and Havoc in the other jeep."

The party promptly divided, each member taking a seat in the appropriate vehicle.

Upshaw reclaimed his position at the wheel.

Blade sat down on the passenger side. "Ready when you are," he commented.

Upshaw glanced at the jets. "What about them?"

"They'll be flying back to Los Angeles in a few minutes," Blade replied.

"I've never seen jets like those," Upshaw mentioned. "What are they?"

"VTOLs," Blade answered. "They can attain supersonic speeds, yet they also possess vertical-takeoff-and-landing capabilities."

"Like a helicopter," Upshaw observed.

"Sort of," Blade said. "They transport us wherever our assignments take us."

Upshaw started the jeep. "I've read about the Freedom Force in the papers, but I never thought I'd meet all of you in person."

"The Force goes where it's needed," Blade remarked. "If trouble develops anywhere in the Freedom Federation, we're sent to deal with the situation."

Upshaw pulled out, heading the jeep to the south. He gazed

in the rearview mirror to insure the second jeep was following him. "The Federation leaders had the right idea when they formed the Force," he said. "Taking one volunteer from each Federation faction and creating a special, elite fighting team was brilliant."

"And necessary," Blade stated. "It's been one hundred and five years since World War Three. The seven factions composing the Freedom Federation face constant threats to the Federation's existence. We needed a combat-ready strike force to deal with the menaces that continually crop up."

Upshaw looked over his left shoulder at the bear-man seated in back of the giant. "I forget. Which Federation faction is he from?"

"I can talk, you know," the bear man declared in a raspy tone. "The name is Grizzly, and I'm from the Civilized Zone."

Upshaw made a coughing noise. "Sorry. I didn't mean to upset you."

"I'll bet," Grizzly cracked dryly.

"You're a mutant," Upshaw noted. "Or more correctly, a hybrid."

"No fooling!" Grizzly retorted. "What was your first clue?"

"You know what I mean," Upshaw said defensively. "We don't see many mutants like you in California. Oh, there are a lot of the wild kind, the mutations produced by the enormous levels of radiation and all the chemical toxins unleashed on the environment during World War Three. We see more than our share of three-headed animals and other deformities. But we don't see many like you."

"That's because I'm the result of genetic engineering," Grizzly said. "Genetically developed hybrids aren't as numerous. We're unique," he added proudly.

Upshaw negotiated a curve in the highway. "It's hard to believe how much the country has changed since World War Three. The government of the U.S. collapsed, and now we have a lot of groups scattered all over the landscape. California was fortunate. We were one of the few states to retain our administrative identity after the war."

"True," Blade spoke up. He reflected on the current state of affairs resulting in his present mission. Seven factions had banded together into a protective alliance dubbed the Freedom Federation. The Free State of California, as it was now called, had been the last member admitted to the Federation. The governor of California, as a token of good will and commitment, had graciously offered to base the Federation's new tactical unit, the Force, in Los Angeles, and to utilize California's VTOLs as the primary means of transport. And here he was, the leader of the Freedom Force, leading his people into action once again. He hadn't expected to be sent on a mission so close to LA. Aguanga was approximately 80 miles from the metropolis.

"I know about the Civilized Zone," Upshaw was saying. "How the remnants of the U.S. government withdrew to Denver during the war and reorganized a new government in the Midwest. I also know about the other Freedom factions." He glanced into the rearview mirror. "Which one is the young lady from?"

"Mr. Upshaw, meet Athena Morris," Blade introduced her. "She's our newest addition to the Force, and she hails from California."

"Really?" Upshaw said in surprise.

Athena leaned forward. "Is there something wrong with having a woman on the Force?"

"No," Upshaw stated hastily. "Of course not. But it wasn't mentioned in the papers."

"I just joined, officially, about three hours ago," Athena disclosed.

"What did you do before you joined the Force?" Upshaw asked.

"I was a journalist for the *Times*," Athena replied.

"Say!" Upshaw exclaimed. "Aren't you the one who's been writing all those features on the Force? I seem to remember your byline."

Athena beamed. "You do, huh? Yep, that's me."

"Why would a journalist want to join the Force?" Upshaw inquired. "You're putting your life on the line every day."

"It's simple," Athena said, lowering her voice conspiratorially. "I'm as crazy as the rest of these turkeys!"

"Speak for yourself, wench," Grizzly chimed in.

Upshaw glanced at Blade. "You have quite a crew, don't you?"

"You don't know the half of it," Blade said.

"Refresh my memory," Upshaw prompted. "Where are the others from?"

"The Indian you saw, Thunder, is a Flathead from Montana," Blade detailed. "The gunman with the revolvers is Boone, and he's from the Dakota Territory. And the soldier, Sergeant Havoc, is the best noncom in the California military. He has black belts in karate and judo and a brown in aikido."

Upshaw's forehead creased. "There are two members from California in the Force? I thought it was supposed to be one from each Federation faction?"

"We've been forced to make some adjustments," Blade said. "We've already lost two men. One was from the Clan, and the second was sent by the Moles, both of which are based in Minnesota."

"Isn't the group you're from based in Minnesota too?" Upshaw queried.

"Yes," Blade confirmed. "The Family lives in northern Minnesota, in a compound designated the Home."

Upshaw grinned. "Quaint names."

"The man who founded our survivalist compound believed in certain basic values," Blade explained. "He incorporated those values when he formed his survivalist retreat."

"I've read a lot about you," Upshaw went on. "They say you were the head of the Warriors, the guardians of the Home."

"I still am the top Warrior," Blade mentioned. "I've been juggling both responsibilities."

"You head the Warriors and the Force?" Upshaw said. "You must be one tough son of a gun."

"Him? He's a cream puff," Grizzly interjected.

"Now that we've satisfied your curiosity," Blade said to Upshaw, "why don't you fill me in on what happened here last night?"

"Gladly," Upshaw said. "Aguanga was hit by the Vampires."

"The Vampires?" Blade repeated quizzically.

"You've never heard of them?" Upshaw inquired.

"Just in passing," Blade said. "When General Gallagher proposed this assignment, he told me a town had been raided by them. But he didn't go into detail. I assumed he was referring to a band of Raiders."

"There wasn't enough time for Gallagher to explain everything," Athena stated in the general's defense. Gallagher had been instrumental in helping her to get onto the Force despite Blade's initial objections, and she felt she owed the general a debt.

"True," Blade conceded. "We were sent out on short notice."

"Besides," Athena stated, "I can fill you in on the Vampires. I know as much about them as anyone. I've seen scores of stories on them."

"Be my guest," Blade said.

"The Vampires first appeared about seventy years ago," Athena elaborated. "They've raided small communities and towns every year or so since then. They always attack at night. They've completely wiped out a few settlements—"

"What is the purpose behind their raids?" Blade asked, interrupting. "Are they after food? Valuables? What?"

"Women, primarily," Athena said. "They've abducted hundreds of wolmen, and a few dozen men, in the seven decades they've been raiding southern California."

"Why do they take so many prisoners?" Blade questioned.

"No one knows for sure," Athena responded. "There are a lot of rumors. Some people say the Vampires suck the blood of their captives."

"Are you serious?" Blade asked.

"According to the rumors, the Vampires feast on the blood of their victims," Athena stated. "We both know how unreliable rumors can be."

"I suppose I shouldn't be shocked," Blade remarked. "After all the cannibals, mutants, scavengers, and other degenerates I've encountered, blood-sucking deviates are nothing unusual."

"Are you familiar with the legend of the Vampires?" Athena inquired.

"No," Blade admitted.

"You told me once that your Family has hundreds of

thousands of books preserved in a concrete building," Athena commented. "Don't any of those books deal with vampires?"

Blade pondered for a moment. "I can recall a book from my schooling days. A friend of mine named Geronimo did a book report on it. The novel was by a writer called Stoker, I believe. The story concerned a vampire, a Count-somebody-or-other."

Athena grinned. "Count Dracula. He was the title character in a book called Dracula published in 1897."

"You seem to know a lot about the subject," Blade noted.

"I'm a journalist, remember?" Athena responded. "Any journalist worthy of the name performs lengthy background research on a story to be covered. I had to write up a few of the Vampire stories for the *Times*, and naturally I conducted a study of the vampire legend in general," Athena explained. "Legends concerning vampires have been around for as long as the human race has been in existence. Traditionally speaking, vampires were regarded as inhuman creatures, either corpses or spirits who arose from the dead to feast on the blood of the living. Scores of books and films featured the vampire in one form or another before the war."

"But vampires aren't real," Blade said.

"So far as we know," Athena stated. "But the legends have persisted for ages. So when the raids began seventy years ago—always at night, and always by creatures seemingly endowed with supernatural powers—it's understandable why the creatures were called Vampires."

"What else do we know about them?" Blade probed.

"Not much, I'm afraid," Athena said. "They usually kill all witnesses to their raids."

"Where do they come from?" Blade asked.

Athena shrugged. "No one knows. The Army has attempted to find their lair without success."

Upshaw cleared his throat. "Some people believe the Vampires come from a Dead Zone."

"What's the Dead Zone?" Grizzly inquired.

"Not *the* Dead Zone," Athena corrected the mutant. "*A* Dead Zone. Dead Zones are areas that sustained a direct nuclear hit during the war."

"My Family refers to them as Hot Spots," Blade said.

"Whatever," Athena declared. "San Diego suffered a direct hit, and Aguanga is only sixty miles away."

"Aguanga was fortunate," Upshaw interjected. "Aguanga was just outside the blast radius, and the prevailing winds blew the radiation to the southeast, sparing the town."

"Why do some people believe the Vampires come from the San Diego Dead Zone?" Blade questioned.

"Because the Army has tracked them to the edge of the Dead Zone twice," Athena answered. "Each time the Vampires had raided a town and taken a lot of captives. Each time the Army used dogs to follow the trail. And each time the trail led into the Dead Zone."

"Did the Army go in after them?" Blade asked.

"Once," Athena replied. "The first time."

"And what happened?" Blade asked.

"The platoon never returned," Athena disclosed.

Blade lapsed into a reflective silence. Was it possible, he speculated, that General Gallagher had deliberately refrained from revealing all the pertinent information pertaining to the Vampires because the general had been afraid the mission would have been turned down? As the head of the Force, Blade exercised veto power over every proposed assignment. Perhaps, knowing the Force had just returned from a deadly strike in Oregon, the general had intentionally withheld the full scope of intelligence available on the Vampires for fear Blade would decide the unit wasn't up to another sustained conflict so soon after Oregon.

Perhaps.

But he lacked proof.

So, for the time being at least, he would extend Gallagher the benefit of the doubt.

"What are you thinking about?" Athena queried.

"Nothing," Blade told her.

"Look!" Upshaw declared, staring at a cluster of buildings ahead. "There's Aguanga."

CHAPTER TWO

Aguanga was a typical community, arranged with a network of side streets encircling a small central business district consisting of a few old-fashioned stores.

Cyrus Upshaw drove through the town until he reached an intersection with a STOP sign. He pressed on the brakes briefly, then took a right. "The southwest section of Aguanga was hit the hardest," he elaborated. "I suspect the Vampires approached town through the Cleveland National Forest. They must have bypassed the Mission Indian Reservation because no one spotted them until they were in Aguanga."

"What tactics did they employ?" Blade inquired.

"They're a crafty bunch, I'll grant them that," Upshaw stated. "They waited until it was late, ten o'clock or so, before they came in. There were dozens of them, and they'd hit an entire street at one shot. Their usual technique involved killing the power to a residence, then entering. All women between the ages of sixteen and thirty, or thereabouts, were taken prisoner. Very few men were taken. Most of the men were killed."

"How many homes were attacked?" Athena asked.

"Forty-four," Upshaw answered. "Aguanga has grown a lot since the war. Our population is slightly over two thousand." He paused and frowned. "The raid could have been much worse than it was."

"How many casualties were there?" Blade questioned.

Upshaw's cheeks seemed to sag. "Seventy-three were slain. Thirty-two women are missing and five men. Surprisingly, they spared the youngest children." He stared at a house on the left, the fourth in a row. "There's the Hogue home. There's a young man here worth seeing. His mother and father were killed last night, and his older sister is one of those missing."

"Why should we see him?" Blade queried.

"He's one of the few who actually got a glimpse of the Vampires," Upshaw replied. "Even tried to shoot one. The fiends nearly split his skull wide open." He executed a tight U-turn and parked alongside the curb.

Blade stared at the homes lining the street. "Did you have guards posted around the town?"

"No," Upshaw said. "What good would it do? The Vampires possess acute senses. They'd spot our guards long before the guards saw them. The guards would have been killed needlessly. They wouldn't have helped last night, and they wouldn't have helped a year ago."

"What happened a year ago?" Blade inquired.

"Three women disappeared," Upshaw responded. "We never did find them despite an extended search. No one saw them being abducted, but everyone believes the Vampires were responsible."

"The Vampires seldom strike the same town twice in a row," Athena commented. "Aguanga is an exception. Usually the Vampires range all over southern California. Predicting their attacks has been impossible."

Upshaw turned the key and the jeep's engine sputtered and stopped. He climbed out. "Do you want to talk to the Hogue boy?"

"How old is he?" Blade asked.

"Nineteen," Upshaw replied.

"Is it all right to disturb him?" Blade questioned.

"The doctor said a short visit was permissible," Upshaw said.

"Okay. But we won't stay long," Blade stated. He emerged from the jeep, then bent over to gaze at Grizzly and Athena. "Wait here."

"I'd like to come," Athena said.

"The fewer who go in, the better," Blade responded. "It sounds like our witness is very seriously injured. We don't want to strain him more than absolutely necessary."

"Do you want us to twiddle our thumbs while we're waiting?" Grizzly quipped.

"You can sharpen your claws," Blade suggested and straightened. He walked to the second jeep, now parked to the rear of the first.

Sergeant Havoc was seated on the passenger side across from the driver. "Orders, sir?" Havoc asked out the window.

"Stay put," Blade directed.

"Yes, sir."

Cyrus Upshaw started toward the Hogue home. "If you'll come with me . . ." he said to the giant.

"Ethan Hogue is a fine young man," Upshaw commented. "I knew his father and mother well. I'll miss them."

Blade followed Upshaw onto the porch. "Tell me," he said. "How were the seventy-three casualties killed? Was the blood drained from their bodies?"

"No," Upshaw replied. "Most of those killed were husbands and the older sons or brothers of the kidnapped women. And women over thirty or so were also killed. Ethan's mother, for instance, was forty-nine. In every case their death was violent, brutal. Either their necks were snapped or their throats were torn apart." He shuddered at the memory.

"Let's go in," Blade advised.

Upshaw knocked on the wooden door and waited.

Within seconds a plump, elderly woman in a gray dress opened the door. "Mayor Upshaw! What a surprise."

"Harriet," Upshaw said, "I'd like you to meet Blade, the leader of the special team the governor sent to take care of the Vampires. Blade, this is Harriet Tofani, Ethan's aunt."

"Hello," Blade stated.

"I'm pleased to meet you," Harriet mentioned. "It's about damn time the Vampires were eliminated!"

"We'll do our best," Blade assured her.

"Harriet, we need to see Ethan," Upshaw informed her. "Doc Cook gave his permission."

Harriet stepped to one side. "Come on in. Ethan is upstairs, resting in bed. Doc Cook says he won't be on his feet again for at least two weeks." Her mouth curled downward. "The poor boy! And to think of sweet Greta in the hands of those monsters!"

Upshaw moved toward the stairway. "We'll only be a few minutes."

"Would you like some tea?" Harriet asked Blade.

"No, thanks," the Warrior responded.

"How about some cookies? Or cake? I have a chocolate cake fresh out of the oven."

"Thank you. But not now," Blade told her. He stayed on the mayor's heels as Upshaw went up the stairs and took a left, proceeding to a bedroom at the end of the hall. The door was open.

Blade towered a foot and a half over the mayor. He could see into the bedroom as they walked down the hallway, and he spied the Hogue youth on a bed against the far wall. Ethan Hogue's head was swaddled in white bandages and his eyes were closed.

Upshaw tapped lightly on the door jamb.

Ethan opened his eyes and swiveled his head in the direction of the doorway, grimacing in discomfort. "Mayor Upshaw," he said thickly, then licked his lips.

"Doc Cook said we could talk to you for a few minutes," Upshaw stated. "Are you feeling up to it?"

Ethan's eyes shifted to the giant.

"This is Blade," Upshaw explained. "He's the head of the Force."

Ethan's eyes brightened. "I've read about you," he said weakly.

"Are you up to talking?" Upshaw reiterated.

"Sure," Ethan replied.

The mayor and the Warrior stepped over to the bed.

"How are you feeling?" Upshaw asked.

"A little better," Ethan answered. "The doctor gave me

something for the pain. Now all I have is a dull ache.'' He tried to grin. ''And twenty-one stitches, of course.''

''Ethan,'' Blade said, ''I'll make this as short as possible. I understand you actually saw the Vampires. Is that right?''

''Yes,'' Ethan confirmed.

''Can you describe them?'' Blade questioned him.

''It was dark,'' Ethan began. ''I couldn't see them clearly. I stood within a few feet of one of them, but I was scared to death at the time. All I remember is very white skin. They were real thin too. And they didn't wear much clothing.'' He paused. ''Oh. They can run like deer. I've never seen anyone run as fast as they can.''

''Did you note any facial features?'' Blade asked the youth.

''No,'' Ethan said. ''Sorry.''

''Don't be sorry,'' Blade told him. ''You were under great stress.''

''Is there anything else you can tell us?'' Upshaw interjected. ''Anything that may be important?''

Ethan reflected for a moment. ''Yeah. The four I went after, the ones who took Grace, were heading to the south.''

''That's good,'' Blade said. ''It narrows down the area we'll need to search to find their trail.''

''There's not much else I can help you with,'' Ethan remarked forlornly.

''Did you see any weapons?'' Blade thought to ask.

''No,'' Ethan responded. ''None of the Vampires carried guns or knives or anything. But one of them did hit me with something.''

''Your Uncle Brice found a big, bloody rock near where he discovered you,'' Upshaw disclosed. ''The Vampire hit you with the rock.''

''I don't have any further questions,'' Blade commented. He turned to leave.

''Blade . . .'' Ethan said softly.

Blade glanced at the young man.

''They took my sister!'' Ethan exclaimed, tears filling his eyes. ''Please don't let them kill her! Bring her home safe and sound!''

Upshaw placed his right hand on Ethan's shoulder. ''Calm

down, son. Blade and his people will do everything in their power to save Greta and the others. You get some sleep now.''

Ethan mustered a feeble smile. ''Okay.'' He closed his eyes and instantly dozed off.

Blade descended to the living room, Upshaw behind him.

Harriet Tofani was sitting in a blue easy chair, knitting. She went to rise.

''Don't get up,'' Blade said. ''We'll let ourselves out.''

''Are you sure you won't have some tea and cake?'' Harriet asked.

''We have work to do,'' Blade stated. He smiled and exited the home.

''Can we lend you any assistance?'' Upshaw inquired as they returned to the jeeps.

''Thanks,'' Blade stated, ''but from here on out, it's up to us.'' He halted on the sidewalk between the vehicles. ''Fall in,'' he barked.

The Force members promptly climbed from the jeeps and formed a single line on the sidewalk as the Warrior backed onto the grass. They stood at attention awaiting their instructions. Athena was on the right, then Grizzly, Boone, Thunder, and Sergeant Havoc.

Blade clasped his hands behind his broad back. ''Thirty-two women and five men were abducted from this town last night by Vampires. Our objective is twofold: to save those who were kidnapped and to exterminate the Vampires.''

''Blade,'' Boone interrupted. ''What in the world are Vampires?''

''I don't know,'' Blade admitted. ''They could be humans, mutants, or hybrids. Whatever they are, they've been raiding southern California for seventy years. The Force is going to put a permanent end to their depredations.''

''Sir,'' Sergeant Havoc declared. ''Do we have an estimate of enemy strength?''

''Enemy strength is unknown,'' Blade answered. ''A conservative guess would be several dozen, minimum. But there could be hundreds.''

Grizzly grinned. ''My kind of fight.''

''Our first step is to find their trail,'' Blade directed. ''Grizzly,

I want Thunder and you to conduct a sweep pattern. Start in the back yard of this house. I doubt the Vampires could completely cover their tracks, not with thirty-seven captives in tow. Get moving.''

Thunder and Grizzly jogged off.

Mayor Upshaw, standing near the second jeep, shook his head. "The Vampires never leave tracks. Our best hunters couldn't find their trail."

"The Army has tracked them twice," Blade noted.

"But they used dogs," Upshaw mentioned.

"Thunder is an outstanding tracker," Blade said. "If they leave so much as a smudge on the ground, he'll find it. And as for Grizzly, his sense of smell is better than a bloodhound's. They'll pick up the trail."

"What about us?" Athena asked.

"We wait," Blade replied. He stared at the lanky gunfighter. "Boone, get General Gallagher on the horn."

Boone knelt, placed his M-16 on the sidewalk, and removed his backpack. He unfastened the upper flap, revealing a compact military radio.

"I understand you're from the Dakota Territory," Upshaw commented while watching the gunman fire up the unit.

"From the Cavalry," Boone said, referring to the Federation faction in control of the Dakota Territory.

"What do you think of California?" Upshaw asked.

"Let me put it this way," Boone said, adjusting a black headset with an adjustable boom mike over his ears. "I can't wait until my hitch is over and I can return to Dakota."

"Force members serve for a year, don't they?" Upshaw queried.

"Don't remind me," Boone stated. He flicked a toggle and began talking into the mike. "Bravo-Lima-Alfa-Delta-Echo to Big Bad Wolf. Repeat. Bravo-Lima-Alfa-Delta-Echo to Big Bad Wolf. Do you copy? Over."

Mayor Upshaw's face betrayed his bewilderment at the military jargon.

A small, square speaker in the upper right corner of the radio suddenly crackled with static. "This is Big Bad Wolf speaking," a gruff voice declared.

"One moment for Sir Galahad," Boone said, removing the headset and extending it to Blade.

Feeling slightly self-conscious at having to use the general's code words, Blade took the headset and aligned the band over his head. "Silent mode," he said to Boone.

The Cavalryman flicked another toggle and the speaker on the unit ceased crackling.

Blade could hear the static in his headphones. He spoke into the boom mike. "Sir Galahad here."

"Do you have something to report?" General Gallagher inquired.

"We expect to start in pursuit shortly," Blade replied.

There were several seconds of silence, as if the general expected additional information. "Is that all?" he demanded.

"Why wasn't I provided with a complete dossier on the Vampires?" Blade inquired bluntly. He could envision the bulldog of a general turning crimson with anger.

"What do you mean?" Gallagher hedged.

"Don't play games with me," Blade said sternly. "You know what I'm referring to."

"Speed was of the essence," General Gallagher maintained. "There wasn't time for a complete briefing before your departure."

"Perhaps," Blade said. "In any event, we're going to have a discussion about this after I return to the Force HQ."

"Whatever you want," Gallagher commented. "I'll be here until the mission is accomplished. If you need anything, just say the word."

"I need more honesty," Blade stated. "Sir Galahad, over and out." He stripped off the headset and tossed it to Boone.

"Do you mind my asking what was that all about?" Mayor Upshaw queried.

"General Gallagher and I don't always see eye to eye," Blade explained.

"Did he rush you down here?" Upshaw asked.

"You can say that," Blade responded.

"Maybe he was justified," Upshaw remarked. "You wouldn't want the trail to become cold."

"Speaking of the trail," Sergeant Havoc interjected and

pointed to the right.

Blade turned. Grizzly and Thunder were running toward him. "Find anything?" he asked them.

Grizzly smirked and nodded. "Let's go kick some Vampire butt!"

CHAPTER THREE

"If it wasn't for the captives," Thunder remarked as he knelt in the middle of a field seven miles from Aguanga, "tracking these Vampires would be next to impossible. They tread lightly and rarely leave even a partial print."

"At least we won't lose them," Blade said. He glanced at Grizzly, standing to his left. "What about the scent?"

"Human, I'd say," Grizzly opined. "Not very pungent, though. Sometimes you humans stink to high heaven, but these suckers don't. They must bathe regularly."

"And we don't?" Athena rejoined.

"I have my doubts," Grizzly replied, then snickered.

"Let's keep going," Blade directed. "We still have plenty of daylight left."

Grizzly and Thunder resumed their tracking, working in tandem.

Blade waited until the mutant and the Flathead were 20 yards ahead before motioning for the others to follow. Athena was behind him, Boone next, and Sergeant Havoc brought up the rear.

"The Vampires have changed direction," Athena remarked.

"I noticed," Blade said. Initially the Vampires' trail had proceeded due south from Aguanga, but six miles from the town the trail angled to the southwest.

"The San Diego Dead Zone is southwest of here," Athena noted.

"Which means the Vampires may be heading for their home base," Blade deduced. "And once we locate it, we can dispose of them."

"Mind if we talk?" Athena inquired.

Blade glanced over his right shoulder. "About what?"

"You."

"Why are you so curious about me?" Blade asked, facing front and watching Grizzly and Thunder enter a stand of trees.

"I'm curious about everyone on the Force," Athena answered. "I need copy for the stories I file on our escapades. The more background information I obtain, the more human interest angles I uncover, the more my readers will like my articles. And we want the public to perceive the Force in a favorable light. You know as well as I that there are those who think the Force is an unnecessary waste of taxpayer dollars. General Gallagher, for one. He opposed the Force when the unit was formed, and he hasn't changed his opinion."

"Gallagher opposed the Force on political grounds," Blade reminded her. "He believes California should not have joined the Freedom Federation. He's an isolationist. He thinks the state is better off by itself."

"Whatever his reasons," Athena said, "he's not our biggest booster."

"He must like you," Blade observed. "He tried repeatedly to persuade me to allow you to join."

Athena elected to change the subject. "How are your wife and son? Have Jenny and Gabe adjusted to life in Los Angeles?"

"Not yet," Blade said, and sighed. "Jenny misses Minnesota. She wants to live at the Home, not in California."

"What will you do if she goes back?" Athena asked.

"I don't know," Blade replied. "I'll cross that bridge when I come to it."

"Maybe you should take her on a vacation," Athena proposed. "We could all use some R and R."

"I think you're right," Blade agreed. "After this mission is over, everyone will receive a two-week leave." He walked into the trees.

"Terrific!" Athena said happily. "Now all I have to do is survive the mission."

"I know I could use two weeks off," Boone interjected. "I'd like to visit some friends in Dakota."

"Are those friends female?" Athena asked impishly.

Boone shrugged. "One or two."

"I thought so," Athena snickered. "Any plans for marriage in the near future?"

"My personal affairs are none of your business," Boone informed her.

Athena looked back at the Cavalryman. "Touchy, aren't we?"

"I'm not a Californian," Boone responded.

"Meaning what?" Athena pressed him.

"Yeah," Sergeant Havoc joined in. "What's wrong with Californians?"

"You want the truth?" Boone asked him.

"What else?" Havoc rejoined.

"Californians, for the most part, have lost their edge," Boone assserted.

"What edge?" Athena asked, delighted the gunman was conversing freely. Usually, Boone was laconic, bordering on silent. Of all the Force members, only Thunder was less talkative. She knew very little concerning the backgrounds of both men, and she was determined to learn more, to uncover their motivations and beliefs.

"I never realized it until recently," Boone said. "The people living before the war must have been soft, flabby, and lazy."

"Why do you say that?" Athena probed.

"Because the people living before the war and Californians today have a lot in common," Boone stated. "Many of them, particularly those in the big cities like Los Angeles, can't hunt or fish worth beans. They'd starve if they ever had to fend for themselves. All their necessities—their food, their clothing, their water, and whatnot—are provided for them. They don't know how to be self-reliant. They let others do their thinking for them." He paused. "If the people living before the war were the same, then it's no wonder their civilization crumbled."

"Are you saying all Californians are the same?" Sergeant Havoc queried.

"Nope," Boone responded. "There are exceptions, like yourself. You can take care of yourself better than most men I know, but you're a professional soldier. You've been in the military all your life."

"And I suppose life is different in the Dakota Territory?" Athena questioned.

"As different as night and day," Boone told her. "Folks in the Dakota Territory know how to live off the land. Living on the frontier hardens people, men and women. We wouldn't fall apart if the grocery trucks stopped delivering food because we can grow our own."

"So you think the people living in the Dakota Territory are superior to those in California?" Athena said, goading him.

"I never said that," Boone answered, correcting her. "I simply said the folks in Dakota are more self-sufficient. We haven't lost our edge. We haven't lost touch with ourselves."

"Interesting," Athena commented.

"There's something I'd like to know," Sergeant Havoc said.

"What is it?" Boone asked.

"If I remember my history, wasn't there a North and South Dakota at one time?" Havoc questioned.

"There was," Boone verified. "But the two merged after the war. Both states became known as the Dakota Territory. The Cavalry controls the southern half, but we're having problems in the north."

Blade, listening to the conversation while keeping his eyes trained on Grizzly and Thunder as the Force weaved through the trees, abruptly halted. He gazed at the Cavalryman. "What kind of problems?"

"Some of our patrols have been ambushed," Boone detailed. "And a few farms and ranches were destroyed."

"By whom?" Blade inquired.

"We don't know," Boone said. "Kilrane is planning to mount a major campaign to find out next month."

Blade's gray eyes narrowed. Kilrane was the leader of the

Cavalry and a friend. "Why wasn't the Federation Council apprised of the situation?"

"We can handle it ourselves," Boone stated.

"After our leave is over, maybe we can fly to the Dakota Territory and show the Cavalry how to kick butt, as Grizzly would say," Athena suggested.

Sergeant Havoc laughed.

"I don't like the idea of Kilrane keeping secrets from the other Federation leaders," Blade said. "Why did we go to all the trouble to form the Federation if we're not going to rely upon one another when trouble arises?"

Boone didn't respond.

Blade looked to the southwest. Grizzly and Thunder were nowhere in sight. Annoyed, he marched after them. The others followed.

Athena surveyed the trees. "Anyone have an ax?"

"Why do we need an ax?" Blade asked.

"To chop down some of these trees. We could carve a couple of dozen dandy wooden stakes."

"Wooden stakes?" Boone repeated quizzically.

"According to legend, the only way of killing a vampire and insuring it stays dead is by driving a wooden stake through its heart." Athena explained. "Legend also has it that you can kill a vampire by chopping off its head, sprinkling it with Holy Water, or exposing it to sunlight. But there is evidence to suggest those means do not dispatch the vampire forever. The best method is the stake."

Boone glanced at the trees. "What did these vampires supposedly look like?"

"They were invariably reported as pale and thin," Athena disclosed. "They possessed long fangs and were incredibly strong."

Blade suddenly recalled the words of Ethan Hogue: "All I remember is very white skin. They were real thin too."

"Vampires were reputed to have the ability to transform themselves into bats in some cultures," Athena was saying. "Their breath was the pits." She paused. "Oh. And they could run like the wind. One report of a vampire in Las Vegas in the 1970's claimed the creature attained speeds of fifty to sixty miles an hour.''

Blade remembered Ethan's statement: ''They can run like a deer. I've never seen anyone run as fast as they can.'' Was it possible, *really* possible, vampires were more than mere myth?

Sergeant Havoc snorted derisively. ''It's all bunk! There are no such things as vampires!''

''Don't let them hear you say that,'' Athena teased. ''They may try to suck your blood tonight.''

''I'd like to see them try,'' Havoc stated. ''I bet a vampire can't suck much blood with a 45 shoved up its nose.''

Boone chuckled.

''I don't think you two have anything to worry about,'' Athena said. ''The Vampires we're after seem to prefer the fairer sex.''

''Don't worry, Athena,'' Sergeant Havoc stated. ''We wouldn't let a Vampire get its grubby hands on you.''

''How sweet! I didn't know you cared,'' Athena quipped.

''We wouldn't want to give the Vampire blood poisoning,'' Havoc elaborated.

The soldier and the Cavalryman enjoyed a hearty laugh.

Blade was pleased to note their newfound sense of amiability. On the first mission, and again during the Reptilian affair, intense friction between them had reduced their effectiveness and threatened the existence of the Force. It was nice to see them getting along for a change. The others had even accepted Grizzly as one of their own, although initially they had resented his presence in the unit. He hoped they would continue to grow in their mutual friendship. If not, they—

A burst of automatic gunfire suddenly erupted from up ahead.

CHAPTER FOUR

Blade galvanized into action at the first sound. He raced in the direction of the shooting, skirting trees and crashing through the underbrush. Irritated at himself for losing sight of his point men, anxious for their safety, he discarded all caution.

A tremendous growl rent the air.

Had Grizzly and Thunder encountered the Vampires?

Blade heard a guttural roar arise 20 feet in front of him. He sprinted around a large tree, covered 15 feet in a mad dash, and plowed through a shoulder-high bush.

There they were!

Thunder was down, prone on the ground, a trickle of blood seeping from his left temple, his M-16 beside him.

Eight feet from the Flathead was the cause of his condition: a mutant. Like so many of the mutations affecting the animal kingdom, this one stemmed from the embryonic deformity produced by the contaminated environment. Radioactive and chemical toxins had leeched in to the soil and entered the food cycle. A healthy, pregnant animal would drink tainted water or consume poisoned plants and thereby drastically alter the formation and development of the embryo it was carrying.

This one, once, would have been a black bear.

Now it was a raving, insatiable demon.

On all fours it stood four feet at the shoulders and was seven feet in length. A coat of ragged, patchy black hair covered its seven hundred pounds of sinews and muscles. In contrast to a normal bear, the mutant's head was outsized, twice the typical length. Most of the hair on its head was missing, exposing dry, cracked, sickly skin. Saliva dripped from its gaping maw, its huge teeth glistening with drool. Between the shoulder blades was an extraordinary hump, a trait characteristic of the grizzly bear, not the black.

Even as Blade watched, the mutant reared up on its hind legs and shuffled toward Thunder.

Standing between the mutant and the Flathead was Grizzly. He had cast his M-16 aside and was crouching with his arms at his sides. His hands suddenly went rigid, his fingers fully extended, and five-inch claws shot from his fingers and thumbs.

Blade had witnessed Grizzly employing those retractable claws before. The claws were housed in the upper portion of Grizzly's hands, above the knuckles. When Grizzly straightened his hands and locked them in place, the claws automatically popped out, sliding down sheaths just under the skin and issuing from underneath small flaps of flesh located behind each fingernail. Once his hands were locked and the claws extended, Grizzly could not use his fingers for anything other than ripping and slashing. Which suited him just fine.

Grizzly abruptly sprang, pouncing on the bear's chest and burying the claws on his left hand in the mutant's chest. He blocked a ponderous swing of the bear's arm with his right, then raked the bear across the eyes.

The mutated bear snarled and tried to embrace its tormentor in a lethal hug.

Grizzly dropped to the grass and ducked to the right. He darted around his foe and vaulted onto the mutant's back.

Blade, fascinated by the furious battle, held his fire for fear of accidentally striking Grizzly. He was dimly aware that the others had arrived and were likewise transfixed.

Grizzly tore into the mutant's neck with a vengeance, tearing and stabbing.

The mutant, growling in rage, lumbered toward a tree. It pivoted and attempted to pin Grizzly against the trunk.

But Grizzly was too quick. He released his grip and jumped to the left, landing and launching himself again in a fluid motion. His claws speared into the mutated bear's eyes, all the way to the fingertips.

The bear stiffened and tottered forward. Its mouth opened and closed a few times.

Grizzly, clinging to the bear's oversized head, raised his right arm overhead, then buried his claws in the bear's left ear.

With a gurgling grunt the bear toppled over.

Grizzly was already dropping to one side. He landed lightly on his feet and straightened. His claws were caked with blood and gore.

The mutated bear was on its stomach, crimson spurting from its ruptured eye and its left ear. It convulsed and wheezed, nearly dead.

Thunder groaned and opened his eyes. He began to rise.

Blade moved to the Flathead's side and used his left arm to assist Thunder in standing.

Athena walked over to Grizzly. "Are you okay?"

"I'm fine," Grizzly replied. "This bear was a wimp. I didn't even work up a sweat."

"What about you?" Blade asked Thunder. The Flathead was sagging against him.

Thunder reached up and gingerly touched his left temple. He ran his fingers over a two-inch cut below the hairline. "I feel groggy," he said. "But I don't believe my injury is serious."

Blade looked at Grizzly. "What happened?"

The hybrid nodded at the bear. "The sucker jumped us. Thunder was in the lead and saw it coming. He got off a few rounds, but the thing never stopped. It clipped him on the head."

"Why didn't you use your M-16?" Blade demanded. "Why did you rely on your claws?"

"Thunder's rounds didn't have any effect," Grizzly replied, then smirked. "Besides, I like the personal touch."

"Overconfidence can lead to disaster," Blade observed. "You shouldn't take unnecessary risks."

Grizzly grinned. "Can I quote you in my biography?"

"Grizzly was magnificent," Athena stated in his behalf. "He saved Thunder's life."

Grizzy beamed.

Sergeant Havoc stepped over to the mutated monstrosity. "I don't see what all the fuss is about. It's just a dinky bear."

"Oh, yeah?" Grizzly said, his eyes narrowing. "I'd like to see you take on a mutant using only your hands."

"I could have wasted this bear with one hand," Sergeant Havoc declared.

"Bet me!" Grizzly rejoined.

"I could," Sergeant Havoc stated.

Grizzly glanced at Blade. "And you think *I'm* over-confident?"

"You don't believe me?" Sergeant Havoc queried in mock surprise.

"Do I look like I was born yesterday?" Grizzly retorted.

"One hand is all it would take," Sergeant Havoc insisted. He reached into his right front pants pocket and removed an oval metallic object. "One *hand* grenade, that is."

Blade grinned, Boone laughed, and even Grizzly chuckled.

Thunder stood fully erect. "I can manage on my own now."

Blade dropped his left arm to his side. "Are you sure?"

"I do not feel any dizziness or sickness," Thunder asserted. "And the weakness in my legs has passed. I can resume my duties."

"You'll take it easy for a while," Blade told him. "In fact, we'll take a ten-minute break." He walked over to the mutated bear. "I wasn't aware that black bears roamed this far south in California," he commented.

"They didn't until a few decades ago," Athena mentioned. "The bears have been extending their range southward ever since the war."

Blade nodded. "It's the same all over the country. With the human population reduced, and with nature reclaiming previously populated tracts of land, the wildlife is proliferating."

"Good!" Grizzly stated. "The less land you humans control, the less you'll screw the environment up."

"What are you talking about?" Havoc demanded.

"I know what it was like before the war," Grizzly said. "You humans had fouled up the environment with your industrial pollution, your vehicle emissions, and your aerosol sprays. Your chemical spills contaminated dozens of waterways and killed millions of fish. Your acid rains ate away at the virgin forests. Your toxic-waste dumps sickened humans and animals alike. And your kind was responsible for the extinction of dozens of species.'' He snorted. ''You humans have a knack for fouling up everything you touch.''

''You can't blame us for the mistakes of our forefathers,'' Boone chimed in.

''Yeah,'' Havoc said. ''I know you don't think very highly of humans, but we have achieved some impressive accomplishments.''

''That you have,'' Grizzly conceded sarcastically. ''I was real impressed when I learned that humans almost destroyed the world. Few things have impressed me as much.''

Thunder knelt and retrieved his M-16, then crossed to Grizzly. He placed his right hand on the hybrid's left shoulder. ''I thank you, brother, for saving my life. I deeply regret my earlier misgivings about having you on the Force. The Spirit-in-All-Things is present in you.''

Grizzly laughed. ''Don't give me that religious mumbo jumbo, Thunder. I saved your hide because you're my teammate. That's all. I'd do the same for any of you dimwits.''

''Not to change the subject,'' Athena said, ''but do you think the Vampires heard the shots?''

Blade gazed to the southwest. ''There's no way of telling.''

''I am ready to continue,'' Thunder declared.

''Grizzly and Havoc, take the point,'' Blade ordered.

''I am fit to take the point,'' Thunder said.

''You'll take it easy for a while,'' Blade instructed him.

Grizzly knelt and wiped his claws clean on the bear's corpse. He slowly relaxed his fingers and the claws slid from sight. ''I'm ready,'' he said, retrieving his M-16. He glanced at the noncom. ''Let's go, soldier-boy. And try not to get lost.''

''I don't get lost,'' Havoc responded indignantly.

They hastened to the southwest.

''Stay in sight!'' Blade called out.

Sergeant Havoc nodded.

Blade let them go 20 yards off before hiking after them. He hefted the Commando and alertly scanned the vegetation. Where there was one wild mutant, there were probably more. Aguanga and vicinity were officially designated as a Cleared Area, an area where the California Army had exterminated most of the feral mutants.

Most.

But obviously not all.

The Force trekked on a southwesterly course throughout the afternoon and early evening hours, penetrating ever deeper into the Cleveland National Forest.

"There once was a state park around here somewhere," Athena mentioned at one point.

"Not any more?" Blade asked.

"No. People don't like to travel too close to the Dead Zone. But I remember seeing the park listed on a map. Palomar Mountain State Park was the name of it. There was a famous observatory near the peak, as I recall. The Mount Palomar Observatory," Athena detailed.

The terrain sloped gradually upwards.

Another half hour brought them to the north shore of a fair-sized lake. Grizzly and Sergeant Havoc were waiting near a large boulder.

"It's getting too dark to see the spoor," Grizzly commented as Blade approached. "Do you want us to go on?"

"No. We'll camp here for the night," Blade said. "I wouldn't want to blunder into an ambush." He surveyed the rocky shore. "No fires. We don't know how far ahead the Vampires are, and we don't want to alert them to our presence."

"They must be miles ahead of us," Athena said.

"Maybe not," Blade disputed her. "The Vampires are engaged in a forced march with thirty-seven prisoners, and they won't be able to travel any faster than the prisoners can. If we start a fire, we run the risk of having it spotted. So no fire."

"I bet I freeze my tootsies tonight," Athena groused. "Nights are chilly at this altitude in April."

"You'll survive," Blade stated. He gazed at each of them. "We'll eat jerky and drink from our canteens, then turn in. I don't want anyone drinking from this lake. The water could be contaminated. After we eat, Athena and I will take the first watch. Grizzly and Sergeant Havoc will take the second. Boone and Thunder the third. Three-hour shifts for everyone.''

''Can we tinkle, or will the noise attract the Vampires?'' Grizzly inquired facetiously.

''Just don't tinkle in the lake,'' Blade advised. ''If the water isn't polluted, we want to leave it that way.''

''I'll be back,'' Grizzly said. He moved toward a jumbled mass of boulders 40 feet off.

Blade sat down on a flat rock and leaned the Commando on a nearby boulder. He removed his backpack.

''Mind if I join you?'' Athena asked, taking a seat to his right before he could respond.

Sergeant Havoc, Boone, and Thunder took seats at the base of the large boulder.

''Do you want me to contact General Gallagher?'' Boone asked.

''Not until we have something to report,'' Blade responded. He opened his backpack and fished inside for the packet of beef jerky. His fingers closed on the smooth plastic and he withdrew the packet.

Athena was doing the same. ''How did you ever convince General Gallagher to supply us with jerky instead of rations?''

''I became accustomed to eating jerky at the Home,'' Blade said. ''Venison jerky is a Family staple. The rations Gallagher gave us tasted like soggy, salty paper. I politely requested to receive jerky instead.''

''I know you better than that,'' Athena remarked. ''What else did you tell him?''

Blade grinned. ''I mentioned noticing a herd of cattle on a ranch near our headquarters. Then I tapped my Bowies. He took the hint.''

Athena laughed. ''He was afraid you'd butcher the cattle yourself.''

Blade unwrapped his packet and bit into a stick of jerky. The tangy meat caused his mouth to water. He chewed heartily and stared at the stars materializing in the steadily darkening sky.

Athena leaned back and viewed the celestial spectacle. ''Do you ever wonder if there are other inhabited planets out there?''

"There are."

"How can you be so certain?" Athena inquired. "We don't have any proof."

"The Family Elders teach us there are many inhabited worlds," Blade stated. "How can anyone gaze at the immensity of the cosmos and believe otherwise? Take a look at our own world sometime, at the abundant life on this one puny planet. The Spirit does not intend for anyone or anything to exist in isolation."

"You're getting metaphysical on me again," Athena said. "You're a Warrior, yet you're also a philosopher. I've never met anyone quite like you."

"That's because thinking has become a dying art," Blade said. "The Elders teach each Family member to think for themselves."

"Well, Mr. Thinker, if there are beings on other worlds, then why haven't they contacted us? Some of their cultures must be more advanced than ours, capable of interstellar travel. Why haven't they shown up?"

"How do you know they haven't?" Blade responded.

"Be serious," Athena said.

"I am. How do you know these beings haven't already contacted certain people on our world? How do you know they don't select qualified individuals to serve as liaisons?" Blade asked.

"You've been reading too much science fiction," Athena cracked.

Blade shrugged and resumed eating.

"Where'd you ever get a crazy idea like that? From the Elders?" Athena probed.

The Warrior nodded.

"I'd like to meet one of the Elders sometime," Athena said. "Maybe one of them would consent to an interview for the *Times*."

Blade chewed on his jerky.

Grizzly walked toward them, his M-16 in his right hand, his backpack in his left. "Did I hear you talking about little green men from Mars?"

Athena chuckled and stood. "You and your hyper-keen

hearing! I think I'll go visit the ladies'." She strolled in the direction of several trees approximately 30 feet distant, her M-16 over her right shoulder.

"Fat lot of good my hearing did me today," Grizzly muttered as he rested his haunches on a rock. "That bear never made a peep before it attacked, and the wind was blowing the wrong way for me to detect its scent."

Blade observed a meteor streak across the heavens.

"I love the forest," Grizzly mentioned. "The animal half of me feels at home here." He sighed. "When my stint in this outfit is up, I think I'll find an uninhabited area where humans never show their ugly faces and settle down."

Blade stared at the hybrid. "Why do you pretend to dislike humans so much?"

"Who's pretending?" Grizzly rejoined archly.

"You are," Blade said. "I know you don't despise humans as much as you claim. You're friendly with us on the Force. And Athena and you are very close."

"Athena's a sweetheart," Grizzly stated. "And as for the rest of you chumps, you're not bad for meatheads. But don't get me wrong. I may like some humans, but as a species you're scum. You're a blight on this planet. The only thing I can compare humans to is a horde of locusts. You destroy everything you get your grubby mitts on."

"That's not true," Blade said. "Humans have their faults, true. But we also strive to achieve spiritual ideals. We have created great art and literature. Many humans have learned to live lives devoted to loving others. A few bad apples don't spoil the whole bunch."

"Tell me this, Bright Guy," Grizzly declared. "If your species is so great, why have humans had so many wars? Why did your kind nearly wreck the world?"

"There have always been power-mongers," Blade said. "And there have always been those who believed in using violence to achieve their ends. Humans have yet to learn how to live in harmony."

Grizzly laughed. "Now there's an understatement if I ever heard one!"

Before their conversation could continue, a horrified scream pierced the night.

CHAPTER FIVE

"Athena!" Grizzly bellowed, and was off like a shot, heading for the trees 30 feet away, forgetting his M-16 and his backpack.

Blade scooped up his Commando but left the backpack on the ground. He sprinted toward the trees.

Thunder, Boone, and Sergeant Havoc were also coming on the run.

A pale form appeared in the trees for an instant, then was gone.

Vampires! Blade gripped the Commando firmly. He saw Grizzly plunge into the undergrowth and a moment later followed suit.

Grizzly was five yards in the lead when he abruptly stopped and leaned down.

Blade reached Grizzly's side. "What is it?"

Grizzly straightened with an M-16 in his right hand. "This is Athena's!"

Sergeant Havoc, Thunder, and Boone joined them, each one armed with their M-16s. Only Havoc had his backpack on.

"The bastards have Athena!" Grizzly hissed, exposing his

teeth and facing to the southwest. He sniffed the air noisily. "I have their scent!"

"We go after them," Blade said. "But first we get our backpacks."

"I'm not waiting!" Grizzly snapped, and took off at a fast springing gait, still holding Athena's M-16.

"Grizzly!" Blade called, to no avail.

In seconds Grizzly was lost to view.

"Damn!" Blade fumed. He glanced at Boone and Thunder. "Go get all the gear!"

They hurried toward the lake.

"How did the Vampires know we were here?" Sergeant Havoc asked.

"Who knows?" Blade replied. "Maybe they heard the shots earlier. Maybe they were checking their back trail. Maybe they have senses we don't know about."

"Want me to go after Grizzly?" Havoc offered.

"No," Blade said. "we'll stick together. Grizzly should have waited. Another minute wouldn't make a difference. We need those backpacks. They have our food and water, not to mention our plastic explosives, spare ammo, and the radio Boone's carrying." He paused. "I'm going to have a long talk with Grizzly later."

"I wouldn't want to be in Grizzly's . . ." Havoc began, about to say "shoes," then corrected himself. ". . . furry feet."

Blade waited impatiently for Boone and Thunder, chafing at every second of delay.

"The Vampires will be expecting us to come after her," Sergeant Havoc noted. "We could walk right into a trap."

"We don't have any choice," Blade said.

They waited in silence until their companions returned. Boone and Thunder were both wearing their backpacks. Boone was holding another in his left hand. Thunder held two extra backpacks and an extra M-16.

"This one is yours," Boone said to Blade.

Blade quickly aligned the backpack on his back.

"One of these backpacks is Athena's," Thunder commented. "The other gear is Grizzly's."

"We'll divide it up," Blade directed. "I'll take Grizzly's

M-16.'' He took the weapon and slung it over his left shoulder. ''Let Havoc and Boone carry the extra backpacks.''

''I can carry one,'' Thunder said.

''Maybe later,'' Blade stated. ''Havoc and Boone weren't clipped by a bear today.''

''I am fit,'' Thunder insisted.

''Later,'' Blade reiterated.

Boone and Havoc took the extra backpacks and slid their left arm through the strap loops, adjusting the backpacks on their left shoulders.

''It's a good thing we travel light,'' Boone quipped.

''Let's go,'' Blade said.

''How will we know which way to go?'' Boone inquired.

''The Vampires have been heading to the southwest all day,'' Blade answered. ''That's the way we'll go.'' He gazed up at the stars, taking his bearings. Like the Flathead, the Cavalryman, and Sergeant Havoc, he was adept at using the alignment of the constellations and stars at given times of the year as a guide for night travel. The celestial arrangement in the California sky differed somewhat from Minnesota; he had spent weeks after his arrival familiarizing himself with the starry realm.

''Does this mean we don't get our beauty sleep?'' Sergeant Havoc joked.

Blade started to the southwest, his eyes constantly scanning the landscape. The night was moonless, the countryside murky. He moved as rapidly as the limited light and the tangled growth allowed. Boone was behind him, then Thunder and Sergeant Havoc.

The minutes dragged by. An hour elapsed. Two. Three.

Blade halted at the crest of a rise and surveyed the valley below for signs of a campfire.

Nothing.

The four men pressed on.

Another hour passed.

Blade mentally debated whether to stop for the night and resume their search in the morning or keep going. All four of them could use some rest. The farther they went, the more convinced he became that they would not catch up with Grizzly and the Vampires before dawn. Even if they did, a firefight against unknown adversaries in the dark gave their enemies the edge. He preferred to tackle the Vampires during the day.

Fifteen minutes went by.

Blade emerged from the trees and found a narrow field in their path. He stopped and stared at the others. "We'll take a break here."

"Shouldn't we stay after them?" Sergeant Havoc asked in surprise.

"We need a few hours' sleep," Blade said. "We won't perform at our peak if we're exhausted. It's already past midnight. Thunder and you will grab two hours of shut-eye, then Boone and I."

"Yes, sir," Havoc responded. He immediately proceeded to lie on the ground.

"I hope you know what you're doing," Boone commented to the Warrior.

"So do I," Blade said.

Grizzly could move at an astonishingly swift pace when he wanted, and he bolted after Athena's abductors with all the speed at his command. He knew he was disobeying Blade, violating procedure, and being insubordinate, but he couldn't help himself. Athena Morris was his one true friend, and he intended to save her at all costs. Of all the humans he'd ever known, she was one of the few who looked at him without a hint of fear or revulsion in her eyes.

The Vampires would pay for taking her!

He tracked them easily, his flaring nostrils registering the unmistakable scent of the Vampires commingled with Athena's sweet womanly smell. The padded soles of his feet seldom made a noise. Leaves and limbs brushed against his fur. His fingers twitched as he envisioned slashing the Vampires to ribbons.

The trail bore to the southwest for over a mile, then inexplicably angled to the southeast, then the east.

What was this?

Why had the Vampires changed direction?

Grizzly ran at a dogtrot, bent over at the waist so he could readily distinguish the odors he was following. The Vampires, he judged, were in a hurry to get somewhere. Their scent hung in the air lightly, as if they were hastening to a definite destination.

But where?

An hour later he found the answer.

Grizzly came up over a low hill and slowed to a standstill. A quarter of a mile distant was a flickering campfire. He doubted the Vampires would light a fire and reveal their location; the fire must belong to someone else.

Who?

Grizzly descended toward the fire, advancing stealthily, craftily employing trees and thickets as cover. The woodland was exceptionally still. Not even an insect stirred.

A bad sign.

He crouched behind a broad tree trunk 40 yards from the campfire and scrutinized the area around the blaze for the slightest movement.

There was none.

Puzzled, Grizzly closed on the campfire. He was within 20 yards of the slowly diminishing flames when the breeze wafted a new scent to his nostrils.

Blood.

Fresh blood.

He held his arms at his sides, prepared to extend his claws on a second's notice, and silently padded toward the fire. Eight yards from the blaze he found a crumpled deerskin tent in a heap on the grass. Two more strides and he spied the first body.

It was a man slumped over a small log, lying on his stomach, his arms outspread, his face twisted to the side, his features locked in an expression of stark fright. Long black hair cascaded over his shoulders. He wore a brown flannel shirt and buckskin pants and moccasins.

Grizzly warily walked over to the corpse. He gingerly touched the man's left cheek and the head dropped at an unnatural angle. The man's neck was broken! Grizzly knelt and examined the victim's face closely.

The dead man was an Indian.

What had happened here?

Grizzly straightened and slowly circled the fire, finding five more bodies, all Indians. Three had died of snapped vertebrae, two of crushed throats. He speculated that the Indians had been hunting in the hills when the Vampires had waylaid them. There was no telling where the Indians hailed from. Prior to the war over a dozen Indian Reservations had existed in the general area: the Mission Indian Reservation, the Pechanga Reservation, the Rincon Reservation, Los Coyotes Indian Reservation, and many, many more. Thunder had mentioned them one night while the Force members were lounging in their barracks.

The fire light glinted off a metallic object to the right.

Grizzly crossed to the object and knelt. A Winchester was partially concealed in a clump of weeds. He picked up the weapon and sniffed the barrel. The gun had not been fired, which meant the Vampires had decimated the Indians quickly; the hapless Indians had been unable to get off so much as a single shot. He dropped the Winchester, unwilling to lug a second firearm along.

How far ahead were the Vampires?

He walked to an Indian with a pulverized throat and placed his left palm on the corpse's forehead. The skin was quite warm, and he estimated the Vampires were less than 30 minutes in front of him. With his neck tilted, he walked in ever widening circles, sniffing the air until he found the Vampire scent again. Casting a parting glance at the Indian encampment, he jogged in pursuit of the Vampires and Athena. He felt a degree of relief at not finding her body in the camp. The Vampires were still holding her prisoner, but at least she was alive.

For now.

His muscles rippling and flowing under his fur, he covered mile after mile. Fatigue nagged at his mind but he refused to acknowledge his body's complaint. He'd sleep after Athena was rescued, not before. The Vampires were again bearing to the southwest. As the hours elasped and his weariness grew and grew, his alertness lessened and lessened. His stubbornness and tenacity supplanted his better judgment and he pressed ever onward instead of resting.

Ultimately, this caused his undoing.

Grizzly followed the spoor into a rocky gorge where the Vampire scent was stronger than ever before. Had he been fully vigilant, he might have wondered why the Vampire odor was suddenly so sharp. But he jogged farther into the gorge, his wariness dulled by his strenuous exertion. Consequently, he didn't realize he was in danger until a lean, pale figure unexpectedly launched itself from a boulder on his left.

The Vampires were waiting for him!

He felt powerful arms close on his knees and he was knocked to the right. Unable to stay erect he toppled over, releasing the M-16.

Snarling, the Vampire lunged at the bear-man's neck.

Grizzly reacted instinctually, avoiding the Vampire's raking fingers and slamming his right fist into the thing's face. Dislodged by the mighty blow, the Vampire was sent rolling to one side. Grizzly heaved to his knees as the patter of onrushing feet sounded to his rear. He tried to turn.

A hurtling Vampire rammed into the bear-man from behind.

Bowled over by the impact, Grizzly found himself with his nose in the dirt and a Vampire clamping its fingers on the back of his neck. He reached over his right shoulder and gripped a cool, clammy wrist. His dense shoulder muscles straining, he wrenched on the Vampire's arm and was rewarded by the creature sailing over his head to crash into a nearby boulder.

Move your butt! his mind shrieked.

Grizzly rose to his hands and knees, intending to unsheath his lethal claws as he stood, but he never got the chance.

Three more Vampires pounced on him.

Borne to the ground by the things piling on top of him, Grizzly twisted and lashed out, striking with his fists, crunching a nose on one foe and pounding the left eye on a second.

Undaunted, the Vampires gripped his wrists, one on each arm, and held fast. The third creature, the one with the busted nose, slugged the mutant on the jaw three times in succession.

Grizzly felt his fury mounting, but he also felt uncomfortably giddy. He struggled to break free, amazed at the strength the thin, seemingly frail Vampires possessed.

Growling wickedly, the third Vampire delivered two more punches to the bear-man's chin.

Pinpoints of light were spinning before Grizzly's eyes. His eyelids fluttered as he attempted to shake off the things one final time. They were immovable. The last sound he heard was a peculiar titter.

CHAPTER SIX

Shortly past noon.

They emerged from the forest on the bank of a stream. Thunder was in the lead, engaged in reading the sign. Blade was a few feet to his rear. Then came Boone and Sergeant Havoc.

Thunder knelt and inspected a footprint impressed in the mud at the edge of the stream. He looked up and saw the strangers. "We have company," he announced.

Blade had seen them.

Six Indians were on the opposite bank of the ribbon of water, standing 15 yards downstream. Each was armed with a rifle. They were attired primarily in buckskins, although a few cotton or wool shirts and a pair of jeans were in evidence.

Thunder stood and smiled.

The Indians whispered among themselves.

"Fan out," Blade ordered softly.

Sergant Havoc moved to the right, Boone to the left.

"I will go talk to them," Thunder offered.

"Let them come to us," Blade stated.

A heavyset Indian in buckskins slowly approached the Force

members. He nervously glanced from one to another and finally focused on Thunder. When he was directly across the stream from the Flathead, he stopped.

"Greetings, brother," Thunder said sincerely. "I am of the Flathead tribe in Montana. My parents named me Thunder-Rolling-in-the-Mountain." He grinned. "My mother believed a long name was distinctive."

The heavyset Indian smiled. "I am called Shadow. My people were once confined to the La Jolla Reservation, but we now claim this land as our own."

"We did not know this is your land," Thunder said. "We apologize if we are trespassing."

Shadow looked at the giant. "Who is your leader?"

"How do you know he is our leader?" Thunder responded.

"He has the eyes of a leader," Shadow said.

"I am Blade," the Warrior declared.

"Why are you here?" Shadow asked.

"We seek those the whites call Vampires," Thunder answered.

Shadow did a double take.

"You know of them?" Thunder questioned.

"Yes," Shadow said. "They are the scourge of my people. We call them the Blood Drinkers."

"A party of Blood Drinkers passed this way during the night," Thunder divulged. "Did you see them?"

Shadow shook his head. "You would be wise to avoid contact with them. They are death to all."

"We must find them," Thunder said. "They have taken one of us, a woman."

Shadow gazed at the stream. "The Blood Drinkers have raided my people many times and stolen many women. Our braves have tracked them to the Red Land where demons dwell. The Blood Drinkers live there."

"Have you gone into the Red Land?" Thunder inquired.

"No one may enter the Red Land and live," Shadow replied. "The demons slay all who do."

"How far are we from the Red Land?" Thunder asked.

Shadow pondered for several seconds. "From the spot where we stand, perhaps twenty miles."

''We thank you for this information,'' Thunder said, ''and we hope we may pass through your land in peace.''

''You may,'' Shadow stated. ''And should you encounter our brothers, tell them that we are looking for them.''

''Your brothers?''

''We are but half of a hunting party,'' Shadow disclosed. ''Six of our brothers went to the east two days ago after deer. They were supposed to meet us this morning, but they did not show up at our meeting site.'' He paused and frowned. ''I hope the Blood Drinkers did not find them.''

''If we see your brothers, we will tell them we saw you,'' Thunder promised.

''Thank you,'' Shadow said. ''And may the Breath Giver guide your footsteps.''

''Yours as well,'' Thunder said.

Shadow nodded and returned to his companions. They conversed for a minute, then melted into the forest.

Boone walked to the edge of the stream. ''Why didn't someone let us know that the Indians have reclaimed this land?''

''I've been wondering the same thing,'' Blade commented. ''Surely General Gallagher or Governor Melnick must know, yet they didn't inform me.''

''Maybe they don't consider it important,'' Thunder speculated. ''What are a few tracts of land compared to the total size of California? Then again, they might not know. Not many whites live in this area. The tribes may have quietly reclaimed the land, without bloodshed.''

''Let's keep going,'' Blade instructed.

Thunder stared to the southwest. ''I fear for the safety of the missing half of that hunting party.''

''Why?'' Blade queried.

''Because I believe some of the Vampires have left the main column,'' Thunder said.

Blade's eyes narrowed. ''What makes you say that?''

Thunder pointed at the mud fringing the stream. ''I was not certain until we reached this spot. The Vampires do not leave many tracks, but some. All morning I found even fewer than yesterday, although the prints of the captives have been easy to read. I suspect some of the Vampires have gone a separate way. Perhaps the ones who abducted Athena last night, the ones sent to check their back trail, did not return to the prisoner column. Perhaps they went elsewhere.''

"After the other half of the hunting party?" Blade deduced.

Thunder nodded grimly. "That would be my guess."

"How many Vampires left the original group?" Blade inquired.

"It's hard to tell," Thunder said. "But not more than ten. I estimate there were three dozen or so originally."

Blade sighed in frustration. "Terrific!" he muttered. "This means Athena is not with the main column. And Grizzly is after the splinter group. They could be anywhere in the forest."

"I am sorry," Thunder apologized. "I should have noticed the exact point where the smaller group of Vampires separated. I should have said something before this."

"Don't blame yourself," Blade said. He stared at Boone and Havoc. "No breaks today. We press on until nightfall. If you get hungry, nibble on some jerky."

Thunder waded across the stream.

Blade stepped into the placid water. His apprehension was mounting by the hour. Barring a fluke, he doubted the Force would overtake the Vampires conducting the prisoners from Aguanga before the mysterious creatures reached the sanctuary of the Dead Zone. And the prospect of Athena being held by another group of Vampires who were prowling through the wilderness in search of new victims caused him intense mental anguish.

Thunder was waiting on the bank ten feet away.

Blade crossed the stream, and together they covered Boone and Sergeant Havoc as the latter two joined them. With Thunder taking point, they struck off to the southwest once again.

The afternoon hours passed slowly, uneventfully. Birds flitted through the trees. Squirrels scampered on the limbs. Rabbits darted from their path. Once a magnificent 12-point buck bounded from a thicket and disappeared to their rear.

Blade gazed at the sinking sun and reflected on the mission. They were approaching the boundary of the Dead Zone; by his calculations, they were no more than two or three miles from their destination. He was not about to go into the Dead Zone after dark. They would spend a restful night in the woods, then penetrate the Zone in the morning. He surveyed the countryside ahead for a suitable campsite.

And spied the . . . animal.

At first glance he thought it was a raccoon. The creature was perched on a log 50 feet in front of Thunder. It balanced its squat body on all fours and stared balefully at the human intruders. A coat of reddish-brown fur covered its upper body, but the color shaded to gray underneath. A bushy tail with six alternating black stripes was visible. The animal appeared to be three feet in height and in the neighborhood of 50 pounds. Blade peered at its face, bothered by an unnatural, freakish aspect to its head.

The thing spun and jumped behind the log.

Blade grinned, blaming his apprehension on a bad case of nerves. Even if the creature was a mutant, what serious harm could a mutated raccoon do to four well-armed men?

Plenty, as events developed.

Especially if the raccoon wasn't alone.

Thunder did not notice the raccoon. He was intently studying the ground for spoor when he came to a small clearing and halted.

"This looks like a good spot to camp tonight," Blade commented as he reached the clearing.

"Fine by me," Boone said. "My feet are killing me."

"You are accustomed to riding a horse," Thunder remarked.

"I wish we had horses now," Boone stated.

Sergeant Havoc, standing closest to the trees, gazed to the right. "Sir, we have company."

Blade swiveled and froze.

Three of the creatures were ten feet off, scrutinizing the Force members with cold, beady eyes. From the neck down they resembled raccoons; from the neck up they were deformed. Their heads were twice the normal size; their eyes were slanted and slightly bulbous; their foreheads protruded from their skulls; and their mouths were ringed with teeth two inches long.

"There are more over here," Boone said, staring to the left.

Blade pivoted to find five more of the things.

"There are five in front of us," Thunder stated.

Blade glanced to their rear and the hairs on the nape of his neck prickled.

Six of the creatures were behind them.

"I don't like this," Boone said softly.

And the clearing erupted in a paroxysm of bloodshed.

The creatures hissed, snarled, and screeched as they launched themselves at the humans.

Blade, poised near the middle of the clearing, tossed his Commando aside as one of the mutants sprang at him. Employing the machine gun at such close quarters would be disastrous. He would risk shooting his men accidentally. Instead, he drew his Bowies, the big knives flashing up and out. He whipped the right Bowie in a tight arc, catching the first mutant on the neck, the razor edge severing the creature's head in a crimson spray of gushing blood.

Thunder, with a clear field of fire before him, leveled his M-16 and fired as the five mutants charged him. The slugs tore into their bodies, slamming them to the grass. Convulsing in their death throes, they still attempted to reach him, to snap at his legs.

To the rear, Sergeant Havoc tried to turn and bring his M-16 into play. But six fierce forms attacked him simultaneously, leaping onto his chest and ramming into his legs. He went down.

Four of the mutants converged on Boone, two from the left, two from the right. The pair on the left missed as the Cavalryman sidestepped their rush, but the duo on the right connected, hurling themselves upward and landing on his backpack, their combined 104 pounds driving him forward onto his knees. One of them, hissing and spitting, clawed its way up and over the backpack. Boone felt a burning sensation on the rear of his head as the mutant's claws sliced his flesh. He deliberately threw himself backwards onto the ground, pinning the raccoon clinging to the backpack between the pack and the turf and upending the mutant clawing at his head. Flat on his back, exposed, and vulnerable, Boone resorted to the weapons he was a master at using.

The Cavalryman flung the M-16 to the left and drew his Hombres.

Boone rolled to the right, rising to his knees with the revolvers held at waist height. The mutant he'd pinned was three feet away, scrambling to its feet. He shot it through the head. A yard beyond were three more, between the Cavalryman and the trees. They charged him in a concerted assault, and they died in the space of a second as the Hombres thundered and belched lead. Boone twisted, and there was Blade impaling one of the mutants on the point of his left Bowie. But another raccoon was in midair, springing at the Warrior's crotch. Boone blasted the creature in the forehead and saw its brain blow out the back of its head. Out of the corner of his eye he detected movement and swiveled in time to see yet another mutant bounding toward him. With ruthless efficiency he shot the animal through the eyes.

Sergeant Havoc was still on the ground, fighting for his life, struggling and thrashing as six of the mutants tore at his body. One was tearing at his right leg, another the left. Three were on his chest and the last was striving to rend his throat. Havoc's hands were clamped on the mutant's neck and he was holding its furious form at bay.

Boone took a gamble. In a millisecond he realized Havoc's grip was slipping, that the noncom's life was on the line. With the thought came an instantaneous response; the right Hombre boomed. The impact of the 44 Magnum slug at a range of only five feet literally tore the mutant from Havoc's grasp, the slug penetrating the center of the raccoon's forehead, passing completely through its body, and bursting out its anus.

Sergeant Havoc, his hands unexpectedly free, swept both arms out and in, his hands rigid, the calloused edges connecting with one of the raccoon's on his chest, one hand just behind each ear. Blood spurted from its nostrils and ears as its neck was crushed. A second mutant snapped at his right wrist but missed. Havoc boxed the raccoon on the right ear, knocking it to the ground.

And then Blade was there, stabbing his right Bowie into the back of the mutant on the ground even as his left Bowie speared into the raccoon on Havoc's right leg.

The remaining mutant on the noncom's chest snarled and went for the human's face.

Sergeant Havoc was faster. His right hand caught the raccoon by the throat and he hoisted it into the air, his left hand thrusting against the creature's chin in a Shotei strike, a palm-heel blow. The raccoon's neck snapped with a loud crack and it slumped in his hand.

A lone raccoon was alive, the one on Havoc's left leg. It abruptly darted toward the trees.

Thunder, waiting for an unobstructed shot, fired once.

The last of the mutant raccoons screeched as it tumbled and rolled several yards, to crash against the trunk of a tree. It gasped once and expired.

The clearing was suddenly, eeerily quiet.

Blade wrenched his Bowies from the raccoons he'd slain and straightened, blood dripping from the blades.

"I always considered raccoons harmless little critters," Boone commented somberly. "I never will again."

Blade knelt alongside Havoc. "Don't move."

Sergeant Havoc rose onto his elbows. "I'm okay, sir."

"Sure you are," Blade stated. "And stop calling me 'sir.' "

Havoc's face and neck were lacerated by a dozen claw marks. His brown T-shirt was torn to shreds, the skin underneath crisscrossed with crimson slashes. The fabric on his fatigue pants had been slit open below the knees and both legs displayed gaping wounds.

Boone and Thunder stepped to the noncom's side.

"I hope those things weren't rabid," Sergeant Havoc remarked.

"I don't think they were," Blade said.

"They weren't," Thunder stated with conviction. He crouched and deposited his M-16 on the ground. "I will tend your wounds. I have medicinal herbs in my backpack."

Blade scanned the forest while wiping the Bowies on his pants. "There doesn't seem to be any more."

Boone began reloading the spent cartridges in his Hombre. "You two take care of Havoc. I'll watch out for the mutants."

Sergant Havoc tilted his neck so he could gaze backwards at the gunman. "Thanks. You saved my life there."

"You would have done the same for me," Boone said.

"That was some shooting," Havoc said, complimenting the Cavalryman. "Better than I could have done."

Boone walked to the center of the clearing. A peculiar rattling emanated from his backpack. He finished reloading the revolvers, holstered them, and unslung both the extra backpack on his left shoulder and his own. His clattered as he lowered it to the grass.

"The Spirit-in-All-Things smiled on us," Thunder mentioned as he removed a brown leather pouch from his backpack. "This could have been much worse."

"A person can't let down their guard for a second," Blade said. He slid the Bowies into their sheaths, then leaned over the noncom to examine the wounds.

"They're just scratches," Sergeant Havoc stated, sounding embarrassed by the attention.

"You let us judge how serious your injuries are," Blade said.

"Yes, sir."

Blade determined the face, neck, and chest cuts were largely superficial. He inspected the right leg. A circular strip of skin approximately three inches in circumference had been bitten off, but the muscles and tendons were untouched. The left leg was another story. Two inches below the knee was a ragged, four-inch strip where the skin and the muscle had been chewed off, exposing the bone. "Can you bend your left leg?" he asked.

Sergeant Havoc slowly lifted the leg, then flexed it gingerly until the leg was bent at the knee. "No problem," he said.

"Lay it down," Blade advised.

Havoc complied.

"We have a problem here," Boone interjected.

Blade glanced at the Cavalryman. "What?"

Boone was squatting with his backpack open between his legs. He reached into the pack and withdrew their radio. Their shattered radio. Wires and broken circuit boards dangled from the fractured casing. "It must have happened when I landed on my back."

"So much for contacting General Gallagher for support," Blade remarked.

Thunder pulled a small glass jar from the brown pouch, unscrewed the cap, and inserted two fingers. A greenish-blue sticky substance caked his fingers when he extracted them.

"What's that?" Sergeant Havoc asked.

"A remedy of my own," Thunder said. He started applying the ointment to the noncom's neck and face, rubbing the substance over the slash marks.

Havoc scrunched up his nose. "Whew! It stinks! What's in it?"

Thunder answered as he administered the medicine. "Ground roots and certain leaves. Bear fat. Mineral water. Eye of a newt. The toe of a frog. Bat wool. And the tongue of a dog. All the usual."

Sergeant Havoc's mouth dropped. "You're kidding, right?"

"Am I?" Thunder answered with a grin.

"You've *got* to be kidding!" Havoc insisted.

"Did I mention it also contains lizard's leg?" Thunder asked with a straight face.

CHAPTER SEVEN

He came awake slowly, his chin throbbing, a dull ache pervading his lower face. His body swayed from side to side, and he received the impression that he was being carried.

The Vampires hadn't killed him!

Why not?

Grizzly opened his eyes to find the sky filled with stars. He must have been unconscious only a short while! His eyes narrowed as he pereceived he was tied to a long, stout pole or limb. His wrists and ankles were bound securely. Craning his neck, he dicovered a Vampire bearing the front of the pole upon its left shoulder. He glanced to the rear and observed another Vampire effortlessly supporting the other end. Both wore dark loincloths.

Where were they taking him?

"So? Sleeping Beauty is awake!" the Vampire to the rear commented in a high-pitched voice, then tittered.

Grizzly recalled having heard that titter before. "You can talk!" he declared.

"No shit, Sherlock!" the Vampire said sarcastically. "You must be a genius!"

Grizzly shook his head, wondering if he was dreaming.

"Don't you have the usual zillion-and-one questions?" the Vampire inquired.

"Who are you? *What* are you?" Grizzly asked.

The Vampire sighed. "How original!"

"Where's Athena, you slime-bucket?" Grizzly demanded angrily.

"Athena?" the Vampire repeated.

"You scumbags grabbed her earlier tonight," Grizzly said. "About an hour or so before you killed six Indians."

"Earlier tonight?" the Vampire stated, and tittered. "You mean last night. You were out cold all day."

All day! Grizzly gazed at the stars again.

"You're lucky," the Vampire said. "If you were human, you'd be dead right now. We would have wasted your ass after we jumped you." He paused. "But we've never seen anyone like you before. Loring thinks we should take you to Corpus."

"Where's Athena?" Grizzly repeated belligerently.

"Is that the bitch's name?" the Vampire responded. "She's with the rest of the foodstuff. We rejoined the others a while ago."

Foodstuff? Grizzly stared at the Vampire. "Do you have a name?"

"Polidori, at your service," the Vampire said in a mocking tone.

"What the hell are you?" Grizzly snapped.

"The humans call us Vampires," Polidori said. "They've been calling us that for years."

"What do you call yourselves?" Grizzly asked.

"The Venesects," Polidori replied.

"Where are you taking me?"

"You'll see," Polidori said.

"What do you plan to do with me?" Grizzly probed.

Polidori tittered. "You'll see."

"I see I'd like to cram that smirk down your throat!" Grizzly declared testily.

"You're not the timid type," Polidori commented. "I like that. It means you have good blood. I think I'll put in dibs."

Dibs? "I want to see Athena," Grizzly stated.

Polidori grinned. "Don't hold your breath."

"I'll remember you when I get free," Grizzly threatened.

"I'm scared to death," Polidori quipped. He stared skyward for several seconds. "We'll reach the Heartland before daylight. Perfect! I won't need to spend another day curled up under some rotten tree."

"You camp during the day and travel at night," Grizzly deduced. "Why?"

"Wouldn't you like to know," Polidori responded.

Grizzly, feeling supremely frustrated, scowled. He'd rate his performance on the mission as less than zero. He was separated from Blade and the others. He had failed to rescue Athena. Worse yet, he'd allowed himself to be captured by a bunch of pasty wimps! He needed to redeem himself, and as he saw it, there were two options. The ropes binding him to the pole were tight, but he knew he could break loose if he applied all of his prodigious strength. Freeing himself, though, was not the wisest course; he was outnumbered, and he did not know Athena's exact location. Since he wouldn't escape without taking her, his other option was to wait for the right moment, to let the Vampires, or the Venesects as they called themselves, take him to the Heartland.

"Do you have any idea how many pints of blood are in your body?" Polidori unexpectedly asked.

"No. Why?" Grizzly responded.

"I was just wondering about the divvy," Polidori answered.

"What's the divvy?" Grizzly questioned.

"Bits and pieces. Pieces and bits," Polidori said and laughed.

Grizzly wanted to wring Polidori's skinny neck. He calmed his boiling temper, holding his emotions in check until the proper time.

Polidori would get his, eventually.

Grizzly intended to see to it personally.

CHAPTER EIGHT

"So this is the San Diego Dead Zone," Boone remarked, sounding utterly unimpressed. "It doesn't look much different from the Dead Zone I saw in the Dakota Territory five years ago."

They were standing on a low hill 50 yards from the Dead Zone. The contrast between the Zone and the prolific vegetation in the forest was startling. The forest was lush and green, the Zone was devoid of plant life. The forest soil was rich in nutrients and a healthy brown, but the Dead Zone earth was parched and reddish.

"It looks like a red desert," Sergeant Havoc mentioned.

"This place is evil," Thunder said solemnly. "A violation of Nature."

Blade scanned the red dunes for a sign of life. Not so much as an insect stirred. "Somewhere in there is where we'll find the Vampires. Does everyone have a full canteen?"

"Yes, sir," Havoc said.

"Mine is full," Thunder replied.

"Same here," Boone stated.

Blade looked at the noncom. "Are you sure you're up to this?

You can wait here for us to return.''

"No way, sir," Havoc asserted. "I've come this far. I'll go all the way."

"Suit yourself," Blade said. "Head on out! Thunder, take the point. No more than ten yards in front. I'll bring up the rear."

They advanced to the edge of the Dead Zone and halted.

"There," Thunder said, pointing. "Following them will be easy."

The surface of the fine red dirt was marked by dozens of footprints, all heading to the west.

"Keep your eyes peeled," Blade advised. He waited as the others marched into the Zone, then trudged after them. He scrutinized Sergeant Havoc.

The noncom walked with a pronounced limp. Thunder had treated and bandaged both legs, thereby preventing infection. By all rights Havoc should be recuperating in a bed. The strain of the prolonged hiking waas aggravating his wounds. He could not apply all of his weight to his left leg, and he hobbled on his left foot as he proceeded gamely into the Zone.

A mile was traversed in silence. The montony of the barren terrain was oddly oppressive, seeming to radiate an aura of menace.

"This place is creepy," Boone commented as they crested a dune.

Ahead was a flat expanse of red earth.

"I hear there are Dead Zones all over the country," Sergeant Havoc said. "All kinds of monsters inhabit them."

"Just what I wanted to hear," Boone cracked.

Blade noticed a mound of red dirt to their right and 40 feet in front of them. The mound was S-shaped, five feet high, and over 20 in length.

They tramped half the distance to the mound.

Blade felt perspiration beading his forehead. The sun, strangely, was baking his skin, as if the red earth served as an oven, reflecting and amplifying the heat. He mopped at his brow with his right hand. How could anything live in such a land? he wondered. How did the Vampires survive and thrive under such harsh, arid circumstances?

Sergeant Havoc glanced over his left shoulder. "It's hard to believe this was once a major city, isn't it, sir?"

"I asked you to stop calling me sir," Blade reminded the noncom. "Blade will do."

"I've spent my adult life calling my superiors sir," Havoc noted. "It's hard to break old habits."

Blade gazed absently at the mound of dirt, then at the far horizon. "Have you ever been in a Dead Zone before?"

"No," Sergeant Havoc admitted.

"I was in New York City once," Blade divulged. "There was red dirt and molten slag everywhere." He paused. "New York City had a population of fifteen to twenty million when the war broke out. Fifteen to twenty million lives were obliterated in mere minutes. It's difficult to appreciate the reality of such total destruction. Here we are, walking where a major city once stood. What was San Diego's population? Close to two million?" He shook his head. "I still can't seem to fully grasp the magnitude of the war."

"I know what you mean," Sergeant Havoc said.

"Every time I think of the war, and of our ancestors, I keep coming back to the same question," Blade stated. "How could they do this to themselves?"

"And what's the answer?" Sergeant Havoc responded.

"The Family Elders teach a course called The History of World War Three," Blade said. "It's very interesting. World War Three, they say, was the result of several factors. One was the absolute incompatibility of capitalism and communism. Capitalism was based on the profit motive and the private ownership of property, while communism vested all ownership in the state and held all property in common. The two systems were diametrically opposed. And the communists were intolerant of other political beliefs. They wanted to rule the world. The man who wrote *The Communist Manifesto*, Karl Marx, stated their goal plainly. He advocated the forcible overthrow of all existing social conditions."

"What other factors were involved?" Sergeant Havoc asked.

"The military factor was one," Blade detailed. "Both sides constantly strived to hold the edge militarily. They poured billions of dollars into ever newer and better weapons systems.

If they had spent half of that money on their social problems, like poverty and illiteracy, they could have cured their social ills. But each side was determined to be King of the Mountain. They perfected the art of war until it became racially suicidal. Their leaders tried to achieve peace through diplomacy and treaties. They failed because neither side trusted the other, they misled each other, and because promises and pledges are no substitute for a genuine craving for peace."

Sergeant Havoc absorbed the Warrior's words thoughtfully.

"Another factor was the spiritual one," Blade went on. "In America the people were free to worship as they pleased. There was religious diversity, although the secular humanists tried to mold a society without a spiritual foundation. On the Russian side, the government, the Communist Party, was officially and actively atheistic. They considered religious beliefs a form of insanity. A godless society can never coexist with a religious one."

Havoc stared at the ground. He was amazed at the Warrior's analysis. What manner of men and women did they raise in the Family? How could Blade be such a skilled fighter, and so ruthless when necessary, and yet be so philosophical—indeed spiritual—at the same time? He did not understand.

The Force members passed within six feet of the mound of S-shaped dirt.

Blade gazed idly at the mound as they strolled by. He noticed the granular texture of the dirt, and the particles shimmering in the sunlight.

They were ten feet beyond the mound when Thunder abruptly halted and crouched, his right hand feeling the impressions at his feet. He looked back at Blade. "They are carrying someone."

"Be specific," Blade directed.

"Two of the Vampires are leaving clear footprints," Thunder explained. "Their feet are sinking deeper in the dirt. Either they are fat Vampires, or they are bearing additional weight. They are walking about seven feet apart. I think they are carrying someone or something between them, probably using a branch."

Sergeant Havoc's mind flashed back to their first mission, the strike against the vile Spider. "The Hatchlings transported me that way after I was caught.''

"Is there any indication the Vampires wear shoes or boots?'' Blade inquired.

"None,'' Thunder responded. "All I've seen are prints of naked feet. Their soles must be solid callus.

"How much of a lead do they have?'' Blade queried.

Thunder studied the tracks for a moment. "These tracks were made during the night. It's ten o'clock now. I'd say they passed here about four in the morning.''

"Maybe we can catch up with them before nightfall,'' Blade stated hopefully. "Head out.''

They resumed their trek into the Dead Zone.

Blade took several strides, then stopped, listening. A weird sort of swishing had sounded for a second or two. He cocked his head and surveyed the Dead Zone on both sides.

Nothing.

Shrugging, the Warrior followed his companions.

The swishing was repeated.

Blade halted.

The swishing ceased.

Was the blistering heat affecting his hearing? Blade slowly turned, scrutinizing the alien landscape. He saw the mound, and the expanse of red earth, and . . .

The mound!

Blade's gray eyes narrowed, his grip on the Commando tightening. The mound had moved! It was no longer S-shaped, but had mysteriously straightened at one end. The end nearest the Force. He stared at the mound for over a minute, waiting for it to move again.

"Is something wrong, sir?'' Sergeant Havoc called out.

Blade glanced over his right shoulder. Havoc and the others were waiting for him 50 feet away. He double-checked the mound, which displayed no hint of movement. "I guess not,'' he yelled. He faced westward and headed for his companions. Perhaps he had misjudged the original shape of the mound. After all, mounds of dirt did not move by themselves. There must be a logical explanation. He gazed at the others and froze.

Sergeant Havoc, Boone, and Thunder were gaping at him in stunned amazement.

No.

Not at him.

Behind him!

Blade whirled, his skin crawling with goose bumps at the sight he beheld.

The mound was moving, the rear portion uncurling into a straight line. And suddenly the mound performed an equally incredible feat; it started toward the Warrior.

Bewildered, Blade pressed the Commando stock against his right shoulder. He squinted to reduce the glare as insight washed over him. The mound wasn't moving: something was coming at him *under the ground!* There was something underneath the surface, something alive, something five feet in height and over 20 feet long.

Dear Spirit! What could it be?

"Blade!" Boone shouted in alarm. "Run for it!"

Blade wasn't about to run. He stood between the thing and his men, and he intended to stop whatever-it-was before it reached them. He saw the red earth ripple as the thing gained speed, the fine grains flowing up and over the thing as if the ground was pliable putty instead of dense dirt.

"Blade!" Sergeant Havoc yelled.

Blade let the thing get within five feet of him before he opened fire, the Commando thundering and bucking in his arms. The slugs smacked into the ground at the leading edge of the thing, dirt flying everywhere.

Whatever-it-was never missed a beat. The front end swerved, bearing to the left and skirting the Warrior.

Blade poured a withering burst into the side of the thing, but it was apparently unaffected.

In a burst of speed the underground denizen bypassed the giant and angled toward Sergeant Havoc.

"Havoc! Look out!" Blade bellowed and took off in pursuit.

Segeant Havoc cradled his M-16 and awaited the thing. His injured left leg precluded any hope of avoiding the behemoth. He opted to make a stand where he stood.

The thing bore down on the noncom with astonishing swiftness.

Pounding after it, Blade knew he could not reach Havoc in time. The noncom would be on his own.

Not quite.

Thunder and Boone raced around Havoc, Thunder on the left, Boone the right. They intentionally put themselves in the creature's path, running 15 feet from the noncom, then stopping.

The behemoth came on like a burrowing express train.

Thunder and Boone fired in unison, their M-16s chattering, their shots plowing into the dirt welling up over the creature's back.

The thing never slowed.

Thunder and Havoc were four feet apart when the behemoth passed between them, the ground tilting crazily and cresting like a wave in the ocean. Both lost their footing and were upended.

Blade, sweat caking his body, the blood pounding in his temples, watched in horror as the creature closed on Sergeant Havoc.

CHAPTER NINE

General M.A. Gallagher was in no mood for interruptions. He stood in the Communications Center at March Air Force Base and glared at the hapless Communications Specialist seated in a chair before him. "I don't care if you've tried a hundred times," he snapped. "You'll keep trying until I tell you otherwise. You got that, Sergeant?"

The soldier gulped and nodded. He swiveled his chair and applied himself to the radio once more. "Bravo-Lima-Alfa-Delta-Echo, this is Big Bad Wolf. Do you copy? Over."

General Gallagher listened to the sergeant, frowning in annoyance. The Freedom Force should have radioed in a position fix at dawn. The ramifications of their failure upset him immensely. If Blade didn't call in soon, he would have to send a platoon of Rangers after the Force.

A young lieutenant approached the general. "Sir, you've been here for hours without a break. Would you care for a cup of coffee or some food?"

Gallagher looked at the lieutenant, his brown eyes narrowing. With his jowly features, stocky body, and crew-cut brown hair, he resembled a pit bull about to bite. "When I'm hungry,

Lieutenant, I'll let you know," he declared testily.

"I just meant—" the lieutenant began.

"I know exactly what you meant!" General Gallagher said, cutting him off. "You just attend to your duties and let me worry about my stomach."

The lieutenant blanched. "Yes, sir." He did an about-face and hurried off.

Gallagher clasped his hands behind his back and stared at the Communications Specialist. "Anything, Sergeant?"

"No, sir."

"Keep trying," Gallagher ordered. He glanced at a blue telephone on the wall to his left, wondering when Governor Melnick would call to inquire about the status of the mission. As the personal liaison between the Force and the governor, he, ultimately, would be praised or criticized depending on how the Force performed. So long as the Force accomplished each mission, he was content to bask in the limelight and savor the attendant benefits to his career. But if the Force failed, if Blade and company bought the farm, Gallagher knew his career might suffer. Governor Melnick, for one, would be extremely unhappy. Not to mention all of the other Federation leaders. A stigma would be attached to his sterling service record, and through no fault of his own. Sure, he'd withheld certain information pertaining to the damn Vampires from Blade. Yes, he'd deceived the Warrior, but Blade would have turned down the mission, would have refused to leave until the Force rested from their Oregon foray if Gallagher had told the complete truth. He'd deliberately given the Warrior the misimpression that the assignment in Aguanga would be a quick in-and-out affair, knowing full well that Blade's sense of dedication would take care of the rest.

Who could have figured Blade would fail?

The thick steel door to the Communications Center opened and in walked a major, a thin man with gray streaks in his hair. He crossed to the general and stood at attention. "Sir! There's someone here to see you."

General Gallagher scowled. "Not now, Major Donovan! Can't you see I'm busy?"

"Sir, this can't be helped," Major Donovan persisted.

"There's someone here to see you who came in on the courier run."

"The courier run?" Gallagher repeated, his thick eyebrows arching.

"Yes, sir," Donovan confirmed. "One of the VTOLs returned from its courier run to Minnesota fifteen minutes ago with an unexpected passenger."

Gallagher's forehead creased in perplexity. When the VTOLs weren't required to shuttle the Force on a mission, they were utilized as a courier service between the Federation factions. The jets did not ferry passengers on a regular basis, except for Blade. The Warrior visited the Home at least once a month. "Who was the pilot?"

"Captain Laslo," Major Donovan answered.

"I'll bust him down to airman for breaking regulations!" Geneal Gallagher stated.

"You'll do nothin' of the kind, honky," said a low, firm voice from the doorway.

General Gallagher pivoted, his mouth slackening. "You!" he blurted.

"Yeah, me," said the newcomer. "Long time no see." He sauntered into the ComCenter with an air of indifferent arrogance, a huge black man with a curly Afro attired in a brown leather vest and faded brown corduroy pants.

"Bear!" General Gallagher exclaimed.

"None other," Bear stated, stepping over to the officer.

"We haven't seen each other since the summit meeting in January," Gallagher noted. "What are you doing here?"

"Can't you guess?" Bear rejoined.

Gallagher reflected for a minute. Bear was from the Federation faction known at the Clan. They lived in the town of Halma, not far from the Family, and their leader was a man named Zahner. Bear was Zahner's right-hand man. He was also a close friend of Blade's.

"Did you figure it out yet?" Bear asked.

"I think so," Gallagher said. "You've volunteered to represent the Clan on the Force. The last man they sent didn't last very long."

Bear nodded at the rows of ribbons adorning the general's

jacket. "Is one of those for smarts? You're right on the money."

"Why did Zahner send you?" Gallagher queried. "You're one of the top Clansmen."

"So? Rank doesn't have any privileges in the Clan," Bear said. "We've all got to serve however we can."

"Blade will be delighted to see you," General Gallagher predicted.

Bear smiled. "Where is he anyway? I want to report to him right away."

General Gallagher coughed. "I'm afraid that's not possible."

"Why not?" Bear demanded, folding his muscular arms across his wide chest.

"Blade isn't here," Gallagher revealed. "He's on a mission and I don't know when he'll be back."

"Where is this mission?" Bear inquired.

"That's confidential information," General Gallagher replied brusquely.

Bear's lips compressed and he leaned forward until his nose was almost touching the officer's. His brown eyes were flinty, and his tone when he spoke was hard. "You listen to me, General, and you listen good!" he said so only Gallagher could hear. "I didn't think much of your scuzzy butt when I was in California for the summit, and I can see that you ain't changed much. You can take all those medals you're wearin' and stuff 'em up your ass! They don't mean squat to me." He paused. "I volunteered for the Force because I happen to like Blade. And I just flew two thousand miles to see him. Now you tell me where he is, or in front of all your troops I'm going to turn you upside down and shake you until you rattle. Got me?"

General Gallagher's face did a marvelous imitation of a beet. His lips worked but no words came out.

"And don't try to pull rank on me," Bear warned. "I'll take my orders from Blade and no one else. If you don't like it, you're welcome to try and do something about it."

Gallagher finally found his voice. "No one talks to me like that!" he hissed. "No one!"

"I said my piece," Bear stated. "What happens next is up to you."

Gallagher suppressed his fury with a monumental effort. He

refused to lose his control in front of subordinates.

"Where is Blade?" Bear repeated.

Gallagher knew that Bear would carry through with his threat. He knew Governor Melnick would frown on an altercation between a top-ranking officer and a lowly grunt. Tact was called for. "Blade is on a mission in the vicinity of San Diego."

"Where exactly?" Bear questioned.

"I don't know, exactly," General Gallagher confessed.

Bear gazed at the banks of communications and computer equipment lining the walls of the ComCenter. "Do you take me for a fool, honky? I may have been raised in the Twin Cities and spent most of my life in a gang, but I'm not stupid. Blade has told me a little about the Force. They always take a radio along, don't they?"

"Yes," General Gallagher verified.

"Then you must know where he is," Bear observed.

Gallagher placed his hands on his hips. "I'll be honest with you—"

"Don't change your personality on my account," Bear said, interrupting.

"I really don't know where Blade is at this moment," General Gallagher continued, ignoring the insult. "We've lost contact with the Force."

"Why don't you send in a backup unit?" Bear suggested.

"I was going to wait a while longer," Gallagher replied.

"Screw waiting," Bear stated. "I'll go after them."

General Gallagher pretended to stare at the floor to disguise his sudden grin of satisfaction. Bear's arrival could be a blessing in disguise. If he sent Bear after Blade, and if Bear failed, then the onus, the discredit, would be on Bear's shoulders. Gallagher nearly laughed. He would be off the hook!

"What about it?" Bear prompted. "Give me some men and I'll find Blade for you."

General Gallagher adopted a contemplative expression, as if he was mulling over the proposition. "I don't know," he hedged.

"Come on!" Bear goaded. "I can do it."

"It would be risky," General Gallagher commented.

"I don't care," Bear stated. "Blade is my friend, and I know Boone real well. They may be in trouble."

Gallagher scratched his chin. "Would you be willing to lead a company of Rangers into the field?"

"When do we leave?" Bear responded eagerly.

General Gallagher smiled. "In an hour. I'll order choppers to airlift you to Aguanga. You'll be on your own from there."

"Aguanga?" Bear said.

"The name of the town the Force was sent to," Gallagher divulged. "You can pick up their trail at the town."

"Looks like I owe you one," Bear said.

"I'm just doing my job," Gallagher remarked.

Bear gazed around the Communications Center. "I can use a bite to eat before I go."

"There's a mess hall outside this building and to the east," Gallagher said.

Bear turned toward the doorway.

"Wait,' Gallagher declared. "There's something I'm curious about."

Bear looked back at the general. "Like what?"

"Where did you ever get the name Bear?" General Gallagher inquired. "It's not a typical, everyday name."

"I picked it up in the Twin Cities," Bear detailed. "I belonged to a gang headed by a scumbag named Maggot. He got his kicks by givin' everybody a nickname, and the nickname he gave me stuck. Everyone has been callin' me Bear for years."

"What's your real name?" General Gallagher asked.

"What's the diff?" Bear responded. "I like my nickname better."

"I was just curious," General Gallagher said. "What is your real name?"

Bear's sheepish response was barely audible. "Harold."

CHAPTER TEN

Sergeant Havoc stood his ground, aimed the M-16, and fired. His rounds stitched into the wave of red dirt surging toward him and the creature underneath swerved to the left, circling him. Havoc emptied the M-16's magazine in the roiling earth.

Blade raced to the noncom's aid. He saw Boone and Thunder scrambling to their feet.

The thing swung toward Havoc again the moment the M-16 went empty. He shuffled backwards, discarding the M-16 and drawing the Colt automatics.

Red dirt started spraying upwards a few feet in front of the noncom, forming a geyser of shimmering particles. The fountain of fine earth rose a full ten feet into the air, choking the air with dust and restricting visibility.

Blade spied a bulky, dark shape rising from the ground at the base of the geyser. The behemoth was emerging from its subterranean domain! "Havoc!" he shouted. "Look out! It's coming up!"

Sergeant Havoc was holding his left Colt in front of his eyes to block the swirling dirt. He squinted at the snakelike form flowing from the hole in the ground. The dust prevented him from seeing the thing clearly. Where was its head? Its eyes? Where was the monster most vulnerable?

The thing arced six feet above the ground, then its front end lunged at the noncom.

Sergeant Havoc threw himself to the right. Something smacked against his legs and he was thrown for a loop. He landed on his back facing eastward, the creature to his rear.

"Roll!" Blade bellowed.

Havoc automatically rolled to the left and something thudded onto the earth in the spot he'd just vacated. He heaved to his right knee and swiveled to confront his adversary.

And what an adversary!

The behemoth was a wormish creature of gigantic proportions, with a girth of four feet and a length five times as great. Its body was brownish-black, laced with narrow folds in the outer skin, and reeking with a sickeningly sweet odor. Headless and eyeless, the worm did possess an enormous, hideous maw consisting of reddish lips and a toothless mouth wide enough to swallow a man in one gulp.

Havoc blasted away with the Colts, a clear fluid spurting from the creature every time he hit home.

Boone and Thunder joined in, their M-16's chattering in unison.

The worm reared higher, swinging its mouth in the direction of this new threat.

And then Blade was there, on Havoc's right, the Commando in the Warrior's right hand, Grizzly's M-16 in his left. He fired them simultaneously, his massive arms absorbing the recoil.

The worm jerked and whipped its body from side to side, its maw opening and closing spasmodically.

Blade unexpectedly ceased firing, dropped the Commando and the M-16, and unslung his backpack.

Sergeant Havoc, Boone, and Thunder poured it on, the Cavalryman and the Flathead ejecting spent magazines and inserting fresh ones in a twinkling.

Havoc expended the last round in his Colts and grabbed for a new clip in his left front pocket. He saw Blade charge the worm. The Warrior was holding his right arm aloft, a packet of plastic explosive outfitted with a timer clutched in his hand.

"Me! Take me!" Blade yelled.

The worm reared up, then plunged its giant mouth toward the Warrior.

Blade heaved the explosive, a perfect toss, the packet sailing straight into the creature's maw and down its throat. "Hit the dirt!" he commanded, then flung himself from the behemoth.

The sensation of swallowing a foreign object had caused the worm to recoil skyward. It was framed against the backdrop of blue sky when the detonator went off.

Sergeant Havoc, in the act of flattening as the explosive occurred, was slammed to the earth by the concussion. Grisly chunks of brown, fleshy gore spattered all over him and the surrounding ground. He hugged the dirt, his back becoming clammy from the worm's sticky fluid raining down. His ears began ringing.

In the aftermath of the explosion the Dead Zone was preternaturally still.

"Is it dead?" Boone asked.

Sergeant Havoc looked up. Blade was rising. Thunder and Boone were already erect.

"It's dead," Blade stated.

The upper third of the worm had been blown to smithereens, leaving a jagged fringe of flesh that was oozing fluid. Its colossal body was twitching. Tendrils of smoke wafted upward.

Havoc slowly stood, brushing the dust from his clothing. "How long was the timer set for?" he inquired, glancing at the Warrior.

"Less than a minute," Blade replied.

Havoc whistled. "You believe in cutting it close!"

"There was no time to lose," Blade said.

Sergeant Havoc scrutinized the worm's repulsive corpse. "And what if you had missed?"

"I would have kept my fingers crossed for a giant robin to show up," Blade joked.

Thunder walked over to the worm, his mouth downturned. "Will we encounter more abominations like this?"

"Probably," Blade answered. "Unless we're very lucky."

Thunder surveyed the Dead Zone. "This land is a blight on Creation. I do not like being here."

''Who does?'' Blade retorted. He retrieved the Commando and the M-16, reloaded both, then slung the M-16 over his left shoulder.

Segeant Havoc recovered his M-16.

''Are you okay?'' Blade asked the noncom.

''No worse than before,'' Havoc replied.

''Then let's move out,'' Blade directed them.

They resumed their trek into the Dead Zone, walking in silence, alert for another attack. Hours passed and none came.

''How large is this Dead Zone?'' Boone queried loudly at one point.

''Twenty miles in diameter,'' Sergeant Havoc answered. ''At least, that's what I was told a few years ago.''

Blade gazed at the red dirt. ''Some cities were more fortunate than San Diego,'' he commented.

Boone looked back. ''How so?''

''San Diego sustained a direct surface burst,'' Blade explained. ''Other cities were hit by air bursts.''

''What's the difference between the two?'' Boone inquired.

''The surface burst is far more destructive and deadly,'' Blade said. ''The blast sucks up tons and tons of dirt and debris, all of which becomes coated with radioactive material in the mushroom cloud. All of these radioactive particles then fall back to the ground, producing the fallout. So from a surface burst there are two devastating consequences. The first is the blast itself, and the area it destroys will depend on the size of the thermonuclear device. The second is the radioactive fallout, which the winds can spread over a wide area.''

''The results aren't the same with an air burst?'' Boone asked.

''No,'' Blade said. ''The air burst won't destroy as large an area as the surface burst. And the air burst produces very little fallout because the blast takes place in the atmosphere above the target. Hardly any dirt or debris is drawn up into the mushroom cloud. In later years, this means less contamination of the soil.''

Boone surveyed the red plain ahead. ''Is this area radioactive?''

''Only slightly,'' Blade responded. ''General Gallagher and I were discussing the war about three weeks ago. He told me the Hot Spots in California are monitored regularly. The radiation level here is higher than normal, but it's not life-threatening.''

"That's a relief," Boone remarked.

Thunder abruptly stopped and pointed to the west. "What is that?''

The Force members clustered around the Flathead.

"It looks spooky," Boone mentioned.

Blade had to agree. A half mile off was a solitary spire rearing heavenward.

I can't make out details," Sergeant Havoc said.

"Let's go see what it is," Blade proposed, taking the lead.

They traversed a quarter of a mile, expectantly fingering their weapons.

Blade was the first to see the rim. He ascended a dune and blinked rapidly at the vista before him, astonished.

The very earth seemed to fall away not 20 yards distant. Beyond was a tremendous crater stretching as far as the eye could discern. Inside the crater was a titanic jumble of molten slag, twisted and rusted girders, ruined buildings, and heaps of rubble.

Blade walked to the crater rim and stared at the tangle of metal and stone.

"Will you look at that!" Boone exclaimed.

"I never imagined. . . ." Sergeant Havoc began, then stopped.

Thunder's lips compressed as he scrutinized the crater. A look of ineffable sadness etched his features.

Blade gazed at the spire, actually all that was left of a once-mighty skyscraper. The scene vividly reminded him of New York City.

"Are we going down there?" Boone questioned. He did not sound too keen on the idea.

"Afraid so," Blade said. "We know the Vampires have their lair in the Dead Zone. Where else could it be?" He studied the slope below the rim. "The incline is gradual. We won't have any problems getting down there."

"It's not getting down I'm concerned about," Boone said. "It's getting back up."

"Since when did you become such a big worrywart?" Sergeant Havoc inquired.

"Ever since I signed up for the Force," Boone replied. "I miss Dakota and I want to see it again someday."

"You will," Blade assured the Cavalryman.

Boone chuckled. "Not at the rate we're going."

Blade stepped onto the slanting crater wall. The rim was only 15 yards from the bottom and he reached the base with ease. As the others slowly descended the slope, with Sergeant Havoc gingerly applying pressure to his left foot, he studied the ruins.

From the crater rim the molten slag, ravaged buildings, girders, and other debris had appeared as a packed, almost solid mass. But closer inspection revealed a maze of openings and passageways penetrating into the gloomy bowels of the ruins. Red dust caked everything. The air was hot and motionless.

"Why do I have the feeling I'm being watched?" Boone queried as the others joined the Warrior.

"I have the same feeling," Sergeant Havoc said.

"I'll go first," Blade proposed.

"Be my guest," Boone quipped.

Blade took four strides toward the ruins.

"Look!" Thunder suddenly blurted.

Everyone froze in midstride.

"What is it?" Boone asked, his eyes darting every which way.

"I saw something move," Thunder said.

Blade scanned the devastation. "Where?"

Thunder pointed at a wide opening in a 40-foot pile of rubble. "There."

"Did you get a good look at it?" Blade inquired.

"No," Thunder answered. "It was big and green. That's all I can tell you."

"How big?" Boone interjected.

"About as big as a horse," Thunder responded.

"Uh-oh," Boone said. "Here we go again."

Blade held the Commando next to his waist and advanced to the edge of the ruins. To his left rose a column of slag and to his right a shattered concrete wall.

Sergeant Havoc came next, then Boone and Thunder.

"I should have known better," Boone muttered. "When

Kilrane asked me to volunteer for the Force, I should have known better.''

"Kilrane?" Havoc repeated.

"The leader of the Cavalry," Boone detailed. "One of my best friends. He asked me to volunteer as a personal favor to him."

Sergeant Havoc grinned. "Some friend you've got there."

"I think the next time I see him," Boone whispered, "I'll pop him in the chops."

Blade entered the ruins.

"Here goes nothing," Sergeant Havoc said, and followed.

Blade proceeded cautiously. The bizarre jungle of metal and stone was emotionally unsettling. He remembered reading about the astronauts and their flights to the moon and elsewhere, and he wondered if the space travelers had experienced similar reactions as they walked upon a totally foreign world. The passage he was on wound ever deeper into the demolished metropolis. Spires, slag, crumbling walls, and vestiges of decimated structures towered overhead. Murky shadows enveloped the landscape. A maze of passageways branched in all directions. He glanced down at the path and halted.

There, outlined by the layer of red dust, was the imprint of a naked foot.

Blade lifted his eyes and discovered a whole series of footprints heading in the direction the Force was going.

The others also noticed.

"Vampire tracks," Thunder stated.

Blade continued onward. After 50 feet he reached a junction and stopped.

The footprints bore to the left.

The Warrior pursed his lips, debating whether to stick with the tracks or take another route.

From above the Force a distinct clicking sounded.

Blade tilted his head and stared upward, searching the crevices and obscure recesses.

Again the noise was heard, a grating click-click-click. Only louder.

"It's coming toward us," Thunder commented.

A misty shower of red dust sprinkled over them.

Blade looked around and spied a section of wall 15 yards to the left. The jagged wall was five feet high and twice that in length. "On me," he declared, jogging toward the promising shelter.

Just as a gigantic, squat form dropped from the upper recesses and landed between the Force and the wall.

CHAPTER ELEVEN

Grizzly paced the dark cell with his fists clenched at his sides, his suppressed anger close to the boiling point.

The room was ten feet by ten, its walls and door constructed of old wood. Devoid of all furniture, lacking even a sink, the cell reeked of sweat and urine. The floor was compact earth.

How long did the Vampires intend to keep him confined?

Grizzly paused and glanced at the door. He'd lost track of the hours spent in the cell, and he was growing increasingly impatient as the time passed. Six Vampires had dumped him in the cell last night, untied the ropes securing him to the pole, then departed with the pole and the ropes. By his estimation it was now the following afternoon, and not one Vampire had shown its ugly face all day. His stomach was growling and he needed to relieve himself, but he had a greater worry.

Where was Athena?

He walked to the cell door and peered out the narrow barred slot situated at eye level. An empty, dim corridor stretched before him. A single lantern was attached to a metal hook ten yards from the door, casting feeble light on the wooden walls and dirt floor. Some of the light filtered in the cell window, affording the only illumination.

Why didn't he just break out? he asked himself.

Grizzly frowned as he stared at the corridor. He knew the answer to that one: He wouldn't do anything to endanger Athena. If he escaped, the Vampires might kill her before he could find her. Locating Athena before he made his bid for freedom was imperative.

Then he would take care of the damn Vampires!

His keen ears detected the quiet padding of naked feet on the dirt floor of the corridor.

A pale figure appeared, heading toward the cell.

Grizzly watched until he recognized the approaching Vampire, then he backed into the darkest corner.

Seconds later a cruel, angular face materialized at the barred slot. "Grizzly?" Waxlike eyes shifted from right to left. "Ahhh! There you are? What are you trying to do? Hide?" the figure asked and tittered.

"To what do I owe this honor, Polidori?" Grizzly asked. He did not mention that standing in the corner had been a purposeful test of the Vampire's vision.

"Would you like some food?" Polidori inquired.

Grizzly moved to the door. "I get to eat?" he rejoined in surprise.

"Of course," Polidori stated. "We don't want you to become weak and sick."

"Why all this concern about my health?" Grizzly questioned.

"The healthier, the bettter," Polidori replied enigmatically. "I'm sure a bright mutant like you can figure it out, Grizzly."

On the verge of telling the Vampire where to shove its sarcasm, Grizzly tensed and placed his hands on the door. "You called me by my name!"

Polidori tittered. "Yep. Definitely a bright mutant!"

"I never told you my name," Grizzly stated. "How did you find out?"

"From your sweetheart," Polidori replied.

"My sweetheart?"

"Athena," Polidori said with a smirk. "I do admire your taste in women. She's a fox."

Grizzly's nostrils flared. "Where is she? What have you done to her?"

"We haven't done anything to her," Polidori said. "Yet. Corpus has given orders she's not to be touched."

"Who is Corpus?" Grizzly asked.

"The head of the Venesects, stupid," Polidori replied.

"If he lays a hand on her—" Grizzly began.

Polidori laughed. "Didn't you hear what I just said? Corpus has ordered us not to lay a finger on her. She's not to be used as foodstuff." He sighed. "Too bad. She's a healthy specimen."

"Why is Athena receiving special treatment?" Grizzly inquired.

"Because of you," Polidori responded.

"Me?"

"Yeah, dummy. You. Corpus has taken a personal interest in your case. And when I told him that you're hot to trot for the bitch, he decided to use her to keep you in line," Polidori detailed.

Grizzly could feel his temper rising. "I want to meet this Corpus."

"You will," Polidori promised.

"When?"

"Tonight. Corpus is holding a banquet in your honor." Polidori snickered. "And the bitch will be there too."

"What about the people you abducted from Aguanga?" Grizzly questioned.

"All of them will be at the banquet," Polidori said. "They'll be the highlight of the night."

"What do you mean?"

"You'll see," Polidori said, then snickered. "Now how about a snack to tide you over until the banquet?"

"I'm not hungry," Grizzly lied. "But I do need to use a bathroom."

Polidori cackled. "A bathroom! What do you think the corners of your cell are for?"

"If I go in here it'll stink up the whole room," Grizzly remarked.

"Poor baby!" Polidori mocked him.

"At least let me out to go somewhere else," Grizzly said.

"No way."

"I won't try to escape," Grizzly stated. "You have my

word.''

Polidori's eyes narrowed. "I don't trust you. But Corpus did say you wouldn't try a thing as long as we have the bitch.''

"So let me out," Grizzly prompted.

"Why should I do you any favors?" Polidori asked. "What's in it for me?''

"Just my gratitude," Grizzly said.

Polidori started laughing. He laughed and laughed, doubling over, his hands pressed against his ribs.

"What's so funny?" Grizzly demanded.

Polidori slowly straightened, his laughter trailing off. He took a deep breath. "You are!''

Grizzly did not respond.

"You're the funniest guy I've met in ages!" Polidori declared. "Do you think I care about your gratitude?''

"Then let me out for another reason," Grizzly proposed.

"Like what?''

"When I get around to killing you, I won't make you suffer," Grizzly pledged. "But only if you let me out.''

Polidori began laughing again.

Grizzly frowned. He knew insanity when he saw it, and Polidori was definitely off the deep end. Perhaps all of the Vampires were tainted by hereditary mental instability.

"You're a regular comedian!" Polidori stated. "And I'll tell you what I'll do. I'll let you out to take your dump, but I'm going to hold you to your promise. I wouldn't want to suffer!'' He burst into a hearty guffaw.

Grizzly waited for the Vampire's mirth to subside. He regretted making his hasty pledge. If anyone deserved to suffer, Polidori did.

"But remember," the Vampire said, suddenly serious. "Any funny stuff and the bitch buys the farm! They're expecting me back soon.''

"Who is?''

"Corpus, Loring, and Minshi," Polidori said. He reached out and slid a metal bolt from its socket, then retreated several paces. "Okay. Come out.''

Grizzly opened the door and stepped into the corridor. His cell was located at the end of the passage.

"Follow me," Polidori instructed. "I'll find you a place to potty."

They walked along the corridor.

"You've mentioned the name Loring twice," Grizzly noted. "Who is he?"

"Loring is second in command to Corpus," Polidori answered. "Loring was in charge of the foodstuff hunt we were on when we captured you. He was the first one who jumped you in the gorge."

"Didn't I break his nose?"

"No. That was Prest. He's pissed about it too. He wanted to finish you on the spot, but Loring stopped him," Polidori said.

"And who is Minshi?" Grizzly asked.

Polidori abruptly halted and glanced back at the mutant. "Minshi is in a class all by himself."

"How's that?" Grizzly queried.

"You'll see." He stepped past the lantern.

Grizzly wanted to learn more information while Polidori was in a talkative mood. "What's with the lantern? You certainly don't need the light to see by."

"True," Polidori said. "Venesects can see in near total darkness. But we keep one lantern in each corridor for the benefit of the foodstuff. They can't see shit in the dark."

"Do you mean the people the Vampires have kidnapped?"

"Of course, moron," Polidori replied.

"They have the run of this place?" Grizzly probed.

"Some do," Polidori responded. "We use them for menial labor. We spare them if they do good work."

"Have any tried to escape?" Grizzly asked.

"No one has ever escaped from the Heartland," Polidori boasted. "And no one ever will."

"Then I'll be the first," Grizzly commented.

Polidori cackled.

They reached another cell door on the right side of the passage.

"Let's try this one," Polidori suggested. He opened the door and peered inside. "This one isn't occupied. Dump in here."

Grizzly entered the cell, a virtual carbon copy of the original.

He crossed to the far right-hand corner, then noticed Polidori was watching him. "Out. I don't need an audience."

"Bashful, huh?" Polidori said. He closed the door.

"No peeking," Grizzly warned as he squatted.

"Are the others as weird as you?" Polidori inquired.

"What others?" Grizzly responded, grunting.

"Your friends. The four men you were with. An Indian, a soldier, another guy in buckskins, and a giant."

"I don't know who you're talking about," Grizzly said.

"Sure you don't!" Polidori retorted. "Maybe it will refresh your memory when you see them at the banquet."

"They're here!" Grizzly exclaimed.

"One of our lookouts spotted them earlier," Polidori revealed. "Corpus ordered them to be captured. You'd better hope my brothers get to them before something else does. There are a lot of mutants in the Heartland, infesting the upper levels."

Grizzly was alarmed at the news. Blade as walking into a trap! Should he try to warn the Warrior? How could he, when he had no idea where to find the Force? "Say," he said casually, "I've been meaning to ask you something. You blindfolded me before you carted me down here. How far are we below the surface?"

The Vampire did not answer.

"Polidori? Did you hear me? How far are we below the surface?" Grizzly repeated.

No reply.

Puzzled, Grizzly finished and stood. Where was a large leaf when he needed one? He walked to the door and attempted to open it.

The cell door was locked.

"Polidori? What is this?" Grizzly demanded. He pressed his nose to the barred slot.

Forty yards off the Vampire's pale figure was gradually receding.

"Polidori! You son of a bitch! You tricked me!" Grizzly shouted, incensed.

Polidori paused long enough to yell a sarcastic reply. "No shit!"

The Vampire's laughter filled the corridor.

CHAPTER TWELVE

The monstrosity, as Thunder had indicated, was as big a horse.

Blade trained the Commando on the creature as it gathered itself to attack.

Eight feet tall at the shoulder and six feet wide, a gargantuan beetle blocked their path. Its six sturdy legs supported an ovoid body covered by green, armorlike fore wings, and an elongated neck and head, both black. Extending an arm's length from the head were two formidable, serrated mandibles clicking together in anticipiation of its next meal.

Blade fired, the Commando thundering eerily, booming and reverberating from the lofty spires, slag, and girders. The wooden stock bucked against his right side as the heavy slugs tore into the beetle.

Chittering in anguish, the creature halted for a second. It lowered its head and charged, absorbing the hail of lead without apparent effect.

Sergeant Havoc, Boone and Thunder were momentarily unable to aid the Warrior; he stood between the beetle and them. Boone darted to the right, Thunder to the left, both intending to provide covering fire. But before either could squeeze off a shot the beetle was on the giant.

Blade, firing all the while, endeavored to leap to the left to avoid the creature's rush. He failed. The beetle swung its head, its right mandible slamming into Blade and sending him sprawling onto his stomach. Before he could rise, the creature pounced.

"Blade!" Boone shouted.

Blade rolled over just as the creature reached him. The Commando was on the ground to his right. Any thought of retrieving the machine gun was instantly curtailed as the beetle's mandibles speared for his neck. He instinctively reached up, catching the mandibles in his brawny hands, gripping them by the outer edges. His muscles bulged as he held them aloft.

A contest of strength ensued, the beetle slowly, inexorably lowering its mandibles closer and closer to its prey as the Warrior struggled to keep them at bay.

Thunder ran to the head of the mutant and pressed the barrel of his M-16 against the beetle's left compound eye, then fired a short burst.

The creature did not so much as flinch, and now its mandibles were within six inches of the Warrior's neck.

Blade's biceps and triceps seemed to be sculpted from steel. Perspiration beaded his forhead, and every vein on his crimson face was protruding.

Sergeant Havoc closed in, his M-16 in his left hand, a metallic object in his right. He swung the automatic rifle like a club, striking the beetle's foreleg.

The mutant wrenched loose from the Warrior's grip and swung toward the noncom.

Havoc frantically backpedaled. "Get away from it!" he yelled. "Get away from it!" He brandished the object in his right hand.

The grenade.

Thunder and Boone dove for the nearest cover.

Blade surged to his feet and sprinted for the jagged wall.

The beetle bore down on the noncom.

And Havoc, hobbling toward a mound of slag, yanked the pin and tossed the grenade overhand. He took a painful, flying leap and landed behind the slag.

Blade was a yard from the wall when the grenade exploded. The concussion felt like a sledgehammer blow to the back as he was picked up and flung into the wall. Agony lanced his ribs as he slumped to the dirt, his senses swirling. He gulped in air and pushed himself to his knees.

The beetle was history, its head, neck, and the front section of its body all gone, the rear portion lying in the dust. Gruesome, pulpy pieces were scattered everywhere.

Boone stepped from in back of a pile of debris. "That was too close for comfort!"

Thunder walked around a twisted girder. He scanned the heights. "There could be more."

"I hope not," Sergeant Havoc muttered, rising from behind the mound of slag. He glanced at the Warrior. "Hey! Are you okay?"

Blade nodded, then stood. He slowly approached the carcass, his gray eyes roving the ground for his Commando. His lips curled downward when he found it. The machine gun had been caught in the blast; the stock was shattered, the barrel split and twisted. "Damn!" he snapped.

The others joined him.

"You still have Grizzly's M-16," Boone offered by way of a condolence.

"I know," Blade said. "But I liked that gun."

Sergeant Havoc stared at the grisly remains of the beetle. "I can't wait to get out of this Dead Zone."

"You and me both," Boone concurred. He gazed at the noncom. "Why didn't you use that grenade on the worm?"

Havoc averted his eyes and mumbled a few words.

"What? I didn't catch that," Boone said.

"I completely forgot about it," Sergeant Havoc admitted sheepishly.

Thunder was scrutinizing the passageways. "We should not stay here. The explosion will attract the Vampires."

Blade unslung the M-16 from his left shoulder. "You're right. Havoc, if you have any problems keeping up, just sing out."

"You can count on it," Sergeant Havoc said.

Blade returned to the junction. The Vampire tracks took the left branch, which might indicate the Vampires would be coming from that direction. He did not want to run into the Vampires just yet. To succeed in the mission he needed to capture a

Vampire. He would pick the time and place. "We'll go straight," he stated, and did so.

The passage proceeded in a direct westerly line for several hundred yards, then curved to the south, winding deeper and deeper into the ruins. Odd noises sounded occasionally: twitters and flutters and barks and growls. Once something howled.

Blade slowed as the passage widened. A spacious circular area appeared, a hundred yards across and ringed by imposing, ravaged edifices. Shafts of sparkling sunlight filtered down. Chunks of concrete, bricks, melted metal, demolished vehicles, and other legacies to humankind's destructive propensities formed heaps of various sizes. A narrow path threaded among the piles.

The air overhead was unexpectedly rent by the flapping of large wings.

Blade looked up, but all he saw was the sunlight and the shadows.

"What was that?" Boone asked in a hushed tone.

"I didn't see it," Sergeant Havoc said.

Thunder, the last in line, was gazing rearward. "We are being followed," he announced quietly.

"How do you know?" Boone questioned.

"I know," Thunder asserted.

Blade knew the Flathead was right. He had sensed someone . . . or something . . . on their trail for the past fifteen minutes. "We'll take cover," he declared, and led them into the labyrinth of debris. Thirty yards further he found the perfect ambush site.

To the right of the path was an antique yellow bus resting on its rusted undercarriage. There was no trace of the tires, all of the windows were missing, and the door was ajar and crumpled outward. The yellow paint was peeling and faded, the body marred by countless cracks.

"There," Blade said. He walked to the door and peeked inside. Some of the seats were still bolted to the floor, the cushions long since deteriorated. Detached seat frames littered the floor.

"What's the plan?" Boone inquired.

"We'll wait in here," Blade stated. "If the Vampires are after us, then we'll spring a little surprise on them. I want one alive."

He stepped into the bus and moved to the center, the floor creaking and rattling underfoot. The side of the bus faced the path, affording an ideal field of fire. He crouched below one of the windows.

Sergeant Havoc, Boone, and Thunder positioned themselves, with Thunder nearest the door. They waited in expectant silence.

Blade wondered if he had bitten off more than he could chew. The Dead Zone was a particularly perilous realm, with lethal manaces seemingly lurking behind every corner. Four men might not be enough to accomplish the mission, not when there could be hundreds of Vampires to deal with, Vampires who knew the Zone well. The Vampires enjoyed a decided, possibly insurmountable, advantage.

A faint footfall terminated his reflection.

The Warrior elevated his head until he could see over the lower edge of the window.

Ten yards separated the bus from the path. Another 15 yards to the rear was the first in a line of Vampires, nine in all. They were in a hurry, the leader with his eyes glued to the path.

Blade waited. He wanted the Vampires alongside the bus before he sprang the trap.

The Vampire leading the pursuit halted abreast of the bus. He knelt and examined the tracks in the dust, then rose and pivoted toward the vehicle.

Blade could see the Vampire's glassy eyes widening in consternation. He raised the M-16 to his right shoulder, sighted, and fired, his initial rounds smacking into the lead Vampire's head and catapulting the ghoul backwards.

Sergeant Havoc, Boone, and Thunder took their cue from the Warrior. Each cut loose with skilled precision.

Caught in the open in a writhing spray of automatic gunfire, the Vampires were decimated. Six dropped in half as many seconds, their bodies riddled with holes. Two foolishly tried to reach the bus and were cut to ribbons. Only one was left alive, and he wheeled and attempted to flee.

Boone was quicker. The Cavalryman drew his right Hombre, his arm a streak, and fired from the hip.

The shot was unerringly on target, the slug tearing into the Vampire's left foot, penetrating his ankle. He shrieked as he went down.

Blade didn't bother with the door. He gripped the upper rim of the window, lifted his legs, and vaulted to the ground. In five bounds he reached the Vampire and shoved the M-16 into the man's face. "Freeze!" he commanded.

The Vampire wasn't going anywhere. He was on his right side, clutching his leg above his splintered ankle and grimacing in anguish. "Finish me, you bastard!" he snapped. "Finish me!" He glared up at the giant.

Blade was surprised to note that the Vampire's nose was disfigured, bent to the left and swollen. "Keep your mouth shut unless I say otherwise!"

The Vampire's eyes were simmering pools of hatred. "Or what? You don't scare me!"

Boone, Thunder, and Sergeant Havoc surrounded their prisoner.

"The rest are dead," Havoc confirmed.

"We don't scare you?" Boone asked the Vampire.

For an answer, the Vampire tilted his head and tried to spit on the Cavalryman's moccasins.

Boone was holding his M-16 in his left hand, the Hombre in his right. He suddenly swept his right arm down, ramming the Hombre barrel into the Vampire's left eye and cocking the revolver.

The Vampire stiffened.

"If I were you," Boone advised in a grating tone, "I'd be real scared. Because if you flap your gums again without permission, your bloodsucking days will be over. Savvy?"

"Ye . . . Ye . . . Yes!" the Vampire stuttered.

Sergeant Havoc looked at Boone and grinned in appreciation.

"Now," Blade stated, "I want some answers. For starters, what's your name?"

"Prest."

"Are there more of your kind after us?" Blade interrogated him.

"Not at the moment," Prest replied, then smirked. "But there will be! Soon! You don't stand a chance!"

Blade gestured at the nearby ruins. "Is this your home base?"

"This is the Heartland," Prest said.

"Why do you call it the Heartland?" Blade asked.

"It was named the Heartland before I was born," Prest responded. "No one ever told me the reason."

"How old are you?"

"Twenty-seven."

"And how many Vampires live here?" Blade questioned.

"I don't know the exact count," Prest said. "The last I heard, there were something like two hundred and eighty."

"That's all?" Blade said skeptically.

"It's more than enough to take care of you four," Prest commented. "You'll never leave the Heartland alive!"

"We'll see," Blade said. "We're searching for two friends of ours. One of them, a woman wearing fatigues, was captured by Vampires. We don't know—"

"Quit calling us Vampires!" Prest interrupted.

"What?"

"We don't like that name," Prest said. "We're Venesects, damn it!"

"You prefer to be called Venesects?" Blade asked.

"You outsiders call us Vampires. It's your word, not ours," Prest stated.

"Venesects it is then," Blade said. "Where will we find your fellow Venesects?"

Prest's eyes shifted nervously. "Here and there."

"Not good enough," Blade informed him. "The Venesects must occupy a certain area in the Heartland, a place you call home. Where is this place?"

"I'll never tell," Prest said defiantly.

Blade glanced at Boone.

The Cavalryman jabbed the Hombre barrel into the Vampire's left eye again. "I'll count to three," he warned.

"I'll never tell!" Prest reiterated.

"One," Boone began.

Prest licked his red lips.

"Two," Boone said.

"Never!!" Prest shouted, his right eye twitching uncontrollably.

"Thr—" Boone said.

"All right! All right!" Prest cried. "I'll talk!"

Boone stared at the Vampire for a moment, then twirled the Hombre into its holster.

"Where will we find your home base?" Blade queried impatiently.

Prest glowered at the giant as he replied. "The lower levels to the south."

"You'll take us there," Blade ordered. "Before we head out, I want to know about our friends, a woman in fatigues and a mutant with the features of a bear."

"That son of a bitch!" Prest spat.

"You've seen him?"

Prest raised his left hand and pointed at his nose. "Who the hell do you think did this?"

"What about the woman?" Blade pressed him. "Have you seen her too?"

"Yeah," Prest admitted.

"Are they alive?" Blade inquired, leaning forward.

"The last I knew," Prest said.

Blade straightened and studied their prisoner. The Vampires, or Venesects, were not fear-inspiring in the daylight. Prest was a prime example; he was more revolting than fierce. His pale skin, crimson lips, and glassy eyes lent him a sickly aspect. His thin frame appeared to be malnourished. Prest wasn't a mutant, but he wasn't entirely human.

"What are you staring at?" Prest snapped.

"Can you walk?" Blade asked.

Prest lifted his left leg. Watery, pinkish blood covered his foot, ankle, and shin. "What do you think, asshole?"

Blade glanced at Thunder. "Find something he can use as a crutch."

"Right away," Thunder said and moved off.

Blade stared upward at the shafts of sunlight. Nightfall would descend in a few hours, and the night was the Vampires' element. He did not relish the prospect of being in the Heartland after dark. In addition to the Vampires there were other dangers to worry about, creepy-crawly things with a craving for flesh. Vile things, unleashed by the transmutative capacity of radiation. Things an unsuspecting prewar world would never have envisioned.

"How about this?" Thunder said, intruding on the Warrior's musing. He held a shoulder-high length of rusty pipe.

"Do you expect me to use that?" Prest demanded.

"You'll use it," Boone stated, "or I'll plug you in the other foot and you can crawl all the way."

Prest's thin lips curled back from his tapered teeth. "You're mine! When the time comes, you're mine!"

"On your feet," Blade ordered.

The Vampire took the proferred pipe, then used it as a brace under his left arm so he could shuffle to a standing position. He dangled his left foot above the ground, his pink blood spattering the dust underneath.

"Move out," Blade directed.

Prest took a tentative step with the makeshift crutch.

"How far must we travel?" Blade inquired.

"Four miles or so," Prest replied.

Sergeant Havoc glanced at Blade. "At the rate he can move with the crutch," he commented, "we'll take all night."

"We'll do the best we can," Blade said. He prodded the Vampire with his M-16. "And if I get the impression you're stalling, I'll let Boone have you."

Prest gazed at the Cavalryman. "Is that your name? Boone?"

Boone nodded.

Prest smiled malevolently. "I'll carve it on your forehead before I'm done with you."

Boone caught a whiff of the Vampire's breath and scrunched up his nose. "Whew! What did you do? Eat a skunk today?"

If looks could kill, Prest would have slain the Cavalryman on the spot.

Sergeant Havoc nudged Boone with his right elbow. "It's easy to understand why these clowns have bad breath."

"It is?" Boone responded.

"Sure. They're full of it up to here," Havoc said, then touched his nose.

CHAPTER THIRTEEN

Polidori halted in front of a pair of huge wooden doors. He turned and grinned at the captive. "Are you ready?"

"Quit playing games and open the damn door!" Grizzly snapped.

One of the four Vampires behind the mutant, one of the quartet assigned to serve as his escort to the banquet, snickered. "He doesn't have much of a sense of humor, does he?"

"No," Polidori mentioned. "It's pitiful." He made a show of sniffing the musty air. "At least he had the decency to put on some cologne."

The quartet laughed.

Polidori faced the doors, gripped the metal knob on the door on the right, then shoved.

Grizzly, expecting a dilapidated banquet filled with slovenly Vampires, was genuinely astounded. He walked through the doorway, surveying the impressive setup.

"Not bad, huh?" Polidori said with evident pride.

"Not bad," Grizzly mumbled.

The banquet hall was enormous, 100 yards wide and 50 yards from the front doors to the rear wall. A vaulted ceiling arched above a white, tiled floor. Eight radiant chandeliers, brimming with candles instead of light bulbs, were suspended from the ceiling at twelve foot intervals the width of the chamber. Large wooden tables, aligned edge to edge, had been arranged in a horseshoe shape with the open end toward the front doors. Hundreds of Vampires and dozens of humans were milling about the hall, males and females.

"Corpus had this built," Polidori said to Grizzly. "Most of the material came from the towns and settlements we've raided."

A bell suddenly peal... ...rant and clangorous.

The Vampires and humans im.... ly took seats at the tables, the humans pulling out the wooden chairs so the Vampires could sit down. Then the humans seated themselves.

Grizzly stared at a veritable sea of pale countenances and sinister eyes, and for a second his confidence wavered. An uneasy sensation developed in the pit of his stomach.

A tall Vampire at the head of the horseshoe was the only one standing. He beckoned with his right arm. "Come in, Grizzly. We have been expecting you."

Polidori prodded the bear-man by slapping his left shoulder. "Get a move on! Don't keep Corpus waiting."

Grizzly walked toward the tall Vampire. He ignored the hungry gazes fixed on him by the Vampires, but he could feel his skin prickling just the same, especially under the fur at the nape of his neck.

"Welcome," the tall Vampire said. "You are our guest of honor tonight." A large golden bell on a metal tripod was visible to his rear.

Grizzly appraised the tall Vampire as he approached the table from the opposite side. This Vampire was different from the rest. Grizzly could see the difference in his handsome, regal facial lines, in the square thrust of his shoulders, in his alert green eyes. He wore a brown loincloth that was immaculate. While not exceptionally muscular, he was superbly proportioned. His long hair, unlike the dark hair of the majority of the Vampires, was white. Grizzly stopped behind a chair directly across from this unique Vampire. He nodded once. "So you're the head scumbag."

Abrupt intakes of breath punctuated the assembled Vampires and humans.

"There is no need to be insulting," the tall Vampire said. "And yes, I am Corpus."

"You're awful polite for a rotten Vampire," Grizzly commented.

Corpus's eyes bored into the mutant. "Why are you deliberately baiting me? I invited you here as my personal guest. No harm has befallen you." He paused. "And please don't refer to us as Vampires. We are Venesects."

"Vampires are bloodsucking leeches," Grizzly said. "If the shoe fits . . ." He let the sentence trail off.

Corpus sighed. "If you persist in this crude behavior, I will be compelled to have you returned to your cell. Which is unfortunate, because I was under the impression you wanted to see Ms. Morris again."

Grizzly tensed. "Athena is here?"

"She will be, shortly," Corpus replied. "Now what will it be? Will you behave in a civilized fashion, or do you want to languish in a miserable cell? The choice is yours."

Grizzly pulled out the chair and sat down. "So what's on the menu?" He noticed four brown leather straps affixed to the table top.

Corpus smiled and slowly seated himself. "A special meal is being prepared for you. I'd like to surprise you."

A thin Vampire with a hook nose and a cleft chin, in the chair to Corpus's right, placed his elbows on the table and folded his hands. "Can you imagine the vitality?" he asked.

"Vitality?" Grizzly repeated quizzically.

"A superb specimen," Corpus said to the hooked-nosed Vampire. "Grizzly, I would like you to meet Loring. He's my right-hand man."

"I've heard about him," Grizzly mentioned.

"Oh?" Loring said.

"From Polidori," Grizzly disclosed. He looked around for the tittering Vampire, but Polidori was gone. A female Vampire ten feet to the right drew his attention. He realized that all the female Vampires covered their breasts with strips of pliable brown leather.

"Have you also heard about my brother, Minshi?" Corpus inquired, nodding at the doors.

Grizzly shifted in his seat, his eyes widening slightly.

A colossal Vampire was coming into the banquet hall. In size and build he strongly resembled Blade. His face, though, was a mask of latent cruelty. Huge hands swung at his sides. His skin tone was extraordinarily white, his eyes pinpoints of feral luminosity. A black loincloth encircled his waist.

"He's your brother?" Grizzly said.

"My younger brother," Corpus responded. "I have the brains, he supplies the brawn. He is most devoted and serves as my official executioner. There were a few Venesects who opposed my plans. Believe it or not, under Minshi's influence all dissension has been eradicated."

"I believe it," Grizzly assured the Vampire leader.

Minshi was within ten feet of the head table when he moved to one side, revealing the woman following him. His immense form had obscured her until that moment.

"Athena!" Grizzly exclaimed, rising.

Athena took one look and raced up to him. She flung her arms around his neck and hugged him tightly. "Grizzly! I didn't think I'd ever see you again!"

Grizzly felt a peculiar constriction in his throat. He coughed and held her at arm's length. "I'm here to rescue you. Have any of them touched you?"

Athena shook her head. "They put me in a small room with just a cot. Polidori visited me once. No one else showed up until a few minutes ago." She glanced at Minshi and shuddered.

"Please have a seat," Corpus stated courteously, standing. "I have looked forward to meeting you. I am Corpus."

Athena studied the Vampire. "Polidori told me about you."

"And me about you," Corpus said. "Have a seat." He pointed at an empty chair to Grizzly's right.

Athena complied, her eyes narrowing as she beheld the leather straps.

Grizzly sat back down, overwhelmed with relief at discovering Athena was unharmed.

Minshi walked up to the table on Grizzly's left.

"Go check on Polidori," Corpus instructed his brother. "We don't want to delay the festivities."

"As you wish," Minshi said gruffly. He spun and departed.

Corpus gazed at Grizzly and Athena. "Would either of you care for some wine before the main course? We have an excellent selection of white and red wines."

Grizzly and Athena exchanged surprised expressions.

"You drink wine?" Grizzly commented in disbelief.

"No," Corpus answered. "But many on our human staff do. Our dietary requirements are quite different."

"I know," Grizzly said. "You specialize in drinking blood."

"Do you hold our nutritional needs against us?" Corpus asked.

"Nutritional needs!" Grizzly declared, then snorted. "There's a good one! Killing innocent people in cold blood isn't my idea of obtaining proper nutrition."

"When I say nutritional needs, I mean precisely that," Corpus stated defensively. He gazed from the bear-man to the woman. "Perhaps an explanation is called for. Are you familiar with the origin of the Venesects?"

"They crawled out from a slimy rock," Grizzy quipped.

"Be nice," Corpus said sternly.

Athena surveyed the banquet hall and the crowded tables. "How did all of this come about?"

"I will gladly provide the details," Corpus offered. "But first, would either of you like some wine? I'm afraid it's the only liquid refreshment we possess for human consumption. We do not bother with storing water because we don't drink it."

"I would," Athena said. "I'd like a glass of white wine."

"And you?" Corpus asked Grizzly.

"No thanks."

Corpus shrugged. "Suit yourself." His right hand disappeared below the table and produced a small golden hammer. "This bell was appropriated from a Spanish-style church near the border," he divulged, twisting in his seat. He reached out and tapped the bell lightly twice.

A door in the rear wall, ten feet to the right, instantly opened. A man appeared, a human dressed in a white shirt, white pants, and an apron. He hurried over to Corpus. "You rang, sir?"

"A goblet of our best white wine for the lady," Corpus directed.

"Certainly, sir." The man in white wheeled and hastened to obey.

Grizzly shook his head in disgust. "Did you house-train him yourself?"

Corpus eyed the mutant for several seconds. "Why should you care for these humans? What are they to you? I am not ignorant, you know. I'm aware of current developments in the world. Most humans dislike mutants, so why should you care for them?"

"I wouldn't say I care for them very much," Grizzly replied. "But I don't like seeing others made into slaves, whether they're humans, mutants, or otherwise."

Athena could sense a friction between the two. Her happiness at being reunited with Grizzly after so many hours of anxiety and terror was tempered by her perception of their predicament. "You mentioned an explanation," she said, hoping to defuse a confrontation.

Corpus leaned back in his chair and surveyed the hall. "We have come a long way since the war, and greater glories are on our horizon."

"The Vampires . . ." Athena began, and then remembered the name Polidori had used during their earlier discussion. "I'm sorry. The Venesects arose after the war?"

"Yes," Corpus confirmed. "We possess the written records of our ancestors. They relate a fascinating tale." He stared absently at the ceiling. "Millions of people were living in San Diego when the nuclear missile hit. Apparently they received twenty minute's advance warning from the authorities. Most attempted to flee. Some resigned themselves to their fate. And a few retired to special shelters, fallout shelters, hoping to survive the nuclear explosion."

The man in white returned bearing a crystal goblet containing white wine. He reached across the table and deposited the goblet near Athena.

"Thank you," she said.

He nodded and left.

"As I was saying," Corpus continued. "A few San Diego residents huddled in below-ground fallout shelters—trembling in fear, no doubt. One of these shelters, located in the southern section of the city, was constructed by a wealthy financier. This particular shelter was one hundred and fifty feet underground and could only be reached by a generator-powered elevator. Thirty-two people were in this shelter when the blast occurred.''

"They survived," Athena deduced.

"That they did," Corpus said. "Only to find themselves buried under tons of debris. The surface was too radioactive for them to venture above ground. They were forced to live like rats under the ruins, building tunnels where necessary, and foraging as best they could. Their stockpiled food eventually was exhausted. They tried subsisting on rodents, insects, and earthworms without success." He looked at Athena and Grizzly and smiled. "And then one of them had an inspiration."

"What kind of inspiration?" Athena queried.

"Using their own bodies as sustenance," Corpus responded.

Athena appeared horrified. "They became cannibalistic?"

Corpus laughed. "No. Nothing so extreme. They wanted to survive, not destroy themselves. One of them, a physician, hit on a novel idea." He stared at Athena. "Liquid nourishment or solid food? Which is more essential to human survival?"

"A person can survive longer without food than without water or another liquid," Athena answered. "The human body is three-fourths water. I read somewhere that the average person can live for up to two months without food and not suffer any irreparable harm. But we can't go much more than a week without water."

"Exactly," Corpus concurred. "So for the survivors, their primary concern was discovering a source of liquid nourishment. And what better source than their own blood?"

Athena's lips curled downward distastefully. "Their blood?"

"What else?" Corpus rejoined. "Blood is exceptionally rich in vitamins and minerals. Take iron as an example. Humans need iron. Four tablespoons of blood can supply the typical adult's daily iron requirement. Blood also contains proteins and sugar. As a source of nourishment for the survivors, blood was ideal. Even more crucial was the fact that blood is constantly being manufactured by the body. Blood is renewable. A healthy person can give a pint of blood every six to eight weeks with no ill effects."

"So your ancestors took to drinking their blood to stay alive," Grizzly remarked in fascination.

Corpus nodded. "Their blood, supplemented by whatever other liquid foodstuffs they could find. The Venesects have existed on this diet for over a century."

Athena gazed at the Vampires to her right and left. "I think I'm beginning to understand. Your ancestors were compelled to live underground for decades because of the excessive radiation. By the time your people could venture safely above the surface, their bodies had adjusted to a subterranean life-style. Their eyes had adapted to the limited light below ground, which meant they couldn't venture abroad in the daylight because the bright sun would damage their vision."

"Excellent," Corpus said. "Most perceptive."

"This explains the reason you conduct your raids at night," Athena went on. "Why you travel at night and rest during the day, avoiding the sunlight as much as possible."

"Any other insights?" Corpus encouraged her.

"Yes," Athena said. "Your pale skin is caused by two factors. One, obviously, is the prolonged period the Venesects have lived underground. The second must be tied to a form of anemia. I'm not a doctor, but I've seen anemic patients at a hopsital. And some of your people are suffering the same symptoms."

"I am impressed,"Corpus complimented her. "You have summarized our problem concisely. About thirty years after the war, our ancestors noticed a marked decline in their health and general vitality. They realized that they could not subsist on their own blood any longer. Their blood had become impoverished through a lack of certain vitamins and minerals. In order to restore their vitality they needed a fresh supply of vitamin-rich blood, a new source of nutrition. They started hunting for foodstuff on the surface at night."

"They started abducting people and bringing the victims down here to feed on," Grizzly interjected testily.

"Rudely put, but accurate," Corpus said. "What choice did we have? Either we acquired a new nutritional supply or we perished."

"Why didn't the Venesects try to live above ground again?" Athena inquired. "Why didn't your people try to wean themselves from their dependence on blood?"

''We did try,'' Corpus stated with a frown. ''We were not successful. Our physiological evolution has acclimatized us irredeemably to our current status.'' He sighed. ''There is no going back. We are what we have become and we will never be as we were.''

''You can't go on like this,'' Athena commented. ''Sooner or later the people on the surface will send in a military force and wipe you out.''

''We took care of the last force sent against us,'' Corpus disclosed.

''That was just a platoon,'' Athena noted. ''What happens if an army is sent?''

''We will cross that bridge when we come to it,'' Corpus philosophized. He looked up in the direction of the front doors, a wide grin creasing his features. ''Ahhhh. They have arrived.''

Grizzly turned in his chair.

Minshi, Polidori, and over a dozen other Vampires were escorting several dozen bedraggled, fatigued humans into the banquet hall. A ripple of excitement animated the Vampires seated at the tables; they began conversing in hushed tones, smiling in anticipation, and a few even licked their lips.

Corpus shifted and struck the golden bell hard three times.

All talking ceased. Every eye in the hall focused on the head Vampire.

''All human attendants will return to their quarters,'' Corpus commanded.

There was a commotion as five dozen humans rose and left the chamber, circling around the incoming captives.

''We don't permit the help to view our feasts,'' Corpus said to Grizzly. ''Many Venesects have taken humans as mates or as personal servants. We wouldn't want to unduly upset them.''

''Personal servants! Don't you mean personal slaves?'' Grizzly queried.

''I'm beginning to believe you're a hopeless case,'' Corpus stated.

Minshi, Polidori, and their crew of Vampires had herded the frightened humans they were escorting into the open space between the arms of the horseshoe.

Two Vampires closed and bolted the huge doors.

"So we won't be disturbed," Corpus remarked.

"Who are these people?" Athena asked, staring at the 37 prisoners.

"They are from Aguanga," Corpus replied.

Athena tensed and glanced at the Vampire leader. "What do you intend to do with them?"

Corpus chuckled. "Please don't act naive."

Athena blanched and stood. "I want to leave."

Corpus's eyes narrowed. "Sit down," he instructed her harshly. "You've displayed an intense curiosity about us. What kind of host would I be if I did not satisfy your curiosity to its utmost?" He surveyed the assemblage. "Let the feeding commence!"

CHAPTER FOURTEEN

"**I** think this turkey is stalling, sir," Sergeant Havoc mentioned.

"I am not!" Prest snapped. "I'd like to see you do any better on one foot."

Blade paused and scanned the corridor ahead. Closed doors lined both sides of the hall. A solitary lantern with a flickering flame cast ominous shadows on the walls.

"I've done what you wanted," Prest groused. "I'm sticking to the corridors we use the least. These rooms are for storage, mainly. You won't find many Venesects in this area."

"How soon will we reach our friends?" Blade asked.

"Soon," Prest assured the Warrior. "They're being held in cells on one of the lower levels."

Boone, who was fourth in line after the Vampire, Blade, and Sergeant Havoc, stared at the ceiling. "We keep going farther and farther underground. I don't trust this guy. He could be leading us into a trap."

"If he does," Blade said, "he'll be the first to die."

"I'm not stupid," Prest declared.

"That's debatable," Sergeant Havoc quipped.

"Up yours!" Prest retorted.

"Keep moving," Blade instructed the Vampire, then nudged him with the M-16 barrel.

"I'm doing the best I can!" Prest complained. He hobbled on the makeshift crutch toward the lantern.

Blade followed, glancing over his right shoulder at his men. Thunder was covering the rear. Boone was tensed, coiled for action. Sergeant Havoc seemed to be taking the strain in stride, and he was walking with a less pronounced limp. So far, so good. But how long would their luck hold? The Vampires were bound to discover their presence.

Unbeknownst to the Warrior, the Vampires already had.

Prest passed the lantern and proceeded to a junction. He took the left fork.

"This place is a maze," Blade commented. "And all the passageways look alike. How do you keep from getting lost?"

"We're born and raised down here," Prest said. "By the time I was ten I knew every tunnel, every corridor by heart. It's impossible for a Venesect to become lost," he boasted.

"Even on the surface?" Blade asked.

"The surface is a different story," Prest stated. "But we've traveled at night for decades. We can read the stars as well as anybody."

"How many guards will be posted at the cells?" Blade questioned.

"That depends on how many prisoners are being held," Prest replied.

In 50 yards they came to another junction.

"We go straight," Prest announced.

Blade noticed the dirt floor was gradually inclining downwards. Fewer and fewer doors appeared. A cool draft blew across his face. Where was the air coming from? Had the Vampires excavated ventilation shafts? He was about to pose the question to Prest when an astonishing thing happened: The Vampire abruptly soared like a bird.

Or seemed to.

One moment Prest was walking down the incline, his head and shoulders partially obscured by the murky blackness. The next he was flying through the air with his arms outstretched.

Blade automatically raised the M-16 and sighted on the aerial Vampire, but before he could squeeze the trigger another amazing happening prevented him from firing.

The floor dropped from under him.

The Warrior felt the dirt start to slide as the entire floor suddenly tilted at a sharp angle, then swiveled inward.

"What the—!" Sergeant Havoc exclaimed.

All four Force members pitched into the abyss below. Boone and Thunder endeavored to grab hold of the wall, their efforts frustrated by the smooth, slippery wood.

Blade realized an entire section of floor served as a gigantic trapdoor, and he envisioned being impaled on rows of pointed stakes or falling into a nest of ravenous mutants. Instead his boots made contact with a brittle, yet oddly resilient surface. Something crunched under his heels as he sank in to his knees. He nearly toppled forward but regained his balance. A putrid stench engulfed him.

Sergeant Havoc, Boone, and Thunder landed near the Warrior, their collective impact creating a racket of snapping, crackling, and popping noises.

Blade looked up. Dimly visible 25 feet overhead were the pale features of the Vampire. Prest's face was stationary, and Blade guessed that the Vampire was standing at the rim of the hole.

Prest uttered a triumphant laugh. "The tables have turned, you bastards!"

"Do you want me to pick him off, sir?" Sergeant Havoc whispered to Blade.

"Not yet," Blade said quietly, then raised his voice to address the Vampire. "That was a slick move, Prest."

"Damn straight it was!" Prest replied.

"How'd you do it?" Blade casually inquired, hoping to derive a clue as to the nature of the hole they were in.

"It was easy!" Prest gloated. "We set you up, chumps!"

"We?" Blade repeated.

Three more Vampires suddenly materialized alongside Prest.

"Where did they come from?" Blade asked.

"They were shadowing us for the past ten minutes," Prest answered. "I led you past one of the few guard posts we have on the lower levels. They hid until we were out of sight, then took a shortcut to reach the pit first.'' He snickered. ''They took care of unlatching the door.''

''The corridor was booby-trapped,'' Blade speculated.

''No, you idiot,'' Prest declared. ''This is our garbage pit.''

''Your garbage pit?'' Blade reiterated in surprise.

''That's right,'' Prest said. ''Let me explain. Decades ago we had a problem with our garbage. All the refuse was dumped in a big hole on one of the upper levels, and the dump became a breeding ground for mutants of all kinds. Bugs. Worms. You name it. They were drawn to the dump like vultures to carrion.'' He paused. ''We decided to do something about it. First we dug this new pit on the very lowest level, as far from most of the mutants as we could get. This corridor is a dead end. One way in, one way out. By posting guards farther up, we can prevent stray bugs from locating it. We even covered the pit with a swinging door to reduce the stench. Sometimes a worm will burrow into the pit, but we've pretty much eliminated the problem.''

''So the guards rigged the garbage-pit door to open when we were on it,'' Blade commented. ''And they covered it with dirt to hide it.''

''You've got it,'' Prest said, smirking.

''But how did you avoid falling in?'' Blade questioned. ''I didn't know Vampires could fly.''

The Vampires laughed.

''We can't,'' Prest stated. He made a motion with his right hand, as if he was tugging on something. ''There's a rope here. It's attached to a beam near the ceiling. We use it to lower down a lantern from time to time to inspect the pit for worms or other mutants. All I did was leap for the rope and swing across the pit while you jackasses were falling in. The guards extinguished the lantern we usually keep next to the pit door. It was too dark for you to see the rope, but I could see it clearly.'' He paused. ''And now you're our prisoners.''

''What do you intend to do with us?'' Blade inquired, then quickly whispered to Sergeant Havoc. ''Can you nail all four with one burst?''

''No problem,'' Havoc responded. ''Just say the word, sir.''

Prest seemed to lean forward. "What's going on down there?"

Blade had forgotten about the Vampire's keen eyesight and hearing. "We're just concerned about your intentions," he replied.

One of the Vampires abruptly disappeared.

"You can cool your heels down there while I go report to Corpus," Prest said. "Our leader will be very pleased."

"I can get those three, sir," Sergeant Havoc remarked in a barely audible tone.

"Not yet," Blade responded. Where was the fourth Vampire? He needed all four on the rim. If just one escaped, the alarm would be sounded and the Vampires would be after the Force en masse. He was relying on Havoc's skill with the M-16 to resolve the dilemma. Boone and Thunder were both expert marksmen. Thunder, in particular, was outstanding with a rifle. But Sergeant Havoc had used M-16's extensively and was the best shot in the California military.

"Keep an eye out for worms," Prest taunted them. "We wouldn't want anything to happen to you!"

A glow of light appeared above the garbage pit, and a second later the fourth Vampire stepped into view holding a lantern.

"Now?" Havoc whispered.

"Wait," Blade directed.

The fourth Vampire turned and attached the lantern to a metal loop imbedded in the wall at shoulder height.

"Get ready," Blade instructed softly.

Prest held his crutch aloft. "I won't be needing this any more. I put another one over on you! I could have walked at my normal speed! My ankle only hurt for a little while. We Venesects are more resistant to pain than you humans. Even serious injuries hardly faze us for long. We're practically impervious to harm," he boasted.

"You're not impervious to death," Blade remarked.

"So?" Prest rejoined.

"So die," Blade said, then shouted to Sergeant Havoc. "Now!"

Sergeant Havoc was cradling the M-16 with the stock pressed against his right hip and the barrel angled upwards. He simply shifted the barrel a few inches and squeezed the trigger.

The lantern light bathed the Vampires in a yellowish-orange radiance, clearly revealing their stupefied expressions as they were struck. The burst stitched their heads from right to left. Prest took the first slugs in the forehead, his mouth drooping, his body starting to slump over. The other three died in a spray of brains, hair, and flesh. Two of them fell backwards. One sprawled to the right. Prest plunged headfirst into the garbage pit.

Blade saw the Vampire's falling form dropping toward him and waded to the right, forcing his way through the reeking refuse.

The corpse slammed into the muck at the spot the Warrior vacated.

"Nice shooting," Blade complimented the noncom.

"They were overconfident," Havoc observed. "They shouldn't have exposed themselves."

For the first time since dropping into the pit, Blade surveyed his surroundings. The garbage pit was ten yards in circumference with sides of red earth. A disgusting stew of bones, excrement, and other sickening waste matter filled the pit to his knees. The lantern light accented every nauseating detail.

Boone was also scrutinizing the pit. "Yuck! Let's get out of here."

Blade gazed at the rim, pondering a plan. He could see the thick rope suspended from the beam, but the lower portion was out of sight. Was the bottom of the rope coiled on the corridor floor? Prest had mentioned using the rope to lower the lantern into the pit, so there must be additional footage. If one of them could reach that rope, escaping the pit would be an easy task.

But how to reach the rope?

"Look at all these bones!" Boone commented. "They look human."

"They are," Thunder said.

Blade spied the way out. The large trapdoor had swung inward and was now flush with one side of the pit, with the lower edge of the door 16 feet above his head. Close to the bottom edge, at the corners, were two metal rings. Normally, he reasoned, ropes were tied to the rings and strung over the beam to suspend the door over the pit. The Vampires must have removed the ropes so the door would drop when sufficient pressure was applied. He peered at the opposite rim, realizing the pit was wider at the bottom than the top by a good seven yards.

"How will we get out of here?" Boone asked.

Blade moved to the side and positioned himself directly under the trap door. "Thunder, come here."

The Flathead stepped over to the Warrior. "Yes?"

"I want you to climb onto my shoulders," Blade directed. "When you're ready, I'll give you a heave. You should be able to grab the bottom of the door. Take hold of one of the rings."

Thunder slung his M-16 over his shoulder. "How will I get from the ring to the top of the pit? There are no handholds on the door."

"Take my Bowies," Blade suggested. "Stick them in the door and use them to climb on."

"You should go," Thunder said. "You are much stronger than I."

"Could you bear my weight on your shoulders?" Blade inquired.

"Two of us could," Boone interjected, joining them. "Put one leg on my shoulder and one on his. We should be able to support you."

Blade pursed his lips in thought. They were right. He stood a better chance of reaching the rim. "Okay. Take this," he said, extending his M-16 toward Sergeant Havoc.

The noncom took the weapon.

Boone and Thunder situated themselves with their backs against the dirt side. The Cavalryman slung his M-16 over his right shoulder and cupped his hands. "Ready when you are."

Thunder cupped his hands and nodded.

Blade stared at the trap door, gauging the distance. He rubbed his hands together. "On the count of three."

"How much do you weigh, by the way?" Boone asked.

"About two hundred and sixty pounds," Blade replied.

Boone grinned. "Sorry I asked."

"One," Blade said, beginning the count. He would need to move as rapidly as possible, especially once he reached the door. His own weight would be a detriment. "Two."

"Good luck," Sergeant Havoc commented.

Boone and Thunder braced their legs.

"Three," Blade said. He placed his right boot in Thunder's hands, his left in Boone's, and quickly clambered onto their shoulders. His nose was nearly touching the earthern wall. Craning his neck, he gazed at the lower edge of the door four feet above his head.

"Hurry!" Boone prompted through clenched teeth. "You feel like you weigh a ton!"

Blade eased his right Bowie from its sheath, tensed his legs, and leaped, his left arm outstretched and grasping for the metal ring in the lower left corner. His fingers closed on the ring, providing the fleetest of purchases, but he was already in motion with his right arm, surging the Bowie up and in. The blade thudded into the wood, penetrating deeply, and held fast.

"You did it!" Boone cried, elated.

The Warrior sagged for a second, girding his strength, his arms rippling, his body flush with the side of the pit. The strain on his shoulders was tremendous! Concentrate! he told himself. Concentrate! The tricky part was next. He released the metal ring, his left hand flashing to his left Bowie and drawing the knife as he started to slump, his right arm laboring to support his entire weight. He drove the left Bowie overhand as far as he could reach, using his right arm to lift himself higher so that the left Bowie sank into the door three feet above the right one. He lifted his left leg and rested his foot on the metal ring.

He couldn't stop now!

Blade grunted as he looked up at the rim.

Six feet to go!

He tugged on the right Bowie, working the blade back and forth until the knife came free. His shoulder muscles bunching into knotted cords, he lunged upward yet again and imbedded the right Bowie in the door.

Dear Spirit! How his shoulders hurt!

Blade ignored the agony and focused on wrenching the left Bowie from the wood. His nostrils inhaled the dank, musty scent of the dirt wall. The left Bowie pulled free, and once more he raised the knife as high as he could and rammed the blade into the wood.

"You're almost there!" Boone yelled.

Breathing heavily, Blade tugged on the right Bowie until it came loose. He propelled himself higher and slammed the knife home, then glanced upward.

The rim was mere inches above his right hand!

He released the left Bowie and clutched the edge of the pit. With a monumental effort he propped his left forearm on the rim. Using his left arm for leverage, he let go of the right Bowie and braced his right forearm on top. Climbing all the way out was accomplished with relative ease, and he perched on the rim, squatting while he caught his breath.

"Don't forget us," Boone quipped.

Blade glanced down at the trapdoor. He would retrieve the Bowies after rescuing his companions.

"The rope!" Boone urged.

The Warrior grinned at the Cavalryman's eagerness to vacate the foul pit.

"Sometime this year!" Boone cracked.

Blade shifted toward the rope. As he'd expected, enough rope was coiled on the corridor floor to reach the bottom of the garbage hole. He rose and walked to the coils, then deftly tossed the rope over the side.

"Thanks," Boone called out.

Blade inspected each of the Vampires to insure they were dead. As he was examining the last one, inquisitively studying its pallid complexion, Boone appeared. The Cavalryman was climbing hand-over-hand up the rope.

"I thought I would be sick," Boone mentioned as he scaled the rim and straightened. "I couldn't wait to get out of there!" He looked down. "I'm up! Who's next?"

Blade walked to the edge.

Thunder was nimbly ascending.

The Warrior turned and gazed along the corridor. "Boone, I want you to go back to the nearest junction. Other Vampires may have heard Havoc's shots. If any show up, get here on the double."

Boone nodded and hastened off.

So what was their next move? Blade asked himself as he watched Thunder mount the rope. Prest had claimed that Athena and Grizzly were both in cells on one of the lower levels, but the Vampire was probably lying. Which meant the two could be anywhere.

The rope shook and swayed slightly as Thunder neared the top. He hoisted his body above the edge, then stepped to solid ground. "I'm up!" he shouted to Havoc.

Blade knelt and began scooping the dirt aside.

"What are you doing?" Thunder questioned.

"What is the trapdoor attached to?" Blade asked.

"I don't know," Thunder responded.

"Neither do I," Blade said. The trapdoor protruded from under the dirt, and six large metal hinges were visible, spaced at intervals on the inner edge. He scraped off the dirt behind one of the hinges and discovered the inner half of the hinge was riveted to a metal plate partially imbedded in a wide concrete foundation. Frustrated, he stood and sighed.

"Is something wrong?" Thunder inquired.

"I was thinking of rigging a booby trap for the Vampires to give them a taste of their own medicine," Blade explained. "But dismantling some of these hinges would take too much time."

Sergeant Havoc came up over the lip of the pit, an M-16 on each shoulder. He swung to the corridor floor and landed unsteadily, his left leg almost buckling. Grimacing, he caught himself and straightened.

"Your leg?" Blade said.

Havoc nodded. "It's worse than before. I twisted my left ankle when I fell into the pit."

"Can you walk?" Blade asked.

"I can manage," Havoc asserted.

Blade took a stride and grabbed the rope. "My Bowies are still in the door," he commented, then slid down until he was next to the top Bowie. He jerked the knife out and replaced it in his right sheath. A few seconds later he recovered the other Bowie, then climbed from the pit.

"Here's your M-16, sir," Havoc said, offering the automatic rifle.

Blade was reaching for the weapon when the shots sounded from the direction of the junction.

Boone!

CHAPTER FIFTEEN

Athena Morris was shocked to the depths of her soul, horrified beyond measure. She saw the Vampires swarm upon the hapless captives from Aguanga. She heard the women and men scream as they were grasped securely, with five or six Vampires to each prisoner, and carted to the tables. Only then did she comprehend the significance of the leather straps attached to the tops of the tables.

Corpus was watching with a demented gleam to his eyes and a flush to his cheeks. Drool formed on his lips.

Polidori, Minshi, and three more Vampires were approaching the head table. They effortlessly carried a young woman between them. Terror contorted her face. She had blonde hair and was wearing a cinnamon-colored blouse and green slacks. Her petrified green eyes locked onto Athena. "Please!" she pleaded. "Help me!"

Athena went to rise, but Grizzly grabbed her left arm and restrained her.

"Don't," he cautioned.

"I should help her!" Athena insisted.

"There's nothing you can do," Grizzly told her. "They'll kill you if you interfere."

Corpus glanced at them. "Move aside!" he commanded with a sweep of his right arm.

Grizzly rose and pulled Athena to the right.

Polidori, Minshi, and the three Vampires arrived at the table with their victim.

"God! Help me!" the young woman cried desperately. She was lifted into the air and deposited on her back on top of the table. Working in concert, the Vampires strapped her wrists and ankles. "Help me!" she screamed.

The banquet hall was a madhouse. Shrieking and sobbing, the captives from Aguanga resisted the Vampires in vain. One by one the prisoners were firmly bound to the wooden tables. The Vampires remained emotionally calm through the bedlam, many licking their lips or exposing their pointed teeth in mocking grins.

Corpus hammered on the bell again after all of the captives were properly restrained. He faced the expectant Vampires and smiled. "Brothers and sisters, feeding time is here! You know the rules. Until the day comes when there is an abundant supply, we must share the foodstuff."

The prisoners had fallen silent at the sound of the golden bell. They listened to the Vampire leader with fear in their eyes.

"No gorging. No quarreling," Corpus went on. "We must be civilized about this," he added sarcastically.

Some of the Vampires laughed.

"I want to leave!" Athena declared.

Corpus looked at her. "Leave? How can you be so rude?"

"I don't want to see you kill these people!" Athena stated.

Corpus grinned. "Who says we're going to kill them?"

"You're not?" Athena responded, perplexed.

"We don't kill our foodstuff outright," Corpus elaborated. "We milk them for all they are worth."

Athena stared at the terrified woman on the table. "Do you mean . . ."

"Exactly," Corpus said with a smirk. "Observe and learn." He turned and tapped the bell twice.

The man in white promptly appeared. "You rang, sir?"

"Yes, William," Corpus said. "Bring the tray."

"At once," William replied. He hurried through the door in the rear wall.

"Why are you making me watch this?" Athena asked.

"The experience should be educational," Corpus told her. "For both of you."

"That works both ways," Grizzly interjected.

Corpus glared at the bear-man. "What does that mean?"

"You've got an education coming," Grizzly said. "Sooner than you think."

"Are you threatening me?" Corpus demanded.

Grizzly shook his head. "No," he said solemnly. "It's a promise."

Corpus leaned on the table. "Pay close attention to the festivities, fool. Your turn isn't far off."

"Dream on," Grizzly quipped.

The man in white returned bearing a large silver tray laden with an enormous pile of odd items. He dutifully placed the tray on the table in front of the Vampire leader, then departed.

"You may find these interesting," Corpus remarked. He picked up a thin, clear plastic tube or hose approximately a foot in length. One end of the tube was open, but the other was capped by a small needle. "Do you know what this is?"

"It looks like an intravenous tube," Athena commented.

"And it is," Corpus confirmed. "We appropriated cases of these from a hospital in Palm Springs. They make our feeding much easier. Originally, our ancestors drank the blood from vials. Later we experimented with straws." He wagged the tube. "And now we have the ideal method."

The young woman groaned.

"Please," Athena said, "I don't want to watch this."

Corpus chuckled. "Too bad."

"Why don't you feed on animals?" Athena asked. "Why use humans? This is barbaric. It's sick!"

"Who are you to judge us?" Corpus retorted. "And to answer your question, we do feed on animals for variety. But it's not the same. We prefer the sweet, delicious taste of humans. Females taste the best."

Athena stared at the young woman in despair.

Corpus handed a second feeding tube to Loring, then slid the tray across the table to Polidori and Minshi. Each Vampire took one of the feasting utensils. The tray was passed to the other Vampires, from one table to the next.

Many of the captives were weeping. Some cursed the Vampires.

The young woman on the head table glanced at Athena. "What's your name?"

"Athena Morris."

"I'm Greta Hogue from Aguanga," Greta said. "If you manage to get out of here, please tell my parents and brother you saw me."

Athena felt a congestion in her throat and swallowed.

Greta closed her eyes, her lips shaping soundless words.

The tray was still making the rounds.

Grizzly was in an emotional quandary. He wanted to tear into the Vampires, to feel his claws ripping their bodies apart. But any aggressive act on his part would undoubtedly result in Athena's death. Her life was his paramount consideration, and he refused to recklessly endanger her.

Greta Hogue suddenly opened her eyes and gazed at the bearman. "I can tell you don't like the Vampires. Will you help me?"

Grizzly spread his hands in a helpless gesture. "What can I do? There are too many."

"A glimmer of intellect," Corpus quipped. "There's hope for you yet."

Greta's face was unspeakably sad.

His shoulders slumping, Grizzly bowed his head and stared at the tiled floor. What should he do? Aid this girl and get Athena and himself killed? To help her would be suicidal. Besides, she was a human, and he was not excessively fond of humans. Except for Athena. But if he stood there and did nothing, how would he feel later? He wasn't like Blade; he didn't believe in all that Spirit nonsense. He relied on his conscience to dictate his actions, to determine between right and wrong. Was it right for him to stand there and do nothing?

Corpus surveyed the chamber. "Everyone has a feeding tube. We can continue." He raised his arms. "Brothers and sisters! Enjoy yourselves!"

Grizzly looked up.

The Vampire leader leaned over Greta Hogue, examining her left arm. He traced his right index finger across her skin and she shivered. "You have fine veins, my dear."

Minshi, Polidori, and the vampiric conclave watched him intently, hungrily.

"This won't hurt much," Corpus told Greta. "The needle may sting a bit."

Greta closed her eyes again. "Please! Don't!"

"Quit whining, bitch," Corpus snapped. He aligned the needle over a bluish vein on the inside of her elbow.

"No!" Greta cried.

Corpus unexpectedly glanced at his second in command, Loring. "Why aren't they here yet?"

Loring's hooked nose bobbed as he did a double take. "Who?"

"The giant and his crew," Corpus said. "I gave orders for them to be captured and brought here. Why haven't they arrived?"

Loring shrugged. "Maybe Nordier, Prest, and the rest took longer than we expected to catch up with the giant."

"And perhaps they ran into trouble," Corpus commented. "Take ten men and go find them."

"Now?"

"Now," Corpus said.

Loring looked at Greta, the tip of his tongue visible between his red lips. "But we're just about to feed!" he complained.

Corpus straightened, his features shifting, becoming bestial. "When I give you an order," he growled, "you will obey it! You will leave now!"

His disappointment obvious, Loring dropped his feeding tube on the table and headed off.

"Pick any ten to go with you," Corpus instructed. "And if they object, they can lodge their protest with Minshi."

Loring walked toward the front doors, pointing at Vampires at different tables, selecting ten to accompany him. Not one lodged a protest.

Corpus waited until Loring and company were gone and the doors were bolted, then he lowered himself above Greta, leering maliciously. "And now, my dear, a truly exquisite experience is about to be yours. Your blood, your essence, will nourish us. And for this treat, we thank you."

Tears welled from Greta's eyes.

True to his word, and ever so gently, Corpus slowly inserted the needle into her vein.

Greta flinched and gasped.

Corpus pinched the plastic tube near the needle to prevent the blood from flowing until he was ready. He insured the needle was fully inserted, then stroked her arm with his left hand. "How beautiful," he said softly.

"Corpus! Don't!" Athena pleaded.

The Vampire leader didn't bother to look at Athena. "If you open your mouth again," he warned, "Minshi will separate your head from your shoulders with his bare hands."

Minshi grinned.

Grizzly caught Athena's eye and shook his head.

"Are you ready, my dear?" Corpus asked Greta. He raised the open end of the tube to his mouth, his lips puckering as they enfolded the clear plastic, and released the pressure near the needle.

Greta Hogue fainted.

His lips moving out and in, as if he was kissing someone, Corpus sucked on the tube as the blood flowed upward. He sighed contentedly when the crimson fluid reached his mouth, savoring the taste, his eyes becoming dreamy with rapture.

The assembled Vampires took their cue from their leader. They inserted needles into the captives and began feeding with undisguised relish.

Athena was unable to turn aside. She was stunned by the grisly scene, her loathing overwhelming.

Minshi and Polidori were eager to quench their thirst, Polidori taking Greta's right elbow as Minshi reached down and gripped the bottom of her right slacks leg. He hardly seemed to strain as he ripped the fabric from the hem to the crotch. Saliva coating his lips, he draped the split material on either side of her leg. Methodically, with total concentration, he inserted his needle and began feasting in great gulps, blood spilling out the corners of his mouth.

"Dear Lord!" Athena mumbled in dismay.

The banquet hall was filled with sucking and slurping sounds as all of the Vampires started feasting. Some of the captives thrashed futilely, others became hysterical, blubbering and babbling, while more than a half-dozen succumbed to shock.

Dizziness flooded Athena's mind. She clutched at the nearest chair for support, and then Grizzly was there, his right arm around her slim shoulders.

"I'm here," he said.

"I can't stand this!" Athena stated. "It's . . . obscene! And they plan to do it to us!"

"I won't let them," Grizzly assured her.

"How will you stop them?"

Grizzly didn't answer. He couldn't answer. Because there was no answer.

CHAPTER SIXTEEN

Boone was standing over a pair of dead Vampires when his companions arrived at the junction.

"Are you all right?" Blade asked, scanning the intersecting corridors for more of the fiends.

"Fine," Boone responded. He prodded one of the Vampires with his M-16, satisfying himself the creature was deceased.

"What happened?" Blade queried.

"They appeared down the hall to the right," Boone explained. "I tried to follow orders and return to warn you, but they ran like the wind. They were at the junction before I went ten feet. I didn't have any choice."

"From here on out we move as fast as we can," Blade directed. "Those shots were bound to be heard. We must locate Grizzly and Athena before reinforcements arrive."

"How will we find them, sir?" Sergeant Havoc questioned.

"We just keep looking," Blade said. "Thunder, the rear. I'll take point. Boone, stay close to Havoc. He twisted his left ankle. Help him if he slows up."

"I don't need a baby-sitter," Havoc declared.

"This isn't a debate," Blade reminded him.

Sergeant Havoc frowned but stifled his disapproval.

"Move out," Blade said. He took the right branch, proceeding at a brisk walk, wanting to put a lot of distance between the two corpses and the Force. Prest had claimed there were hundreds of Vampires inhabiting the Heartland. If so, where were they? He was mystified by their absence. The Force had encountered only a handful, and the rest had to be close by.

But where?

He came to another intersection and paused, waiting for the others.

"Which way?" Boone inquired.

Blade glanced at the noncom. "How are you holding up?"

"No problem," Sergeant Havoc replied.

"Okay. We go straight," Blade directed, then led off. A lantern ahead revealed more of the same: an empty corridor with wooden walls and a dirt floor. A door appeared to his left and he angled toward it. His right hand gripped the knob and turned, and he was surprised to discover it wasn't locked. Inside were stacks of boxes and crates.

"Anything?" Boone asked.

Blade shook his head and resumed his search. At the next intersection he took a left. At the one after that a right. His frustration was mounting with every stride. He now believed that he'd committed a major mistake by venturing into the Vampires' sanctum. The network of passages was bewildering; a person could seemingly wander in them forever.

A junction materialized 40 feet in front of him.

What was that?

Blade stopped and crouched, his eyes narrowing as he scrutinized the junction. Vague, pale forms were moving through it. Vampires! He counted ten or eleven, his finger on the M-16's trigger, expecting to be spotted at any moment. But the party of bloodsuckers never noticed him. He received the impression they were in a hurry. Prudence was necessary, so he counted to 20 before rising and advancing to the intersection. A quick glance to the right confirmed the Vampires were gone. Relieved, he stepped from concealment.

Boone, Sergeant Havoc, and Thunder joined him.

"Did you see them?" Blade whispered.

Boone nodded. "Do we go after them? They could lead us to Athena and Grizzly."

"Too risky," Blade said. "Their senses are better than ours. They may spot us. Let's see where they came from." He marched into the left fork.

This corridor was unusual. Two lanterns were attached to the walls instead of one. The dirt was well trampled, indicating the hallway was used frequently. A row of doors lined both sides and a few were open.

Blade stared at the first door to his right, and he was startled to see light emanating from the doorway. He cautiously approached to within a yard, the M-16 leveled.

Without any warning, a woman stepped from the room. She was a brunette, her shapely figure clad in a brown loincloth and a strip of leather across her large breasts. Her brown eyes widened at the sight of the giant. "Who are you?" she blurted out loudly.

"Keep your voice down," Blade advised. "We're here to help you."

"Who are you?" she repeated.

"We're from the outside," Blade said. "We're going to rescue you."

"Like hell you will!" the woman said.

"What?" Blade asked, not certain he'd heard her correctly.

"I'm not leaving Heartland, mister," she stated.

"Why not?"

"I like it here," she said.

"Have the Vampires brainwashed you?" Blade queried.

"Give me a break!" she responded indignantly. "I want to stay because I have it real good here. I'm Loring's squeeze and he treats me like a princess."

"I don't understand," Blade admitted.

"I understand, sir," Sergeant Havoc commented from the Warrior's rear. "This woman is nuts."

"Loring is my mate," she disclosed. "I won't leave him. I can't."

"You're in love with a Vampire?" Blade inquired in amazement.

"Lots of the Venesects have human mates," she said. "It's not that unusual."

"And what do you think will happen down the road?" Sergeant Havoc demanded. "Will this Loring love you forever or just as long as it suits his purpose?"

"He does love me," she insisted. "He'd never hurt me. He's treated me special from the day he took me from my home in Fallbrook."

"Did you have a family?" Blade asked.

"A husband," she replied. "A foul-mouthed, alcoholic, wife-beater. Compared to that son of a bitch, Loring is a swell guy."

"Loring is a Vampire," Havoc remarked. "Vampires drink human blood."

"And humans kill animals for food," she retorted. "We eat their meat and drink their blood."

"Humans don't drink animal blood," Havoc said.

"Oh? Haven't you ever eaten a raw steak?" she countered.

"Are you positive you won't come with us?" Blade pressed her.

The brunette shook her head, sadness tinging her features. "I can't."

"You won't," Havoc said.

"I can't," she repeated. "I'm pregnant."

For a moment no one said a word.

"I'll have to ask you to go back in your room," Blade stated. "I can't let you warn the Vampires. We'll tie you up and gag you, but I'm sure someone will free you before too long."

The brunette looked into his eyes. "I can't let you do that," she said softly. Without any warning, she whirled and dashed down the corridor. "Help! Help! The Heartland is under attack!"

"Damn!" Blade fumed, starting in pursuit.

Boone darted past the Warrior, his lean legs flying. He overtook the brunette within ten feet. She looked over her left shoulder, about to shout again. Boone slammed the stock of his M-16 against her head and she sprawled onto the floor. He clubbed her again when she tried to rise.

More humans appeared, gaping at the Force members and the unconscious brunette.

Blade realized the entire corridor was occupied by the human mates of the Vampires. He didn't see any of the ghouls, but they had to be nearby. "In your rooms!" he bellowed, waving the M-16 as he jogged ahead.

The men and women promptly obeyed, door after door swinging shut.

"Now what?" Boone questioned as the Warrior came abreast.

"We haul butt," Blade advised. Taking the time to bind all of the humans would be impractical. He ran toward a junction at the far end of the hall.

A human male in a brown loincloth emerged from a door on the left, a hatchet in his left hand. "Stop!" he cried.

Blade shot him in the forehead, the single round propelling the man over a yard to crash onto his back. The Warrior sprinted past the body and reached the intersection without further interference. To his right was a dark passageway, to his left a hall containing several mesmerized humans who had heard the shot and were gawking at the giant in astonishment. Directly ahead was a well-lit, empty corridor. He went straight ahead.

Where in the world were all the Vampires?

The Warrior covered 50 yards. At the next junction he took a right, sticking to the passageways with the most illumination. The more illumination, he reasoned, the more human traffic. And the more human traffic, the more likelihood of Vampires also frequenting the area. He wanted to capture another Vampire and extract the whereabouts of Athena and Grizzly. But he had to find a few Vampires first, the fewer the better, making a capture easier.

The Vampires, however, found the Force sooner, and there were more than a few.

"Blade!" Thunder suddenly called out. "We have company!"

Blade stopped and spun.

A pack of Vampires was bounding toward the Force. They had just turned the corner at the last junction, their faces grim, their speed incredible.

Blade counted six. He crouched and motioned for Boone, Thunder, and Sergeant Havoc to form a line across the corridor. Havoc was limping badly. Blade sighted on the pack 20 yards away, impressed by their courage. Unarmed, the Vampires were confronting four automatic rifles without a hint of fear. What else besides bravery would compel the six to make such a reckless assault when the Vampires must know the inevitable result? The Vampires were strong, their bodies immune to pain to a large degree, but they weren't invincible.

For a fleeting instant Blade admired them.

And then another motive abruptly occurred to him and he tensed. What if the Vampires were *not* acting recklessly? What if there was an ulterior motive to their frontal attack? These Vampires were coming from the corridor the Force had vacated moments ago. Was it possible this was the same party he'd seen earlier? If so, there had been ten or eleven. Where were the rest? If the frontal charge was a ploy, then the rest must be . . .

Blade pivoted, his lips compressing at the sight of five more Vampires bearing down on the Force from the rear. They were less than seven yards distant and closing fast, their mouths open, their teeth exposed. ''Behind us!'' he shouted, and fired on full auto.

The Vampire nearest the right-hand wall was caught in the chest by the burst and hurled onto the floor, twitching and gurgling.

Boone twirled and cut loose, downing a second Vampire.

Thunder and Sergeant Havoc were concentrating their fire on the Vampires in front of them. Two of the six dropped soundlessly.

Blade shot another Vampire to the rear.

And then the two remaining Vampires were within six feet. Pouncing range. One came at the Warrior, the other hurtled at the Cavalryman.

Blade tried to swivel the M-16 barrel to shoot his opponent in the stomach, but the Vampire, a man with a hook nose and a cleft chin, swiped the barrel aside and clamped his hands on the Warrior's throat. Blade surged to his feet, astounded by the Vampire's strength. He could feel steely fingers digging into his neck. Releasing the M-16, he reached up and grabbed the Vampire's wrists, then attempted to pull those viselike hands from his throat.

Boone, meanwhile, was literally thrown for a loop. His foe gripped the M-16 and wrenched the weapon loose, tossing it to the floor with a contemptuous sneer. The Cavalryman went for his Hombres, but the revolvers were clearing leather when the Vampire seized the front of Boone's buckskin shirt with both hands and swept the Cavalryman up and over. Boone sailed over the Vampire's head and tumbled through the air before smashing onto his right side, dazed, the Hombres still clutched in his hands.

Without missing a beat, the Vampire lunged at Thunder, looping his right arm around the Flathead's neck and hauling Thunder backwards.

Sergeant Havoc suddenly perceived he was the only one firing. He shot one more in front, then twisted to see Blade grappling with one of their adversaries, Boone down, and Thunder being choked. He aimed at the Vampire choking Thunder.

Footsteps padded behind him.

Havoc never got off the shot. A white arm appeared over his right shoulder and tore the M-16 from his grasp. He attempted to turn, but a hand grabbed the back of his neck and hoisted him to his feet.

The last two Vampires closed on Blade.

The Warrior suddenly found himself the target of three Vampires. He saw them coming and managed to swing around, interposing the one with the hook nose between himself and the onrushing pair. Drawing his right arm back, he planted a tremendous blow on Hook Nose's chin. The Vampire, staggered, loosened his grip. Blade punched his foe a second time, his malletlike fist rocking the Vampire's head and causing Hook Nose to stagger back several feet.

Snarling and hissing, the last two Vampires bypassed Hook Nose and leaped, each gripping one of the Warrior's arms.

Blade's muscles bulged as he fought to fling the Vampires from him. They clung to him with all their might, but he was able to lift them from their feet and ram the one on his right into the wall. The Vampire started to sag. Before Blade could repeat the maneuver the battle was lost.

Hook Nose scooped up one of the M-16's and pointed the barrel at the giant. "Freeze or die!"

Blade's gray eyes flared and he hesitated.

"I mean it!" Hook Nose said. "I may want you alive, but I'll kill you and all of your friends if you don't do exactly as I say."

The Warrior observed Thunder in the grasp of a Vampire, on the verge of passing out. Sergeant Havoc was being held from behind by the neck and the right elbow, vainly endeavoring to swing his left elbow around and clip his captor.

"What will it be?" Hook Nose demanded.

Blade knew further resistance would be futile. He relaxed his arms in resignation.

"That's better," Hook Nose said. "What's your name?"

"Blade."

"I'm Loring."

"My displeasure, I'm sure."

"Save your insults," Loring stated. He looked at the Vampire holding Blade's left arm. "Collect their weapons and packs."

Blade, Havoc, and Thunder were stripped of their backpacks, guns, and knives. The Vampire finished frisking Thunder, who was lying on his back on the floor, and glanced up. His forehead creased as he gazed down the corridor. "Wasn't there another one?"

The Vampire responsible for subduing Thunder turned. "Yeah. There was a guy in buckskins. I took him down."

"He must be hiding in one of the rooms down the hall," the first Vampire commented. "Should we look for him?"

Loring reflected for a moment. "No. We don't want to keep Corpus waiting. You know how impatient he can become, and what happens when he loses his temper. We'll take these three to the banquet hall. I'll send a detail back here to find the guy in buckskins. He's just one human. He can't do much harm."

The Vampires let go of Blade and Havoc. Loring covered the giant and the soldier while his companions gathered the gear. One of the Vampires slung Thunder over his right shoulder.

"Let's go," Loring said. "I'll tell you the way. And remember, we're right behind you. Go straight, the way you came."

Blade complied, Havoc at his side.

"I can't believe Boone ran out on us," the noncom remarked.

"You know Boone better than that," Blade declared.

"We've made a mess of this mission, haven't we, sir?" Sergeant Havoc mentioned.

"That's the understatement of the decade," Blade responded

bitterly.

Sergeant Havoc's lips curled downwards as he limped along.

"How's the leg?" Blade inquired.

"Worse than ever."

"No more talking!" Loring snapped.

They walked a dozen yards in silence.

"Hey!" Loring said. "I want to know something."

Neither Blade nor Havoc responded.

"Didn't you hear me?" Loring demanded.

"You said not to talk," Blade replied.

"Very funny," Loring commented. "I want to know which one of you slugged Bernice?"

"Bernice?" Blade said.

"My mate. One of you bastards knocked her out. She was on her knees when I found her. Which one of you is responsible?"

Blade and Havoc ignored the question.

"That's okay. Play your little games," Loring said. "I'll find out which one, and when I do, you'll pay! I think I'll peel strips of skin from your body and watch you beg for mercy."

Sergeant Havoc glanced at Blade and grinned. "What a swell guy!"

CHAPTER SEVENTEEN

The grand feast was winding down.

A majority of the Vampires had finished feeding and were seated in their chairs, their expressions serene, their eyes placid, their mouths rimmed with a red film. The captives from Aguanga, weakened by the sudden loss of pints of blood and emotionally ravaged by their traumatic ordeal, scarcely moved. They moaned and groaned pitiably, trickles of blood seeping from the puncture marks left by the needles.

Corpus sat in his chair at the head table, leaning back, his arms draped at the sides of his chair, his eyes glassy, a twisted smile conveying his contentment.

Minshi and Polidori, sitting across from Corpus, were equally satiated.

Grizzly and Athena were two of the few still standing. His right arm encircled her shoulders. "I'm sorry," he said.

"What are you sorry for?" Athena asked weakly. Her shoulders were slumped, her chin on her chest, tears moistening the corners of her eyes.

"I should have done something," Grizzly stated softly.

"There was nothing you could do," Athena said, disputing him, sniffling.

Grizzly gazed at the limp, crimson-speckled women and men on the tables and frowned, his eyes focal points of torment. When he spoke, his words were barely audible. "I was wrong. I should have tried to save them."

"You would have been killed," Athena said.

"Probably," Grizzly agreed. "But I'm a member of the Force. I'm pledged to protect the people from every Federation faction. I volunteered to serve. No one forced me." He sighed. "I've learned a valuable lesson here today. We can't turn from our responsibilities. We can't shirk our duties. We have to try, no matter what the cost. There's no way of knowing if we'll succeed or not, but failure isn't the same as shame. True shame comes from not trying. Do you see my point?"

Athena looked at him in respect. "Yes, I do."

Grizzly stared at Greta Hogue. Her eyes were fluttering, her breathing ragged, and periodically she uttered a feeble whine. "Too bad for her that I learned my lesson too late."

A sarcastic snicker sounded from the other side of the table. "How pathetically noble!" Corpus cracked.

Grizzly glared at the Vampire leader.

"Spare us your sentimental garbage!" Corpus stated. "You're fooling no one but yourself. Face facts."

"What facts?" Grizzly responded.

Corpus smirked. "You're a coward."

Athena could see Grizzly's jaw muscles twitching as he removed his arm.

"I'm not a coward," Grizzly said.

"You didn't even make an attempt to help these wretches," Corpus declared. "And you have the gall to talk about your responsibility? Hypocrite."

Athena expected Grizzly to fly across the table in a fit of rage; instead, he bowed his head, his body sagging.

"You know I'm right, don't you?" Corpus gloated.

A hard pounding on the front doors brought an end to the conversation.

"Open the doors!" Corpus bellowed.

Two Vampires moved sluggishly to the huge doors and slowly undid the bolts.

Athena thought she would swoon.

Blade and Sergeant Havoc entered the banquet hall, Havoc hobbling on his left foot. Escorting them were five Vampires, including Loring. One of the Vampires was carrying Thunder. There was no sign of Boone.

Grizzly had turned as the doors swung wide. His face lit up at the sight of his colleagues.

"More company, I see," Corpus said, rising. He nodded at Minshi and Polidori, both of whom rose and stepped to the left, studying the new arrivals. Minshi seemed particularly interested in Blade.

"You apprehended them. Good," Corpus remarked as Loring's party neared the head table. "But weren't there four of them?"

Loring walked to the right, past the Warrior and the soldier. "Yes. One got away. But he can't get far. I'll send a search squad after him right now."

"See to it," Corpus instructed. "Lead them personally."

Loring hastened toward the tables on the left side of the chamber.

"I am Corpus," the head Vampire announced.

"Whoop-de-do," Sergeant Havoc quipped.

Corpus ignored the soldier and stared at the giant. "Your name, sir?"

The Warrior was surveying the room in dumbfounded stupefaction. His eyes roved over the victims of the gruesome blood feast, his lips slightly parted.

"Your name, sir?" Corpus repeated.

The Warrior's burning gaze shifted to the Vampire. "You're the one responsible for this?"

"I can't claim all the credit," Corpus said humbly.

"I hope you can count," Blade said.

Corpus seemed puzzled. "Why?"

"Because your days are numbered."

Surprisingly, Corpus laughed. "I appreciate a sense of humor. But you still haven't told me your name."

"Blade," the Warrior disclosed.

"What an odd name," Corpus commented.

The Vampires carrying the backpacks and weaponry stepped forward. "The name fits," one of them said. "You should see what he was packing."

"Show me," Corpus directed.

Relieved at being able to deposit all the gear on the table, they piled the backpacks, M-16's, knives, and 45's in a heap. One of them held aloft the Bowies, one in each hand, then set them down.

Corpus whistled. "You go in for big knives."

"The better to gut you with," Blade said.

Corpus chuckled. "A luxury you shall never enjoy."

Blade glanced at Athena and Grizzly. "Are you two okay?"

"Fine," Athena replied.

Grizzly didn't answer.

"Who sent you?" Corpus asked the giant. "Why are you here?"

"To exterminate the Vampires," Blade answered bluntly.

"Never happen," Corpus said. He gestured at one of the chairs across from him. "Have a seat and I'll tell you why."

The Warrior stood still.

"Why engage in this childish behavior?" Corpus asked. "I could have you killed now. All of you! But I have better plans for you, and I'm offering my hospitality. If there is more than solid muscle between those ears of yours, you will graciously accept. Unless," he said and leaned on the table, "you want to antagonize me and spoil my mood. In which case I might change my mind and exterminate some of *you* right this instant." He looked at Athena as he spoke.

Blade reluctantly walked to the table and stood behind the chair.

"Make room for them," Corpus commanded, sitting.

Several other Vampires relinquished their seats.

"All of you! Sit down!" Corpus instructed the giant's associates. "You must be hungry. I will have food brought."

"I won't be able to eat for a week," Athena mentioned as she took a seat.

Grizzly sat down next to her.

Sergeant Havoc moved to Blade's left, waited for the Warrior to sit, then eased into a chair, keeping his left leg as straight as possible.

Corpus pointed at the Indian. "Revive him."

One of the Vampires held the Flathead as a second slapped his cheeks lightly. Thunder took a deep breath and his brown eyes opened.

"Join us," Corpus stated, indicating a chair to the soldier's left.

Manifestly confused, not quite fully recovered, Thunder stumbled to the wooden chair and sat, his questioning gaze on Blade.

"How cozy," Corpus quipped. "Would you care for your food now?"

"No thanks," Blade replied.

"It won't be poisoned," Corpus said. "I assure you."

"No thanks," Blade reiterated.

"I see you possess an obstinate streak," Corpus mentioned. "Very well. Suit yourself. Just remember this was your idea when morning arrives and you're famished."

"Why are you toying with us?" Blade asked.

"Who's toying?" Corpus retorted. "Can't your dim intellect conceive of a higher purpose to my curiosity? A person in my position makes many enemies. In order to survive, I must grow to understand my enemies as well as I understand myself. Ignorance breeds weakness."

"What will you do to us?" Blade inquired.

"Please, let's dispense with morbid affairs," Corpus responded. "The aftermath of a feeding invariably results in a euphoric high. I like to savor the sensation." His eyes narrowed in contemplation. "Now about exterminating the Venesects—"

"You will be annihilated," Blade said, interrupting. "It's inevitable."

"Nothing in life is inevitable except dying," Corpus said. "And the Venesects will never die out. We're here to stay."

"Your time is running out. Sooner or later the California Army will invade the Dead Zone with a battalion or more. You won't stand a chance," Blade stated.

"You exaggerate, my friend," Corpus disputed the giant. "There are endless passages under the Heartland, and only the Venesects know every one. If an army invaded, we would see them coming miles off. We would secret ourselves and never be found. They could try bombing us or using artillery, but this far underground we wouldn't even be fazed. And if, for the sake of argument, they successfully launched a sneak attack and penetrated the Heartland, they wouldn't kill all of us. Some of us, you can be sure, would escape. And those who did would perpetuate our bloodline through the millennia.''

"You have this all thought out," Blade noted.

Corpus smiled. "I try." He thoughtfully considered the giant. "So who sent you? The governor of California?"

"I'm not at liberty to say," Blade replied.

"How rude," Corpus declared. "And here I am, trying to be so polite. My major flaw is my excessive kindness."

Blade pointed at the woman on the table. "You call this kindness?"

"No. She comes under the category of tasty treats," Corpus said, then laughed.

"Her name is Greta Hogue," Athena interjected. "She's from Aguanga."

Greta Hogue! Ethan's sister! Blade stared at her, realizing she was in shock.

"Do you know her?" Corpus asked.

Blade shook his head.

"I think you're lying," Corpus stated. "And I weary of your arrogance! You cease to amuse me! I have changed my mind. Dawn is several hours off. You have until one hour before daylight!"

"What happens then?" Blade questioned.

Corpus grinned wickedly. "Some of us will enjoy a snack before retiring for the day!"

CHAPTER EIGHTEEN

The agony in his right side was slowly subsiding.

Boone leaned his back against the wall and closed his eyes. He hoped his ribs weren't fractured or busted. The pain would slow him down when it counted the most, when it came time to go after Blade, Thunder, and Havoc.

He couldn't wait much longer.

How long had he been in the darkened room? Boone wondered. He regretted temporarily leaving his friends, but he hadn't had any other choice at the time. That toss through the air had rattled him but good. He vividly recalled lying on the floor in intense anguish, his right side feeling numb. Rallying his strength, he'd looked up to see Thunder out of commission, Sergeant Havoc in the grip of a Vampire, and Blade on the verge of being subdued by three more of the bloodsuckers.

His right side lanced by exquisite spasms, and unable to shoot accurately, he'd done the only thing he could: saved himself so he could later save them.

Boone remembered forcing his body to move, to roll away from the fight, simply intending to put some distance between the Vampires and himself. His action had been instinctive, not predicated on any clever scheme. When the open doorway had materialized on the right side of the corridor, he'd immediately rolled into the unlit room and collapsed, the torment in his right side almost unbearable. He'd waited with baited breath for the Vampires to find him.

Amazingly, they hadn't come.

Boone had listened to the Vampires depart with his companions. He'd overheard the comment the one called Loring had made about sending a detail to locate him, and he wasn't about to wait around for them to arrive.

Maybe he could manage now.

Boone opened his eyes and struggled erect, using his elbows to brace himself as he rose. With a firm grip on the Hombres, he sidled to the doorway and peeked outside.

The corridor was deserted.

Pleased his strategy was working, Boone stepped into the hall. Which way should he go? The Vampires would likely expect him to head for the hills, to continue away from the ambush spot. They'd probably check every room, every hiding place, beyond the site of the fight. But what about rooms in the opposite direction, in the direction the Vampires had taken their prisoners? Would the sons of bitches reckon on a frontal attack from one man?

Not very likely.

Boone shuffled to the first junction, his stride increasing the farther he went. The exercise was helping his side, reducing the discomfort. He halted in the intersection and debated on the proper branch. On a hunch he stuck with the corridor he was in, going straight. At the next junction he took a right.

And froze.

Far off, someone laughed.

Boone jogged forward, seeking a door. He found one on the left, holstered his left Hombre, and tried the doorknob.

Locked.

Undaunted, he proceeded another 15 feet and discovered a door on the right. He grasped the knob and turned, grinning in triumph when the door opened.

More laughter, but much closer.

Boone eased inside the dark room, listening for the telltale evidence of an occupant, but all was quiet. He closed the door until a crack afforded him a glimpse of the corridor.

Voices in conversation became audible.

". . . see the look on her face when I stuck the needle in her neck? I thought she'd shit her pants!"

"I hate it when they do that."

"I wish we didn't need to track down this bozo. I like to sleep after a feed."

"The foodstuff tonight was terrific."

"Ever tried to feed from a penis?"

"Once."

"What happened?"

"The prick pissed in my face."-

Feed from a penis? Boone aligned his eyes with the crack just as a party of Vampires walked past the door. He counted 12, and thought he recognized the one in the lead as one of those involved in the ambush. Loring maybe?

"Think we'll get to feed on the giant and his buddies?" a Vampire asked.

"Are you kidding?" responded another. "Corpus will save them for the inner circle."

"Quiet!" the leader barked.

Boone waited until he was certain the Vampires were long gone. He cautiously opened the door and looked both ways before stepping into the passage. The remark about feeding on a giant had alarmed him. So far as he knew, Blade was the only giant in the Heartland. Which meant the Vampires intended to feed on the Warrior, and soon. He resumed his hunt, listening intently.

What if he had miscalculated?

What if he reached Blade and the others too late?

He wouldn't be able to live with himself.

The fear of failing his friends motivated him to move faster. He passed door after door, and three junctions, without encountering anyone.

If only his luck would hold!

Boone was approaching an intersection when a tremendous commotion erupted ahead, as if dozens and dozens of people were talking at once. He took a sharp left at the junction, dashing to the first door on the right.

It was already open, and a lantern was visible on a wall to the left.

Boone ducked inside, then peered along the hallway to the junction. Vampires came into view, dozens of them. He quit tallying the number at 73 and estimated over a hundred filed through the intersection. Where were they all going? After him? He doubted they would send so many after one man. Were they on their way to a big shindig or coming from one? He stiffened as a small group appeared and headed in his direction.

No!

He closed the door and pressed his right ear to the panel.

". . . don't think it's fair," commented a Vampire.

"Tell that to Corpus and he'll let Minshi handle your complaint. You know what will happen then."

"I still don't think it's fair," the first one said. "Why should we be denied the privilege of feeding on those newcomers? Why should Corpus, Minshi, Polidori, and Loring receive special treatment? Aren't all Venesects created equal?"

"Some are more equal than others," the second Vampire stated.

Boone guessed the group was right outside his door.

"Corpus may be the best leader we've ever had," yet another Vampire remarked. "But one day he'll go too far. He's too dictatorial for my tastes."

"Don't let any of his friends hear you say that," advised a different one.

"I bet that giant has prime blood."

"And what about the mutant? Did you see his fur? I think he was cute." This voice sounded feminine.

"You would, Lamia."

"How would you find a vein through all that fur?" asked another male.

"You could always shave the fur off."

"Where there's a will, there's a way."

The voices trailed off as the group went beyond hearing range.

Boone knew the Vampires were referring to Grizzly. He was about to turn, to inspect the room, when someone else spoke sternly behind him.

"Who are you? No one is allowed in here!"

Boone was holding his right Hombre in front of his body at wasit level. He tightened his grip and glanced over his right shoulder, grinning broadly.

"Who are you?" repeated a man in a white shirt, pants, and apron.

"Howdy," Boone said. Five feet separated the two, and he wanted the man to move a little closer before making his move. Plugging the guy was out of the question; the Vampires would hear the shot.

"Does Corpus know you are in here?" the man asked belligerently.

"Of course he does," Boone lied, scanning the room. He recognized he had stumbled into a large kitchen; pots and pans were stacked on shelves along the right wall, sturdy wooden tables spotted by bloodstains were in the center, and a pair of white sinks were in a corner on the left. On one of the wooden tables was an open cardboard case, and beside the case was a pile of strange clear tubes.

"I don't believe you," the man said. "What is your name?"

"Boone. I was sent to lend you a hand," Boone responded.

"Now I know you're lying!" the man in white declared. "I will inform Corpus of this intrusion." He pivoted and took a stride.

The Cavalryman took one bound and pounded the man in white on the back of the head with the Hombre revolver.

Staggering forward, the man clutched at the nearest wooden table. He shook his head in a vain effort to retain his mental clarity.

Boone wasn't about to give the fool a chance. He closed in and swung the revolver three more times. His first blow caught the man on the back of the head again; his second smacked into the right ear as the man tried to swivel and confront him; his third lashed the man across the temple, splitting the skin and drawing blood.

The man in white sprawled onto the white tile floor.

Boone took a deep breath and scrutinized the opposite side of the kitchen from the hall door. He spotted a stove in a corner to the right, and slightly to the left of the stove was a closed door.

What was on the other side?

He advanced to the door and gingerly tried the knob. It rotated easily enough, but as he went to open the door he heard voices from the far side.

Vampires?

Boone released the doorknob and pondered his next step. There were too many Vampires abroad in the corridors to risk continuing his search for the time being. The wise thing to do was to stay put. The guy in white was out for the count, and the kitchen, apparently, was off limits to most everybody. This would be a safe place to hole up for a spell.

But he couldn't take too long.

The lives of his friends were on the line.

CHAPTER NINETEEN

An hour and a half before dawn.

Shadow and his five fellow braves were sleeping the slumber of deep exhaustion. The evening before they had finally found the missing half of their hunting party. Animals had nibbled at a few of the bodies, rendering the facial features on one of the dead braves indistinguishable and gnawing the fingers from two others. Awash in grief, Shadow and his companions had conducted the appropriate ceremonies to expedite the passage of the departed spirits to the realm of the Breath Giver. Hours were spent in digging graves, and then the weary braves had turned in, leaving one of their number on guard. But that worthy, seated next to the roaring fire, succumbed to his fatigue and dozed off, his chin on his chest.

Hours elapsed. Beginning to toss fitfully in his sleep, Shadow opened his eyes and gazed absently at the fire. He was lying on the ground ten feet to the rear of the guard, and everything looked as it should. Slipping into repose, he did not realize the sentry had fallen asleep until much later when he again opened his eyes and beheld the black man. For a minute he believed he was dreaming. Few blacks lived near the land of his people, and Shadow had encountered them only a few times when on trips to the towns of the whites. This one was a huge black, almost as big as the white giant called Blade, very muscular, dressed in a brown leather vest, brown pants, and black boots.

"Hi, there," the black said with a smile. He was crouching an arm's length from Shadow, an M-16 cradled in his arms.

Shadow started to rise, and suddenly the barrel of the M-16 was nearly touching his nose.

"Do it slow, my man," the black advised. "Real slow. I'm not alone." He gestured with his left arm.

Shadow was startled to see dozens of somber men ringing the camp, all soldiers, all armed.

"Stand up," the black said. "Slowly." He stood.

"As you wish," Shadow stated, rising with his hands in the air.

"You can put down the hands, bro," the black said. "I ain't here to waste you."

The other braves were rousing from their sleep. Soldiers detached from the ring and stood over the braves with their M-16's extended. The sentry at the fire jumped up and was promptly covered by three automatic rifles.

"Behave yourselves and no one will be hurt," the black declared for everyone to hear.

"What do you want?" Shadow inquired.

"I'm lookin' for some friends of mine," the black said.

"What is your name?"

"Bear," the black said. "And yours?"

"I am Shadow."

"Well, Shadow, I'm sorry to disturb your beauty rest, but we need to talk," Bear stated. "I've been trampin' all over these woods searchin' for an outfit known as the Force. Ever heard of 'em?"

"No," Shadow said.

"You sure? Their leader is a big bozo by the name of Blade," Bear mentioned. "There are others with him. One is a cowboy I know called Boone. Another is an Indian, Thunder. There's a soldier, Sergeant Havoc. And a mutie named Grizzly and a woman named Athena."

Shadow nodded. "We ran into some of them."

Bear stepped closer to Shadow. "You have? When? Where? Which ones?"

"We saw them the day before yesterday, east of here," Shadow detailed.

"Where were they headin'?"

"Toward the Red Land. They said that one of them, a woman, had been captured by the Blood Drinkers," Shadow answered.

"The Red Land?" Bear repeated quizzically.

"The whites refer to it as the Dead Zone," Shadow explained. "But it is not dead. Many demons inhabit the Red Land, as do the Blood Drinkers, those the whites call Vampires."

"So you saw all of the Force except Athena?" Bear probed.

"I did not see a woman with them," Shadow replied. "Nor did I see a mutant."

Bear pursed his lips. General Gallagher had shown him photographs of each Force member he didn't know before his departure for Aguanga. Blade, of course, was an old friend. Boone too was a prior acquaintance. Bear had enjoyed the Cavalryman's company at the Home on several occasions, and the two had attended the summit meeting in Anaheim back in January. But Thunder, Havoc, Grizzly, and Athena were all new to him.

"They are your friends?" Shadow asked.

"Blade and Boone are," Bear responded. "I'm going to be joinin' up with them, but first I have to find them."

Shadow pointed at the row of freshly dug graves, at the mounds of dirt. "We will assist you, if you want. The Blood Drinkers killed some of our brothers."

"Sorry," Bear said. "I'd like to take you, but we need all our spare room on the Choppers for when we find the Force."

"Choppers?"

"Our helicopters. They're waiting to hear from me at Aguanga. I'm going to radio for them to pick us up and airlift us to this Dead Zone. Is there a big clearing around here?"

Shadow nodded to the south. "Two minutes from here."

"Good. It's about time these Vampires learned they can't be messin' with folks and gettin' away with it," Bear stated.

"May the Breath Giver preserve you," Shadow said.

"Huh? Yeah. Sure. Stay cool. And don't take no crap from the scuzzy lowlifes!"

Shadow watched the black and the soldiers melt into the trees, and he experienced a twinge of regret. He would have liked to get to know the black better. Bear was most . . . colorful. And the black employed a marvelous vocabulary.

What, for instance, were "scuzzy lowlifes."?

CHAPTER TWENTY

"**W**here is Loring?" Corpus demanded impatiently. "I will not wait much longer! Dawn will break in less than an hour."

"He must not have found the one who got away," Polidori commented. "Knowing Loring, he won't return until he does."

"Then he will miss our bedtime snack," Corpus said with a sneer.

Blade shifted in his chair and stared over his left shoulder at the 20 Vampires gathered near the head table, awaiting the word from their leader. The Aguanga captives had been removed earlier, and Corpus had dismissed most of the Vampires, then spent his time expounding on how the Venesects would inevitably conquer the humans.

The Force members had listened in stony silence, with only Blade venturing to reply whenever Corpus became especially obnoxious. Obviously, the Vampire leader loved to hear himself talk. Blade had also used the time to study his associates, to gauge their readiness for what was coming. There was no way Blade would allow the Vampires to feed on his people without a fight, and while the Force was badly outnumbered, they could take a lot of Vampires with them.

Thunder took Corpus's diatribes in stride, his arms folded

across his chest. Sergeant Havoc had reacted passively,
constantly rubbing his left leg, seemingly preoccupied with his
injuries. Athena alternated between glaring at the Vampire
leader and casting apprehensive glances at Grizzly. And Grizzly,
quite uncharacteritstically, sat slumped in his chair in a dejected
attitude.

Blade was perplexed by the hybrid's melancholy behavior.
Normally, Grizzly was extroverted in the extreme. What could
have transpired to so drastically modify his attitude? How
effective would Grizzly be when the moment of truth came?

"Are you religious?" Corpus unexpectedly inquired.

Blade looked the Vampire in the eyes. "Yes."

"Then you will have a few minutes to make amends with
whichever deity you worship," Corpus offered.

"The Spirit," Blade said.

"What?" Corpus said testily, as if he hadn't expected a
response.

"Where I was raised, we believe in the dominance of the Spirit
in our lives," Blade elaborated. "Living the will of the Spirit
should be our paramount concern."

"Your Spirit must not reciprocate your devotion," Corpus
said sarcastically. "Why doesn't this Spirit protect you? Where
is this Spirit now, when you are on the brink of dying?"

"A person with genuine faith never dies," Blade declared.

Corpus laughed uproariously. Minshi and Polidori, standing
to the left of the Warrior and slightly behind him, chimed in.

Blade idly stared at the pile of Force gear on the table in front
of him, just out of reach. His Bowies were on the top of the
heap. One lunge and they would be his.

"How can anyone believe all that religious gibberish?"
Corpus said, mocking the Warrior. "Where was the God of
all those Christian denominations—the Catholics, Presbyterians,
Lutherans, and Baptists—when World War Three broke out?
Where was the Allah of the Moslems? What happened to the
Lord of the Quakers and the Mormons? Where was this God
when all his precious children were having their buns fried to
a crisp?"

"You misunderstand the nature of the Spirit," Blade
remarked.

"How so?" Corpus asked. "Enlighten me."

Blade held his hands out, palms up. "Pick one."

Corpus did a double take. "What is this? Some childish game?"

"Pick one," Blade reiterated.

Corpus pointed at the giant's right hand. "There. So what?"

"So now you know why the Spirit did not intervene to prevent World War Three," Blade said.

"You're not making any sense," Corpus said.

Blade placed his hands on the edge of the table, slightly nearer to the pile of weapons. "You just exercised your free will, the same free will everyone has, the free will to live according to the will of the Spirit or to live according to the dictates of our own conscience, our own precepts of right and wrong."

Grizzly's head snapped up, and he cocked his head as he listened to the Warrior.

"If everyone lived consistent with the Spirit's will, if we all strived for perfection, if we all loved one another as the spiritual leaders of humankind have enjoined down through the ages, this world would be a Utopia," Blade asserted. "But very few live spiritual lives. They give lip service to the Spirit, then go their merry way. They allow their actions to be controlled by their fluctuating feelings, by their frame of mind at any given moment." His hands inched a fraction closer to the pile.

Corpus leaned forward. "Fascinating! I had no idea you are a religious fanatic. But tell me. How does this free-will business tie in with World War Three?"

"The Spirit bestowed on us the free will to make this planet a paradise or to destroy it," Blade said. "The choice is ours."

"A puerile assessment, if ever I heard one," Corpus remarked. He looked at Polidori. "I hope his blood doesn't contaminate ours with his stupidity."

Polidori cackled.

"I'll be damned!" Grizzly abruptly exclaimed.

Every face focused on the mutant.

"The coward speaks!" Corpus quipped.

"I think I understand you," Grizzly said to Blade.

"You do?" Blade responded.

"Yeah," Grizzly declared. "And now I know what I've got to do." His eyes narrowed. "Do you get my drift?"

Corpus glanced from the mutant to the giant and back again.

"Don't try anything foolish! You're outnumbered four to one."

Grizzly glowered at the Vampire leader. "I can count, asshole. And the odds are two to one."

"Oh?" Corpus rejoined, starightening. "You have allies I don't know about?"

"As a matter of fact, I do," Grizzly stated, slowly rising.

"Sit down!" Corpus commanded.

Grizzly raised his arms, tilting his forearms in the direction of the Vampire leader, his hands almost vertical. "Up yours!" he retorted, his fingers going rigid and locking in place, his five-inch claws sliding from under the flaps of skin behind each fingernail. He snarled, stepped onto his chair, and vaulted onto the head table, all in a quick, fluid motion.

"Stop him!" Corpus shouted, too late.

Grizzly launched himself through the air, slamming into Corpus's chest, the impact toppling the Vampire leader's chair backwards and sending them both to the floor.

Pandemonium erupted.

Minshi grabbed the tabletop, preparing to leap to his brother's assistance.

Blade came out of his chair in a rush, tackling the huge Vampire, and both went down, grappling for an advantage.

Sergeant Havoc, Thunder, and Athena started to grab for weapons from the pile of gear, but the 20 Vampires to their rear swarmed in. One grabbed Thunder's wrists, and another took hold of Athena. For a moment it seemed like their desperate bid for freedom was doomed.

Until an unforeseen wild card entered the fray.

A gunman named Boone, charging through the door in the rear wall, an Hombre in each hand. Both revolvers thundered once, and the Vampires gripping Thunder and Athena were each struck in the forehead and flung backwards. The Hombres boomed again and two more died.

For a few seconds the total attention of the 16 remaining Vampires was focused on the Cavalryman and his deadly guns.

Which was all the distraction Havoc, Thunder, and Athena needed. They snatched the handiest weapons from the heap: Thunder an M-16, Athena an M-16, and Havoc a pair of 45's. They swiveled, rising, and blasted away at point-blank range.

Wrestling with Minshi in a ferocious struggle on the floor,

Blade heard the gunfire and renewed his efforts to break loose and aid his friends. But the gigantic Minshi had other ideas. His left hand locked on the Warrior's throat, Minshi struck Blade a devastating blow to the chin. Stars exploded before the Warrior's eyes, and he doubled over as a knee drove into his groin.

Minshi growled and stood, pulling Blade after him. He effortlessly lifted the Warrior into the air, clear overhead, and hurled Blade onto the table.

Blade gasped as his left shoulder was jarred by the unyielding wood. Pain engulfed him. His head bumped an object and he twisted, his eyes brightening at the sight of the pile of Force gear, his Bowies now lying at the outer edge of the heap. He seized the knives and twisted onto his back.

Just as Minshi pounced, leaping onto the table top and diving at the Warrior.

Blade instinctively extended his arms, the Bowie tips straight out.

Minshi couldn't check his plunge. The Bowies caught him high on his chest, penetrating to the hilt, and he collapsed on top of the Warrior, his eyes quivering, wheezing.

Grunting with the effort, Blade tossed Minshi to one side, to the right, onto the table, and wrenched the Bowies out. He rose to his knees, his eyes flicking in all directions, assessing the battle. Ten of the Vampires were sprawled on the tile floor near the head table. Sergeant Havoc and Thunder were engaged in hand-to-hand combat, Thunder swinging his M-16 like a club, Havoc using his martial-arts skills against three Vampires as they tried to pin his arms. Athena was on the floor, straddled by a Vampire intent on choking the life from her. And Boone was frantically reloading his Hombres as a trio of Vampires scrambled over the tables toward him. Blade tensed his legs muscles, about to go to Athena's succor.

"Surrender or Corpus dies!" roared a raspy voice.

The Vampires abruptly ceased fighting, their eyes on the two figures on the far side of the head table.

Grizzly had his left hand, the claws retracted, encircling the Vampire leader's throat. The claws on his right hand were brushing Corpus's eyelashes. Slashes marked the Vampire's cheeks, chest, and arms, and rivulets of pink blood crisscrossed his torso. "Back off!" Grizzly barked. "Or I'll snuff this prick right now!"

Some of the Vampires complied. Others looked at their leader. "Do it!" Corpus ordered.

The ten Vampires backed away from the Force members.

Blade slid off the table and stepped to Athena's side. He replaced his left Bowie in its sheath and looped his left arm around her shoulders as she endeavored to stand, her knees wobbly. "I've got you," he said.

Grizzly looked at the Warrior. "You call the shots, boss man. What do we do?"

Blade was ever the realist, and his pragmatic side prevailed. "We get out of here and go for help. We'll take Corpus with us as insurance."

"What about them, sir?" Sergeant Havoc asked, nodding at the ten Venesects.

"We'll tie them up," Blade said. "It will buy us some time."

"Where's Polidori?" Grizzly queried. "I don't see that tittering idiot anywhere, and I know he was here when the fight began."

Athena straightened and pointed at the open front doors. "I saw him take off."

"He's going for reinforcements," Sergeant Havoc remarked.

"That's right!" Corpus gloated. "He'll come back with more Venesects than you can possibly handle! We'll rip you to pieces!"

Grizzly jabbed his claws into Corpus's right cheek. "If you open your mouth again, I'll cut out your tongue."

The Vampire leader clammed up.

"Okay!" Blade declared. "Grab your gear! We're leaving."

Moving with a sense of dire urgency, the Force members reclaimed their backpacks and weapons. They inserted fresh magazines into their M-16's and made sure their Colts were loaded.

Thunder slid an M-16 across the table to Boone, who slung the automatic rifle over his left arm, preferring to rely on his Hombres.

"All loaded?" Blade asked after a minute.

"All set, sir," Sergeant Havoc said. "Do you want me to tie these guys?"

"There's no time to waste," Blade said. He leveled his M-16 and fired. Only eight feet away, the Vampires had no time to charge and nowhere to flee. They were decimated on the spot, some screeching and flopping as they hit the floor. In seconds it was all over.

"You son of a bitch!" Corpus cried, enraged.

"Let's go," Blade said grimly, starting toward the huge doors.

"Wait!" Boone called. "We can skedaddle through the kitchen."

The Warrior glanced at the rear door. "Good idea. Over the tables! Move it!"

Thunder, Sergeant Havoc, and Athena climbed onto the tables, angling toward the kitchen door.

Blade followed them, watching the front.

Boone dashed to the rear door and threw it open, and only his superb reflexes saved his life.

The man in white was there, clutching a carving knife in his right hand, a maniacal expression contorting his face as he stabbed at the Cavalryman's chest.

Boone threw himself backwards, bumping into one of the tables, the Hombres at waist height. He thumbed back the hammer on the right revolver and planted a slug in the man's right eye, the force of the impact bowling the man in white over.

The Force members darted through the doorway, Blade bringing up the rear behind Grizzly and Corpus.

"You'll never get away with this!" Corpus snapped at the Warrior.

"I told you to shut your face!" Grizzly warned.

They reached the hallway, exited, and paused.

Blade glanced at Corpus. "Which way to the surface?"

"Go to hell!" Corpus replied.

"Grizzly," Blade directed. "Cut out his tongue."

"With pleasure!" Grizzly said, tapping the Vampire leader's lips with his claws.

Corpus stared into Grizzly's eyes for a moment, then looked at those razorlike talons. "Take a right."

CHAPTER TWENTY-ONE

They emerged from the ruins near the east rim of the crater to find the sky filled with stars and a tinge of yellow lining the horizon.

"This is where we came in!" Sergeant Havoc exclaimed.

"How'd we get here so fast?" Boone questioned in disbelief.

"It pays to have someone who knows all the shortcuts," Athena said, glancing at Corpus.

Grizzly, standing behind the Vampire with his claws pressed against Corpus's neck, looked at the stark slag and girders to their rear. "And he isn't the only one. We're in for it now!"

Blade heard them too. The hubbub of many excited voices on their trail. The Vampires, not far off and closing.

"You won't escape!" Corpus boasted.

"To the rim!" Blade commanded. "Hurry!"

They raced to the crest of the crater. Sergeant Havoc, who had been hard pressed to keep up during the flight from the kitchen, practically dragged his left leg after him.

Blade stepped onto the rim and turned, his mouth a thin line as he surveyed the Heartland. "Leave Corpus with me and take off," he instructed them.

"Do what?" Grizzly responded.

"Did I hear you right?" Boone asked.

"You heard me," Blade said. "I'll hold them off as long as I can. Dawn is in ten minutes, and we know the Vampires can't tolerate the sun. If I can pin them there in the crater, you'll be able to escape."

"The noble sacrifice!" Corpus stated, and laughed.

"I'm not leaving you," Boone declared.

"Nor will I," Thunder concurred.

"None of us will," Athena said. "We're a team, right? The Force. We stick together through thick and thin."

Blade gazed affectionately at each of them. "I appreciate your sentiments. I really do. But this isn't the time to argue. Some of us must make it out of the Dead Zone. We've been down there. We know what's going on. We can bring an end to the reign of terror by getting word to General Gallagher. The Vampires must be stopped! Tell Gallagher to invade the Heartland with a regiment and all the firepower he can muster." He paused. "The lives of countless people depend on your getting through."

"I don't know," Athena said.

"Go!" Blade barked. "And that's an order!"

Athena looked at Grizzly. who nodded. She frowned, then started to the east.

Thunder gazed at the Warrior for a second before jogging after her.

"You too, Boone," Blade said.

The Cavalryman balked. "You're my friend."

"I am," Blade agreed. "And if you are really mine, you'll do as I say. Get."

Boone nodded once and took off after the others.

"Your turn, Sergeant Havoc," Blade remarked.

"No, sir."

Blade scrutinized the noncom. "*You* are disobeying a direct order?"

Sergeant Havoc sighed. "Not by choice. This leg of mine has had it. I can't go any farther, Blade."

"You could try."

"They'd overtake me, and you know it," Havoc said. "I'd rather make my last stand here."

Blade knew the noncom was telling the truth. "Okay. You can stay. But no sleeping on the job."

Havoc grinned and settled to the rim in a prone position.

"That leaves you," Blade addressed Grizzly.

"Forget it."

"I'm ordering you to leave."

"You're wasting your breath."

"Damn it, Grizzly! Listen for once!" Blade declared.

"No can do," Grizzly responded wistfully. "It's partially my fault we're in this fix. I'm seeing it through to the end."

"What are you talking about?"

Grizzly stared at the ruins. "A mutant's got to do what a mutant's got to do."

"You won't leave?"

"Nope. You can boot me off the Force later, if you want."

"Later then," Blade said, and faced the Heartland.

The babble of roiling voices was much louder.

Blade lay down a few yards from Sergeant Havoc and slanted his M-16 over the rim. "Wait until they're on the slope."

"Yes, sir," Sergeant Havoc said. He drew his right Colt and offered the automatic to Grizzly. "Here. You don't have a gun."

"I don't want one," Grizzly replied. "My claws are all I need. Thanks, though."

Corpus, standing on the rim to the right of Havoc, with Grizzly to his rear, gazed longingly at the inky contours of the Heartland. "Do you hear them? They'll be here soon. Do yourselves a favor and surrender while you have the chance."

"Do't make us laugh!" Grizzly retorted.

"You'll die here. You know that, don't you?" Corpus queried. "The three of you will be crushed like the gnats you are!"

Grizzly looked at Blade. "Can I shut this turkey up?"

Before Blade could respond, the Venesects poured from passages at the base of the ruins, streams of pale figures flowing into the crater and milling about.

"Which way?" one of them yelled to no one in particular.

"Up here!" Corpus suddenly shouted. "It's a trap!"

Grizzly plowed into Corpus from behind, his arms around the Vampire's thin waist, and together they pitched over the edge and tumbled down the slope.

"Grizzly!" Havoc cried.

The Venesects surged en masse toward the east side of the crater.

Frowning at his failure to terminate Corpus while he had the opportunity, annoyed because his arguments with the others had distracted him from his duty, Blade sighted on the leading row of Vampires and squeezed the trigger. There was no waiting for the Vampires to reach the slope, where Grizzly was now battling Corpus. The Vampires would overwhelm the mutant in an instant, and Blade was determined to see that they didn't. His initial burst took down over a half dozen, but it wasn't enough to slow them.

Sergeant Havoc joined in, his M-16 chattering, every shot connecting as he raked the front row. Five, six, seven Vampires toppled to the red dirt and the line wavered.

Blade continued firing, the white, scarecrow forms making excellent targets. He aimed at their heads, at the most vulnerable part of their anatomy, knowing a shot through the brain was the best bet to kill them. Eight more keeled over in half as many seconds.

Unnerved by the deadly fusillade, staggered by the loss of so many of their companions in the opening moments of the battle, the Vampires retreated into the passageways to regroup.

"They won't be so easy to stop the next time," Sergeant Havoc mentioned, replacing the magazine in his M-16.

Blade was engrossed in the fight on the slope.

Grizzly and Corpus were on their feet, exchanging a flurry of fist and claw blows, their postures awkward because of the incline. Corpus, taller and with the greatest reach, was landing powerful punches to the bear-man's face. In the banquet hall Grizzly had pinned the Vampire leader under the table, where Grizzly's shorter arms and claws had given him the close quarters advantage. But here on the open slope, able to maneuver and maximize his superior size, Corpus enjoyed the upper hand.

Backpedaling, Grizzly blocked a boxing strike intended for his throat. He was frustrated by his inability to land a lethal swipe of his claws and feeling exposed, perched on the incline with a horde of Vampires about to charge again at any second.

Corpus intuitively sensed his foe's trepidation and smirked. "This time the outcome will be different! No false bravado will save your hide!''

Grizzly ducked under another swing and backed up a step.

"A mutant's got to do what a mutant's got to do!" Corpus mimicked the bear-man. "What drivel! You're blaming yourself because you didn't even try to help those wretches from Aguanga.''

Astounded by his adversary's insight, Grizzly took another stride backwards. "I am not," he said, but his tone lacked conviction.

"Who are you kidding?" Corpus retorted, pressing his psychological attack. He realized the mutant was emotionally disturbed, a weakness he planned to exploit to gain the deceptive edge. "Do you know why you didn't help them?"

Instead of responding, Grizzly lashed out with his right hand.

Corpus easily evaded the sluggish swat. "Is that the best you can do?" he taunted. "It's not an answer to my question."

Grizzly tensed, waiting for Corpus to come at him.

"I'll tell you the reason," Corpus stated derisively. "You didn't help them because you're in love."

"In love?" Grizzly blurted out, inadvertently straightening.

Corpus coiled his leg muscles for the final spring. "Yes! In love with that bitch Athena!" he asserted.

The effect on Grizzly was worse than any physical blow could have been; his mouth slackened, his eyes widened, and he lowered his guard, his arms dropping to his sides. He was, for the space of a few seconds, thoroughly confounded and momentarily defenseless.

Which was exactly what Corpus wanted. He hissed as he sprang, digging his fingers in the mutant's neck and ramming his right knee into the bear-man's crotch. The momentum of his rush bowled the hybrid over, and they landed with Grizzly on his back and Corpus straddling his enemy's chest, his legs pinning Grizzly's arms to the ground. The Vampire leader's eyes blazed as he applied pressure on the throat, gouging his fingernails into the flesh. "And now, you damn nuisance, we end this farce!"

Grizzly attempted to buck the Vampire off, without success.

"Did you really believe you would defeat the Venesects?" Corpus scoffed. "You pathetic fool! The Venesects are indestructible!"

Struggling to regain his composure, his self-control, Grizzly thrashed and tried to extricate his arms, squirming from side and side. He was experiencing difficulty breathing, and there was a tremendous pain in his chest and neck.

"When I'm done with you," Corpus declared, "I'll take care of those two morons on the rim!"

Grizzly tugged on his right arm, his concentration disjointed. What was the matter with him? Why couldn't he get his act together? Was it because he knew, deep in his heart, that the damn Vampire was right? His affection for Athena had prevented him from performing as he normally would. Anxiety over her safety had turned his resolve to mush, had tempered his feral intensity with debilitating indecision. Was the truth that hard to admit? What was so traumatic about being in love? Was it because Athena was . . . human?

Corpus, confident of victory, dug his nails in even more. "And then do you know what I'll do?" he demanded harshly. "I'll have your bitch tracked down and brought to me! Yes! And I'll feed on her myself! Just me! Wouldn't that be poetic justice?"

Corpus feed on Athena? Grizzly gritted his teeth and held his breath, saving what precious little air was left in his lungs, and jerked on his right arm.

"It's better this way," Corpus assured the mutant through taut lips. "The bitch and you would never have worked out! Can you imagine the monsters you'd breed?" He paused and sneered. "Funny, though. I've never heard of a mutant with the hots for a human piece of ass before!"

An inarticulate bellow of sheer rage burst from Grizzly's mouth. His right arm pulled free in a herculean effort, and he speared his claws up and in, burying them in the soft tissue under the Vampire's chin.

Corpus stiffened and grunted, then heaved himself backwards, tearing free of the claws, falling onto his back and rolling to the right. He rose, his left handing clutching at the punctures in his neck, his blood spraying over his fingers.

Grizzly was already erect. He roared as he took one bound and swiped his left hand across the Vampire's face, his claws ripping through Corpus's cheeks and nose, leaving stringy sections of dangling skin and lacerations oozing crimson gore.

Gurgling, in a panic, Corpus staggered backwards. He glanced at the Heartland and started to turn, to flee.

Grizzly wouldn't let him.

The mutant moved in close and drove his right claws into the Vampire's abdomen just above the loincloth. His right arm bunched, the muscles rippling under his fur as he tore his claws upward all the way to the sternum, effectively slitting Corpus open. Still in the grip of his blood lust, Grizzly drew both arms back, then lanced his claws into the Venesect's groin.

Corpus shrieked and beegan to sag, his right hand on his ruptured stomach, his left reaching lower.

With a savage twist, Grizzly yanked his claws from the Vampire's privates.

"No!" Corpus blubbered feebly as he sank to his knees, his left hand covering his crotch, his right endeavoring futilely to check the spilling of his internal organs as they gushed through the gaping slit in his abdomen. His intestines squished out and plopped onto the turf. "No!" he whined.

Grizzly stepped back and eyed the Vampire disdainfully.

His features a mask of torment, Corpus doubled over, then looked up at Grizzly in astonishment. "You . . . !"

Grizzly leaned down until his face was next to Corpus's. "You had me," he said, scowling. "No one has ever come closer to nailing me than you. But you blew it. You should never have mentioned Athena."

Blood poured from Corpus's mouth, spurting over his lower lip and down his chin.

"Funny, though," Grizzly said, mimicking the Vampire. "You were right. I do love Athena. But only you and I know it."

Corpus wobbled, his eyes glazing.

"I'd like to keep it a secret," Grizzly mentioned softly. "I'll never tell a soul. How about you?"

A convulsion racked the Vampire's body, he breathed one last, ragged breath, and pitched onto his face at the mutant's feet.

"I guess you won't tell anyone either," Grizzly remarked, gazing at the corpse. "Thanks. I appreciate that." He sighed, stared at the rim ten yards above him, then at the ruins.

Just as the Vampires launched their second attack.

CHAPTER TWENTY-TWO

"**W**hat was that all about?" Sergeant Havoc asked as Corpus slumped to the dirt.

"I don't know," Blade said, his forehead creased in thought.

"What was all that talking they were doing?" Havoc queried. "I only caught a few words. Do you know what they were saying?"

Blade looked at the noncom. "I—" he began.

And a wave of Venesects poured from the demolished structures and raced toward the east rim.

The Warrior rose to his knees. "Grizzly! Get up here! We'll cover you!" he yelled.

Instead, Grizzly faced the onrushing Vampires.

"What the hell is he doing?" Havoc blurted. "He can't take them all on by himself!"

Blade raised his M-16 to his right shoulder. "Concentrate on those who get near to him. Give him some fighting room."

"He's crazy," Havoc declared, taking aim.

The Vampires were 20 yards from the mutant when Blade and Sergeant Havoc cut loose. With the steadily brightening sky now a pale blue, and the golden arc of the sun barely visible above the eastern horizon, the slope and the crater floor were bathed in a rosy light. The Vampires were perfect targets. Over a dozen in the center of the front of the wave, those barreling toward Grizzly, were killed in the first few seconds. As they fell, those to their rear bore to the left or the right, bypassing the bodies. Some went after the mutant, but the majority sprinted for the east rim.

Grizzly, crouching on the incline, went on the offensive, snarling as he charged. His claws flashing, his body a whirlwind, he met the Venesects head-on.

Blade saw the mutant shred a Vampire's throat, and then he was compelled to focus on the lines of white forms racing up the slope toward him. He sent a withering spray of lead into the foremost row.

Sergeant Havoc was likewise engaged, his marksmanship unerring. Vampire after Vampire dropped.

The left side of the wave abruptly changed direction, angling away from the giant and the soldier, heading for a point on the rim 20 yards off. Their strategy was clear. They would flank the two humans and come in from the side.

Blade pivoted, devoting his attention to the left flank. The magazine suddenly went empty and he swiftly ejected it and slapped home a new one. During Grizzly's fight with Corpus, Havoc and Blade had removed their spare magazines from their backpacks and crammed them into their pockets. The backpacks they had left lying on the rim.

The left side of the wave was almost to the crest.

Blade waited until 10 to 15 of the Vampires were just rising above the rim. He wanted them slightly off balance, in the act of stepping to the higher ground. At that precise instant he fired, sweeping the M-16 in an arc, going for their heads.

The ploy worked.

Outlined against the lightening sky, the leading line was silhouetted as they absorbed the rounds. Some screamed, others threw their arms in the air, and all except one was knocked backwards onto those scrambling up the slope. A domino effect toppled one after the other, dozens tripping over their companions, creating a jumble of legs and arms. The left flank was in confusion, their momentum checked.

Blade reached down and scooped his backpack into his right

hand, dropping the M-16. He pulled an explosive packet with a timer from the pack and swiftly adjusted the setting for one minute. The state-of-the-art packets could stop a tank cold. One was sufficient to blow a tank to smithereens, and Blade carried enough explosives in his backpack to destroy ten tanks.

Move! his mind shrieked.

He ran to the left, making for the rim above the floundering Venesects, holding the backpack and the packet at chest height.

Some of the Vampires saw him coming and tried to claw their way to the top.

Blade reached the edge directly above the mass of Vampires. He stuffed the packet into the backpack, then tossed the backpack overhand into the middle of the muddled bloodsuckers.

Move!

He spun and dashed toward Sergeant Havoc. "Hit the dirt!" he shouted, his legs pumping.

Havoc, striving to arrest the advance of the right flank up the slope, firing like a man possessed, glanced at the Warrior.

"Down!" Blade yelled.

The noncom promptly obeyed, diving onto his stomach.

Move!

His mind ticking off the seconds, Blade knew he had run out of time. He was in the process of leaping, attempting to put a few more feet between the slope and himself, when the detonator went off.

The explosion was stupendous, shaking the ground like an earthquake.

Blade felt the concussion slam into his back and he was flung for a loop, landing with a jarring impact.

For a moment the terra firma seemed to be airborne, as if the very planet was gasping in anguish. A colossal dust cloud soared heavenward, and seconds later the rain began, the pelting of red dirt and clumps of sod, the shower of pink droplets and body parts: severed arms and legs, decapitated heads, detached feet, and pieces of Vampire torsos.

Blade slowly stood, doubling over, the swirling dust stinging his eyes and causing him to cough. He squinted, covered his mouth with his left hand, and moved cautiously toward the rim. The dust obscured everything. He wasn't even certain he was heading in the right direction.

"Blade?" Havoc called out, not more than a yard distant.

The Warrior distinguished the noncom's crouching form in the billowing red dust. "Here!" he responded, stepping to the soldier's side and dropping to his knees.

"Where are the Vampires?" Havoc asked, craning his neck to the right and left. "I don't see them!"

"We'll have to wait for the dust to settle," Blade said, scanning the nearby ground for his M-16. He spotted the weapon lying at the edge and retrieved it.

"Did you see what happened to Grizzly?" Havoc questioned anxiously.

"No," Blade said, hoping the mutant had been far enough from the center of the blast to be spared.

They waited impatiently. The dust seemed to take forever to sink to the ground or disperse on the westerly breeze. Slowly visibility improved.

"I can see the right side!" Havoc exclaimed. "The Vampires are gone."

Blade swiveled to the left, his eyes narrowing.

A secondary crater now marred the slope of the great crater. Tendrils of smoke wafted upward. Blasted bits of pale bodies were everywhere. Piles of corpses served as a demarcation for the circumference of the explosion. A few Vampires still moved, twitching and groaning.

"There's Grizzly!" Sergeant Havoc stated.

Blade swung to the center.

Dozens of dead littered the slope and the ground below, and at the base of the incline was Grizzly, on his stomach, his arms outstretched, unmoving.

"Do you think he's—" Havoc started to say.

But the Warrior was in motion, sliding over the rim and speeding down the incline, covering yards with each stride, threading a path among the corpses, the M-16 in his left hand. He glanced at the ruins and saw no sign of the Vampires. Either the ghouls had thrown in the towel and were retreating into the bowels of the Heartland or they were reorganizing for yet another assault. For the moment, though, the coast was clear.

Lifeless Venesects encircled Grizzly in stacks two to four

bodies high. Each one bore testimony to the unbridled ferocity of the bear-man in the form of wicked claw marks; some had their throats slashed to shreds, some their eyes punctured, and some lay with their pulpy entrails on the ground beside them.

Blade skirted the last intervening Vampire and reached Grizzly's side. He crouched and gripped the mutant's right shoulder. "Grizzly?"

The bear-man didn't stir.

"Grizzly?" Blade said, then rolled the mutant over carefully.

"Blade!" Sergeant Havoc shouted. "The Vampires!"

Blade looked up and glimpsed white figures moving in the rubble. So the Vampires hadn't left! They were preparing for one more charge.

A moan suddenly passed Grizzly's lips.

Blade bent down and shook the mutant's shoulder. "Grizzly? Can you hear me."

Grizzly's eyes flicked open. He focused on the giant and shook his head. "What the hell hit me?"

"I used explosives," Blade explained.

"The least you could do is warn a guy," Grizzly muttered, pushing himself up on his elbows. He surveyed the carnage and grinned. "Not bad. I haven't had this much fun in ages."

"Are you hurt? Can you stand?" Blade inquired.

"I'm fine," Grizzly insisted, rising.

Blade stood, shifting his attention to the ruins. "They're getting set to try again. We're better off on the rim." He headed upward.

Grizzly followed, his tread unsteady.

"Are you sure you can manage?" Blade questioned.

"I'm fine," Grizzly reiterated. "Just woozy. A few deep breaths and I'll be as good as new."

Blade stared to his right and spied the remains of Corpus. "You did a number on him," he remarked.

"The sucker had it coming!" Grizzly responded.

"I thought he was trying to talk you to death at first," Blade mentioned casually.

"He did love to flap his gums," Grizzly agreed.

"What were you two talking about?" Blade asked.

"Nothing much."

Blade, his broad back to the mutant, grinned.

Sergeant Havoc was on his knees when the pair climbed over the edge. "I'm glad to see you made it," he said to the mutant.

"Not half a glad as I am," Grizzly replied.

"There's a lot of activity down there," Havoc informed Blade. "They won't stop for anything this time."

"We have your backpack," Blade noted. "We'll give them another explosive surprise."

Grizzly glanced at the Warrior. "Anything I can do?"

"Leave."

"What?" Grizzly asked in surprise.

"Leave," Blade repeated. "Get out of here while you still can. We've held the Vampires long enough to insure they can't catch Athena, Boone, and Thunder. Now I want you to leave." He nodded at the battlefield. "I estimate there were over one hundred and twenty after us initially. I don't know how many we've killed. Half. Maybe more. But that still leaves a lot down there, and they'll be fired up, thirsty for our blood. Havoc is right. They won't stop this time. And for all we know, more could show up."

"So why aren't *you* leaving?" Grizzly demanded.

"I would if I could," Blade said. "There's no need to buy the others time. But I won't desert Havoc, and he can't run with his injured leg."

"Well, if you're not leaving, I'm not leaving," Grizzly declared. "And that's final."

"I don't want either of you to stay on my account," Sergeant Havoc interjected.

"I'm the head of this unit," Blade reminded the noncom. "I don't abandon my people."

Sergeant Havoc gazed over his left shoulder at the eastern horizon. "The sun's coming up. The Vampires will want to get this over with as quickly as they can."

"Then let's make sure they don't," Blade said, kneeling and putting a new magazine in the M-16.

"I guess I'll take a snooze," Grizzly quipped. "Wake me if you need me."

"We need you," Blade said. He picked up Sergeant Havoc's backpack and rummaged inside for one of the packets of explosive with a timer and detonator.

"You want me to lob that thing?" Grizzly deduced.

Blade removed a packet and hefted it. "When I give you the word, set the timer for one minute. Don't throw it until I say so."

"Just don't forget I've set the timer," Grizzly cracked.

Blade tossed the packet to the mutant, then shoved the backpack over. "Stay behind us. I don't want you hit."

"With a big lug like you in front of me," Grizzly said, "they won't even see me."

"That's what I'm counting on," Blade stated.

Sergeant Havoc lifted his M-16. "Here we go again."

The Venesects began their third concerted attack. Their features set in grim lines, their legs flying, they glided over the terrain in a compact mass, the point of their column going straight for their foes on the eastern rim. The crater wall partially shielded them from the light of the rising sun.

Havoc sighted on the column. "I want to thank the two of you for sticking with me," he commented.

"I've got nothing better to do," Grizzly said.

Blade took a bead on the front cluster of Vampires. "When they're at the base of the slope," he stated.

"Got you," Havoc acknowledged.

"I need to tinkle," Grizzly remarked.

A cry of collective rage erupted from the swarm of Venesects as they reached the foot of the incline.

"Now!" Blade bellowed.

The Warrior and the noncom leaned over the edge, firing indiscriminately.

This time the frenzied Vampires did not even slow down. As those first in line fell, those to the rear scrambled or vaulted over their comrades. Their earlier failures had served to arouse their wrath to a fever pitch. They were not accustomed to losing in combat, and being repulsed twice by a pair of humans and a mutant was more humiliation than they could bear.

Blade emptied his magazine and grabbed for another. He was smacking it home when he spotted the trio leading the upsurging horde: Polidori, Loring, and . . . Minshi! The enormous Vampire was still alive! He suppressed his amazement and glanced over his right shoulder at Grizzly. "The timer!"

Grizzly nodded and began turning the black dial.

Blade resumed firing, aiming at the three leaders. He sighted on Loring and squeezed the trigger, and was rewarded by the Vampire catapulting backwards onto the slope. Polidori was next. Blade shot him squarely in the face.

The Venesects were halfway to the rim.

"Throw it!" Blade bellowed.

Grizzly stepped to the edge and heaved the backpack with all of his strength.

All three Force members hit the dirt.

Footsteps were pounding close to the edge of the crater when the explosives detonated. Again the ground shook and bucked, only worse than before. A scorching blast of air engulfed Blade, Havoc, and Grizzly, to be replaced moments later by the dense, swelling dust cloud.

Coughing, with particles of red dirt in his nostrils and his lungs, Blade staggered erect, his ears ringing. He peered into the cloud, wondering if the explosion had stopped the Vampires, had sent them scurrying for the cover of the ruins.

It hadn't.

Murky forms materialized in the whirling red dust.

Vampires. With Minshi at their head.

Blade and the huge Venesect were less than a yard apart when they saw one another.

Minshi reacted instantly, lunging and grabbing the barrel of Blade's M-16, then twisting his body to the left as he pulled on the weapon.

Blade released the M-16. There was no time to waste in grappling for the rifle when more Vampires were coming over the rim. He whipped out his Bowies and took a step toward Minshi as the Vampire cast the rifle aside and backed up two strides.

What was this?

Why would the big Vampire back off?

Blade crouched, his Bowies extended, taking a wary step forward.

Minshi unexpectedly smiled, his right hand drifting behind his back, and when it reappeared a second later, his fingers were wrapped around the handle of a large carving knife.

The Warrior's gray eyes narrowed in bewilderment. The Vampire was offering him a fair fight! But why would—

Minshi suddenly swept the carving knife in a curving strike, then again as Blade evaded the keen edge. The Vampire tried to seize the upper hand with a wild series of swings and thrusts, ever the aggressor, constantly driving the Warrior backwards.

Blade caught sight of Grizzly and Sergeant Havoc to his right, side by side, taking on seven or eight Venesects. He saw Havoc slam the palm of his right hand into a Vampire's nose. The distraction proved costly. In the fraction of a second that the Warrior's eyes alighted on his friends, his adversary sprang forward and stabbed the carving knife up and in. Blade tried to jerk his upper body to the rear, but too late.

Minshi's carving knife sliced into the Warrior's left shoulder, penetrating the black leather vest and scraping his collarbone.

The Warrior dodged to the left, searing agony lancing his shoulder. He felt his blood spreading across his shoulder, upper back, and chest.

Minshi smirked and came on, the carving knife coated red.

Blade had to rely on his right arm, parrying four lightning stabs before he held his ground, refusing to retreat any farther. The Bowie and the carving knife produced muted clangs as the blades met again and again. Blade held his left arm at his side, conveying the impression it was useless. He wanted Minshi to step in closer or feint to his left.

Minshi feinted.

And Blade was ready, his grip slightly slippery because of his dripping blood. He held fast and plunged the left Bowie to the hilt in the Vampire's chest.

Minshi gasped and doubled over.

Blade had learned his lesson from their first fight. He'd stabbed the Vampire twice in the chest earlier, and yet Minshi had survived. So one more chest strike was nothing more than a minor inconvenience. Blade wanted to end their conflict permanently. His right Bowie flashed up, spearing into the Vampire's left eye, imbedding the upper third in the socket.

An almost comical expression of astonishment etched the Vampire's face. He voiced a strangled cry of baffled desperation and reached for the Warrior's right arm.

Blade tugged the Bowie free.

Tottering backwards, Minshi placed his left hand over his ravaged eye. He tottered all the way to the brink of the crater. The dust had settled sufficiently to reveal the baleful gleam in his right eye as he toppled over the edge and vanished.

The Warrior turned to the right.

Grizzly was holding his own, his claws hacking and ripping in fearless abandon.

Sergeant Havoc was on his left knee, valiantly resisting the pummeling of three Vampires.

Blade started toward the noncom when a pair of strong arms enclosed his ankles and he tumbled onto his stomach. Something heavy struck the back of his head and the world seemed to spin and tilt. He managed to look over his left shoulder to find a Vampire with an M-16 in its hands. *His* M-16!

The Vampire was holding the rifle by the barrel. He growled and raised it for another blow.

And a strange thing happened.

A horizontal pattern of pink holes blossomed across the Vampire's chest and he was propelled through the air for over five feet.

Still dazed, and now confused, Blade was glancing in the direction of his companions when he saw a charging line of five Venesects cut in half at the waist as they appeared on the rim. A new sound filled the air, a pronounced whump-whump-whump, from overhead. Blade looked upward, and not until that moment had he appreciated how beautiful a helicopter could be.

There were four of them, one hovering over the three Force members, the others swooping over the crater in strafing runs, their big .50-caliber machine guns thundering in rhythmic precision.

Blade rose, realizing every Vampire on the rim was dead, and moved to the edge of the crater.

It was a slaughter. The choppers were picking off the Venesects as they attempted to reach the shelter of the Heartland. Heaps of perforated bodies littered the slope and the area between the incline and the ruins. A few of the Vampires succeeded in reaching cover, but for every one who did, five didn't.

Someone was laughing.

Blade looked to his right and discovered Grizzly and Sergeant Havoc a few feet from him, the mutant supporting the noncom under the left arm.

Grizzly gave an elated whoop. "Look at those turkeys run! We did it! We won!"

"Hey, Blade!" someone called down from above.

The Warrior tilted his head back.

Boone, Thunder, and Athena were in the chopper overhead, in the open bay. The helicopter was hovering at an angle. They smiled and waved.

Blade waved once, then stared at the floor of the crater.

There wasn't a living Venesect in sight.

CHAPTER TWENTY-THREE

The four helicopters were on the ground 50 yards from the east wall of the crater. Green tents had been pitched near the rim. Sentries were on duty on all sides to safeguard against a surprise counterattack. The afternoon sun was hot, and a warm wind stirred the red dust.

Blade and Bear emerged from a tent in the middle of the row and walked to the edge. The Warrior stared at the ruins, reflecting, and sighed.

"What's the matter with you, bro?" Bear asked.

"This was sloppy," Blade said.

Bear scrutinized the floor of the crater. The burial detail had spent the previous two days digging mass graves, and the majority of the Venesects were now decomposing under mounds of earth. "What are you talkin' about? We whipped their butts."

"But we didn't win."

"I think that knock upside your head rattled your brains," Bear commented with a grin.

"We defeated the Vampires," Blade said, "but we didn't win. How can we call any victory complete if some of the Vampires are still alive?"

A squad of Rangers marched into the daylight from the mouth of a passageway.

"Here comes Sergeant Montalbano," Bear observed. "Maybe he has some good news."

"I hope so," Blade said.

The squad passed the mass graves and ascended the incline. Segeant Montalbano, a wiry man with a clipped black mustache, saluted the Warrior.

"Report," Blade directed.

"The sweeps of the lower levels are continuing," Montalbano detailed. "Captain Ryan intends to spend another night down there to finish the mopping up."

Blade gazed at the solitary spire a half mile distant. Captain Ryan was a seasoned, competent officer, and the 190 Rangers in the Company were dedicated personnel. He recalled the relief he'd felt as the big helicopters had landed and disgorged their complements of about 50 men apiece. The Rangers had been spoiling for combat with the Vampires, but the Venesects were nowhere to be found.

"One more thing, sir," Sergeant Montalbano mentioned.

"Yes?"

"Captain Ryan found more humans," Montalbano divulged.

Blade looked at the trooper. "Alive?"

Sergeant Montalbano frowned. "No, sir. They were dead, like all the rest. Captain Ryan believes they were prisoners. They had those needle marks all over their bodies." He paused. "They were torn apart."

"The Vampires vented their wrath on the captives," Blade speculated.

Sergeant Montalbano reached into his right front pocket. "Captain Ryan asked me to give you this."

"What is it?"

Montalbano pulled a small brown wallet into view. "Captain Ryan told me to give this to you. He said it concerns the woman you mentioned. He said you'd understand."

Blade took the square of brown leather and flipped it open. A faded color photograph, tucked into a plastic strip, drew his attention. The picture showed a young boy and girl, both in their early teens or thereabouts, smiling broadly into the camera.

Their eyes conveyed their vitality and happiness, and they were hugging one another in sincere affection.

Bear leaned toward the Warrior for a glimpse of the photo. "Who are they?"

"The boy is Ethan Hogue," Blade answered softly. "The girl was his sister, Greta."

"Strange, the way she died," Sergeant Montalbano remarked.

"You saw her body?" Blade asked.

"Yes, sir," Montalbano responded. "In a room with four others. Their necks had been broken, their arms ripped from their bodies, and two were mutilated." He nodded at the photograph. "But not her. She wasn't mutilated. She died a clean death."

"How do you mean?"

"She was the only person we've found who was stabbed," Montalbano revealed. "All the others died horribly, but there she was, her arms folded in her lap, lying on the floor with a knife in her left eye."

Blade stiffened. "A what?"

"A knife," Sergeant Montalbano said. "A big carving knife. It was really strange."

Bear noticed a ripple of . . . something . . . register on the Warrior's face for a second. "What is it?"

Blade looked at the photograph, then at Montalbano. "Is there anything else?"

"No, sir," Montalbano said. "With your permission, I'd like to return to Captain Ryan."

"Go ahead," Blade ordered. "We don't need you topside."

Sergeant Montalbano started to turn.

"Sergeant?"

"Yes, sir?"

"Would you stop at the graves and find the sergeant in charge of the burial detail?"

Montalbano nodded. "Sergeant Harrell, sir?"

"That's his name," Blade said. "Would you ask him to report to me on the double?"

Sergeant Montalbano saluted. "Yes, sir." He wheeled and led his squad down the incline.

"What was that all about?" Bear inquired.

"Maybe nothing," Blade replied.

"Uh-huh," Bear said. In all the years he'd known the Warrior, he'd never seen this kind of reaction. It was weird.

Blade clasped his hands behind his back and surveyed the Heartland. "Where are the others?"

"Grizzly and the bunch?"

The Warrior nodded.

"In the mess tent, the last I saw," Bear said. "The medics have tended to Havoc. They say his leg will be as good as new in a couple of weeks." He chuckled. "They were real surprised."

"At what?"

"Those herbs Thunder used," Bear replied. "The herbs saved Havoc's life. Prevented the infection from spreadin' any worse than it did."

Blade watched as Sergeant Montalbano approached Sergeant Harrell.

"So tell me true," Bear stated bluntly. "What do you think of 'em?"

"Who?" Blade responded absently.

"Grizzly and the others," Bear said. "I volunteered to serve a year in your outfit. I'd like to know what I'm getting myself into."

"I'd stake my life on any one of them," Blade declared.

"That says a lot," Bear commented. "They're quite a crew. I think I'll get to like 'em."

"You will."

Sergeant Montalbano and Sergeant Harrell conversed briefly, and Sergeant Harrell jogged toward the east rim.

"Where do we go when we're done here?" Bear asked.

"To the Force facility north of LA," Blade answered.

"I'm lookin' forward to gettin' some time off later," Bear mentioned. "I hear they have some stone foxes in Los Angeles."

"The foxes are nice," Blade agreed, his voice subdued. "But I liked the elephants better."

Bear did a double take. "Say what?"

"Jenny and I took Gabe to the LA zoo," Blade explained. "We'd never seen a zoo before. Gabe had a great time."

Bear stepped over to the Warrior and nudged Blade's left elbow. "Hey. What's eatin' you?"

The Warrior glanced at his friend. "Nothing. Why?"

"You're a lousy liar," Bear noted. "And you haven't been payin' attention to a word I said."

"I did too," Blade insisted.

Sergeant Harrell came over the crest and walked up to Blade. He saluted. "You wanted to see me, sir?"

Blade stared at the mounds of dirt. "Yes, sergeant. Have all the Venesects been buried?"

"Almost, sir," Harrell answered. "We have a few left. And there's a pile of legs and arms and stuff. That's it."

"Good," Blade commented. "I don't want the rotting corpses to attract any more mutants."

"Yes, sir," Sergeant Harrell said. "We had a hell of a time with those three bugs the first night."

Blade pursed his lips.

"Was that all?" Sergeant Harrell questioned, appearing perplexed.

"Did you notice anything unusual about any of the Vampires you buried?" Blade inquired.

"Unusual, sir?" Sergeant Harrell repeated. "No. They all looked pretty much the same to me."

"Did you happen to see a Vampire larger than all the rest?" Blade asked. "One about my size?"

"No, sir," the Ranger replied.

"Would you check with your men? I'd like to know."

Sergeant Harrell shrugged. "I'll check, sir, but it might not do much good. We've been busting our butts, carrying all those bodies to the graves and throwing them in. After you do ten or twenty, you stop paying much attention."

"I understand," Blade said. "But check for me."

"Yes, sir." Harrell saluted and trotted off.

Blade unclasped his hands and looked at Bear. "They won't find his body."

"Whose body?"

"A Vampire by the name of Minshi," Blade stated.

"So what's the big deal over one Vampire?" Bear probed.

"It isn't every day that I kill someone and he doesn't die," Blade responded.

"What?"

"Nothing," Blade said, shaking his head. His eyes roamed over the Dead Zone to the east. "Too bad there aren't any trees around here?"

"Trees?"

"Yeah," Blade confirmed. "Maybe we should have used wooden stakes after all." He walked toward the tents.

Wooden stakes? Bear scratched his chin as he followed the Warrior. There was no doubt about it. His buddy was gettin' downright weird.

EPILOGUE

She found him standing near the helicopters, his shoulders slumped, his arms at his sides, staring into space. "There you are! I've been looking all over for you."

Grizzly turned, his features softening at the sight of her. "Hi, Athena."

"Why'd you take off all by yourself?" Athena asked. "I missed you."

"You did?"

"Of course, dummy," she said.

Grizzly coughed lightly.

"I need your advice," Athena informed him. She gazed at the nearest chopper. "Those pilots sure can handle those babies, can't they?"

Grizzly nodded.

"What's with you?" Athena demanded. "Are you in one of your moods again?" She stretched, beaming contentedly. "We're alive! Do you realize how sweet life is? For a while back there, I was beginning to wonder if any of us would see daylight again."

"Is that why you're so cheerful?"

"That, and another reason," Athena told him. "Which is why I came looking for you."

"Oh?"

"Yep." She inhaled the air. "You and I are becoming quite close. Or didn't you notice?"

"I've noticed," Grizzly said quietly.

"Definitely," Athena stated. "I think you're the best friend I have."

Grizzly's eyes narrowed slightly. "Friend?"

"And as my friend, I expect you to be honest with me," Athena said.

"I'd never lie to you."

"I know." She glanced around to ensure they were alone. "So I need your advice."

"About what?"

Athena smiled. "One of the pilots has asked me out."

Grizzly's cheeks twitched. "Oh?" he commented nonchalantly.

"Yeah. And you know the reputation these fly-boys have," Athena noted.

"What kind?"

"A woman can't trust one as far as she can throw him," Athena said.

Grizzly cleared his throat. "So what advice do you need?"

"It should be obvious," Athena responded. "Do you think I should go out with him after we get back?"

The bear-man conducted a study of the knuckles of his right hand. "You're a big girl, Athena. You do what you want."

"What kind of advice is that?" Athena questioned. "I thought you'd be happy for me. You know I haven't been on a date in ages."

Grizzly raised his right hand and shielded his eyes from the sun. "I'm happy for you."

"Really?"

"Really."

"You don't sound happy."

Grizzly chuckled. "I guess I was hoping you'd want to go out with *me*."

Athena laughed and placed her hand on his shoulder. "I'll go out with you anytime. We're friends, remember?"

"I'll never forget it," he assured her.

"Aren't you glad fate threw us together?" Athena commented.

"If Fate was here in person," Grizzly remarked, "I'd gut the sucker."

She laughed again. "You're crazy! You know that?"

Grizzly nodded. "That's me. A wild and crazy guy."

Athena started toward the tents. "I'm going to tell the fly-boy yes. Want to come along?"

"I wouldn't want to intrude on you two lovebirds."

"Lovebirds? We haven't even been on our first date yet!"

"You know how fast those pilots work," Grizzly observed wryly.

Athena paused. "You're not going to stay out here the rest of day, are you?"

"I thought I'd work on my suntan."

She giggled. "Be serious."

"I'm always serious."

Athena shook her head. "You *are* in one of your moods again. What brings these mood swings on?"

"Hormones."

She stared at him for a moment. "Don't stay out here too long. Please. As a favor for me."

"Your wish is my command," Grizzly said.

"See you soon," Athena stated, and blew him a kiss. She strolled away, whistling.

Behind her, Grizzly's shoulders moved in a peculiar up-and-down fashion.

PIPELINE STRIKE

Dedicated to...
Judy & Joshua & Shane.
To the memory of Roy Rockwood,
who set the tempo.
To the memory of Otis Adelbert Kline,
who set the style.
And to the memory of H.G. Wells,
who showed us that reality and speculation
can be fused superbly.

PROLOGUE

The frigid blasts of wind howled at them from out of the frozen north, chilling both men to the bone despite their thermal underwear, their green fatigues, and their insulated green parkas.

"Damn, it's cold!" exclaimed the lanky lieutenant, his head buried in his parka hood, his hands hidden in bulky gloves, as he stomped his boots to maintain his circulation.

"What did you expect, Tyler?" responded the second man, who was similarly attired except for a green scarf he had wrapped around the lower portion of his face to protect his lips from the numbing weather. He held his binoculars pressed to his eyes. Slung over his left shoulder was an M-16.

"I knew this mission would be a ball-buster, Captain," Lieutenant Tyler said, "but I never expected it to be this bad." He slid his right hand along the leather strap to the M-16 slung over his right shoulder, his movement slightly restricted by his clothing.

"To tell the truth," admitted the captain, "neither did I."

"I wish I was back in L.A.," Lieutenant Tyler commented.

"Keep your mind on our assignment," the captain advised.

"If we make any mistakes now, we're dead."

"Yes, sir," Tyler replied dutifully.

They were standing on the southernmost of a pair of ridges bordering a narrow valley. Captain Bowen scanned the binoculars from right to left. "I hope we have the correct coordinates."

Lieutenant Tyler surveyed the snow-covered landscape below the ridge they were on, noting the sea of white with a frown. "Are you as sick of snow as I am?"

"I sort of like it."

Lieutenant Tyler snorted. "Are you serious, Captain Bowen?"

"Yeah," Bowen answered. "We never saw snow in Los Angeles. In the old days, before the war, L.A. received snow every now and then. But none since."

"World War Three screwed up the climate everywhere," Tyler remarked.

"World War Three screwed up the entire planet," Captain Bowen declared. "The climate changed. Governments collapsed. Massive amounts of radiation were unleashed. Chemical weapons polluted the environment for centuries to come." He paused. "And worst of all, the mutants multiplied like rabbits."

Tyler glanced over his shoulder at the plain of snow to their rear, at the line of tracks they had made. "Do you think there are any here?"

"Mutants?"

"It's probably too cold for them here, right?"

"Wrong," Captain Bowen said. "There are mutants everywhere. Even in Alaska."

Lieutenant Tyler stamped his feet again to disguise his nervousness. "What *kind* of mutants?" he asked softly.

Captain Bowen shrugged. "Who knows? No one can predict how the toxins will affect embryonic growth."

"Have you ever wished you'd been born before the war?" Tyler inquired.

"No, not really," Captain Bowen responded, his binoculars fixed on the valley. "Have you?"

"At least once a day," Tyler disclosed.

"Why?"

"Are you kidding me? Haven't you heard about the life those people led? They had it easy. There weren't any mutants around back then. The criminal element was held in check by the law-enforcement authorities. A person could travel anywhere they wanted without having to be on the lookout for scavengers and raiders. If they were hungry, they went to the store or to a restaurant—"

"We have stores and restaurants in California," Captain Bowen said, interrupting.

"But they're not the same," Tyler said. "Our stores offer the necessities and very few luxuries, and even the necessities are rationed whenever there's a shortage. And our restaurants aren't as ritzy as the restaurants before the war. I was told there were some that had golden arches."

"Golden arches?"

"Yep. Had something to do with their architecture. Imagine that! Golden arches!"

"I find it hard to believe," Captain Bowen commented.

"I'm only relaying the information I was told," Lieutenant Tyler mentioned.

Captain Bowen swiveled the binoculars to the right. "Well, I don't know if I would have liked living then. They may have enjoyed an easier lifestyle, but easier isn't always better."

"It is in my book, sir."

"You're like most people I know," Bowen said. "You believe the prewar society was some sort of Utopia. It wasn't. They had their problems too."

"Name one, sir?"

"They were a society of addicts."

"How do you mean?"

Captain Bowen lowered the binoculars and glanced at Tyler. "Study the history books sometime, and you'll see I'm right. The people suffered from countless addictions.

Drugs, alcohol, caffeine, nicotine, television, and sex.''

"They were addicted to sex?" Tyler asked, and laughed.

"Some were," Captain Bowen replied.

"How can someone be addicted to sex?"

"When all you think about is sex, when all you read about is sex, when every time you look at a member of the opposite gender you want to go to bed with them, then you're addicted to sex," Bowen stated.

Lieutenant Tyler smirked. "Then I must be a first-class sex fiend."

"I wouldn't doubt it," Captain Bowen said with a grin.

"Are you serious?" Tyler queried.

"Very."

"Where'd you hear about all of this?"

"From my wife. She became interested in taking night courses at the university. I guess she got tired of sitting at home, what with all our kids in their teens and seldom there. One of the classes she took was called Prewar Culture."

"Maybe everything they taught her is true," Lieutenant Tyler remarked. "Even if it is, so what? If I had a choice to make between being a sex addict and being attacked by mutants, I'd rather be the sex addict."

Captain Bowen smiled and shook his head. "You're hopeless."

Tyler gazed at the valley, then over his right shoulder at the heavy backpack containing his field rations and the radio. "How much longer do we have to look? I'm freezing my butt off."

"If we haven't spotted the Pump Station within two hours, we'll return to the rendezvous site and call for a pickup."

"Now you're talking," Tyler said happily. "I just hope they're monitoring our frequency."

"General Gallagher won't let us down," Captain Bowen said. He started to the west along the rim of the ridge. "Our main concern is the possibility our coordinates might be wrong."

"Figures," Tyler muttered as he trudged after his superior officer.

''We can't blame the general,'' Bowen commented. ''The map we're using was printed over one hundred and five years ago, just prior to the war. The same buildings might not be standing. Maybe Holtmeyer has constructed his own facility. Who knows?''

''What do you know about the guy?''

''Only what was in the briefing papers,'' Bowen said. ''He claims his name is Eric Holtmeyer. We know nothing concerning his place of origin, his background. We don't even know his age.''

''Then why is the Federation Council taking him seriously?''

''Can they afford to treat him as a quack, considering the offer he's made?'' Bowen asked.

''*If* the guy is for real,'' Tyler remarked. ''He could be trying to pull a scam.''

''Of this magnitude?'' Captain Bowen said.

''The bigger, the better.''

''He'd have to be crazy to try a stunt like that,'' Captain Bowen observed. ''He knows the entire Federation will retaliate if he tries a fast one.''

Lieutenant Tyler squinted at a black speck on the western horizon, a dark dot situated in the center of the valley floor. ''Maybe this Holtmeyer has a getaway all planned. Maybe he'll take off for parts unknown.''

''The Federation will find him.''

''What if he heads overseas? No one has traveled abroad since the war. We have no idea what's on the other side of the Pacific. The territories over there could be just like our Outlands, overrun with mutants and all types of scuzz-buckets.''

''The Federation will find him if he attempts to swindle us,'' Captain Bowen reiterated. ''They'll probably send the Force after him.''

Lieutenant Tyler smiled. ''Blade and company will waste his sorry ass but good.''

''Let's hope Holtmeyer is telling the truth,'' Bowen said. ''The Federation could use the oil.''

"I can understand the reason California would need the fuel," Tyler commented. "California has thousands of cars and trucks and aircraft still in use. But why would the other Federation factions want in on the deal?"

"For the same reason California does," Captain Bowen answered. "California has placed a high priority on maintaining its vehicles and its copters, planes, and jets. The Civilized Zone to the east also has a large number of vehicles."

Tyler gazed at the thing in the valley, noting the increase in the inanimate object's size as they slowly drew nearer.

"The Family, the Clan, the Moles, the Flatheads, and the Cavalry don't own many mechanical means of transportation," Captain Bowen mentioned. "But just think of what the deal would mean to them."

"Sir, do you see that down there?" Lieutenant Tyler inquired, pointing into the valley.

"I spotted it a minute ago," Bowen said.

"What do you make of it?"

"A building."

"The one we're looking for?" Tyler asked hopefully.

"Could be. We won't know for sure until we're a lot closer," Captain Bowen stated. He unslung his M-16 and held the automatic rifle in his left hand. The binoculars dangled from a strap around his neck.

"At last!" Tyler remarked.

Bowen surveyed the valley floor, seeking any evidence of conveyance tracks: jeeps, trucks, snowmobiles, sleds, anything. The snow appeared to be undisturbed.

So far, so good.

"Should I break out the radio?" Tyler queried.

"Be patient," Bowen said. "When I'm ready to contact General Gallagher, I'll let you know."

"Sorry, sir."

Captain Bowen scrutinized the opposite side of the valley, examining the north ridge for sign of movement. All seemed serene. He trudged through the knee-deep snow, oblivious to the cold, intent on completing their critical mission.

"Something moved!" Tyler exclaimed.

Bowen halted and looked at his subordinate. The lieutenant was clutching his M-16. "What moved?"

"I don't know," Tyler admitted, nodding at the valley. "I saw something move down there."

Captain Bowen faced the white vale. "Where?"

"About a hundred yards from the base of this ridge," Tyler disclosed. "Directly out from our position."

Bowen's brown eyes narrowed. "All I see is snow."

"Something moved. I swear it," Tyler stated.

"An animal maybe," Bowen suggested.

"Could have been," Tyler acknowledged. "But if it was, where is the animal now? Polar bears don't up and disappear."

"Maybe it was an arctic fox," Bowen suggested. "One would be hard to spot from up here. They're small, and their white coats would blend right in with the snow."

"This is only October," Tyler said. "Do their coats change color this early?"

"I'm no zoologist," Captain Bowen replied. "Keep your eyes peeled."

"You don't have to tell me twice," Tyler said.

Captain Bowen resumed hiking westward. The rim of the southern ridge was irregular, with sharp drop-offs interspersed with gradual, sloping inclines. The ridge varied in height, averaging 60 feet above the floor of the valley. Five hundred yards separated the north and south ridges, 500 yards of a stark, milky blanket. He came to a spot across from the structure in the valley and stopped. Below him was 50 feet of moderately angled slope.

"Are we going down?" Lieutenant Tyler asked.

"What do you think?"

"I think I should have enlisted in the California Navy instead of Special Forces."

Bowen grinned and started down, gingerly trying each step before placing his full weight on his foot.

"Something moved again, sir," Tyler declared as he followed.

"Where?" Bowen queried, checking his descent.

"Below us, and forty yards to the east," Tyler said.

Again Captain Bowen looked, and again he failed to discern any indication of life. "Your imagination is playing tricks on you."

"I know what I saw," Tyler responded.

"What?"

"I don't know exactly."

Bowen shook his head and walked toward the base of the ridge, his leg muscles tensed in case his combat boots should slip and he would be forced to jump to one side to avoid plunging the rest of the way.

"May I ask a question, sir?" Lieutenant Tyler said.

"Certainly."

"Why, exactly, did I *volunteer* for this mission?"

"You were picked because of your expertise," Bowen said, treading cautiously as his left heel slid a few inches.

"I wasn't aware I had any," Tyler responded.

"Didn't you work at one of the two refineries California has in operation?"

"Yes, but—"

"And weren't you employed there for two years before enlisting?"

"Yes, but I didn't do much. I was responsible for checking the pipes for leaks. You know. Inspecting welds and such."

"Now you know why you were selected to volunteer," Captain Bowen stated. "We could have used a civilian expert, but the governor and the general didn't want to endanger lives unnecessarily. And believe it or not, we don't have any personnel in the military who are experts when it comes to the production process. No need for them, I guess. We deal in tactical issues. So you're the best we've got."

"Then we're in serious trouble," Tyler quipped.

Bowen chuckled, the sound muffled by his scarf. "Your job is to inspect the pipe. That's all."

"If it's there."

"We'll know in a few minutes," Bowen said. "If all goes

well, we can be on our way home within an hour."

"On my next leave I plan to go to the beach and lay on the sand for a week," Tyler remarked. "I'll need that long to thaw out."

Captain Bowen descended to the base of the ridge, his finger on the trigger of his M-16. The snow on the valley floor rose to his waist. Undaunted, he plowed toward the building, which appeared to have been constructed of corrugated metal.

"Do you think Holtmeyer knows about this Pump Station?" Tyler inquired.

"Let's hope he doesn't," Bowen said. "General Gallagher needs verification."

"How did we find out about the Station?"

"From an old map," Bowen revealed. "After Holtmeyer sent his emissary to Governor Melnick, the governor ordered a search to be conducted of every library in the state. They even checked every old industrial file they could lay their hands on, and in the records room of a former conglomerate they found the map."

"If we have a map, Holtmeyer must have a map."

"Leave it to you to look at the bright side," Captain Bowen cracked.

They proceeded through the snow in silence, their breathing labored. Sheltered by the ridges, the valley was spared the onslaught of the icy wind. They forged ahead steadily, enjoying the respite.

"Captain!" Tyler shouted suddenly.

Bowen spun in alarm. "What?"

Lieutenant Tyler was gazing to the east, his eyes wide. "What the hell is that?"

The hairs on Bowen's neck tingled as he stared in the same direction.

Forty feet off was a large hump in the snow, a circular mound three feet wide and two feet in height, and *the mound was moving*!

Captain Bowen gripped his M-16 tighter. Something was

traveling through the snow like a shark through water, staying hidden under the surface, leaving a rippling white wake as it headed to the north.

"What is it?" Tyler asked again in a whisper.

The mysterious mound abruptly altered course, turning to the west.

Coming at them.

"Damn!" Tyler declared.

Captain Bowen crouched and raised his M-16. No known animal could perform such a feat. By the process of elimination, the creature could only be one type: a mutant.

"There's another one!" Tyler said.

Sure enough, a second, smaller mound had materialized 20 feet behind the first.

"I don't like this," Tyler stated.

Bowen glanced at the Pump Station, estimating their chances of reaching the building unmolested.

"Let's get out of here, sir," Tyler proposed.

Before Captain Bowen could reply, a loud noise emanated from beyond the south ridge, a whomp-whomp-whomp.

A gleaming golden helicopter arced into view, sailing over the ridge and dropping into the valley in one smooth motion, demonstrating the pilot's superior skill. The craft hovered 20 yards above the snow, not more than 60 feet from the soldiers.

Bowen raised his right hand to shelter his eyes from the stinging snow lashed by the copter's rotor blades. He tried to catch a glimpse of the occupants, but the chopper was a streamlined model with a tinted bubble. As he watched, a booming voice addressed them from a metal, funnel-shaped speaker affixed to the underside of the craft.

"Greetings, gentlemen. I've been expecting you."

Bowen and Tyler exchanged puzzled looks.

"Do you realize you are trespassing on private land? This property is owned by Holtmeyer Industries, International."

"That's a woman's voice!" Tyler declared.

"But of course you already are aware of the fact. Why

else would you be here? Unfortunately, you've arrived too soon. We won't begin remodeling this Pump Station for another four days.''

"What's she talking about?'' Tyler asked.

"Your government displays a reprehensible lack of trust by sending you,'' the woman went on. ''If I was an overly sensitive person, I'd be offended.'' There was a harsh laugh.

"What do we do?'' Tyler whispered.

"This breach of protocol cannot be tolerated. We offered to allow Federation representatives to openly inspect our facilities, but instead they sent the two of you.''

"We're official representatives of the Federation,'' Captain Bowen lied, shouting at the top of his lungs. "We were on our way to the Deadhorse Airfield when our plane went down.''

The woman in the helicopter evidently did not hear the captain's response. There was a clucking sound, and the grating laugh. "I intended to punish you myself, but I see Nature will tend to the matter for me.''

"What does she mean?'' Tyler questioned.

"Have you observed the pair of humps, gentlemen?''

Captain Bowen surveyed the stretch of snow in front of them, spying the mounds approximately 30 feet away and to the left. Whatever was under the snow had started to veer away as the chopper swooped in, then froze. Both mounds were visible, but they were lower than before, as if the creatures had gone deeper, perhaps to hide from the helicopter.

"Many fascinating varieties of mutations have developed since the war,'' the woman in the aircraft stated. "Some are quite harmless. Others are decidedly dangerous, as you're about to discover. I bid you adieu.''

The helicopter banked and soared off to the north, vanishing over the north ridge within seconds.

"Who was she?'' Tyler asked.

Bowen's eyes were on the mounds, and his pulse quickened as they began moving anew. "Forget her! Get out of here on the double!'' He turned toward the south ridge and ran as fast as the snow would permit.

Tyler looked at the humps and bolted, the snow flying as his legs thrashed. ''I knew I shouldn't have volunteered!'' he groused, confident he could attain the ridge before the things under the snow caught him. He glanced over his left shoulder and did a double take.

The mutants were surging forward at twice their previous speed!

''They're gaining!'' Tyler yelled.

Bowen knew. And he was exerting himself to the maximum, frustrated by the heavy snow, his temples pounding as he covered five yards, then ten. The base of the south ridge was still 25 yards distant.

''Captain!'' Tyler shrieked.

Bowen stopped and whirled, bringing the M-16 up.

Lieutenant Tyler was buried to his neck and shoulders, his features conveying his shock, his M-16 in his left hand, his right clawing at the snow in a futile effort to gain a purchase. ''Something's got my legs!'' he shouted.

''Hold on!'' Captain Bowen declared, taking a stride.

Too late.

Tyler was abruptly sucked under the carpet of snow, uttering a gurgling grunt as he disappeared.

''No!'' Captain Bowen cried, lunging, plunging his right hand into the snow in a frantic bid to grab his friend.

The lieutenant was gone.

''Tyler!'' Bowen bellowed, probing as low as he could reach.''Tyler!''

A mound appeared ten feet to the right.

Captain Bowen straightened and fired from the hip, the stock tucked into his side, the parka absorbing the minimal recoil. A dozen rounds stitched the mound, sending puffs of snow flying, and the hump sank from sight.

Where was the second one?

Bowen backpedaled hastily, every fiber of his being alert, scarcely breathing. What *were* those things? How had they managed to snare Tyler so swiftly?

A commotion erupted less than 20 feet to the north, a flurry of snow amid an indistinct, ominous shape. Within seconds the disturbance subsided.

Captain Bowen took off for the south ridge, casting repeated glances over his shoulders and on both sides, expecting to see one or both of the telltale humps.

Nothing.

He traversed ten yards.

Fifteen.

A smile creased his lips in anticipation of his escape from the valley. Once on the rim, he'd take his bearings and return to the rendezvous site. Even without the radio, without the signal, General Gallagher was bound to send in the VTOL. He'd be—

A hissing sounded to his rear.

Bowen pivoted and fired instinctively, sighting on a large hump bearing down on him. The slugs smacked into the snow, and as before, the mound promptly vanished.

He wasn't out of the woods yet!

Bowen jogged toward the ridge. Were his shots having any effect on the creatures? If they were flesh and blood, if they were mutants, they could be killed. Unfortunately, some of the mutants were tenacious beyond belief. They were endowed with an augmented resistance to pain, and they could sustain supposedly lethal wounds and keep coming back for more.

Five yards to go.

Captain Bowen cast a last look over his right shoulder, and as he did his right boot collided with an object in his path, an object under the surface, a yielding but firm . . . thing.

No!

He felt his right leg gripped, and he experienced a stinging sensation as claws or teeth sliced his pants and ripped the skin underneath. Desperate, he aimed the M-16 at the ground, estimating the mutant's position and squeezing the trigger, hoping the creature would release him when he fired a burst.

And it did.

But another one clamped onto his left leg from behind.

Captain Bowen twisted, poked the M-16 barrel under the snow, and fired. The M-16 shot four times and went empty. He reached into the left pocket of his parka, his fingers closing on one of his spare magazines.

Something started to pull his left leg down.

Bowen wrenched and strained as he tried to eject the useless magazine and insert the new one. He succeeded in releasing the spent magazine, and he was slamming the fresh one home when his leg was unexpectedly freed.

Move!

He shuffled toward the ridge and salvation, his right leg hurting terribly.

Where were they?

Why had they let him go?

Bowen wanted to shout with joy when he reached the base of the ridge. He laboriously lifted his right leg, about to clamber from the valley, when he distinctly heard a swishing behind him. His skin prickled as he attempted to rotate, and he glimpsed a pair of humps surging his way. An instant later his left leg was secured in an iron grasp, and in the twinkling of an eye he was hauled beneath the white mantle.

CHAPTER ONE

The giant wearing the black leather vest and the fatigue pants leaned back in his office chair and propped his black combat boots on the desk. His gray eyes studied the report he held in his brawny right hand. Strapped around his waist were a pair of Bowies, and he absently rested his left hand on the hilt of his left knife as he read.

Personnel Update

General Miles Gallagher:

Per your request, here is the status update on the Force personnel. This information is For Your Eyes Only.

We still don't have our full quota of volunteers. As you well know, each Federation faction was to send one volunteer to serve for a period of one year. The Moles have yet to send a replacement for their man slain months ago. Athena is filling in nicely for our missing member, but she can't be considered as the Mole's representative because she's from California. More on her in a bit.

BOONE: The Cavalryman has become increasingly

moody of late, and I suspect he misses his friends in the Dakota Territory. He has adjusted to our system of training and living, but he can't wait for his enlistment to be over so he can go home.

BEAR: The Clan finally chose a competent man. His dedication to the Freedom Force and his performance have been outstanding.

THUNDER: The Flathead Indians can be proud of their volunteer. When he returns to Montana, I'll send a letter commending his service. He has been spending a lot of time with Grizzly lately, and the pair of them have been honing their tracking skills.

GRIZZLY: I'm concerned about him. Since our last mission, he has been exceptionally sullen and testy. He was making progress in overcoming his prejudice against humans, but now his attitude has taken a strange reversal. Except for Thunder, he won't associate much with the others, not even Athena. I intend to resolve this soon.

SERGEANT HAVOC: Still the finest overall recruit. Your selection, I must say, is the best of the bunch when it comes to taking orders and doing his duty. His professional military background undoubtedly helps in this respect.

ATHENA MORRIS: My initial reservations about her are gone. She has proven herself on all three of our strikes. As our Public Relations Liaison, she saves me from having to deal with the media.

Overall, our drills, practice sessions, and mock combat exercises are going well. But our ability to function as a unit will be impaired if we don't receive an assignment soon. This is October. Five months have elapsed since our last mission. Surely the Federation Council must have a job for us? Kindly confirm at your earliest convenience.

BLADE

* * *

Blade lowered the report, his lips compressing in annoyance as he contemplated his unit's period of inactivity. When Governor Melnick of California had initially proposed forming a special strike force composed of a volunteer from each of the seven Freedom Federation factions, Blade had envisioned that the unit would continually be in the field, constantly responding to threats against any of the Federation members. The reality of the situation, however, was quite different. Except for their first three missions, the Force had spent most of its time in training. Training, training, and more training was the order of the day. He knew the drilling was important, a vital necessity if they were to learn to function as a unit. But all the practice in the world amounted to nothing if they were unable to hone their skills in combat. A target silhouette was a poor substitute for an enemy returning fire. Practice was good, but experience made perfect.

Was the Force even needed?

He reflected on the formation of the tactical squad. The Freedom Federation had been in the process of admitting the former state of California into its ranks. While most of the country existed in barbaric chaos, the consequence of the widespread devastation caused by World War Three, there were now seven organized regions or outposts dedicated to preserving civilization and restructuring society.

California was the largest geographically. One of the few states to retain its administrative integrity after the war, California came the closest to resembling prewar America culturally. California maintained an Army, Navy, and Air Force. With its abundant natural resources, the general standard of living was higher materialistically than most other areas. And when California had been admitted into the Federation nine months ago, Governor Melnick, as a token of appreciation, had graciously offered to foot the bill for constructing a unique facility near Los Angeles, northwest of Pyramid Lake, to house the proposed strike force.

The heads of the other Federation factions had gladly accepted the offer.

The Flathead Indians controlled the land once known as Montana. Freed from dominance by the white race because of the war, they had reverted to the tribal practices of their forefathers. They were determined to never be subjugated again, and they had readily assented to the formation of the Freedom Force to protect the vested interests of the Freedom Federation.

Roaming the wide plains and hills of the Dakota Territory were the rugged horsemen known collectively as the Cavalry. In a sense, the honest, God-fearing people of the Dakotas had also been freed by the war, liberated from oppressive government interference in their lives, from incessant over-regulation. Like the Flatheads, they had reverted to a simpler way of life. They ranched and farmed and raised their families to enjoy the fruits of true freedom. Their leader, Kilrane, had sent his best friend, Boone, as their representative on the Force.

During World War Three, the government of the U.S. had reorganized in Denver, Colorado, and forcibly evacuated thousands of citizens from the Midwest and East into the Rocky Mountain States. Later dubbed the Civilized Zone, this faction was second in size to California. The Civilized Zone included an unusual element in its population demographics, dozens of genetically spawned mutants. They had sent one of their mutants as a volunteer.

The last three Federation factions were all based in Minneosta.

Most reclusive were the Moles, a group living in an underground complex in northern Minnesota, the descendants of a survivalist group that had dug and utilized a network of tunnels as their survival retreat. Their recruit had been killed on the first Force assignment, and they were apparently in no great hurry to dispatch a second.

Also in Minnesota, in the northwest corner of the state, was the faction known as the Clan. They were all refugees from the ravaged Twin Cities, who had been led by the Family to a better life in a rural setting. Their first volunteer had also been slain, but they had sent a replacement, Bear, as soon as they could.

Finally, the smallest faction numerically but the most influential when the Federation leaders met in periodic Council deliberations, there was the Family. Numbering nearly 100, they resided in a walled survivalist compound designated the Home. Eighteen Family members served as protectors of the Home and preservers of the Family, and these eighteen were called Warriors. Their reputation as fighters had spread far and wide, and contributed to Blade being selected as leader of the Force. He was also the head of the Warriors, and his extensive prior experience qualified him for the Force post when the Federation leaders opted to go along with Governor Melnick.

But was the Force needed?

Governor Melnick had introduced the idea of the Force back in January. Here it was October, and the unit had seen action three times. Perhaps, Blade speculated, General Gallagher had been right all along. The general, a confidant of the governor's and the ranking military man in California, had opposed the formation of the Force from the start. Blade frequently found the general's abrasive demeanor difficult to tolerate, but he admired the officer for his unflinching honesty. Gallagher claimed the Force was a waste of time and resources, that the individual Federation factions could function effectively without having to rely upon a special crisis team. And maybe Gallagher was correct.

Blade lowered his legs and rested his elbows on the top of the desk. He had to be careful. He might be allowing his personal feelings to interfere with his objective judgment. After all, he *was* weary of traveling back and forth between the Home and California once a month. He also missed his wife and son unbearably, and he longed to be with them on a full-time basis. Jenny and little Gabe had ventured to California with him after he accepted the post as chief of the Force, but Jenny's chronic depression over being separated from her loved ones and friends had proven too

much for her to bear; she'd decided to return to the Home
and live there permanently. Blade saw them during his
monthly visits, and he had taken to extending those visits
to weeks at a stretch. When he was away from them, he felt
inexpressibly lonely. He often wished the Federation
leaders, the Council, would select someone else to lead the
Force. If missions weren't soon forthcoming, he might be
able to persuade the Council that the Force was, as General
Gallagher believed, nonessential. Or he could talk them into
activating the Force whenever a danger loomed, and allowing
the Force members to live with their respective factions until
such a time as their services were required.

He placed the Personnel Update on the desk and stood,
his seven-foot frame rippling with muscles. Inactivity was
anathema to his personality. He wanted—he needed—action.
The Warriors, in recent years, had seldom seen a month
elapse without action of some kind. Maybe he should—

Footsteps pounded on the stairs leading from the bunker
door down to his office. Someone rapped three times on the
closed wooden door.

"Come in," Blade directed.

The door was shoved wide, and in stepped a lanky man
attired in buckskins. Six-foot-three, with shoulder-length
brown hair and brown eyes, the visitor wore a matched pair
of Hombre revolvers, one in a holster on each hip. His
rugged features conveyed his concern as he spoke. "We've
got a problem."

"What is it, Boone?"

The Cavalryman jerked his right thumb at the doorway.
"You'd better get outside. Sergeant Havoc and Grizzly are
about to mix it up."

Blade was around the desk in an instant, hastening up the
stairs and through the outer door. Twenty feet away were
the other Force members, none of whom were looking in
his direction.

Athena Morris and Bear were on the right. Athena was
a singularly attractive woman, even when clothed in

camouflage fatigues. Fine brown hair fell past her shoulder blades; her cheekbones were prominent, her lips thin, and her keen brown eyes were fixed on the duo in the center with transparent anxiety. Beside her, a study in contrast, was the towering black man sent by the Clan. Bear's curly Afro enhanced his imposing presence. His powerful physique was dressed in black boots, brown pants, and a brown leather vest.

Standing on the left was the volunteer from the Flathead Indians. Thunder-Rolling-in-the-Mountain, like Boone, wore the typical postwar frontier garb, buckskins. Only his were fringed, and he wore moccasins instead of brown boots. His black hair was braided and dropped below his broad shoulders. An oval face, handsome by any standards, and alert, dark eyes contributed to the impression he unconsciously projected of inherent nobility.

In the middle stood the two objects of all the attention, Sergeant Havoc and Grizzly, glaring at one another.

Havoc had been handpicked by General Gallagher to serve on the Force. As a professional soldier, with experience in the Rangers and Special Forces, Havoc was eminently qualified for the position of honor. He was a qualified marksman and weapons master, and he had acquired black belts in karate and judo, and a brown in aikido. Six feet in height, he packed 200 pounds of muscle on his wiry form. His black hair was trimmed in a crew cut, his blue eyes were steely. He wore camouflage fatigues and combat boots.

Grizzly was unlike any of his peers. As a genetically created mutant, he possessed human and bestial traits in equal mixture. His name came from his bearlike features. Only five feet eight, he nonetheless radiated sheer power. His body was completely covered with light, brown fur, and his torso and limbs were exceptionally thick for his size. His arms and shoulders, in particular, were endowed with bulging muscles. Feral eyes blazed from his unique countenance; his chin was pointed, his cheeks slightly concave, his nostrils elongated, his brow receding, and his ears small and circular.

His mouth, in comparison, was wide, his lips thin, and his teeth, exposed as he snarled at the noncom, were tapered.

Blade took several strides forward, his hands on his Bowies.

"—last time I'll say it," Sergeant Havoc was saying. "I didn't mean to insult you."

"Humans are always insulting others," Grizzly responded in his gravelly voice. All he wore was a black loincloth.

"Why are you making such a big deal out of this?" Havoc asked.

"Maybe it's no big deal to you, but it is to me," Grizzly declared, raising his hands, his knuckles toward the noncom. "And if you don't apologize, I'll gut you like a fish."

Blade tensed. The threat was serious. Grizzly possessed a remarkable set of retractable claws. Housed in individual sheaths above the knuckles in his huge hands, the five-inch claws automatically slid out from under flaps of skin just behind his fingernails whenever he extended and locked his fingers. As long as he kept his fingers locked, the claws would stay out. Incredibly strong and resilient, those claws could carve an ordinary man to mincemeat. There was only one drawback to their use. When his fingers were extended so he could employ his claws, Grizzly could not grip anything. Once he relaxed his hand, even slightly, the claws would retract.

"Don't threaten me," Sergeant Havoc said.

"And what if I do?" Grizzly retorted. "What are you going to do about it?"

"I'll kick your hairy ass," Havoc stated.

Grizzly's nose was an inch from Havoc's. "You and what army, turkey?"

"Please!" Athena interjected. "There's no need for this."

"Butt out!" Grizzly thundered at her. "This is none of your business!"

"Yo! Chill out, man," Bear said, trying to placate the mutant.

"I'm not a *man*!"

Thunder stepped nearer. "What has come over you, my brother?"

"I'm not your damn brother," Grizzly responded.

"Did you wake up on the wrong side of the bed today?" Sergeant Havoc quipped.

Grizzly extended the fingers on his right hand, his claws popping into view. "Don't make fun of me, dirt bag."

"Make your move whenever you're ready," Sergeant Havoc said, adopting the Kokutsu-tachi, the back stance.

Blade had heard enough. He stormed toward them, his expression livid. "*Attention!*"

First to respond was Sergeant Havoc. Conditioned by his years of military service, he snapped to attention, halting a yard from Grizzly.

"I said *Attention*!" Blade ordered, halting a yard from Grizzly.

Thunder, Athena and Bear obeyed, standing stiff as boards. Grizzly, however, simply continued to glower at the sergeant.

"Did you hear me?" Blade demanded.

The mutant looked at the giant. "Yeah, I heard you," he muttered.

"Then stand at attention," Blade directed. "Now!"

Grizzly wagged his claws at the Warrior. "And what if I don't?"

"The choice is yours," Blade said, and drew his Bowies.

CHAPTER TWO

For a moment the tableau froze.

Grizzly stared at the gleaming knives, then the Warrior. He saw Boone standing a few yards behind Blade and to the right, and he noticed the Cavalryman's hands were draped near the Hombres.

"What's it going to be?" Blade demanded.

"I wouldn't really gut Havoc. After all, we're all on the same team," Grizzly said sarcastically. He slowly relaxed his fingers, and the claws slid silently into their internal sheaths.

Blade replaced his Bowies. "I want to talk to you. Now. In my office."

Grizzly nodded and walked to the command bunker, one of three bunkers located in the center of the 12-acre compound. To the east was the long bunker used as the barracks, and to the west was the supply bunker. He went inside the concrete building without commenting.

"What the hell was this all about?" Blade inquired.

No one answered.

"I asked a question and I expect an answer," Blade declared. He looked at Sergeant Havoc. "Who started it?"

"I can't recall, sir," Havoc responded.

"Do I look like I was born yesterday?" Blade queried.

"You sure don't," Bear answered. "Not unless your momma had a womb the size of an elephant's. Sir."

Everyone grinned, and the tension promptly evaporated.

"At ease," Blade instructed them, his gaze fixed on the noncom. "I'm waiting for an explanation."

Sergeant Havoc sighed and glanced at the command bunker. "I inadvertently set him off, sir."

"How?"

"It wasn't Havoc's fault," Athena chimed in. "Bear, Havoc, and I were on our way to the barracks for lunch, and we ran into Thunder and Grizzly. I invited them to join us. Thunder said yes, but Grizzly told us he was going to catch a rabbit." She paused and grimaced. "You know how he likes to eat his meat raw and bloody."

Blade nodded. "Go on."

"That's when I made my mistake," Sergeant Havoc said, continuing the narrative. "I wasn't trying to insult him. I merely suggested he'd be better off if he allowed his human self to predominate."

"The sucker blew his cool," Bear mentioned. "He went off the deep end and tried to push Havoc into a fight."

"You know how he's been lately," Blade said to Havoc.

"Yes, sir."

"I should give you my Dummy-of-the-Day award," Blade remarked with a smile.

Boone gestured at the command bunker. "What else are we supposed to do? Treat him with kid gloves all the time? Keep our mouths shut so we won't tick him off? He's been behaving like a jerk ever since our last mission against the Vampires, and he's getting worse every day. If something isn't done, and soon, there *will* be a fight one of these days. You won't always be on hand to rein him in."

Blade pursed his lips. The Cavalryman had hit the proverbial nail on the head. Something must be done about Grizzly. But what? "I'll handle this," he said. "The rest of you go eat.''

Thunder, Bear, and Sergeant Havoc headed for the long barracks.

Boone hesitated. ''Do you want me to stay with you?''

''Thanks. But I don't need a baby-sitter.''

Shrugging, the Cavalryman turned and ambled off.

''I'd like to talk to you before you see Grizzly,'' Athena said, moving closer to the Warrior.

''Do you have some light to shed on his behavior?'' Blade inquired.

''Maybe,'' Athena responded uncertainly.

''I'm all ears,'' Blade said, prompting her.

Athena stared at the command bunker pensively. ''Boone's right, you know. Grizzly has been acting worse and worse since the Dead Zone assignment. Until then, he was actually making progress in his relations with us. His usual bigotry against humans had subsided. At the time, he and I were the best of friends. He confided in me a lot.'' She gazed at the ground. ''Something changed, though. After we returned from San Diego, he withdrew into a shell. He wouldn't talk to me unless I spoke first. I tried to draw him out, to discover the reason for his behavior, but he wouldn't tell me.''

''And you don't have a clue?''

''Just one. As I said, we were the best of friends. But I started dating a helicopter pilot, Captain Slater. I didn't have as much time to spend with Grizzly, and I think he took it personally. I think he decided our friendship wasn't genuine.''

''And you were his only friend,'' Blade noted. ''He wouldn't open up to the rest of us.''

''Exactly,'' Athena concurred.

''But he has been spending a lot of time with Thunder,'' Blade observed.

''They share mutual interests,'' Athena said. ''Thunder has lived with nature all of his life. He knows the habits of the wildlife, and he's an expert hunter and tracker. Grizzly began spending time with Thunder after I became involved with Captain Slater.'' She looked at the giant. ''Deep down, Grizzly's human half craves companionship. He told me so himself.''

''For someone who craves companionship, he has a pitiful way of showing it,'' Blade commented.

Athena reached out and touched Blade's right arm. ''Don't be too hard on him. Please. We must put ourselves in his position. Being a hybrid must be a frustrating experience. Half animal, half human, and not truly at home in either world.''

''I'll be as hard on him as I need to be,'' Blade said. ''I can appreciate the turmoil he must go through, but I can't allow his conduct to disrupt the Force.''

''I understand,'' Athena stated.

''Why don't you go grab a bite to eat?'' Blade suggested. ''I'll take care of Grizzly.''

Athena nodded and walked toward the barracks.

Intrigued, Blade watched her enter the bunker, immersed in thought.

Was it possible?

No.

Couldn't be.

Could it?

He turned and walked to the command bunker. Funny he hadn't seen the connection sooner. But then, it was the last development he would have expected. He opened the door and descended the stairs to his office. Inside, Grizzly was pacing back and forth. Blade moved to his desk and sat down. ''Why don't you have a seat?'' he queried, indicating a chair in front of the desk.

''I'd rather not,'' Grizzly replied.

''Sit down anyway,'' Blade said sternly. ''I don't want you to wear a rut in the floor.''

Grizzly frowned, but complied. He sank into the chair with a glum expression. ''We don't need to talk,'' he said.

''I'll decide if we do or we don't,'' Blade declared.

''Are you going to smack my fingers for being so

naughty?'' Grizzly cracked.

"No. We're both adults. Theoretically, anyway.''

"Look, would it help if I apologized for what happened? I want to get out of here and go for a walk in the woods.''

Blade leaned back in his chair and studied the sullen mutant. Grizzly spent most of his time in the northern section of the Force facility. While the southern part contained a hangar and the runway for the VTOLs, the nothern area was preserved in a natural, wild state for training purposes. Grizzly would disappear for hours at a stretch in the forest. "No,'' Blade said. "We're going to talk this out whether you like the idea or not.''

"See if I ever join a military outfit again,'' Grizzly muttered.

"I'm surprised you remember.''

"Remember what?''

"That this is a military outfit. We adhere to military procedure and enforce a strict discipline. We don't go overboard, mind you. I don't require my people to wear uniforms if they don't want to, but they are expected to conduct themselves in a professional manner.''

Grizzly's nose twitched. "And I haven't been?''

"What do you think?''

The mutant's fists clenched and unclenched. "My problem is personal.''

"Any problem that disrupts the Force becomes my problem too,'' Blade said. "I want to hear about it.''

"Fat chance.''

"Anything you say will be held in confidence.''

Grizzly said nothing.

"I thought our personnel problems were over when we lost our last troublemaker. But you, apparently, have decided to take his place.''

"I'll be fine if everyone just leaves me alone.''

"We're expected to mesh as a unit, to function as a tight-knit team. One bad apple ruins the bunch. I can't have you picking fights every time my back is turned. I want to know what's bothering you.''

"It's personal," Grizzly reiterated.

"Does it have anything to do with Athena?"

Grizzly reacted as if an electric shock had transfixed his body. He straightened abruptly, his eyes widening in surprise. "Why do you say that?" he blurted out.

"I can add."

"Add?"

"I can put two and two together," Blade said. "You started behaving like a jackass shortly after Athena began dating a pilot. Is there a connection?"

"Of course not," Grizzly responded gruffly.

"Oh?"

"There's nothing between Athena and me," Grizzly asserted.

"You were close friends once."

"Once."

"But no longer?"

"She's too busy for me now," Grizzly said.

"Do you wish it was otherwise?" Blade asked.

The mutant uttered a low growl. "Don't pry," he warned.

"You like her, don't you?"

"I told you not to pry."

Blade scrutinized the hybrid for several seconds. "Do you have a woman in your life, Grizzly?" he inquired casually.

Grizzly came off the chair in a rush, his claws sliding out as he stepped to the desk. "Damn you!" he roared. "No one meddles in my private life!"

Slowly, calmly, Blade folded his arms across his chest.

"Stand up!" Grizzly snapped. "I won't hold back this time."

"Sit down," Blade directed softly.

"Like hell I will! Stand up, damn it!"

Blade's flinty eyes narrowed. "Sit down."

Grizzly glowered at the giant, his neck muscles quivering.

"Sit down," Blade ordered for the third time.

Reluctantly, his enraged countenance gradually returning to normal, Grizzly took his seat. His claws were grudgingly retracted.

"That's better," Blade said. "Does Athena know how you feel?"

"No," Grizzly responded, the word barely audible.

"Haven't you told her?"

"Are you crazy?"

"If you love her, let her know. It's better than simmering inside, waiting for an excuse to explode."

Grizzly snorted contemptuously. "You should hear yourself."

"I don't make sense?"

"Can cows fly?"

"I don't understand," Blade admitted.

"How could you? You're not a mutant."

"What does that have to do with anything?"

Grizzly's shoulders slumped. "Everything." He took a deep breath, his chin on his chest. "You have no idea what it's like to be a mutant, to be different from everyone and everything. I'm not fully human, and I'm not an animal. I'm somewhere in between. To the animals I'm just another predator. To humans, I'm a freak—"

"I doubt that Athena views you as a freak."

"Maybe she doesn't. But she also doesn't feel about me the way I feel about her. The idea is ridiculous."

"Why?"

Grizzly looked Blade in the eyes. "Have you ever seen a mixed couple, a human and a mutant together?"

Blade had to think for several seconds. "No," he admitted. "I never have."

"And you never will. What woman in her right mind would allow herself to become romantically involved with a walking, talking fur ball? She'd be the laughingstock of the whole damn planet. Worse, she'd be the target of every bigot around."

"As I recall," Blade said, "you have a bit of a reputation in that regard yourself."

"Hey. I've always believed humans were scum. But I haven't tried to hide my feelings. I've been up front about it," Grizzly responded.

"And now?"

"Now I'm not so sure. I've grown to like the clowns I work with on the Force. And in Athena's case, well . . ." He stopped and stared at the floor.

"Are you open to some advice?"

"Go ahead. It can't hurt."

"You can't keep doing this to yourself," Blade counseled. "You're tearing yourself apart."

"Tell me something I don't know."

"Whether you let Athena know is up to you. I wouldn't presume to meddle in your private affairs. But you must quit flying off the handle at every little provocation. I can sympathize with you, but I won't tolerate having the Force morale affected by your temper. You just said you like the other Force members. If you give them half a chance, you might find that they're the best friends you've got. So loosen up. Chill out, as Bear would say. Your situation with Athena will resolve itself eventually. Time has a way of resolving all problems, of healing all wounds," Blade said. "So lighten up, rocks-for-brains."

A grin creased Grizzly's features. "I guess I had that coming. I have been a pain in the ass, haven't I?"

"A momumental pain in the ass," Blade corrected him.

Grizzly smiled. "All right. I won't blow my cool again." He smiled even wider. "Unless it's for a real good reason."

"Fair enough," Blade said. "And all the best with Athena. To be honest, I don't know what I'd do if I was in your shoes. I don't envy you."

"Maybe you should shut up while you're ahead. You had me feeling okay there for a while," Grizzly quipped. He rose and offered his right hand.

Blade stood and shook.

"Thanks," Grizzly stated. "I won't forget this."

"Part of my job," Blade said.

The mutant turned and strolled from the office.

Would wonders never cease! Blade sat back down and smiled. He'd actually solved his major personnel problem, although the solution promised to be only temporary. And he was pleased at his deductive insight concerning Grizzly and Athena. If he'd been on his toes, he might have noticed sooner. Still, one problem down, a zillion to go. Foremost was what to do about the Force. Should he advocate disbanding the unit on the grounds a strike squad wasn't needed? Or should he roll with the flow and see what happened next? And what about Jenny and Gabe? He was no closer to solving his personal dilemma, and he was tired of straining his brain and coming up empty-handed.

What he wouldn't give for some action!

The sound of someone pounding down the office stairs shattered the Warrior's reverie.

Blade leaned forward, recognizing the person's distinctive heavy tread. Was it the answer to his prayer?

Without bothering to knock, General Miles Gallagher marched in. "Your vacation is over," he brusquely announced. "Enough of this goofing off. I have a mission for you."

CHAPTER THREE

The leaders of the Federation factions had selected General Miles Gallagher to function as the personal liaison between themselves and the Force. California's Governor Melnick would relay the results of the executive sessions to the general, who would promptly convey their requests to Blade. By virtue of his bulldog tenacity and his uncompromising dedication to his superiors, plus his overt concern for the welfare of his troops, Gallagher was widely respected. He was as tough as they came, a man who believed in applying the principle of the direct approach to every assignment. He could also be devious and self-serving on occasion. His appearance tended to mirror his character. A stocky man with brown eyes and crew-cut brown hair, he possessed a square, jutting chin, and a pug nose.

"Hello to *you*, General," Blade said dryly.

"There's no time for the amenities," Gallagher declared, halting in front of the desk next to the chair. "Have your people get their butts in gear. I have a mission for you."

"So you said," Blade responded.

"Then what are you waiting for? An engraved invitation?"

"You're forgetting yourself."

"What?"

"*I* decide which assignments we'll take," Blade reminded the officer. Prior to accepting the post as head of the Force, he had stipulated a number of conditions: he was to be responsible for the training of the volunteers, he would instill discipline as he saw fit, and ultimately, he exercised the final say over all proposed missions.

"This one is critical," General Gallagher said. "Time is of the essence."

"Then you should have arrived here sooner," Blade replied. "Five more minutes won't matter. I want to hear every detail before I commit the Force."

Gallagher frowned. "You can be a real hard-ass sometimes, you know it?"

"So I've been told," Blade acknowledged. "Now what about this critical mission?"

The general sat down and placed his hands in his lap. "Where do you want me to begin?"

"The beginning would be nice."

"That would be three weeks ago, when an emissary from Holtmeyer Industries showed up at the capital and requested an appointment with the governor."

"Back up a bit," Blade said, interrupting. "What is Holtmeyer Industries?"

"A business conglomerate run by a man named Eric Holtmeyer. Apparently, his business connections are international in scope."

"A conglomerate? International?" Blade repeated in surprise. "Since when? I thought the war put an end to the era of the industrial enterprises."

"Evidently not."

"Why haven't we heard of him before?"

"Will you let me finish?" General Gallagher snapped. "I'll give you all the information I have, which isn't much."

"Go ahead," Blade said.

"According to Holtmeyer's representative, Holtmeyer has a business empire spanning Europe and Asia. The man specializes in huge financial ventures. He must be the last of his breed, a big-time entrepreneur. Holtmeyer wants to expand into North America, and he's presented an undertaking on a grand scale as his first venture.''

"None of this makes any sense," Blade declared. "Did Europe and Asia survive the war in better shape than America? Are businesses there flourishing? What is Holtmeyer's background?''

"There you go again," General Gallagher commented. "This is the first we've heard about alleged business activities in Europe and Asia. And we know nothing about Holtmeyer's background.''

"Why did he contact Governor Melnick?''

"Holtmeyer has made an incredible offer," Gallagher detailed. "He's activating the Alaska Pipeline.''

"The what?''

"Do you mean there's one thing they didn't teach you at that Home of yours?'' Gallagher asked sarcastically.

"They taught me how to hack off ears," Blade replied. "Would you care for a demonstration?''

The general ignored the barb. "The Trans-Alaska Pipeline was constructed decades before World War Three as part of America's plan to become energy self-sufficient. Huge oil reserves were discovered under the North Slope of Alaska, enough oil to make the U.S. independent of foreign influence and manipulation. So facilities were built near Prudhoe Bay on the North Slope, and an enormous pipeline was constructed to carry the oil to a southern Alaskan port.''

"I recall reading about the Pipeline in history class," Blade mentioned.

"Then perhaps you recall the outcome of the effort," Gallagher said. "The Pipeline was never utilized to its full potential. The government, in effect, put a lid on the flow of oil with stringent rules and regulations designed to hamper production. Some people claimed the government was deliberately shutting off the Alaskan oil in an effort to bankrupt the oil companies and force them into nationalization. Others

believed the government wanted to create a false energy crisis
to increase government control over the population.''

''Did the government really do that?''

Gallagher shrugged. ''I only know what I read. At any
rate, World War Three put a stop to the reduced flow of oil
and shut down the Pipeline.''

''And this Holtmeyer wants to get the oil flowing again?''

''So he claims,'' Gallagher disclosed. ''He's made a deal.
He'll get the Alaska Pipeline running again, carrying oil all
the way to California, in exchange for one hundred million
dollars in gold.''

Blade sat up straight in his chair. ''What?''

''That's the deal.''

''He must be insane.''

''He's not as crazy as you'd think,'' Gallagher said.

''Where would California, or the entire Federation for that
matter, find one one hundred million dollars in gold?'' Blade
queried.

''We already have it,'' Gallagher replied calmly.

''You what?'' Blade declared, flabbergasted.

''Let me give you a short lesson in economics,'' General
Gallagher stated. ''California still operates on the free-
enterprise principle. The state mints its own money, and we
back up our paper and coin with our gold reserves. The early
leaders of the Free State of California were pretty smart.
They knew America's economy had gone to the dogs after
the U.S. abandoned the gold standard. Any economy without
a solid backing will fall apart sooner or later. So the state
collected all the gold it could lay its hands on, paying
exorbitant rates to private collectors and melting down gold
artifacts and jewelry. Eventually, approximately one hundred
million dollars worth of gold was accumulated.''

''Where is the gold now?''

''Stored under heavy guard at our mint in L.A.,'' Gallagher answered.

''California has one hundred million dollars in gold?''

''That's what I just said.''

"And Holtmeyer asked for *exactly* that amount in exchange for getting the Alaska Pipeline running again?" Blade inquired suspiciously.

"Strange, isn't it?"

"How did he know California has the gold?"

"The fact the state possesses a gold reserve is common knowledge," General Gallagher said. "The exact amount, however, is not. Only certain employees of the mint and a few government employees have been privileged to know the information."

"Would they divulge it?"

"They were all pledged to secrecy, but one of them might have turned traitor for the right price."

"Have you investigated to try and find the leak?"

"We're in the process of tracking the leak now," Gallagher responded. "It will take a while unless the idiot comes right out and confesses."

Blade scratched his chin and leaned back. "How would Holtmeyer have known which employee to contact?"

"California has Freedom of Information laws. Anyone can waltz into the Records Division and search the files."

"That's sort of careless security, isn't it?"

"If we clamped a lid on the files, the media would scream bloody murder. One of the disadvantages of living in a republic is having to put up with liberals, bleeding-heart civil rights activists, and the self-righteous press."

Blade smiled and returned to the subject at hand. "Getting back to Eric Holtmeyer. Why would he make such an offer?"

"For the gold, supposedly," General Gallagher said. "One hundred million is nothing to sneeze at. He also wants a percentage of future profits."

"Did Governor Melnick tell Holtmeyer to take a flying leap?"

"The governor is seriously considering accepting the proposal," Gallagher said.

"You're kidding."

"Do I look like I'm kidding?" Gallagher stated solemnly.

"But why?"

"Economics again. California has had to struggle over the decades to keep its cars, trucks, planes, and ships running. We've rationed our fuel since the war. Do you have any idea what an unlimited supply of crude oil and natural gas would mean to the state?"

"There's natural gas under the North Slope too?"

"Yes. But the crude oil is our main interest. If we could acquire an unlimited supply, our own industrial capacity would be able to expand tremendously. Our standard of living would rise. We could return to the lifestyle the state enjoyed before World War Three. And this wouldn't benefit only us. The Civilized Zone has a lot of operational vehicles. In the long run, this would improve the lot of every Federation faction. The possibilities are mind-boggling."

"There's something I don't understand here," Blade said. "If getting the Trans-Alaska Pipeline running again is so important, why hasn't your state done so before this? California is the Federation member with the highest technological level of development. If anyone could do it, your state could."

"The answer is so simple you won't believe it."

"Try me."

"We never thought of it."

"What?"

"Our government assumed the Pipeline was knocked out of commission during the war," General Gallagher explained. "We had no reason to believe it could be repaired and rendered functional. Besides, until twenty years ago or so, we were strictly involved with merely picking up the pieces and trying to restore the basic necessities to our people."

"So was everyone else," Blade noted.

"Another reason California never attempted to rebuild the Pipeline stems from the logistics involved. The North Slope is a long, long way from our state. We're talking in the neighborhood of three to four thousand miles. And we don't possess the tankers required to transport the crude from Valdez, the southern Alaskan port I referred to, to one of our ports."

"Does Holtmeyer possess tankers?"

"So he claims."

"Can he transport the oil from Prudhoe Bay instead of Valdez?"

"No. At least, they couldn't before the war. Too much ice. It's right on the Arctic Circle."

"I've noticed the words you've been using," Blade mentioned. "Supposedly. Evidently. Alleged. Claims. I get the impression you're skeptical of Holtmeyer."

"The son of a bitch is lying through his teeth," General Gallagher declared.

"Does Governor Melnick share your view?"

"Melnick is a politician. He'd give a convicted ax murderer the benefit of the doubt if he thought he'd get a vote out of the deal."

Blade grinned.

"Actually, Melnick can't afford to dismiss Holtmeyer outright. There's always the slim chance that Holtmeyer can do what he claims. And the governor must weigh the potential advantages to the people of the Freedom Federation if, just if, Holtmeyer can deliver."

"Has Melnick informed the Federation leaders?"

"Yes. They've advised him to proceed with negotiations and to serve as the official Federation representative in all deliberations. If it looks like a deal will be struck, a summit meeting will be called in L.A."

"Is the deal close to being finalized?"

"Not by a long shot. Verification is holding us up."

"What do you mean?"

"Governor Melnick is not about to hand over one hundred million in gold unless he can verify the Trans-Alaska Pipeline is working and Holtmeyer can supply the crude."

"Won't Holtmeyer allow verification?"

"He says he will, but he's been stalling. He wants

Governor Melnick to visit Prudhoe Bay personally. Then they'll sit down and iron out the details of the agreement.''

"Is Melnick going?''

"Yes.''

"And where does the Force come into the picture?''

"I want the Force to be the governor's personal bodyguard while he's in Alaska.''

"But Melnick already has a police branch protecting him.''

General Gallagher nodded. "The California Secret Service. The branch was created by the legislature about ninety years ago after one of our early governors was assassinated. The Service is patterned after the federal branch used to protect the prewar Presidents and other officials.''

"Then why don't you use them?''

"They're not specialists like the Force,'' General Gallagher said. "Sure, they protect the governor twenty-four hours a day, but they don't specialize in killing to the degree the Force does.'' He mustered a rare smile. "They don't kick ass like you do.''

"That's it? We baby-sit Governor Melnick in Alaska?''

"Not quite.''

"I knew it,'' Blade stated. "What else?''

"The governor wants to do some stalling of his own. He wants the Force to be our advance site-inspection team. You'll go up first and check the Prudhoe Bay facilities.''

"With or without Holtmeyer's permission?''

"By whatever means necessary, if you get my drift.''

Blade studied the officer. "Knowing you as well as I do, I'm surprised you haven't already tried to verify Holtmeyer's claims.''

General Gallagher frowned. "I have.''

"What happened?''

"I didn't want the governor walking into a trap of some kind,'' Gallagher detailed. "I doubt Holtmeyer wants to assassinate Melnick. This is too elaborate to be an assassination scheme. Holtmeyer could hire a marksman to do the job at a lot less expense, if all he wants is the governor dead.''

He paused. "I decided to verify the Pipeline is working on my own initiative. I sent in two of my best men."

"What did they find?"

"I don't know. They never came back."

"Holtmeyer had them killed?"

"Again, I just don't know. We located an old map of the Prudhoe complex, and on it I found a reference to a Pump Station south of Prudhoe Bay. A computer check turned up an officer with a couple of years of refinery experience under his belt. Lieutenant Tyler was his name. His superior was Captain Bowen, one of the most reliable men I've ever known." He stopped and sighed. "A VTOL dropped them off, and that's the last we saw of them."

Blade was favorably impressed by the officer's evident remorse over the loss of the two men. "There's always the chance they're still alive. Maybe Holtmeyer is holding them prisoner."

"Maybe," General Gallagher said doubtfully, then focused on the giant. "So what's it going to be? Will you accept this mission?"

"The Arctic Circle, huh?"

"Just think, polar bears and caribou."

Blade glanced around the office and chuckled. "Darn. Wouldn't you know it. I forgot to bring my long johns."

CHAPTER FOUR

The pride of California's military establishment consisted of a pair of exceptional aircraft, two VTOLs. Known as Hurricanes, the jets were capable of vertical takeoffs and landings. They combined the abilities of a helicopter with the aerodynamic excellence of a supersonic craft. Manufactured prior to the nuclear holocaust, the Hurricanes received special-priority treatment. No expense was spared in ensuring spare parts were always available and fuel was on hand. The VTOLs were utilized extensively, primarily as a shuttle and courier service between the Federation members and as the preferred method of transport for the Freedom Force. Each Hurricane could accommodate five passengers and a pilot. On extended flights, midair refueling was routinely conducted by tanker aircraft. The Hurricane could travel anywhere at incredible speeds. They were indispensible.

Blade thought about the importance of the craft as the two streaking VTOLs arced out of the southern sky and angled toward Prudhoe Bay.

"Everything looks so small from up here," Boone commented from the seat to the Warrior's right. The seating arrangement in the Hurricanes positioned the pilot at the forward end of the cockpit, and then came two rows of two seats apiece. Behind them was a solitary seat.

"It changes your perspective," Blade responded, glancing over his left shoulder at Thunder and Sergeant Havoc. He could see the rear seat, piled high with their gear.

"How so?" Boone asked.

"You can't have a swelled head at fifty thousand feet," Blade remarked.

Boone's forehead knit as he thought about it. After a bit he grinned. "I see what you mean. Never thought of it that way."

Blade reached up and adjusted his flight helmet.

"Whatever you said to Grizzly must have worked," Boone mentioned.

"Why?"

"The first thing he did after leaving your office was apologize to Havoc."

"Grizzly apologized?"

"Yep. Surprised me too."

"Give Grizzly some time. He'll work his problem out eventually," Blade stated.

Sergant Havoc leaned forward and stuck his head in the foot of space between Blade's seat and Boone's. "What exactly is his problem, sir? If I may ask."

"You may not."

"Sorry, sir," Havoc said, and settled back. "I didn't mean to pry."

The Warrior looked at the noncom. "You weren't prying. Your concern is understandable. We must all depend on one another in life-or-death situations, and if one of us isn't up to par, everyone is endangered."

"Grizzly's path is a difficult one," Thunder interjected. "I am grateful to the Spirit-in-All-Things that I was not born a mutant."

The pilot banked the Hurricane to the east. Captain Peter Laslo was his name, and he was one of the best pilots in

California. "I made a loop so we can approach Prudhoe Bay from the west," he announced into his helmet ComLink.

"Acknowledged," Blade replied.

"I'll decelerate when we're close to the facilities," Laslo said. "If you want to hover over anything, just say the word."

"No hovering," Blade directed. "I don't want to arouse any suspicion. Just take it nice and slow."

"You've got it."

Blade stared straight ahead and spied the blue waters of the Bay. To the north was the Beaufort Sea, which in turn blended into the Arctic Ocean. He reached into the right pocket on his green parka and extracted the copy of the map given to him by General Gallagher. After spreading the map on his thighs, he removed a blue pen from an inside parka pocket and gazed at the landscape below. According to the research papers Gallagher had supplied, the ground in the area of Prudhoe Bay was frozen all year long. It was called permafrost. The ground was frozen to the average depth of 2,000 feet.

The VTOL settled lower slowly.

His fingers gripping the pen, Blade squinted to detect the outlines of the structures now visible a mile distant. A white blanket covered the permafrost, and the dark buildings stood out in stark contrast.

"I have never seen so much snow," Thunder commented.

"I did some skiing a few years ago," Sergeant Havoc said. "The Mt. Baldy Ski Area east of L.A. is a popular spot for skiers from all over California. I went there to learn to ski and had a great time. The state doesn't receive much snow anymore except at the higher elevations, and I had only seen snow a couple of times before I went to Mt. Baldy." He shook his head in wonder. "But it was nothing like this."

"The Dakota Territory gets a lot of snow in the winter," Boone mentioned. "Four years ago a blizzard left twelve-foot drifts, so this isn't new to me. This country reminds me of Dakota in one other respect."

"Because it's flat?" Havoc asked.

"Dakota isn't all flat," Boone said. "We have rolling hills and valleys too. No, this land reminds me of the Dakota Territory in another way. This is the kind of land that makes or breaks a person. Rugged. Hard. The kind where I was born and raised."

"Then you should feel right at home here," Sergeant Havoc remarked. "And every time you see a polar bear, just pretend it's a buffalo."

Blade smiled and concentrated on their approach to Prudhoe Bay. He surveyed the land to the south and north, and on the latter side he spotted a building. But which one was it? Dozens were marked on his map. How could he tell which was which from the air?

The Hurricane suddenly descended even lower, until Captain Laslo was flying the VTOL at a height of 500 feet.

More buildings appeared, located to the north, east, and south, situated at varying distances from one another and connected by a network of roads. Blade studied a complex just to the north, and decided they must correspond to the cluster on his map designated as GC-2. As the VTOL continued on its slow, easterly course, the magnitude of the operation became startlingly clear. The Prudhoe Bay setup was enormous. Fortunately, the placement of the structures corresponded exactly with the coordinates on Blade's map. He recognized the Sohio OPS Center and the GC-3 buildings. With special interest he circled the Central Power Supply facility on the map.

Captain Laslo veered the VTOL to the southeast gradually.

Blade craned his neck for a better view of the roads and the structures ahead. The A.R. Company OPS Center was to the northeast. They flew over Central-Pad 1 and headed for Deadhorse Airfield.

"I didn't know the Pipeline was above ground," Boone commented.

"Part of the Pipeline is above ground, part underground,"

Blade said, relating information supplied by General Gallagher. "Why? Did you see it?"

Boone nodded and indicated his side of the canopy with a jerk of his right thumb. "Back there a ways."

"There's an airport," Sergeant Havoc declared, pointing ahead.

"Deadhorse Airfield," Blade informed them.

"Why would anyone name an airport Deadhorse?" Havoc inquired.

"I'd like to meet the dummy," Boone said. As a Cavalryman, he appreciated the value of a well-trained horse and had spent hours every day in the saddle. "Must be a city slicker."

"We have a reception committee waiting," Sergeant Havoc declared.

Deadhorse Airfield was a bustle of activity. A half-dozen vehicles were lined up near a section apparently reserved for the VTOL. In front of the vehicles, facing the landing strip, were two rows of men dressed in white uniforms and carrying automatic rifles. Ground-crew personnel were scurrying to and fro. To the east of the VTOL area rested three craft: a sleek jet, a large transport plane, and a golden helicopter. No snow was on the strip.

"I'm taking us down," Captain Laslo told them. "Be ready for anything."

"That's my line," Blade said. He twisted and gazed to the rear, spying the second Hurricane a quarter-mile off and winging toward the Airfield. On board were Grizzly, Athena, and Bear. He'd deliberately placed Grizzly and Athena on the same Hurricane, hoping they might be able to discuss their relationship if they were forced to share a cramped cockpit for hours.

"I sense danger," Thunder unexpectedly proclaimed.

"Brilliant deduction, Sherlock," Sergeant Havoc quipped. "We're about to set down in potentially hostile territory, we're outnumbered a hundred to one, and you sense danger. What was your first clue?"

"The danger I sense is not the obvious danger," Thunder responded.

"What sort of danger?" Blade asked, replacing the map.

"My people believe in developing our intuition to enhance our communion with the Spirit-of-All-Things. And my intuition is impressing on me a feeling of great danger. I can not yet identify the source of this danger."

"If you do, let me know,"Blade instructed the Flathead. He was feeling extremely uneasy himself.

The Hurricane slowed to a virtual stop, hovering above the landing strip, its engines roaring.

Blade glanced at Sergeant Havoc. "Pass out our weapons," he ordered. Each of them was already armed with a pair of Colt Stainless Steel Officers Model 45's, except for Boone, who preferred his Hombre revolvers. Blade wore his 45's in shoulder holsters. Each Force member had been issued a parka, and all were wearing thermal underwear under their clothes and heavy boots. Blade had reluctantly put on a fatigue shirt and annoyed General Gallagher by wearing his black leather vest over the shirt.

Havoc turned in his seat and reached into the back. One by one, he grabbed two M-16's and handed a rifle to Thunder and Boone, then slid a third one between his legs. Grunting, he took hold of Blade's M-60 and handed the large machine gun to the Warrior. "Here you go. Leave it to you to carry a gun this size."

Blade hefted the weapon and smiled. "This gets the job done, and that's what counts." Three and a half feet in length, weighing close to 20 pounds, using standard 7.62-mm ammo, and able to fire 200 rounds per minute in the rapid-fire mode, the M-60's devastating firepower could be a critical factor in combat. Blade wore two ammo belts crisscrossed over his chest, under the parka.

"Those guys look like they mean business," Boone mentioned, gazing at the two rows of men flanking the Airfield. He counted 24 in each row.

"They're professionals, all right," Sergeant Havoc

concurred. "Mercenaries, probably." He began distributing backpacks.

"Maybe Eric Holtmeyer has his own private army," Blade speculated. He took his backpack and squeezed it on.

"Is that him near the limo?" Sergeant Havoc queried.

Blade scanned the vehicles and saw a golden-hued limousine parked in the center of the row. Two jeeps and a pickup were parked to the right of the limousine, and three more jeeps were to the left. Standing two yards from the limo, between the car and the troopers in white, stood three persons. One of the trio was uncommonly tall. Before Blade could observe further details, the VTOL dropped to the landing strip. He removed his flight helmet.

"Here we go," Boone said.

"Action, at last," Havoc stated happily.

Thunder was trying to see the trio clearly.

"Thanks for flying California Air Express," Captain Laslo joked. "The fare will be one thousand dollars. Kindly pay the stewardess on your way out." So saying, he activated a toggle switch on the control panel and a small door located under the middle of the canopy on the outside of the Hurricane swiveled open. The VTOL had been specifically designed to ferry strike teams into fire zones. Consequently, the canopy was never opened while the Hurricane was unloading. Doing so would expose the pilot to enemy fire. To safeguard the pilot, and ensure the tactical squad could reach the ground quickly and safely, the small door had been incorporated into the Hurricane models manufactured in the years preceding World War Three.

Blade hastily unfurled a green rope ladder lying on the floor next to the exit, then unhooked his restraint belt and started to slip through the doorway.

"Remember," Captain Laslo said. "We'll be back in two days with Governor Melnick if we receive the go-ahead from you." He looked at Blade with concern. "Even if we don't get the green light, we'll be making a pass over Prudhoe Bay in two days. If you can, signal us somehow. We'll come in and haul your butts out.''

"You'd return for us without authorization?" Blade inquired, his head and shoulder poking through the doorway.

"We never desert anyone," Laslo affirmed. "All of the pilots feel the same way. If we drop you off, then you can be damn sure we'll be back to get you unless something unexpected delays us.''

Blade thought of the time the Russians shot down one of the Hurricanes, stranding two other Warriors and himself in Florida. He fervently hoped he'd never be stranded again. "Thanks. We'll be looking for you.''

"Take care," Captain Laslo advised.

With a nod, Blade clambered down the taut ladder, the M-60 clutched in his big left hand. The bottom rung of the ladder was weighted so the ladder would not sway in the wind while the strike team was descending. He dropped the final five feet and turned, cradling the M-60, then stepped to the left, out of the way of the men following him.

The rows of soldiers in white abruptly parted, the six troopers in the middle of each line closing formation to allow the trio near the limousine to advance toward the Hurricane.

Its engines thundering, the second Hurricane was coming in for a vertical landing to the east of Laslo's VTOL.

Blade kept his eyes on the three figures.

One was an extremely beautiful woman attired in tight white pants, a fur-lined white coat, and white boots. Her face was heart shaped, her lips a bright red. She moved with unconscious sensual grace, her hips swaying gently with every stride. Her green eyes scrutinized the giant intently as she approached.

The second figure was a man of average height and build. He wore a bulky, brown fur coat covering him to his ankles. On his feet were polished brown boots. His features were set in a haughty expression. Thin brows peaked a pair of piercing blue eyes. His blond hair formed a golden, curly halo. He walked with an air of arrogance, his hands in the pockets of his fur coat.

Blade studied the third figure, his finger on the M-60's trigger, experiencing a palpable sensation of menace as the man drew near.

This was the tall one, and he stood at least seven feet high, equal to the Warrior. His frame was leaner, his musculature evidently more compact. He strolled with a measured tread, an intentional economy of movement, his arms draped loosely at his sides. Of particular interest were his face and hands. His countenance was decidedly Oriental. Short, black hair crowned an impressive face with slanted eyes, narrow brows, and pronounced cheekbones. His visage was as cold as the snow bordering the airstrip.

Blade peered at the Oriental's hands.

The man possessed thick, bony fingers and blunt nails. His hands were twice the size they should be, with each digit the diameter of four ordinary fingers, and his knuckles resembled the knots on a tree. He wore a black shirt and black pants, both of lightweight construction, and seemed impervious to the chilling wind.

That was when Blade noticed the Oriental's feet.

They were naked!

Blade glanced at the Oriental's face, then the feet again. How could the man walk around at the Arctic Circle in the winter without any shoes or boots? His eyes narrowed. Like the hands, the feet were outsized, calloused, and bony. They were virtual clubs.

"What is this?" Sergeant Havoc quipped from Blade's right elbow. "National Giant Month? That bozo looks like he'd give you a run for your money."

Blade looked to the right at Havoc and Boone, then to the left at Thunder. All three were holding their M-16s in the ready posture. He glimpsed Bear climbing from the second Hurricane, then faced front.

Just as the trio arrived.

The man in the fur coat smiled smugly and pulled his right hand from his coat pocket. "Greetings," he said urbanely. "I'm Eric Holtmeyer."

CHAPTER FIVE

Blade extended his right hand and shook, noting Holtmeyer's firm grip and unflinching gaze. "I'm Blade."

"Your reputation precedes you," Holtmeyer said, releasing the Warrior's hand. "I recognized you immediately. Men of your stature are few and far between, although, as you can see, I employ someone whose reputation is the equal of your own. Only his was established in the Far East." He indicated the Oriental with a nod of his head.

"Hello," Blade said to the man in black.

The Oriental did not respond. He simply stood there impassively, just behind Holtmeyer.

"Cat got your tongue?" Blade queried.

"He doesn't speak English," Holtmeyer stated.

"Does he own shoes?"

Holtmeyer burst into laughter, the genuine, hearty mirth of a man who appreciated a sense of humor. "No, as a matter of fact, he doesn't." He swung toward the woman. "This is my business associate. Ms. Pruty."

"Call me Lalita," the woman said softly, offering her right hand. Her hair was platinum with a blonde streak down the middle.

Blade shook, feeling the warmth she generated, his own fingers tingling from the cold. His gloves were in his left parka pocket.

"My!" Lalita declared. "The poor baby is freezing."

"We should retire to my lodge," Holtmeyer suggested. "We can conduct our business better where it's warm."

"Your lodge, Mr. Holtmeyer?" Blade repeated quizzically.

"Please, call me Eric," Holtmeyer said. "And yes, I have a lodge. The old A.R. Company Operations Center has been refurbished and converted into my personal headquarters and living quarters."

Blade stared at the rows of troopers. "You seem to have a knack for organization."

Holtmeyer nodded curtly, the act of a man confirming a fact and not extolling his ability. "Organization, Blade, is the key to success in life."

"We have jeeps waiting for you," Lalita mentioned. "If you'll be so kind, we'll escort you to the lodge."

"Lead the way," Blade said.

Holtmeyer and Lalita pivoted and headed for the vehicles, the Oriental trailing Holtmeyer like an obedient mastiff.

Blade turned around. Grizzly, Athena, and Bear had joined them. Much to Blade's surprise, the mutant had elected to wear fatigue pants, combat boots, and a parka. Blade was mystified. Grizzly *never* wore clothes, except for the black loincloth. So why was he wearing them now? Blade doubted the weather would adversely affect the hybrid. Grizzly's fur enabled him to withstand the harshest of elements. "Okay. You heard the man. Let's pile into those jeeps."

The Force members trudged off, each with a camouflage backpack snug on his back. Sergeant Havoc's backpack contained their radio.

Bear hesitated, waiting for the others to proceed. "I want to thank you, bro," he remarked sarcastically.

"For what?" Blade asked, making for the jeeps.

"For stickin' me in with Grizzly and Athena," Bear said, walking on the giant's left.

"How was the flight?"

"It sucked."

"Why? Were they quarreling all the way?"

Bear snorted. "You've got it all wrong. They hardly said a word."

"Did they sit next to each other?" Blade asked.

The black nodded. "They sat behind Captain Wilson, and I was behind them. I could hardly get a peep out of them. Athena would mumble a couple of words when I talked to her, but Grizzly was a clam. All he could say was yes or no." He paused. "I was twiddlin' my thumbs the whole trip."

"I was hoping they'd talk," Blade commented.

"Why? What's up?"

"I can't say."

"You can't tell your old buddy? I thought we're friends."

"We are, but I gave my word."

"Say no more," Bear said. "Grizzly did try to tell her something once or twice. I saw him look at her and open his mouth, but he always changed his mind. Is he warm for her form?"

"I gave my word."

"Say no more," Bear reiterated. "I was so bored, I was wishin' I had a book. And I hate to read."

"I'll fly back with them," Blade volunteered.

"Fine by me. Just take a pillow," Bear cracked. "You know, they act as if they're lovers on the outs. Are they?"

"My word, remember?"

"Say no more," Bear declared. "You don't have to tell me twice. If it's private, it's private."

Blade smiled and looked at his companion. "If you want to know the truth, ask Grizzly."

"Are you nuts?" Bear responded. "That crazy sucker would chop off my balls if I stuck my big nose in where it doesn't belong."

"He just might," Blade agreed.

"Hey, did you see the melons on that fox?" Bear inquired enthusiastically.

"Melons?"

"Yeah. Melons. Boobies. Grapefruits. Hooters. Bazongas. Tits."

"Are you referring to the lady's breasts?"

"I ain't referrin' to her feet."

Blade chuckled. "For a man who hates to read, you're a walking thesaurus."

"A what?"

"Never mind."

"Is that good or bad?"

Blade slowed as they drew near to the troopers, all of whom were standing stiffly at attention. "It's good," he said absently.

"Really? No one's ever called me a thesaurus before."

Eric Holtmeyer, Lalita Pruty, and the Oriental were waiting near the gold limousine.

"What the hell is a thesaurus, anyway?" Bear asked.

"Not now," Blade said, scanning the row of soldiers as he passed them, registering their clean, neat white uniforms and white parkas, their hard-bitten visages, and their recent-vintage assault rifles. The configuration of the rifles was unfamiliar, and he mentally reviewed the many books and magazine articles he'd read on automatic rifles in the huge Family library in an effort to identify them. One style stuck in his mind. If he was right, these troopers were outfitted with Beretta AR 70/90s. And if he *was* right, the implications were profoundly disturbing. Were the AR 70/90s still being manufactured? If so, by whom? Where was the production facility located? Europe? Asia? Was Eric Holtmeyer's claim to ownership of an international business empire legitimate? If so, the Force would need to hoe a fine line to avoid antagonizing a possible ally to the Freedom Federation.

"Which jeeps should we take?" Bear queried.

They had caught up with the rest.

"You must be hungry after your long flight," Holtmeyer declared. "I will have a smorgasbord prepared."

"Don't trouble yourself on our account," Blade said. "We have field rations."

"Why should you eat your miserable field rations when you can enjoy my hospitality?" Holtmeyer replied. "We must get off on the right foot if we're to have a long-term business association." He nodded at the Oriental, who immediately opened the limo's passenger-side rear door. Holtmeyer leaned inside, and when he straightened a moment later he was holding a cordless telephone in his left hand. He dialed a number and raised the phone to his left ear. "Varney? Yes, our guests have arrived. I want the table in the dining room set up. We'll be there—"

A tremendous din drowned out Holtmeyer's words as the Hurricanes rose from Deadhorse Airfield.

Blade gazed over his right shoulder, watching the sleek aircraft climb into the azure sky and bear to the south. When he shifted his attention forward again, he found that Holtmeyer had replaced the phone and was staring at the departing VTOLs with a barely perceptible frown.

"They were welcome to remain," their host remarked.

"They'll return in two days if I send them a coded message confirming everything is okay," Blade mentioned.

"Governor Melnick is a very cautious man," Holtmeyer commented.

"Which is why we were sent on ahead to inspect the site," Blade said. "Once we've verified the flow of crude, the governor will arrive for the negotiations."

"Does he mistrust everyone this way?"

"You must know how much the oil means to our Federation," Blade stated. "The governor must be certain before getting the hopes of the people up."

"I meant no offense," Holtmeyer said.

"None taken."

"Then let's drive to my lodge," Holtmeyer stated. "I'll see all of you there." He eased into the limo and smiled at them before sliding to the far side of the car.

Lalita entered, and the Oriental promptly closed the door and moved to the driver's door. He yanked the door wide and compressed his towering form behind the steering wheel.

Blade looked at each of his people. There were five jeeps

available, but he didn't want any of the Force members riding alone. "Buddy system," he announced. "Havoc and Athena. Bear, you'll ride with Boone and Thunder. Grizzly, you're with me. Take any jeep."

They complied.

Blade climbed into the closest jeep. The door was held open by the driver, one of Holtmeyer's soldiers. He sank into the confined rear seat and waited for Grizzly to do likewise.

In seconds the driver had the loud motor running, and in short order the caravan was en route to the lodge.

"How was your flight?" Blade asked, too low to be overheard.

Grizzly was slumped in the seat, his head shrouded by his parka hood, his hands in the pockets. "Just peachy," he replied morosely. An M-16 was slung over his left shoulder.

"Were you able to work anything out with Athena?"

"That's none of your buisness."

"I'm afraid it is," Blade countered. "I was hoping you would resolve this before we arrived. I need the two of you at peak efficiency during this mission."

"I'm at peak efficiency."

"I know better."

"Who appointed you as my mother?"

Blade leaned nearer the mutant. "Grizzly, I told you before and I'll tell you again. I can't allow the Force to be disrupted, especially not now. So either clear the air with Athena tonight, or forget the whole thing until after we return to California."

"I'll think about it."

"You'll *do* it," Blade commanded. He gazed out the window at the barren, snow-encased scenery. The roads were paved and had been plowed. At intervals they drove past various structures, most lacking identifying numbers or letters. He recalled the information General Gallagher had provided concerning the construction of the Prudhoe Bay complex. Huge, self-contained units, virtually cities unto themselves, had been airlifted by gigantic Hercules aircraft to the North Slope. These prefabricated units were then erected on gravel pads. There were living quarters, offices, eating areas, workshops, and more.

"I couldn't do it," Grizzly said softly.

Blade looked at him. "Do what?"

"Tell her how I feel. I tried. I really did. But I couldn't get a word out."

"Then put your feelings on the back burner until we're all safe and sound," Blade advised.

Grizzly simply nodded.

The Warrior looked at the driver, wondering if he could elicit any pertinent news. "Say, driver?"

"Yes, sir?" the trooper responded, glancing into the rearview mirror.

"Is it always this cold here?"

"Only in the winter."

"You've probably seen a lot of snow. How long have you been here?"

"I can't remember, sir."

"Where do you come from?" Blade probed.

"I've traveled all over, sir. I've been to so many places that I forget where I was last."

The Warrior smiled. "And I suppose you don't know how many people are stationed at Prudhoe Bay?"

"I certainly don't, sir."

"Ignorance is bliss," Blade cracked.

"Will there be any more questions, sir?" the driver queried politely.

"No. I got the message."

"Message, sir?"

"My compliments to your training officer. He's done a superb job," Blade said.

The driver grinned. "That would be Colonel Varney. You'll meet him at the lodge."

"I can hardly wait."

Grizzly looked at Blade and spoke in a hushed tone. "Do you want me to interrogate this turkey? I can make him talk."

He held his right hand up for emphasis.

"Not yet," Blade said.

"I hate these games," Grizzly muttered.

"We can't make any overt, hostile moves until we verify whether Holtmeyer is sincere," Blade stated.

"If he's sincere, I'm Little Bo Peep."

"You don't trust him?"

"My mutant senses are hyper-sharp. I can see and hear better than you humans. And I can also sense danger at times. I feel it coming before it hits." He paused. "I have this feeling the shit is really going to hit the fan here."

"First Thunder, and now you," Blade said.

"And you?"

"And me."

Grizzly chuckled.

"What's so funny?"

"This came at the perfect time. I'm in just the right mood to rip somebody to shreds. I'm not fussy. I don't care who it is. But I can't wait to sink my claws into something."

"You may get the chance sooner than you think."

CHAPTER SIX

Blade came to several conclusions during the drive from Deadhorse Airfield to Eric Holtmeyer's "lodge." First, Holtmeyer had spared no expense in repairing and activating the Prudhoe Bay oil-production facilities. Crews were everywhere, working industriously. The network of roads connecting the wells, pads, and centers had been repaved where necessary. Power was supplied by a fully restored Central Power Supply building. Plows and dump trucks were on hand to keep the Airfield and the roads free of the intermittent snow.

Second, Holtmeyer had a large private army at his disposal. The 48 soldiers at the Airfield were just the tip of the iceberg. Blade observed dozens more on the way to the lodge, some marching alongside the road, others patrolling the perimeters of the structures, and others in troop transports or jeeps, driving here and there.

Third, Blade began to seriously doubt that Holtmeyer was attempting to deceive Governor Melnick and the rest of the Federation. The man would not go to so much trouble to restore the Trans-Alaska Pipeline if he wasn't the bona-fide article. The cost of overhauling Prudhoe Bay must have cost millions, by any monetary standard.

Which presented a perplexing dilemma.

If Holtmeyer was legit, then why were the Force members so uneasy? Was their collective intuition wrong? Was there really a danger, or were they *wishing* there was a danger after so many months of stifling inactivity? Everything about Prudhoe Bay, from the repaired roads and remodeled buildings to the private army, strongly suggested Holtmeyer's proposal was genuine.

The only recourse was to wait and see.

After following the roads to the northeast, in the direction of the Bay, they came to the converted OPS Center, a huge edifice surrounded by a new chain-link fence topped by three strands of barbed wire. Ten troopers guarded the metal gate situated in the center of the western section. More guards, many with leashed dogs, Dobermans and German shepherds, patrolled the grounds. Four jeeps with swivel-mounted machine guns were parked in the large lot in front of the main structure, a three-story edifice.

On the outside, the lodge was no different from the other buildings, consisting of beige, prefabricated walls and a roof. Once the Force members were escorted inside by Holtmeyer's party, they entered a world of wealth and luxury.

"Wow! What a spread!" Bear said as they stood in the wide main corridor, after entering through double doors guarded by four soldiers.

"The governor's mansion isn't this opulent," Athena remarked.

Blade, standing at the head of his team, marveled at the thick gold carpet, the lustrous mahogany furniture, and the painted, gold walls adorned with works of art. He unzipped his parka.

Eric Holtmeyer, Lalita Pruty, and the Oriental stood a yard from the Warrior. Holtmeyer smiled at their comments and nodded at the corridor. "I believe a man's home should reflect his personality. My lodge reflects mine."

"You enjoy the finer things of life," Blade commented.

"Who doesn't?" Holtmeyer responded.

"Some people like a simpler existence," Blade said. "The love of their family, a roof over their head, and a full stomach is all they ask out of life."

"Fools," Holtmeyer declared. "I have no tolerance for simpletons. We are allotted a limited span on this planet, and we should make the most of our time. Those who settle for less are depriving themselves of the experience of knowing life to its fullest."

"I never thought of it that way," Blade admitted. "Are you a student of philosophy?"

"I dabble," Holtmeyer said. He motioned with a wave of his left hand. "Come. You must be famished."

"You can leave your weapons here, if you like" Lalita interjected.

"We'll hold onto them," Blade replied.

Lalita smiled, exposing her even, white teeth under those red lips. "Suit yourself. But you will not be harmed during your stay. I guarantee you."

"Thanks just the same."

Holtmeyer led them down the corridor for 15 yards, then he halted beside a brown door on the left.

The Oriental quickly shoved the door open.

"This way," Holtmeyer said, beckoning them to enter.

Blade advanced to the doorway and surveyed the chamber within. He expected a moderately sized room with a modest selection of food. Instead, he found an immense chamber containing an enormous mahogany table holding tray after tray of varied foodstuffs. The aroma was tantalizing and made his mouth water. There were trays of beef, turkey, and chicken. Trays of vegetables and fruits. Trays of bread and cakes. Enough to feed 50 people.

"Help yourselves," Holtmeyer said.

Blade walked to the right and stood behind a chair. Athena came in next and took the chair to his right, and so it went around the table, with Bear, Thunder, Boone, Sergeant Havoc, and Grizzly taking seats at every other chair, leaving gaps in case they should need to maneuver in an emergency.

Holtmeyer strolled in, noted their seating arrangement, and smiled at the Warrior. "Your caution is commendable, but your distrust is misplaced."

"Trust is like friendship," Blade responded. "Both must be earned."

"True," Holtmeyer conceded, moving to the head of the table. He waited for the Oriental to pull out the chair, then sat down. The Oriental took up a post on Holtmeyer's left, Lalita Pruty on the right.

"Won't you join us?" Blade asked her as he lowered himself down and leaned the M-60 against his right leg.

"She ate before you arrived," Hotlmeyer answered.

Blade swept the table with an appreciative glance. "Your cooks whipped this up on the spur of the moment for us?"

"We've been expecting you," Holtmeyer said. "They were instructed to have adequate snacks prepared beforehand. All I had to do was inform my aide-de-camp to have the table laid out once you arrived."

"You call all of this a snack?"

Holtmeyer grinned. "My philosophy encompasses the food I eat."

"Who's your aide-de-camp?" Blade inquired casually.

"I am," declared a newcomer, and a heavyset man in a white uniform stalked into the dining room. He was six feet tall, solidly built with square shoulders and a square chin. His eyebrows and crew-cut hair were both white. Gold insignia were affixed to his collar. Oddly enough, the man was not armed.

"Ahhhh. Colonel Varney," Holtmeyer said, twisting in his chair and smiling. "Please join us."

The colonel halted near the table, to Holtmeyer's right, beside Lalita.

"Pleased to meet you," Blade stated, rising and offering his right hand.

"Likewise," Colonel Varney said, taking the Warrior's hand in his own.

Blade's eyes narrowed slightly. The colonel's grip was an iron vise. He applied equal pressure and saw the corners of Varney's thin mouth curl upwards.

Colonel Varney nodded. "You're everything I expected."

"You know about me?"

"The colonel is my chief of intelligence," Eric Holtmeyer declared. "He ran background checks on all of you."

"All of us?" Blade said.

"Of course," Colonel Varney stated, and looked at Holtmeyer. "With your permission?"

Holtmeyer gave an imperious flip of his right hand.

"The exploits of the Force are quite well known," Colonel Varney mentioned. "Thanks to the stories written by Ms. Morris, the whole world is familiar with your previous assignments."

"The whole world?" Blade asked.

"You've read my reports?" Athena spoke up.

"As part of my background investigation," Colonel Varney said. "I know you were a journalist before signing on with the Freedom Force, and I know you still write columns detailing their exploits for the California papers. You're their press agent, so to speak. And you must be quite a lethal lady in your own right, or Blade wouldn't have accepted you on the Force."

"What do you know about me?" Blade inquired.

"Where should I begin? You're the head of the Warriors and the leader of the Force. You've beaten the Russians, the Technics, the Gild, the Superiors, the Vampires, and the Reptiloids, just to mention a few—"

"I had help," Blade said, interrupting, puzzled by Varney's detailed knowledge. True, Athena had chronicled their escapades for the media, but she had only written about the missions of the Force. He'd fought the Russians, the Technics, and the Superiors with his fellow Warriors. So how had Varney learned about those missions?

"You're too modest," Colonel Varney said. "In certain circles, you're viewed as one of the deadliest, the most dangerous of men."

"Dangerous to whom?"

Varney ignored the query. He looked at Athena. "Your association with the Force stems from the time they helped you revenge yourself on the Spider."

"I covered the Spider Strike in depth," Athena acknowledged.

Colonel Varney swiveled his gaze to Bear. "And you, sir, are the newest addition to the Force. I must admit I know very little about you, except for the fact you hail from the Clan."

"Blade and I go back a long way," Bear said.

"Really?"

"Yeah. I spent most of my life in a gang in the Twin Cities. Blade and some of the other Warriors saved hundreds of us from a life of sheer hell. I owe him. Anyone messes with my bro, they mess with me. Got it?"

Colonel Varney grinned. "I understand, and I admire your loyalty." He glanced at Thunder. "You, sir, must be the Flathead. Your people must view the war as a blessing."

"We are free again," Thunder replied. "We live in harmony with the Spirit-in-All-Things."

"Freedom is cherished above all else," Colonel Varney said. "But freedom is only maintained through vigilance. Your people are living in the same manner as their fore-fathers, I hear. Is that wise?"

"Wise?" Thunder repeated, baffled by the question.

"An agrarian lifestyle is no match for technological might," Colonel Varney said cryptically.

"Colonel Varney," Holtmeyer declared with a tinge of annoyance in his tone.

Varney tensed. "Sir?"

"Nothing. Continue the introductions."

Blade glanced from one to the other. What was that exchange all about? Varney had said something Holtmeyer didn't approve of, but what was the significance of Varney's remarks?

The colonel turned his attention to Boone. "Are you the Cavalryman?"

"Yep."

"The gunman on the Force," Varney said. "I'm told you're as good as the Family's gunfighter, the Warrior named Hickok."

Blade straightened. How did Varney know about Hickok?

"No one is as good as Hickok," Boone responded. "He's in a class by himself."

"You belittle yourself, sir."

"I tell it like it is."

Colonel Varney gazed at Sergeant Havoc and grinned. "Ahhhh. Havoc. I've looked forward to meeting you. The papers claim you're the best man in the California military."

"Athena likes to exaggerate."

"Athena perhaps. But General Miles Gallagher was quoted as saying you're the best damn soldier he's ever known. Did he exaggerate also?"

"You know how officers are, sir," Havoc said wryly.

Colonel Varney laughed and nodded. "Spoken like a true grunt. You're a qualified marksman, I believe, and you're skilled in the martial arts."

"I've kicked a few butts, sir."

Blade was surprised to see the Oriental display a hint of a reaction to the conversation. Until now, the man in black hadn't budged a muscle. He stood next to Holtmeyer as if he were chiseled from stone. But when Varney mentioned the martial arts, the Oriental's eyes flicked briefly to Sergeant Havoc, then focused straight ahead.

"I too enjoy the martial arts," Colonel Varney said. "I'm not the equal of my esteemed associate from the East, but I have my moments." He stared at Grizzly, who was slouched in his chair. "And you're the famous mutant."

"What of it, pal?" Grizzly responded testily.

"The newspaper accounts refer to claws you possess. I'd like to see them."

"If you ever do, they'll be the last thing you see."

"You won't show me?"

"I don't like being treated like a freak," Grizzly stated.

"I meant no insult."

"None taken."

Blade looked at Holtmeyer. "Apparently, you know a great deal about us, but we know next to nothing about you, about your staff."

"How remiss of me," Holtmeyer remarked. He nodded at the officer. "Colonel Varney has been with me for ten years. He has extensive combat experience, and his record is flawless."

"Where did you obtain your prior experience?" Blade asked the officer.

"Colonel Varney has plied his trade on every continent," Holtmeyer answered. "Europe. Asia. Africa. You name it, he's been there."

"I'd like to hear more about the conditions overseas," Blade said. "The Federation knows very little concerning the status of the rest of the world."

"I'll gladly fill you in later," Holtmeyer stated, "but generally speaking, the rest of the world is no different than North America. World War Three caused global chaos. None of the major governments survived intact. And now different groups are struggling to achieve dominance."

"What groups?"

"You are aware of several of them. The Technics, the Superiors, the New Order of Mutants. There are many others."

"Are you aligned with any of them?"

Holtmeyer averted his eyes for a second, then smiled warmly. "I work for myself." He swiveled in his chair and indicated Lalita Pruty with a nod. "Ms. Purty is an administrator *par excellence*. She has a knack for handling complicated business arrangements with consummate ease."

Blade glanced at the Oriental. "Does he help her count with his toes?"

"No," Holtmeyer said with a smile. "Allow me to

introduce my bodyguard and manservant, Kan Tang. He never leaves my side.''

"Doesn't it get crowded in the shower?" Blade quipped.

Holtmeyer grinned. "Tang is a Thai. I discovered him in Kamphaeng Phet, in western Thailand.''

"Discovered him?''

"Tang is, without a doubt, the best martial artist alive,'' Holtmeyer boasted.

Sergeant Havoc made a snorting sound.

"I first saw him at a muay thai match. Are you familiar with the techniques they use?''

"No,'' Blade confessed. He had studied the martial arts under the skillful tutelage of a Family Elder. While he was adept at dealing death with his hands and feet, he wasn't the top martial artist in the Family. That honor went to another Warrior, Rikki-Tikki-Tavi.

"Muay thai is the Thai style of boxing,'' Holtmeyer was saying. "As we both know, there are dozens of styles of disciplines in the martial arts. Karate, kung fu, judo, savate, and many, many more. Muay thai employs elements common to all styles: kicks, punches, elbow and knee blows, handsword strikes, and others. Practitioners of muay thai specialize in one type of kick, which they call the heavy round kick. It is virtually unstoppable.''

Again Sergeant Havoc snorted.

"Tang has attained the highest rank in muay thai,'' Holtmeyer disclosed. "His entire body is a lethal weapon. Here. Let me show you.'' Holtmeyer looked at Tang and spoke a few words in an unfamiliar tongue.

"You speak the Thai language?'' Blade asked.

"I speak eleven languages,'' Holtmeyer replied. He addressed Tang again.

The Thai stepped to the table and held his hands out, palms down.

"Take a close look at his hands,'' Holtmeyer told the Warrior. "Go ahead.''

Blade leaned over and inspected Tang's hands. Close up,

they were even more extraordinary. The bottom edge of each hand consisted of a half-inch of solid callous. Each knuckle was a bony protuberance an inch in width. And every finger resembled a miniature club. Blade had never seen the like.

"His feet are the same way," Holtmeyer said proudly. "All bone and callous. He can break ten cement blocks with one blow."

"Big deal," Havoc muttered.

"Permit me to indulge in a demonstration," Holtmeyer stated, gazing at the nearest empty chair on his left. He spoke in Thai.

Kan Tang glided around his employer and moved behind the empty chair. He waited, his arms at his sides, his features inscrutable.

Blade watched with keen interest. The mahogany chair was extremely sturdy, with stout arms and a rear panel three-quarters of an inch thick. Mahogany was an exceptionally hard, reddish-brown wood. Breaking any part of the chair would not be easy.

Or so he thought.

Eric Holtmeyer barked a one word command in Thai.

Tang nodded, took a step backwards, and kicked with his right leg. The motion was a blur. His right foot smashed into the rear panel with a resounding crash, and splinters and fragments of wood flew across the table. He stood straight, breathing evenly, awaiting the next order. The panel was demolished.

"What do you think?" Holtmeyer asked the Warrior.

"I know who to see if I want firewood chopped," Blade responded.

"With all due respect, sir," Sergeant Havoc declared, "anyone can go around breaking chairs."

"Would you care to give it a try, Sergeant?" Holtmeyer inquired.

Sergeant Havoc glanced at Blade.

"Be my guest," Blade said.

Havoc smiled and rose. He removed his backpack and set

it on the floor, then stripped off his parka and draped the coat over his chair. He stepped behind the empty chair between Grizzly and his.

Eric Holtmeyer placed his elbows on the edge of the table and scrutinized the noncom intently.

Blade noticed that Tang was also engrossed in Havoc's performance.

"Show these bozos how it's done," Bear urged.

Sergeant Havoc dropped into a horse stance, his fists tucked at waist height, his face a study in determination. He inhaled and exhaled slowly, focusing on the center of the rear panel. With a piercing kiai, he delivered a hammer blow to the middle of the chair. A loud crack sounded, and the rear panel split and buckled inward. Havoc straightened and stared at the Thai.

Kan Tang gave a slight bow.

Havoc returned the honor.

"My compliments, Sergeant," Holtmeyer said. "Tang seldom accords another martial artist the bow of respect. Perhaps one day the two of you will engage in a friendly contest to test your mettle."

"I'd like that," Sergeant Havoc replied.

"Well, now that the entertainment is done with, why don't we enjoy our meal?" Holtmeyer suggested cordially. "There's plenty for every—"

Holtmeyer's statement was abruptly interrupted by the blaring of a strident siren.

"What's happening?" Athena asked anxiously.

Holtmeyer stood and started from the dining room. "The lodge perimeter has been breached. You can stay or come. It's up to you." He hastened out with Tang, Lalita, and Colonel Varney in tow.

"Let's see what's going on," Blade directed.

The Force members hurried from the chamber.

All except for Grizzly. He loitered near the head of the table, waiting for the rest to leave. Once he was alone, he faced Holtmeyer's chair and extended his fingers, enabling his five-inch claws to slide from their internal sheaths. He glanced at the doorway, double-checking, then raised both arms above his head. His hands streaked downward, his claws flashing from the top of the chair to the bottom of the rear panel. Without bothering to examine his handiwork, he turned and ran out.

A moment later the back of the mahogany chair fell to pieces.

CHAPTER SEVEN

Eric Holtmeyer sprinted down the wide corridor to the left, heading away from the front entrance. He covered 40 feet and barged through a set of double doors on the right with Tang beside him and Colonel Varney and Lalita Pruty right behind.

Blade and the Force members followed moments later.

The Warrior halted just inside the large room, amazed at the array of sophisticated electronic equipment lining three walls and filling most of the floor space. Narrow aisles permitted passage among the computer banks, monitoring terminals, consoles, and diverse apparatus. Rows of 24-inch video screens lined three walls, each displaying a separate outdoor scene, some showing the perimeter fence, others depicting roads and various buildings. Dozens of technicians, each in a white smock, manned the equipment. Occupying the middle of the chamber was a command console on an elevated platform, five feet above the floor.

Holtmeyer and his entourage dashed up a short flight of steps to the platform.

Blade glanced at the third wall, in reality an enormous, tinted window. Beyond was the front of the estate and a flurry of activity. Soldiers were jogging in the direction of the fence, many with dogs straining at the leash. Two of the jeeps outfitted with machine guns were roaring toward the gate. Small red lights, affixed to the top of the fence at 30-foot intervals, were flashing.

"It looks like they're under attack," Athena remarked.

Blade moved closer to the platform.

Seated at the sole seat in front of the command console, Holtmeyer was flicking toggles and pressing buttons while looking repeatedly at the video displays. "Where are they?" he bellowed. "Where the hell are they?"

"They breached the north fence," a technician sitting at a computer terminal to the right of the platform replied. "Six HS and two K-9s reported down, sir."

"Where are they *now*?" Holtmeyer snapped.

"Unknown, sir," the technician responded.

"What about the heat sensors?" Holtmeyer asked, staring at a technician to his left.

"No readings, sir," the man answered. "They must have sounded."

Colonel Varney moved to a monitor on Holtmeyer's right and studied the screen.

"Initial readings indicate four," the technician on the left announced.

"Four? We've never had four before," Holtmeyer said. He gazed out the window, scanning the field of snow between the lodge and the fence.

"All HS are deployed," Colonel Varney declared. "K-9s are scouring the area."

"Where *are* they?" Holtmeyer queried yet again.

Blade walked to the base of the steps. "Do you mind if I ask what's going on?"

"Not at all," Holtmeyer said, and beckoned the Warrior onto the platform.

"Keep your weapons ready," Blade instructed his squad, then ascended to Holtmeyer's side.

"This happens at least once a month," Holtmeyer stated.

"What's happening? What's out there?" Blade inquired.

"You're familiar, of course, with the proliferation of mutants since the war," Holtmeyer commented.

"Who isn't?" Blade mentioned.

"Have you ever encountered a snow shrew?"

"Can't say as I have."

"Well, you're about to witness four of the reasons I was compelled to double the size of my HS staff above my early projections," Holtmeyer said.

"Your HS staff?"

"Oh. Sorry. HS is our in-house abbreviation for Holtmeyer Security, the branch of Holtmeyer Industries International responsible for all internal policing functions and external-threat eradication. Colonel Varney is their commander."

Blade's forehead creased. External-threat eradiction? Translation: hired killers.

"To be quite honest, I never expected to find so many mutants this far north," Holtmeyer went on. "I should have known better. Increasing my HS contingent to provide effective security for Prudhoe Bay almost doubled the budgetary allotment I initially calculated. Excuse me, Lalita initially calculated."

Blade gazed at the window. "So what are snow shrews?"

"What do you know about shrews in general?" Holtmeyer rejoined.

"They're small. They look like mice with teeth. And they must eat twice their body weight every day or they'll die."

"Not bad. Yes, an ordinary shrew is no more than seven or eight inches long with a pointed snout, razor-sharp teeth, and five claws on all four feet. And yes, they're fierce, hyperactive hunters. Their metabolism is such that they have to feed at least every three hours, night and day. They'll eat anything they can kill, and in a frenzy they'll kill more than they can eat." He paused and scrutinized the video screens on the right-hand wall. "The snow shrews are a mutation, possibly of the common arctic shrew. Imagine a shrew about two feet high and a yard long, weighing close to one hundred pounds, and you have an idea of what we're up against."

"One hundred pounds?"

"And that's not all. These things can burrow through snow and dirt with the same ease you and I would swim through water. They're fast and deadly. I can't believe they mutated from the arctic shrew."

"Why?"

"Because the arctic shrew is a docile little animal. But my scientists claim the radiation altered the species' gene transmission and deranged their embryonic development. I'm not a scientific expert. If my scientists say it could happen, then it could happen. All that matters to me is the cost to my operation."

Blade stared through the window at a jeep patrolling the drive, coming from the front gate toward the headquarters building. "I didn't notice this window when we arrived," he mentioned.

"The window is composed of shatterproof, one-way glass," Holtmeyer said. "On the outside, it looks just like part of the wall."

"I'm getting a reading!" the technician on the left cried. "Two targets twenty feet inside the fence, approximately forty-five yards south of the gate. Depth, ten feet."

"There are heat sensors implanted in the ground along the fence and under the snow between the fence and the lodge," Holtmeyer explained to the Warrior.

"I don't understand why you call this a lodge," Blade said idly, focusing on the general vicinity of the targets.

"Remind me to show you our game room," Holtmeyer replied.

"The targets are rising," the technician declared. "Eight feet. Six."

Blade saw an HS patrol near the spot, six men and a Doberman strung out in a skirmish line, the trooper with the Doberman ahead of the others. The second soldier in the line carried a walkie-talkie.

Colonel Varney grabbed a small microphone from the console. "Sergeant Fifer, two targets are about eight feet from you, to the south. Do you copy?"

"Copy, sir," came the reply from a square speaker near the officer's left elbow.

"Four feet and still rising," the technician announced.

"They're four feet under and climbing," Colonel Varney relayed the information to the sergeant.

"Copy."

Blade observed the patrol halt. Two of the men held machine guns, the rest AR 70/90s. The Doberman appeared to be going crazy, snarling and pulling on its leash.

"Do you hear anything?" Colonel Varney inquired urgently.

"Not yet, sir," Sergent Fifer responded.

Holtmeyer looked at the tech manning the heat-sensor station. "Where are the other two targets?"

The tech studied a green screen covered with a grid of lines and numbers. "They don't register, sir. They may be below sensing range."

"Give a yell the second you see something," Holtmeyer ordered.

"Yes, sir," the tech said, peering at the grid. "The first pair have stablized at two feet under and six feet from our patrol."

"They're stationary," Colonel Varney said into the mike.

"Copy, sir."

The tech stiffened. "Targets are moving again! They're attacking!"

"They're attacking!" Colonel Varney warned.

Enthralled, Blade watched as a pair of mounds materialized in the snow six feet from the HS patrol. The mounds surged toward the soldiers and the dog, each mound trailing a rippling ridge of snow as the shrew underneath burrowed at its prey.

"Look out!" Colonel Varney shouted.

The soldiers began firing into the mounds, and Blade could hear the muffled, metallic chatter of their weapons through the tinted glass. Both mounds disappeared as the shrews submerged.

"They're descending—" the tech said. "No! They're rising again!"

This time the shrews came up directly under their victims. Two of the soldiers suddenly started sinking into the snow as their legs were gripped by poweful claws. Their fellow troopers tried to aid them, but the two were sucked from sight before their companions could help.

"Damn!" Varney fumed.

"Any sign of the other shrews?" Holtmeyer queried impatiently.

"Not yet, sir," the tech answered.

The drama outside was still unfolding. Apparently not satisfied with their catch, the mutants were coming back for more. A mound crested within two yards of the trooper and the Doberman and bore down on them. The soldier released the dog, and the trained canine leaped onto the mound and commenced digging frantically. A dark form broke from the snow, its front claws slashing, and the Doberman was hurled aside, a ripped, shredded carcass. One of the HS men snapped off a few rounds, but the dark form was already sinking from sight.

"Code 99," Colonel Varney directed. "Code 99 forty yards south of the gate. All perimeter personnel will respond immediately. Repeat. Forty yards south of the gate."

Troopers and dogs were converging on the scene on the double. One of the jeeps was slewing through the white powder at a reckless clip.

"The first pair are ten feet down and not moving," the heat sensor technican said.

"They're probably feasting," Holtmeyer remarked.

The tech leaned closer to the grid. "Two new targets, sir!"

"Where?" Holtmeyer inquired.

"It can't be," the tech responded in astonishment.

Holtmeyer rose, his face livid. "Where are they?"

The tech looked at the floor. "They're under us!"

"Can they get in here?" Blade asked.

"Our floor is solid concrete," Holtmeyer disclosed. "They can't burrow their way through cement."

"They're in motion," the technician stated. "Heading for the east side of the building, seven feet down. The readings are faint and fluctuating because of all the structural mass."

"Look!" Colonel Varney exclaimed, pointing at a video monitor on the left-hand wall.

Blade swiveled. The officer was pointing at a monitor showing four HS troopers walking toward a closed door positioned five yards to the right of the surveillance camera.

"Warn them," Holtmeyer said.

"They don't have a radio with them," Colonel Varney replied.

"Where are they?" Blade inquired, puzzled by Holtmeyer's and Varney's obvious concern.

"On the east side of this building," Varney answered.

"Sir! The targets have increased speed," the tech informed them.

Holtmeyer looked at the colonel. "Get our internal people there now."

"Attention all lodge security," Varney said, the mike an inch from his mouth. "Code 99 at rear door number seven. Repeat. Code 99 at rear door number seven."

Code 99, Blade deduced, must be the HS code word for a critical situation requiring an immediate response.

The four troopers were within ten feet of the rear door.

"I've lost the targets," the tech declared.

Eric Holtmeyer pounded the console in frustration. "No!"

One of the troopers was suddenly pulled under the snow, vanishing in the blink of an eye. The remaining three gawked at the spot where he had stood, then opened fire wildly with their automatic rifles. A second HS man was yanked beneath the powder. He dropped his weapon and tried to grab the legs of his nearest companion, but he slipped from sight, thrashing and screaming, before he could get a grip.

"How can the snow shrews dig so fast?" Blade queried, astounded at the rapidity with which the mutants could strike.

Holtmeyer was watching the final two troopers as they

blasted indiscriminately at the ground. "The fools. They should head inside." He paused. "My scientists told me that a common shrew can burrow at the rate of a foot and a half per minute. Moles, which are only a bit bigger, are even faster. They can cover a foot a minute. And those are the little buggers. These things are huge."

On the screen, a third soldier was sucked under. The fourth bolted for the door and was able to clutch the knob. He tugged the door open, twisting to glance over his left shoulder, and in so doing he tripped over his own feet and sprawled forward, onto the corridor floor, his legs protruding through the doorway, the door swinging all the way out.

"Close the door!" Holtmeyer shouted at the monitor.

The HS soldier tried. He rose to his knees and lunged for the doorknob, but a pair of brown, hairy forms broke the surface and pounced in concert, bowling the trooper over, and all three passed beyond the surveillance camera's range as the soldier was borne into the hall.

"Damn. They're inside," Colonel Varney stated.

"Heat-sensor readings?" Holtmeyer demanded.

"We can't pick them up inside the building," the tech said.

Holtmeyer glanced at the colonel. "I want you to lead the search-and-destroy squads. Get going."

Varney nodded and hurried from the room.

"Have you ever had a snow shrew inside before?" Blade questioned.

"No," Holtmeyer said. "But my men will find the creatures. There's no danger to us, I assure you."

Just then a technician entered the Command Center, and as he pushed the double doors inward, from the bowels of the building wafted a piercing, terrified shriek.

CHAPTER EIGHT

All activity in the room was suspended as the scream drowned out the subdued conversation, the humming of the computers and the terminals, and the clicking and clattering of the banks of diverse equipment.

"Close those doors!" Holtmeyer thundered.

The tech in the doorway stepped inside quickly and sheepishly hastened to his post.

"We can help," Blade offered.

"No," Holtmeyer responded.

"We're trained to handle situations like this," Blade noted. "Allow us to assist your security people."

"I wouldn't think of it," Holtmeyer said. "You're official representatives of the Federation, here at my request. I would be remiss in my duties if I exposed you to peril."

"As you wish," Blade said.

"Sir, the pair outside are on the move again," the heat-sensor technician interjected.

"Which way are they heading?"

"Toward the fence."

"Then we can forget about them for the time being," Holtmeyer said. "Try to isolate the location of the pair in the building."

"But we can't—" the tech began.

"Never use the word *can't*," Holtmeyer declared. "If you think negative thoughts, if you use negative words, you'll inevitably fail to achieve positive results. Repeat after me. I know I can. I know I can."

"I know I can?" the technician said.

"There. Remember my advice every time you're presented with a difficult task," Holtmeyer commented courteously. He leaned on the console and raised his voice. "Now locate those mutants or you'll regret the day you were born!"

"I would if I could, sir," the tech responded stubbornly. "But the heat sensors won't register life-forms inside the building."

Holtmeyer was livid. "You *dare* talk back to me?"

"He has a point, Eric," Lalita Pruty stated sharply. "The heat sensors won't pick up the shrews while they're inside."

To Blade's surprise, Holtmeyer abruptly composed himself.

"If they won't, they won't," Eric said. "Our HS will find them."

The square speaker on the console crackled. "This is Varney. I'm with a squad scouring the bottom floor. There are squads on the second and third floors too. So far, no sign of the shrews. They could be anywhere. This place has so many damn halls."

Lalita picked up the small microphone. "Acknowledged, Colonel Varney. Keep us posted."

"At least you can understand why my security costs on this project are so astronomical," Holtmeyer mentioned. "The total cost of repairing the Pipeline and activating Prudhoe Bay runs in the millions of dollars. My asking price for delivering the crude is justified."

"Why did you specify gold?" Blade quizzed.

"Gold has served as a precious commodity for millenniums. Amass gold, Blade, and you amass power. And power rules the world."

"Our Family Elders teach that love rules the world."

Holtmeyer threw back his head and laughed, then looked at the Warrior and did a double take. "You're serious, aren't you?"

"Yes."

"Incredible," Holtmeyer said, cocking his head to the right and studying the giant the way someone might inspect a new form of mutant. "I'm amazed that someone with your reputation belives in such an infantile philosophy."

"What's infantile about it?"

"Everything. You're denying reality if you truly swallow such a fallacy. Take a good look at the state of the world. Love is hardly the dominating factor."

"It is," Blade disagreed, "and you just don't see it."

"You're talking in riddles," Holtmeyer stated. "Elaborate."

The speaker blared to life again.

"Command Center! Command Center!"

Lalita was still holding the microphone. She pressed a button on the console. "This is Command. Calm down. Who is this?"

"Captain Emba, Exalted One."

Lalita Pruty scowled. "This is *Pruty,* Captain Emba. Do you copy?"

There was a momentary pause. "Yes, Ms. Pruty. Sorry."

"Report," Pruty directed.

"I'm on the second floor, in hall fourteen. My squad was just attacked by a shrew."

"Losses?"

"One man was killed."

"Where is the shrew now? Did you kill it?" Lalita inquired.

"Negative. It went back into the vent."

"The vent?"

"It came out of a ventilation vent, grabbed Private Grissom, and dragged him in. We tried to nail it, but it's long gone."

"Continue your sweep," Lalita instructed.

"Roger."

"How did they get into the ventilation system?" Holtmeyer asked.

"I don't know," Lalita said. "Maybe they found an open shaft Maintenance was working on. They now have access to every room in the building."

"Can we send men into the shaft after them?" Holtmeyer wanted to know.

"No. The ventilation shafts must resemble the tunnels the shrews use. They're at home there. They have the advantage. A man would be cramped inside a shaft, and wouldn't be able to employ his weapons effectively," Lalita said, and paused. "We must draw the shrews out into the open."

"Any ideas on how?" Holtmeyer queried.

Lalita smirked. "We could use you as bait, *sir*."

"Very funny," Holtmeyer muttered.

"Could you post a squad at every vent in the building?" Blade proposed.

"I wish we could," Lalita said. "But you've seen the size of our headquarters, and there are vents in every room."

"We made a major mistake when we revamped and enlarged this building," Holtmeyer said. "We should have installed cameras inside to monitor the halls. If we hadn't already spent so much money—"

"My offer for the Force still holds," Blade commented.

"And my refusal still stands," Holtmeyer replied. "I can't allow any of you to be harmed. The Federation might look unfavorably on my request to supply oil if their representatives were harmed." He stared at the Warrior. "It's bad enough that Governor Melnick sent you instead of coming in person, although I can understand his reluctance to commit himself until he's satisfied that his negotiating party will be safe."

More shots blasted, closer this time.

"At least allow us to guard the doors to the command center," Blade proposed. "You wouldn't want one of those things to get in here." He noticed Lalita Pruty nod.

Holtmeyer mulled the matter for a bit. "Okay. Thanks. I won't need to recall some of my own men to cover the doors. But stay alert."

"I doubt any of us would want to take a nap right about now," Blade quipped. He turned and moved to his team.

"What's up, bro?" Bear inquired.

"How much longer are we going to stand around twiddling our thumbs?" Boone asked.

"Into the corridor," Blade ordered. "I'll explain there."

They tramped through the double doors and clustered about the giant.

"So what gives?" Bear persisted.

Blade glanced both ways to ensure they were temporarily alone. "I told our host we'd guard these doors," he informed them.

"Makes sense to me," Bear said. "Those shrews will probably start attackin' the doors as soon as they run out of people."

"I want Thunder, Athena, Havoc, and Bear to stay put. Grizzly and Boone will come with me."

"What? Why can't we all go?" Athena demanded.

"Someone has to guard the doors," Blade said. "And I want you to slow our host down if he tries to stop us."

"Stop us from what?" Boone inquired.

"You'll take this floor," Blade instructed him. "Grizzly, take the second. I'll go up to the third. Go from door to door, opening every one you find. Make a note of what you see, and we'll compare notes later."

"Hey," Bear commented. "How do you want us to slow Holt-face down? Shove a barrel up his nose?"

"Talk him to death," Blade said. "Just buy us as many seconds as you can. He may be so engrossed with the hunt for the shrews that he might not notice we're gone for a few minutes. I want to know what's in this building from top to bottom."

"Talk him to death, huh?" Bear responded. "Athena will have to handle that."

"Why me?" Athena queried.

"You're a woman, ain't you?"

"What, exactly, is that supposed to mean?" she retorted testily.

"This is our cue," Blade said, nodding at Boone and Grizzly. He jogged deeper along the wide corridor.

"How will we get upstairs?" Grizzly asked.

"Find a stairway or an elevator," Blade said. "There has to be a way."

A shut door appeared on the left.

"Catch you later," Boone said, angling to the door and gripping the knob.

"Be careful," Blade advised.

Boone opened the door and slid inside.

"Holtmeyer will want your hide for this," Grizzly predicted, keeping pace with the Warrior.

"Maybe," Blade said. "But I doubt he'll retaliate in any way. If something happens to us, he knows his deal with the Federation will be on the skids."

They dashed past several closed doors and reached a brown one at the end of the corridor. Without hesitating, Blade twisted the metal knob and flung the door inward.

"A stairwell," Grizzly declared.

Blade led the way upward, taking three steps at a stride. They reached the second-floor landing without bumping into an HS patrol.

"Here's where I get off," Grizzly said, and moved to the door.

"Watch your back," Blade stated, and continued his ascent. He bounded up the stairs to the third floor and entered a hall. The lighting was dimmer than on the first floor, and after the hustle and bustle of the command center, this floor was strangely quiet. Midway along the hallway was an open door, but no security personnel were in evidence.

Perfect.

Blade hurried to the first door on the right and opened it. Within was a small storage closet crammed with cleaning supplies. He closed the door and advanced to the next, which turned out to be filled with white uniforms hanging on a series of metal rods.

What was this?

Was the third floor reserved for storage purposes?

He took three strides and halted at a junction. A narrower hall forked to the right and the left, and he decided to investigate both forks if he had the time. Holding the M-60 in his left hand, he walked to a door on the right and grasped the knob.

Something growled.

Blade tensed and spun, bringing the M-60 up, his finger on the trigger.

The growl was repeated, emanating from the room with the open door farther down the hall.

He eased toward the door, his senses primed, striving to catch the faintest noise. A muted cracking sound arose. With supreme caution, he stepped to the edge of the doorway and halted, girding himself. Be calm, his mind urged. Exercise self-control. The snow shrews were fast, and their claws and teeth were deadly, but they were nothing more than mutations, deviate animals. They could be slain.

The cracking was louder.

Blade took a breath and whirled into the doorway, leveling the M-60, prepared for anything.

Or so he thought.

The spacious room contained row after row of file cabinets, all a dull, metallic gray. There were also ten dead troopers, their milky uniforms spattered with blood, sprawled in the aisles between the cabinets, some of which had toppled onto corpses. On the far side of the file room, in the center of the wall near the ceiling, was an open ventilation shaft. The grill was lying on a cabinet underneath. And perched on top of the third row from the left, busily gnawing on a human arm, its body to the door, was a snow shrew, a hideous, furry beast.

Blade took a pace nearer for a clearer shot, and as his left foot came down, his heel contacted a slippery substance on the tiled floor.

Blood.

His heel produced a faint squishing sound.

With astounding swiftness, uttering a viperous hiss as it released the partially clothed arm, the shrew twirled and charged.

CHAPTER NINE

Athena Morris gazed down the corridor and frowned. "They're taking too long."

"They've only been gone five minutes," Sergeant Havoc said.

"Yeah. Unwind, sugar lips," Bear added. "They'll be fine. Those three can take care of themselves like nobody's business."

"I know they can," Athena responded. "And don't call me sugar lips."

"How about hot-to-trot?" Bear quipped.

"How about if you suck on my M-16 while I squeeze the trigger?" Athena countered.

Bear laughed. "You're one mean momma, foxy. I'll grant you that. Grizzly and you will make a righteous pair."

Athena did a double take. "Grizzly and me?"

"Yeah. It's as plain as the nose on your face that the two of you are havin' a lovers' spat."

"Uh-oh," Sergeant Havoc mumbled.

Athena stepped in front of Bear. "What the hell are you babbling about?"

"I saw the way you two were actin' on the flight here,"

Bear mentioned.

"Meaning what?"

"Meanin' the two of you are close to gettin' tight."

"Are you implying what I think you're implying?"

"I ain't implyin' dog dip. I'm tellin' it like it is," Bear said.

"For your information, Grizzly and I are friends. At least we were."

"Yeah. Sure. Right."

"Are you saying I'm lying?" Athena demanded.

"You're callin' it like you see it," Bear replied.

"Exactly."

"Which may not be the way it is."

"Make sense," Athena stated, her tone tinged with annoyance.

"Do you want it straight out?" Bear asked.

"That would be nice."

"Grizzly and you are in love," Bear declared.

Sergeant Havoc and Thunder focused on Athena, assessing her reaction.

For several seconds Athena appeared stunned, and finally she gave a brittle sort of snicker and shook her head. "Where did you ever get a crazy idea like that?"

"It's the truth, and you know it."

"I know nothing of the kind," Athena insisted. "The idea is ridiculous."

"For a journalist lady, you have a hard time acceptin' the truth," Bear said.

"Grizzly and I in love?" Athena queried, and chuckled. "In case you haven't noticed, Grizzly is a mutant."

"So?"

"So I'm a human."

"So?"

"So mutants and humans do not fall in love."

"Says who?"

"What?"

"Who says humans and muties can't fall in love?" Bear inquired earnestly.

Athena glanced at Thunder and Havoc. "Do you believe this big dummy?"

Neither responded.

"Have you ever heard such a preposterous notion in your entire life?" Athena asked, prompting them.

"Love is not preposterous," Thunder asserted.

"Oh. Great. Thanks, Blade, Junior," Athena said.

"Why do you deny your feelings?" Thunder queried.

"You too?" Athena responded, and looked at Havoc. "What about you? Don't tell me you subscribe to this nonsense?"

The noncom pursed his lips and gazed at Bear, then Thunder. "They may have a point."

"What a bunch of morons," Athena snapped.

"Now that they mention it, there could be a connection to Grizzly's behavior recently," Sergeant Havoc elaborated.

"How so?"

"Didn't he start acting up about the same time you took to dating?" Havoc asked.

Athena recoiled at the implication. "Yeah. So what? Are you saying there was more to our relationship than friendship?"

"Could be," Havoc said simply.

"You're nuts. All of you."

"You could do worse," Bear commented.

Athena glanced at the Clansman.

"Grizzly might be a fur ball," Bear noted, "but he's got soul."

"And we have company," Thunder announced.

A door 15 yards from the end of the corridor opened, disgorging Colonel Varney and ten HS men.

"Play it cool," Bear advised, staring nonchalantly at the opposite wall.

Varney and the troopers hastened toward the command center.

"The colonel doesn't look very happy," Athena remarked.

"Remember, we've got to buy Blade time," Bear said.

"Stall. And no matter what, we can't blow any of these dudes away."

"Who died and left you in charge?" Sergeant Havoc joked.

"We can't start wastin' these suckers until Blade gives the go-ahead," Bear replied. "You know that. So we hang loose until he gets back. Do like I do. Be calm and collected."

Colonel Varney and company were ten yards distant.

"And if this bozo tries to ask us questions, act dumb," Bear suggested.

"This should be right up your alley," Athena said.

"What are you doing in the hall?" Varney called out.

"Hi," Bear responded, giving a wave of his left hand. "How's it hangin'?"

Colonel Varney came within seven yards of the Force members. "What are you doing out here?" he repeated.

"Gettin' some fresh air," Bear said.

"In the corridor?"

"We didn't want to stray too far," Athena said.

Colonel Varney looked from one to the other. "Three of you are missing. Where's Blade, Grizzly, and Boone?"

"They needed to use the rest room, sir," Sergeant Havoc answered politely.

"Does Mr. Holtmeyer know you're here?" Colonel Varney asked.

"He was the one who sent us out," Athena replied.

"But the nearest rest room is inside the command center," Varney mentioned. "For your own safety, don't budge." He moved toward the double doors.

"Our own safety?" Athena inquired.

"The shrews haven't been found yet," Colonel Varney said. "So for your own safety, don't go anywhere. My men will protect you."

"We don't need protectin'," Bear observed.

"You've never fought snow shrews, have you?" Varney asked.

"No," Bear responded.

"Let me assure you that there's safety in numbers,"

Colonel Varney said. "You're better off with my men." He turned the knob and stepped inside.

Athena smiled at the ten soldiers.

One of them, a hefty man with a Beretta, returned the smile. "Hi, there."

"Hello," she said.

The HS man glanced at Bear and Thunder, then gazed at Athena. "What's a classy broad like you doing with a mangy outfit like the Force?"

"Mangy?" Athena said.

"Yeah. How can you work with so many lowlifes?"

"Lester, you'd better lighten up," a second trooper cautioned. "The colonel won't like this."

"Who's going to rat on me?" Lester demanded. "You?"

The second trooper shook his head.

"Then clam up," Lester said.

Sergeant Havoc took a step toward the hefty trooper. "Did you just call us lowlifes?"

"Not you," Lester responded. "I was referring to the dirt bags you're with."

"We aren't dirt bags," Thunder stated.

"You sure are, Indian," Lester said contemptuously. "You and the Tar Baby."

"The Tar Baby?" Thunder repeated, perplexed.

"Yeah," Lester declared, motioning the Beretta at Bear. "The nigger there."

Bear shot him.

One moment Lester was smirking at the Force, and the next a round from Bear's M-16 penetrated his forehead and burst out the rear of his cranium, flinging him into the far wall and spattering his brains and blood over the gold paint and the gold carpet.

The shot triggered a general melee.

Four of the ten troopers automatically raised their weapons, but as fast as they were, Sergeant Havoc was faster. He shot each of them in turn, downing each soldier as the HS man attempted to bring a Beretta into play.

Galvanized to action by the death of their comrades, the remaining six endeavored to join the fray and were summarily dispatched. Not one got off a shot. Athena, Thunder, and Bear sprayed the troopers with fire, causing the men in white to totter backwards, thrashing and convulsing, and to collapse in perforated heaps.

"We've got to get out of here!" Sergeant Havoc cried, heading for the rear end of the hall and the doorway Blade and Grizzly had taken. What else could they do? Behind them was the command center. To the left were the double doors guarded by four troopers outside.

Veering to the right was their only option.

But not for long.

They were 15 yards from the dead troopers when the rear door opened suddenly and security personnel filed into the corridor.

"This way," Havoc shouted, reversing direction and sprinting for the front doors.

The Force members bolted, all except for Bear. He aimed and sent a half-dozen shots into the trooper at the forefront of the line.

Taken unawares, the foremost soldier tumbled to the floor.

Bear spun and dashed after his friends.

"Nail the bastards!" an HS man bellowed, and the troopers raced in pursuit, some firing on the run.

Sergeant Havoc glanced back once, then increased his speed. He didn't want to be trapped in the corridor. Although the weather was blustery cold, at least outside they would have room to maneuver. He was ten feet from the entrance when the doors swung inward.

There, framed in the doorway, were the four other guards.

Havoc threw himself to the right, to the floor, raking them as he dove, his marksmanship skills enabling him to stitch a pattern across each guard's chest, the impact flinging his targets backwards to topple into the frigid snow. Havoc rolled as he landed, coming up against the wall, and surged erect. Move! his mind commanded. He barreled through the doors and paused, surveying the field between the building and the fence.

Patrols were still searching for the first pair of snow shrews, crisscrossing the field in organized rows. Dogs barked and tugged on their leashes. A few troopers close to the headquarters were gazing at the front doors, puzzled by all the gunfire.

Havoc smiled and waved.

Athena and Thunder pounded out the doorway, followed a moment later by Bear.

Sergeant Havoc glanced at the Clansman. "Play it cool," he muttered. "Be calm and collected."

"Nobody calls me a nigger," Bear said. "Nobody."

"So much for Mr. Self-control," Havoc quipped, and jogged to the left. "This way." There were too many HS men and jeeps scouring the field. Maybe, if they swung around toward the rear of the building, they could find a place to lay low and plan their next move.

"Hey! What's going on there?" a trooper 30 feet away yelled.

"Just this," Bear said, and sent a round into the man's head.

"Damn!" Havoc quipped. "Haven't you ever heard of subtlety?"

"Suttle-who?"

They ran all out for the corner of the lodge.

"Halt!" a soldier ordered.

"He's got to be kiddin'," Bear stated.

Havoc saw ten or 12 HS men head after them, and he wondered why the troopers weren't cutting loose with the Berettas. The Force members were sitting ducks, outlined against the backdrop of the outer wall. He—

No!

Not the outer wall.

The window!

With a start Havoc realized they were racing past the command-center window, the window camouflaged as a wall, the tinted window through which Eric Holtmeyer was undoubtedly looking at that very instant. He looked at it and grinned. The HS men weren't about to risk firing until the Force was past the window. True, Holtmeyer had claimed the glass was shatterproof, but a sustained volley could conceivably crack the panes. He poured on the speed, looking over his right shoulder at a loud noise from behind.

The troopers from the corridor were crowding through the front doors.

"After them!" one shouted.

The Force members were almost to the corner.

Thunder came abreast of the noncom. "What about Blade and the others?"

"They're on their own," Havoc replied.

"We can't leave them," Thunder said.

"We can't help them if we're captured. First, we escape. Then we'll return after dark."

"This mission is going badly," Thunder remarked.

"Cheer up," Havoc said. "What else could go wrong?" He attained the corner and took a sharp left.

And blundered smack-dab into a six-man HS patrol with two Dobermans.

CHAPTER TEN

Boone eased the door shut and took his bearings. He was in a small, paneled anteroom containing two chairs and a wooden rack that was filled with magazines and attached to the left-hand wall at shoulder height. He peered at one of the titles. *Skin Galore*. A scantily clad young woman was depicted on the cover, licking her rosy lips and cupping her breasts in her hands. Curiosity almost compelled him to reach for the magazine, but he restrained himself and moved to a closed door across the anteroom.

Where did this lead?

Before turning the knob, he slung his M-16 over his right shoulder and shoved the already unzipped front of his green parka aside, exposing both Hombres on his hips.

Now he was ready.

Boone twisted the doorknob slowly and inched the door outward, his ears detecting a peculiar whining noise commingled with loud humming and buzzing. He peeked around the edge of the door and discovered a narrow, short hall leading to yet another door that was slightly ajar.

The strange sounds came from beyond the door.

The Cavalryman stepped softly to the next door and

flattened his back against the right-hand wall. Through the three-inch gap he could see a large table supporting complicated electronic equipment. He wished Blade or Havoc was with him. They were knowledgeable about such apparatuses; he wasn't. He knew about horses and guns and life on the plains. Electronic gizmos were as alien as life on Mars.

Someone coughed.

Boone drew his right Hombre and cocked his right ear to the gap.

"Whiskey-Hotel-Oscar," a masculine voice declared.

There was more whining and buzzing.

"Whiskey-Hotel-Oscar,' the voice repeated. "Alfa-Romeo-Echo. Yankee-Oscar-Uniform."

A crisp crackling arose, and then a different, fainter voice responded. "Alfa-November. Alfa-Lima-India-Echo-November."

"Roger," the first man said.

Were they using some sort of code? Boone placed the fingertips of his right hand on the door and nudged, and he was glad the hinges worked soundlessly as the door swung inward a yard.

"Goldmane reports operation underway," stated the man in the room.

"Has the Force arrived?"

"Yes, sir."

Boone poked his head inside, surveying the ten-by-twelve-foot chamber. Seated at a hardwood table, his back to the doorway, was a man dressed in a white smock, white pants, and black shoes.

"Identify parties and factions," directed a voice emanating from a square black speaker positioned on the table to the left of the man in the smock.

"Confirming indentities," the man said. "Blade from the Family. Athena Morris from California. Havoc from California. Boone from the Cavalry. Thunder from the Flathead tribe. Grizzly from the Civilized Zone. Bear from the Clan."

"Does Goldmane anticipate any delays in conforming to the time schedule?"

"No, sir."

"Toxin status?"

"The TX-9 will be ready in twelve hours. Mixing will commence at 0300."

"Excellent. Reiterate to Goldmane our concern over the massive expenditures this project has entailed. There is no margin for error, and failure will not be tolerated."

"Message will be relayed, sir."

"The Conclave is unanimous in its decision."

"I will inform Goldmane, sir."

"Is Janus available now?"

"Not at the moment, High Lord."

A sigh emitted from the speaker. "Very well. We will expect the next update in three hours. To the Lords of Kismet."

"To the Lords of Kismet," the man said, repeating the verbal salute.

Static sputtered and crackled for several seconds, until the man in the smock flicked a silver toggle switch on the console in front of him. He breathed a sigh of relief and sat straight in his chair. "Man, I'm glad that's over," he said aloud to himself. "Those High Lords scare the crap out of me."

"How do you feel about loaded revolvers?"

The radio operator, startled by the unexpected question from right behind him, started to turn. And suddenly he was staring down the business end of a handgun and heard the hammer click as it was thumbed back.

"Howdy," said the man in buckskins and a green parka.

"You!" the operator blurted out.

"You know me?"

"You're Boone, the guy from the Cavalry."

"I had no idea I was so famous," Boone quipped. "What's your name?"

"Winslow. Corporal Winslow."

"That was a very interesting conversation you had there,

Corporal Winslow,'' Boone remarked.

The corporal did not reply.

"How about if you explain it to me," Boone said.

"I can't."

Boone smiled and pressed the Hombre barrel against the operator's nose. "I wasn't asking you. I was telling you."

"I can't. If I do, they'll kill me."

"Who will?"

"The Lords of Kismet. You don't mess with them. No one messes with them."

"Why not?"

"They'll send an executioner after your ass," Corporal Winslow stated. "They . . ." he began, and caught himself.

"You were saying?" Boone prompted.

"Nope. Not another word out of me. My lips are sealed."

Boone tapped Winslow's nose with the barrel. "If I were you, I'd spill the beans real quicklike."

"You won't do anything to me," Winslow stated.

"I won't?"

"Nope. One shot, and you'll have half the security force in here. You're bluffing."

"Am I?"

"You know it," Winslow said arrogantly.

"I like a man with confidence," Boone commented.

Winslow smirked.

"But I don't much admire a man who has the brains of a gnat," Boone added.

"Are you talking about me?"

"Do you see any other gnats in here?"

"I don't get it."

"You will," Boone said, and whacked the radio operator across the nose with his Hombre. There was a distinct snap.

Corporal Winslow doubled over in torment, blood flowing from his nostrils, and placed his palms over his nose. "Damn!" he cried, the word distorted by his hands. "You broke my nose!"

"Would you like to try for your teeth?"

Winslow glanced up at the gunman, his eyes widening in fright as he finally recognized the latent menace in the lanky frontiersman. "You would, wouldn't you?"

Boone smiled.

The corporal coughed and sputtered as the blood flow increased, and he grit his teeth as the pain intensified. "I need a doctor!" he wailed.

"You'll need a dentist too if you don't start cooperating," Boone mentioned.

"What do you want to know?"

"Who's Goldmane?"

"Janus Goldmane holds the title of Exalted Executioner for the Lords of Kismet."

"Is Goldmane here at Prudhoe Bay?"

Winslow looked at the Cavalryman. "Yeah."

"Where would I find him?"

Winslow managed a peculiar grin. "Goldmane could be anywhere."

"Who are the Lords of Kismet?"

Sniffling and wiping his nose with the backs of his hands, the corporal sat up. "You've never heard of them?"

"No."

"I thought everyone knew about them."

"Who are they?" Boone asked testily.

"The Lords of Kismet rule Asia."

Boone's brown eyes narrowed. "Asia? *All* of Asia?"

"Yeah," Winslow answered, tilting his head back and gingerly holding his nose with his right hand.

"How many Lords are there?" Boone probed.

"Seven."

"Seven men control all of Asia?" Boone said skeptically.

"I never told you they were men."

"What are they?"

"They're the Lords of Kismet."

"Don't play games with me," Boone warned. "Are the Lords of Kismet mutants?"

'I've never seen them," Winslow replied. "But I hear

they're half and half.''

Boone pondered the information for a bit. ''What's the Conclave?''

''The Conclave of the Lords of Kismet. That's what they call their executive council, when they all get together,'' Corporal Winslow disclosed. He groaned and bent over again, his left arm dropping alongside his leg, his left hand curled near the bottom of his pants.

''What's TX-9?''

''You heard that too?''

''What is it?'' Boone demanded.

Winslow slid his left hand under his pants leg and gripped the hilt of the surival knife strapped to his ankle. ''TX-9 is a chemical toxin.''

''What's it used for?''

''To kill people,'' Winslow said, slowly sliding the five-inch blade free from its leather scabbard.

''How does TX-9 kill?''

''I'm no chemist,'' Winslow retorted.

''You know more than you're telling me,'' Boone said. ''And you'd best begin 'fessing up, right now.''

Winslow pretended to cringe. ''What do you want to know?''

''I want to know how all of this ties into Prudhoe Bay,'' Boone stated. ''Why is Janus Goldmane here? What is he planning to do with the poison? And what involvement do the Lords of Kismet have in this whole affair?''

''I'm a Communications Specialist,'' Winslow said. ''They don't confide in me.''

Boone scanned the room for something he could use to bind the operator and spied a spare extension cord coiled on the table to his right.

''What will you do with me?'' Winslow inquired.

''Tie you up,'' Boone said. ''And don't make a peep until long after I'm gone, if you know what's good for you.'' He moved to the extension cord and reached for the coils with his left hand.

The Communications Room was abruptly rocked by the retorts of gunfire from the main corridor.

Boone turned in the direction of the shots, and as he did he caught a gleaming streak of light out of the corner of his right eye. He shifted to the left and felt something tear at his parka, and then he saw the corporal raising a knife for a second strike.

The blade never connected.

Boone rammed the Hombre barrel into Winslow's neck and squeezed the trigger, the blast propelling the corporal backwards and sending both the radio operator and the chair tumbling to the floor with a crash.

Winslow rose to his knees, his hands clamped to his ravaged throat, vainly striving to prevent his blood from spurting over his chest and spraying the communications room. He gurgled and gasped, his terrified gaze locked on the Cavalryman. His mouth twitched and he tried to speak, but only a reddish spittle issued forth.

Boone stepped up to the corporal, touched the Hombre barrel to Winslow's temple, and fired.

The corporal flipped onto his back, convulsed for half a minute, and was still.

The gunfire in the corridor had risen to a crescendo.

Boone hurried from the radio room, examining his parka on the run. The blade had torn a six-inch gash in the fabric but had missed his skin. He reloaded the two spent rounds as he dashed to the hall door, and then paused, listening.

All was unexpectedly quiet.

What had happened?

He clasped the knob, then froze as another round of metallic chattering erupted from the corridor.

"Nail the bastards!" someone yelled.

His companions must be in trouble!

Boone turned the knob and cautiously looked out. He could see a column of HS men racing toward the front entrance, and he stepped into the hall for a better view in time to glimpse Bear disappearing out the double doors.

What was going on?

The pack of troopers was in rapid pursuit.

Boone began to follow the soldiers, when the last one in line happened to look to the rear. He saw the man's double take, and the trooper endeavored to whirl and bring a Beretta into play. Boone drilled the man in the forehead.

Because many of them were firing at the front entrance, the majority of the HS guards did not hear the sound of Boone's lone shot. But five did, and they stopped and spun, leveling their automatic rifles.

Boone squeezed off five shots in half as many seconds, backpedaling as he did, heading for the rear door, and each shot left a soldier sprawled on the gold carpet. He bumped into the door, reached back with his left hand and twisted the knob, and darted into a stairwell.

As another column of HS troopers appeared at the landing above.

CHAPTER ELEVEN

Grizzly glided down the second-story corridor, his nose twitching as he tried to detect the scent of the snow shrews. He had never hunted shrews before, and he was unfamiliar with their odor, but any scent other than that of humans or dogs would be suspect. He held his hands at his sides, his fingers loose, ready for action. The hallway was quiet.

Where was everyone?

He came to an intersection a third of the way along the corridor and, on a whim, took a left. Human scent was strong here, and he easily distinguished the odors of Eric Holtmeyer and Kan Tang. The Thai was one of the most formidable humans Grizzly had ever seen, and he wondered if he would have the opportunity to test his mettle against the Oriental's martial-arts prowess.

Not that it would be much of a contest.

What chance would Tang have against ten razor-sharp claws, each a lethal weapon, collectively able to slice through bone or wood with the same ease a hunting knife could cut through butter? His claws weren't indestructible; they couldn't put a dent in metal, and he'd broken one, once, when he attempted to hack through a metal door. The claw had taken six months to regrow, and now seemed sturdier than before.

Wait a minute.

What was that?

Grizzly was a few feet from a closed door on the right, and a peculiar scent caused his nostrils to quiver. The odor was unlike anything he knew, with an odd, musty, diffuse quality. He thought he recognized fox, deer, and bear, but the individual scents were commingled and unlike those with which he was familiar. He moved to the door and tried the knob.

The door was unlocked.

He crouched, pushed the door wide, and darted into the room to the left, staying low to reduce the target he presented to potential enemies. A quick glance verified he was the only occupant, and he straightened slowly, his eyes widening as he beheld the dozens of glassy, lifeless orbs returning his gaze.

The chamber was spacious and homey. Gold carpet covered the floor, gold paint the walls. Plush easy chairs were scattered about, with a few luxurious sofas interspersed for good measure. Situated in the center of the north wall was a large fireplace constructed of smooth, glistening stones and gold-colored mortar.

Grizzly hardly noticed.

He walked farther into the room, his attention riveted to the wall decorations.

Son of a bitch!

So this was the reason the headquarters building was called the "lodge"!

He wanted to rip Holtmeyer's guts out.

Ringing the walls, spaced at three-foot intervals, mounted on polished wooden plaques, were 36 animal heads. Exquisitely preserved, their features and pelts intact, they presented the remarkable illusion of being alive. No two were alike. There was an arctic fox in the blue phase, a huge polar bear, a caribou with a magnificent rack, a black bear, a grizzly, a moose, a musk-ox, and a Dall sheep—a tremendous ram. Mammals from other continents were on display, including a male African lion, a Siberian tiger, a South American jaguar, a gorilla, a chimpanzee, and an orangutan. Australia was represented by a red kangaroo and, of all things, a harmless koala. Mixed in with the ordinary types were a few decidedly grotesque abnormalities; mutations of common species, such as a two-headed cougar and a wolverine with four eyes.

Grizzly went from head to head, his eyes blazing, his hands partially clenching and unclenching.

This was Holtmeyer's handiwork.

He just knew it.

Which meant that Holtmeyer must consider himself to be some kind of sportsman, a collector of trophy game, a big man with a gun.

Grizzly grinned wickedly. He'd like to turn the tables on Eric Holtmeyer, to hunt the man down and kill him just like the bastard had slain so many innocent animals and mutants. Give the creep a taste of his own medicine. Maybe even mount Holtmeyer's head on a wooden plaque.

Wouldn't that be great!

He walked to the doorway, pausing to cast a last glance at the game room. An Indian elephant was mounted on the wall to his right, and under the head was an engraved golden marker. Curious, he strolled toward the elephant head until he could read the engraving. *To Janus: With Love. Eric.*

Interesting.

Who was Janus?

Grizzly exited the chamber and turned to the right, continuing until he found another door. He shoved it open and ducked within.

Another dead end.

The room contained 14 bunk beds with footlockers at the base of every bottom bunk. He guessed it was a sleeping quarters for some of the in-house security personnel. On the left-hand wall was a rack filled with Beretta AR 70/90s.

Not much of interest.

He was about to leave, in the act of closing the door, when his gaze fell on one of the footlockers.

What was inside?

Grizzly crossed to the locker and knelt. The lid was not locked, and he lifted the top and studied the contents. Folded uniforms were stacked on the right side. On the left were trays of personal items. He ran his left hand over the objects in the uppermost tray: a pen, a pencil, a small notepad, eight pieces of yellow candy in transparent wrappers, a green ring made from a shiny green substance, and a pile of photographs.

He sorted through the pictures. Most showed a lovely woman wearing an exotic skirt and tight top. Her complexion was dark, and in the center of her forehead was a bizarre blue dot.

What in the world?

He studied her photo, perplexed. In all his travels he'd never seen attire like hers, and he certainly had never observed humans wearing dots on their forehead. Humans were weird, but he never expected them to waltz around with decorator dots adorning their faces.

Then again, they *were* humans.

Grizzly replaced the photographs and picked up the notepad. He flipped back the brown cover and stared at a page written in a foreign language. Perhaps he had made a mistake. He hadn't paid much attention to the HS personnel, and possibly he should have noted their appearance. Like Tang, some apparently came from overseas. How many? And how did Holtmeyer recruit them? The man was more of an enigma with each revelation. He wondered . . .

There was a scratching noise from the hallway.

Moving quickly, he replaced the notepad and lowered the lid. In two bounds he was at the doorway, peering into an empty hall. He extended his fingers, enabling his claws to slide free.

Were his ears playing tricks on him?

He debated whether to unsling the M-16, and decided against using the weapon. He preferred his claws over an automatic rifle any day, and the relatively cramped quarters in the corridor were perfect for his fighting style.

The scratching was repeated, faintly, from the far end of the hallway.

Bingo.

Grizzly slid along the hall, his hands in front of his waist, the nape of his neck tingling. He needed a good fight to take his mind off Athena.

He got one.

Eight feet from the end of the corridor was an air vent on the left wall, within six inches of the ceiling.

Grizzly neared the vent with supreme vigilance, his eyes glued to the grill. If there was a snow shrew up there, the thing might try to come at him in a rush. He advanced to within a yard of the vent and halted, sniffing the air and listening.

The grill exploded off the vent as a heavy body hurtled into the thin parallel bars from the other side, and both the grill and the furry form dropped to the floor, the grill with a crash, the furry form with silent, supple grace.

For a moment they measured one another.

Grizzly took in the tapered snout, the serrated teeth revealed by a feral snarl, the crimson-coated claws on both front feet, and the matted brown hair in a glance. He experienced a fleeting surprise that the shrew was brown and not white, and then there was no time to think, no time for anything but ferocious, primal combat.

The shrew hissed and lunged, snapping with its slavering jaws and swinging its claws with elemental abandon. Each snap was propelled by steely muscles, each swing was lightning fast. Had its foe been human, the shrew would have disemboweled its adversary in the opening seconds of the fight.

But Grizzly was more than human. Endowed with the strength and reflexes of his namesake, Grizzly evaded the shrew's raking claws and countered with slicing swipes of his own. He backed up, intentionally giving ground, forcing the shrew to reach farther, hoping the beast would become careless and expose its neck.

No such luck.

The shrew fought with a savage intensity directed by its shrewd, bestial mind. It attacked again and again and again, but it never committed a reckless act, never allowed itself to be drawn within killing range of Grizzly's claws.

The longer the fight progressed, the more uncomfortable Grizzly felt. The parka was impeding his movement, restricting his blows. Even worse, the combat boots were affecting his balance and speed. He was not accustomed to wearing clothing, and he wished now that he hadn't. All because he wanted to impress Athena—

Growling deep in its throat, the shrew tried to spear its opponent's left leg.

Grizzly barely avoided those flashing claws. Concentrate! he berated himself. This was hardly the time for romantic introspection. He stood firm and blocked several blows, his claws clacking against the shrew's. His adrenaline was pumping, and he could feel his muscles loosening, his ferocity mounting. He forgot about Athena, forgot about his clothes, and focused exclusively on the battle, supplanting his conscious deliberation with sheer instinct.

Their claws streaked and arced in the corridor light, and each one nicked the other over a dozen times. But neither scored a decisive blow until the shrew landed a lucky strike.

The beast stabbed at Grizzly's chest with its left claws, and as its foe stepped backwards to dodge the swipe, it followed with a swing of its right. Although the shrew missed Grizzly's body, its claws snagged in the parka, ripping into the fabric and catching, and in the process causing its enemy to stumble forward and almost trip.

Grizzly flung himself to the rear, too late. He experienced a burning sensation in his abdomen, and he knew the shrew had managed a hit. Blocking another slash at his stomach,

he attempted to retreat, but the shrew's claws were stuck
in the parka material, and now he was locked in a life-or-
death struggle and unable to retreat.

Which suited him just fine.

Grizzly slammed into the shrew, bowling the creature over,
his arms whipping in tight circles, burying his claws in the
hairy body repeatedly, piercing the beast's face and neck and
chest. He struck in a frenzy, a chill, killing rage, and he
swung and swung until his arms began to tire, until the red
haze before his eyes subsided and he could see the shrew
clearly, until he realized he was hacking away at a corpse.
He allowed his claws to retract.

The shrew had been dead for over a minute.

He straightened, breathing deeply, observing the creature's
claws still stuck in his coat. Disgusted, he removed his M-16,
45's, and backpack, then stripped off the parka and dropped
the garment onto the floor. The shrew's body was a mass
of slashed ribbons, oozing blood from cut after cut. Its mouth
was set in a defiant growl, its eyes rapidly becoming as glassy
as those on the trophies in the game room.

Damn.

He'd done it!

Grizzly stood slowly, his left combat boot slipping on a
patch of crimson. His temper flared, and he stripped off the
boots and the pants in short order and threw them down the
corridor. He vowed never to wear clothing again. His loincloth was all he needed, all he wanted.

"You can stop right there," said someone behind him
sarcastically. "We don't care to see your pecker, misfit."

Grizzly turned.

Eight feet distant, their Berettas leveled, stood a pair of
troopers.

CHAPTER TWELVE

Blade squeezed the trigger on the big M-60, the machine gun bucking in his arms, the thunderous blasts music to his ears as the heavy slugs smacked into the charging shrew and stopped the mutant in its tracks. Geysers of blood erupted from its body as it thrashed and convulsed, shrieking like a banshee. He stalked forward, unrelenting in his determination to exterminate the ravenous brute and prevent it from ever killing again.

The shrew, its body riddled with gaping holes, toppled from the cabinets, out of sight.

Had he finished it?

Blade moved to the left swiftly, past three rows of file cabinets, and halted at the head of the aisle into which the beast had fallen.

Four HS corpses littered the floor.

But no shrew.

He stepped to the left and checked the next aisle.

No shrew.

Where could the mutant have gone, as hurt as it was? The thing must be on its last legs. What kept it going? A thirst for revenge?

Blade stepped to the left again and gazed down the last aisle, frowning at the empty stretch of tile. He glanced at the open vent. Would the shrew attempt to escape the way it had entered? Was it back in a corner somewhere, dying?

Neither.

Hissing horribly, the shrew rounded the fourth row of cabinets on the right and hurtled at the Warrior.

Blade pivoted and cut loose when the shrew was only two feet off. The M-60 drove the shrew to its knees on the spot, riddling the mutant again and again. Still the beast endeavored to bite its prey, crawling forward, its jaws snapping. Blade pointed the M-60 at the creature's head, watching dispassionately as the cranium was perforated and chipped away by his rounds.

The shrew uttered a final cry of defiance and slumped over.

Blade let up on the trigger and moved cautiously to the mutant's side. He nudged the beast's head with his left boot, ensuring the genetic deviate was dead. Satisfied, he straightened and scrutinized the file room for sign of the second shrew.

Evidently the mate was elsewhere.

He walked to the nearest prone HS man and crouched, examining the trooper's features in profile. The complexion was swarthy and rugged, and reminded him of photographs of Arabs he'd seen in a book on the Middle East, one of the hundreds of thousands of volumes stocked in the Family library by the Founder. Was this man really Arabic? If so, how had he wound up in Holtmeyer's employ? Did Holtmeyer recruit his HS troopers from around the globe?

There were so many questions and not enough answers.

And he wanted—he needed—answers.

Blade rose and stared at the file cabinets to his right, reading the labels affixed to the center of each drawer. R-T. U-W. X-Z. Personnel records, perhaps? He opened the X-Z drawer and found it crammed with green files. Attached to the upper left corner of every file was a red label imprinted with a name. He flipped through them, noting the names.

Uger.
Uhrich.
Umbriaco.
Valdez.
Vancaneghem.
Vaughn.
Wakely.
Wallis.
Watanabe.

Blade closed the drawer and exited the room, contemplating the significance of the names. He wasn't an expert, but they appeared to be a cross-sampling of diverse nationalities—or what would have constituted nationalities prior to the war. The more he delved into Eric Holtmeyer's organization, the more convinced he became that Holtmeyer Industries was, indeed, international in scope.

He took a left at the next junction, and then a right, wanting to put distance between the file room and himself in case reinforcements should show up to investigate the firing of the M-60. Once he was satisfied no one was after him, he slowed and opened the next door he came to.

The room was 15 feet wide, 20 feet long. A narrow table was positioned in the middle, ringed by folding chairs. On the far wall was an enormous map of the world, and stuck in the map were over a hundred multicolored pins, reds and blues and greens.

Was this a briefing room? Why was it located on the top floor instead of on the bottom, in general proximity to the Command Center? And what was with all the pins?

Blade crossed to the wall and peered at the map, and as he did a pattern emerged. The pins were all stuck in cities, and the majority were in Asia. Europe had only eighteen pins, Africa twelve. There were none marking South America, and only four in all of North America.

What did the pins denote?

Most of the pins in Asia were red, intermixed with a few blues and greens. Curiously enough, most of the pins in

Europe were blue or green. In North America, there was a green pin in Miami, a green pin in Atlanta, another green pin in Chicago, and a red pin at Prudhoe Bay.

Why the variation in colors?

Why were the reds concentrated in Asia?

The mystery grew every second.

He scratched his chin with his left hand, pondering the map. Previous runs with his fellow Warriors had taken him to Miami, Atlanta, and Chicago. Miami was a haven for drug dealers; drugs were now legal there, and a cartel supplied the residents with an unlimited quantity of any kind the people desired. Atlanta was a city-state ruled by autocratic humanists, where free thought and expression had been replaced by strict adherence to a rigid manifesto to so-called human rights. And Chicago was in the control of dictatorial technocrats who treated their citizens as material commodities, and who had forsaken any pretense at adhering to basic, traditional values.

What connection was there between Holtmeyer Industries and those three cities?

Why were the pins in Miami, Atlanta, and Chicago green, but Prudhoe Bay's red?

Blade walked to the door and gave a last glance at the map. He wondered if the others had discovered any important clues to Holtmeyer's operation. Still musing, he closed the door and ambled down the corridor until he reached a junction.

He'd taken much longer than he should have. Which way now?

The decision was made for him by the sound of gunfire, a muted series of retorts emanating from his right. He jogged to the end of the hall, stopping between a door on either side. Opting for the left-hand door, he shoved it open to find a lounge with a picture window on the opposite wall.

The shots were louder.

He hurried to the window and stared out. Unlike the Command Center window, this one wasn't tinted. He could see a flurry of activity three floors below, with over 20 troopers and half as many dogs converging on the building at the run.

Why?

Blade craned his neck for a glimpse of the base of the lodge, but the angle prevented him from ascertaining the reason for the tumult. Uneasy for the safety of his companions, he dashed from the lounge and tried the right-hand door, which afforded access to a stairwell. This was not the same stairwell he'd climbed earlier, he realized, and he took the steps three at a stride. At the bottom was a door with a small window in the upper panel. He was about to fling the door wide, when he happened to glance through the window and spied the three people on the other side. Instantly he ducked down, fingering the M-60's trigger.

Had they seen him?

He counted to ten and inched upward until he could see the trio again. They were engrossed in a conversation and had not observed his face at the window. He peeked in both directions, judging that he was on the north side of the wide corridor adjoining the Command Center, and about seven feet from the front entrance to the building. Soldiers were hurrying back and forth, giving the three figures a wide berth.

What were they saying?

Blade grasped the knob and ever so slowly rotated it until he could ease the door inward a crack. He pressed his right ear to the edge and eavesdropped.

"—one of them has been captured," Colonel Varney was talking. "I just received word the mutant is in custody."

"Is that all?" Eric Holtmeyer responded.

"We're lucky we've caught even one," Lalita Pruty said. "We're not dealing with amateurs here."

"What the hell started it?" Holtmeyer queried angrily.

"We don't know yet," Varney replied.

"Who cares?" Lalita asked. "We have more important matters to concern ourselves with."

"Such as?" Holtmeyer said.

"Such as not allowing any of the Force to leave Prudhoe

Bay alive,'' Lalita stated. ''Such as adhering to our time schedule, and ensuring the first batch of TX-9 is properly mixed at 0300.''

''Do you think they found out about the TX-9?'' Holtmeyer inquired.

''How could they?'' Lalita rejoined. ''They have no idea what we're up to.''

''Will the mixing always be performed at the ten-mile Pump Station?'' Colonel Varney asked.

''Of course,'' Lalita said.

''Why don't we set up the mixing machinery at the Alyeska Pump Station?'' Holtmeyer wanted to know. ''It's closer.''

''The mixing is a continuous operation. TX-9 must continually be added to the crude,'' Lalita replied. ''What if there's a mistake?''

''I—'' Holtmeyer began.

''If done incorrectly, we could end up with a toxic cloud on our hands,'' Lalita cut him off. ''Every living soul at Prudhoe Bay would be wiped out.''

''But—'' Holtmeyer said.

''Never forget the scope of our operation,'' Lalita chided. ''The cost is staggering, but think of the rewards. North America will be ours after we succeed!''

''I didn't mean to—''

''We'll proceed exactly as planned, gentlemen,'' Lalita declared. ''If we could have added the TX-9 to California's own crude, we would have done so. But we require unregulated mass production to succeed.''

''Our success hinges on the Federation's acceptance of the deal,'' Colonel Varney commented.

''They'll accept,'' Lalita said.

''How can you be so certain?'' Holtmeyer queried.

''They can't afford not to accept our proposal,'' Lalita mentioned.

''But the Federation leaders will be suspicious if the Force is killed,'' Holtmeyer observed.

''Not if we can come up with a believable excuse.''

"Like what?"

Lalita Pruty laughed. "Must I think of everything? Can't you attend to one piddling detail?"

"There have been several polar bears hanging around the dump," Colonel Varney said. "We could arrange to have the bodies of the Force mauled."

"Only if they don't die of gunshot wounds," Lalita responded. "We'd have a hard time disguising a bullet hole."

"Not if the corpses were partially eaten," Varney said.

"Hmmmm," Lalita replied. "Your suggestion has merit. Let's wait and see if they're taken alive, as I ordered."

There was the sound of boots thumping on the floor, drawing nearer.

"Yes, Captain?" Colonel Varney said.

"I've located a witness to the initial shooting."

"Is this him?" Varney asked.

"Yes, sir," the captain replied.

"What's your name and rank, boy?" Varney demanded.

"Tech First Class Ruark," a new voice answered.

"And you saw the shooting begin?" Colonel Varney asked the tech.

"Yes, sir. I was just about to leave the Command Center to go get a new box of computer paper."

"What did you see?" Varney pressed him.

"I saw the big black guy shoot one of our men. I couldn't believe it. The black just up and shot him."

"The black Force member? Bear?"

"Is that his name? All I know is that he was a large black."

"And you're positive that he shot one of our men first?"

"Yes, sir."

"Did you overhear their conversation?"

"No, sir. I only had the door open a crack, and I closed it right away. And then all that gunfire broke out. I was so stunned, I didn't know what to do. I heard you get on the horn and order a squad to the main corridor, and seconds later Mr. Holtmeyer and you rushed past me, but by then the Force was outside. I'm sorry."

"You did well," Colonel Varney said. "You're a tech, not a trooper. You're not accustomed to bloodshed."

"You can say that again, sir."

"That will be all. Continue with the search, Captain."

"Yes, sir."

The boots hastened away.

"Why would Bear shoot one of our men?" Holtmeyer inquired, obviously perplexed.

"Why do you persist in asking such stupid questions?" Lalita retorted. "The reason for the shooting is unimportant. What *is* crucial is that we compensate and forge ahead as planned."

"What should we do about our prisoner?" Colonel Varney queried.

"I will question the prisoner personally," Lalita Pruty declared.

"I could handle it," Holtmeyer offered.

"You couldn't handle a wet dream."

"Why are you getting on my case?" Holtmeyer asked. "I'm doing exactly as you said."

"Yes, you are playing the part magnificently. But never forget that you are a very minor player in the grand scheme of things. My scheme. And if you foul up, I'll feed *you* to the polar bears."

"I won't foul up."

"We'll see," Lalita said.

There was a commotion as someone ran in from the front entrance. "Colonel!"

"Yes, Sergeant."

"The woman has been taken. Her three comrades are pinned down a mile east of here. And one of them is injured, sir."

"Excellent. Which one has been injured?"

"The black, sir."

"How fitting."

"Sir?"

"Nothing. Lead the way. I want to be there when we nail

the sons of bitches.''

"Yes, sir.''

Blade heard Varney and the sergeant hasten out the double doors. His forehead creased as he tried to make sense of the conversation. One fact was evident and filled him with alarm; his team was in dire straits. Grizzly and Athena were prisoners, and Bear and two others, probably Havoc and Thunder, were trapped a mile away. Who should he try to help first? He had no idea where to find Grizzly and Athena, and HS troops were swarming. . . .

He suddenly knew he wasn't alone.

A feeling of impending danger caused him to spin, to turn toward the stairs, and his pulse quickened as he spotted the looming presence of Kan Tang perched on the bottom step. He tried to rise, to bring the M-60 to bear, but his contemplation had dulled his awareness and retarded his reflexes. He saw the Thai's right foot arcing at his head.

The universe exploded in brilliant pinwheels of bright lights and dazzling hues as a ten-ton boulder slammed into his right temple, and then he was devoured by a black hole.

CHAPTER THIRTEEN

Sergeant Havoc took out the Dobermans first with a burst from his M-16, then whipped the barrel in a semicircle and flattened the six troopers before they had a chance to return his fire. He kept going, vaulting over a prostrate form and heading to the east.

Another group of soldiers and three dogs were 70 yards to the south and approaching on the run.

Havoc glanced back. Thunder was a yard behind him, and Athena and Bear were just rounding the corner. "Move it!" he urged them, racing all out. He could see the eastern perimeter of the fence, 100 yards to the east. If they could get past the fence, if they could get into the open, they'd be better able to lose their pursuers. The south wall of the headquarters building was 50 yards in length, so for 50 yards they would be screened from threats to the north. They were still vulnerable on three sides, but three was better than four.

Twenty-five yards were covered as the Force grimly raced for their lives.

"Behind us!" Athena suddenly yelled.

Havoc looked around, his eyes widening at the sight of a jeep sweeping around the southwest corner, its tires spinning, snow flying in a powdery spray. "Get down!" he shouted.

They dove for the ground, and not a moment too soon.

The trooper manning the .50-caliber machine gun mounted behind the driver's seat opened up, blasting at the Force as the jeep slewed to the right. The vehicle's motion caused the swivel gun to sway, throwing the gunner's aim off. His rounds punched into the wall three feet above the members of the Force.

Thunder propped his elbows in the snow, aimed, and squeezed off a single shot.

Reacting as if a sledgehammer had smashed into his forehead, the gunner threw his arms into the air and catapulated from the jeep.

Thunder fired again.

The windshield dissolved in a shower of splintery fragments, and the driver pitched to the right, slumping down. Undirected, the jeep looped to the right, its speed diminishing to a crawl.

"Go!" Havoc barked.

The Force members were up and running in an instant.

Sergeant Havoc looked to the south, concerned. The jeep had delayed them, and now the pack closing in was only 60 yards away.

"There're more behind us!" Athena cried.

"Keep going!" Havoc responded. He could hear the crack-crack-crack of the HS weapons and the loud thumps as the wall to his left was hit repeatedly. Miniature geysers of snow spewed into the air near his feet. Sooner or later, the HS men would get the range. He preferred later.

Athena and Bear spun and fired short bursts to discourage the troopers on their tail, then resumed sprinting eastward.

So far, so good.

Sergeant Havoc slowed slightly as he neared the southeast corner of the structure. There could be soldiers lurking on the other side. He abruptly ran faster, and when he was within six feet of the corner he launched himself forward, twisting to the left as he cleared the building, his finger on the trigger.

His prudence paid off.

A pair of troopers were waiting in ambush around the corner. They had their Berettas to their shoulders, ready to fire at chest-height or higher targets.

Havoc sailed into view at waist level, spraying them as he dropped, his slugs ripping into their abdomens and doubling them over. They were flung to the ground, the tallest of the duo screaming, the second clutching his stomach and blubbering hysterically. Havoc landed and immediately surged erect.

Thunder, Athena, and Bear joined him, and they paused for a second, surveying the surrounding fields, taking their bearings.

There were HS to their rear.

There were HS to the south.

And a squad of troopers abruptly materialized to the north, coming into view around the northeast corner.

"This ain't my idea of fun," Bear quipped.

"The fence," Sergeant Havoc said, and they were off.

An HS sergeant to the south unexpectedly halted and cupped his left hand to his mouth. In his right was a walkie-talkie. "Take them alive if possible! Goldmane wants prisoners!"

"Who the hell is Goldmane?" Athena asked, puffing as she ran.

"Whoever the sucker is, you owe him a kiss," Bear remarked.

"I don't owe anybody anything," Athena responded.

"Except Grizzly," Bear said.

"Don't start," Athena warned.

"How can you two idiots argue at a time like this?" Havoc asked, his legs thrashing in the knee-deep snow.

"Women can argue anywhere," Bear replied. "It's in their nature. They're a bunch of bitchy wenches."

Athena glared at the Clansman. "When this is over, I plan

to bop you on the mouth.''

"See what I mean?" Bear declared.

They sprinted in silence for 20 yards.

"The pricks ain't gainin' on us," Bear commented.

"They're in no rush," Sergeant Havoc said. "They know the fence will slow us down enough for them to catch up."

"Will it?" Athena queried anxiously.

"Maybe not," Havoc told her. "I have four surprises in my pockets."

"Is it food?" Bear inquired.

"No."

"Too bad. I'm hungry."

"We have an army on our tail and you're thinking of food?" Havoc said.

"He can't help himself," Athena remarked. "He's a man. All men ever think about is food and sex."

"I'm a man, and I think about more than food and sex," Thunder mentioned.

"You don't count," Athena said.

"Why not?" the Flathead asked.

"You have a brain."

"Are you sayin' I don't?" Bear demanded.

"Let me put it this way," Athena quipped, forging through the snow. "If you're ever short on cash, you can rent out the space between your ears for storage."

They traversed another 20 yards.

Sergeant Havoc looked at the fence, 30 feet distant, and then at the HS troopers bearing down on them. He estimated the nearest soldier would be 50 feet off when the Force reached the chain-link enclosure. There wouldn't be time to try and cut a hole, as he'd expected. He would have to use one of his surprise packages.

"Unleash the dogs!" someone hollered to their rear.

"I'll waste the mutts," Bear volunteered, slowing.

"That won't be necessary," Sergeant Havoc stated, and halted, his right hand reaching into his parka pocket.

The others stopped and watched him quizzically, nervously.

Havoc produced a hand grenade and smiled. "This is our ticket out of here."

"Let 'er fly," Bear said.

Three dogs, a Doberman and two German shepherds, were bounding toward the Force from the south.

"Down!" Havoc yelled, pulling the pin and lobbing the grenade at the fence. He flattened, placing his arms over his head for added protection.

"They have grenades!" one of the HS men exclaimed.

The explosion was tremendous, and shards of metallic fencing, bits of barbed wire, and snow were blown in all directions.

Havoc felt the concussion buffet his clothing, and then he was up and running for the gaping hole in the fence. He leaped over a twisted section of chain-link and turned, intending to cover his teammates. None of the HS had fired a shot since the sergeant's proclamation about taking the Force prisoner, and Havoc hoped their luck would hold.

It didn't.

The three dogs had stopped when the grenade detonated, but they now sprang toward the fleeing quartet, rhythmically rising and falling as their lean forms loped gracefully across the field. They were seasoned canines, superbly trained, and acclimatized to the wintery terrain. Barking fiercely, they seldom floundered as they narrowed the gap.

Thunder halted alongside Havoc.

"Go!" Athena urged, waving them on. "We'll take care of the dogs."

Havoc reached into his parka pocket again. "I can use a grenade."

"Save the grenades for when we really need them," Athena advised. "Now go!"

Havoc and Thunder hesitated.

Athena spun, aimed, and fired.

Bear cut loose from the hip.

Two of the charging dogs were knocked offstride and toppled into the snow. One of the German shepherds veered to the left, unscathed.

"My dog!" an onrushing HS trooper cried, and squeezed off three rounds.

"We want them alive!" the sergeant bellowed.

Sergeant Havoc was about to resume his race for freedom. His eyes turned to Bear and he froze.

The Clansman was bent over, his left hand pressed to his right shoulder, gritting his teeth in anguish, his M-16 on the ground.

"Bear!" Havoc declared, and reached him in three strides. "You've been hit!"

"What was your first clue?" Bear asked, and winced.

"How bad is it?" Havoc inquired.

"Bad," Bear admitted. "It hurts like hell."

Sergeant Havoc looped his right arm under the Clansman's left arm. "Come on. I'll support you."

"Get out of here," Bear said. "You'll never get away lugging me along."

"We will if we work together," Thunder chimed in, stepping close to Bear's right side and bracing the Clansman about the waist. "Let's hurry."

Havoc and Thunder propelled Bear to the east. The noncom looked back.

"Athena! Move your butt!"

She was standing in the center of the ravaged section of fence, her features grim. "Go! Get Bear out of here! I'll hold them for a minute."

"No," Havoc said.

"There's no time to debate the issue," Athena stated. "Just go!"

Havoc frowned and gripped Bear tightly. "Let's go." They bore the big man for 25 yards, and Havoc glanced over his left shoulder.

Athena was holding her M-16 at waist level, eyeing the line of soldiers cautiously converging on her.

"Shoot!" Havoc said. "Why doesn't she shoot?"

She finally did, raising the automatic rifle and firing a half-dozen rounds. Four troopers dropped. She unexpectedly lowered the weapon, staring at the M-16 in evident frustration, her left hand tugging on the magazine.

"Something's wrong," Thunder declared.

"Get out of there!" Sergeant Havoc yelled.

Athena tossed the M-16 aside and pivoted, her eyes locking on her three companions. She took several paces in their direction.

"Come on!" Bear said softly. "You can do it!"

The German Shepherd streaked out of the south, seeming to appear out of nowhere, slamming into Athena and bowling her over. The dog clamped its powerful jaws on her left wrist, holding her down as she struggled in vain, punching the shepherd with her right fist.

"Let's help her!" Bear stated, trying to move to her aid.

"No," Havoc said, forcing the Clansman backwards. "There's nothing we can do for her now. Later, maybe."

"That's what you said about Blade and the others," Bear groused.

"And I'm right," Havoc insisted.

They hastened to the east. Minutes elapsed.

Thunder looked back, his brow furrowing. "They are not chasing us."

"What?" Havoc responded, stopping and turning his head.

"Why'd they let us go?" Bear asked.

"I doubt they did," Sergeant Havoc answered. "They must have an ace in the hole."

"Perhaps they expect the snow shrews to do their work for them," Thunder commented.

Havoc scanned the sea of snow encompassing them. "I forgot all about them. We'd better find a defensible position."

"In the middle of nowhere?" Bear said.

"If we have to, we'll build a snow cave to hide in," Havoc proposed.

They trudged onward.

"I didn't realize the land is so flat up here," Sergeant Havoc observed after five minutes.

"Flat and *cold*," Bear said. "Who would want to live in a land like this?"

"Eskimos," Havoc replied.

"Eski-who?"

"The Eskimos," Thunder repeated before Sergeant Havoc could answer. "They were the original inhabitants of this land, until the whites came along and shouldered them aside."

"Are there any of these Eskimos left?" Bear inquired.

"I don't know," Thunder said. "Perhaps the radiation killed them. Perhaps they all traveled to the south after the war."

"Or maybe Holtmeyer wiped out any Eskimos living in the vicinity of Prudhoe Bay when he arrived," Sergeant Havoc speculated.

Five more minutes expired.

"How are you holding up?" Havoc asked Bear.

"Just dandy."

"We should take a look at your wound."

"It can wait."

"Are you sure?"

"The pain ain't as bad," Bear said. "I can keep going. You can let me go now."

"Not yet," Havoc stated, and grinned. "We don't want you falling down on the job."

Thunder stopped and raised his head. "Listen."

"I don't hear anything," Havoc said.

"Me neither," Bear added.

"Listen," Thunder reiterated.

Havoc cocked his head and waited, and a second later an odd buzzing arose from the west.

"I hear something now," Bear commented. "Sounds like a herd of bumblebees."

Sergeant Havoc released the Clansman and faced their back trail. "I knew they had an ace in the hole."

"What makes that noise?" Thunder queried.

"You'll see in a moment," Havoc said. "This is as far as we go."

Thunder and Bear exchanged puzzled expressions.

Dark dots became visible to the west, rapidly growing larger as they neared the three Force members. The buzzing increased in volume, a raucous intrusion on the pristine wilderness.

"What *are* those things?" Bear asked in wonder.

"Snowmobiles," Sergeant Havoc declared.

Bear marveled at the speed the snowmobiles displayed. He removed his left hand from his shoulder and grimaced. "Looks like we're in serious doo-doo."

CHAPTER FOURTEEN

"Keep staring at me, you turkeys, and I can guarantee I'll rip your eyes out after I get down from here."

One of the quartet of HS troopers posted as guards laughed. "Do you hear this chump?" he asked his companions. "This jackass thinks he'll be alive when we take him down!"

All four soldiers expressed mirth at the notion.

"By the time Goldmane is done with you, there won't be enough of you left to fill a shoe box," the first guard taunted.

Grizzly gritted his teeth and glared.

"Ohhhh, my!" the first guard said in a whining falsetto. "You're scaring poor little me to death!"

"Have your fun while you can," Grizzly growled. "My time will come."

"You're out of time, stupid."

Grizzly looked down at the floor, striving to control his mounting rage. Not yet! Not yet! He was close to the edge emotionally, and he knew what would happen if he went berserk. Patience was called for, at least for the time being. He surveyed the chamber for the tenth time since his incarceration, reviewing his capture and noting the dimensions of the room in preparation for his escape.

The pair of HS responsible for capturing him had escorted

him to the nearest stairwell, wisely keeping their distance, never allowing him to get closer than eight feet. They prudently maintained a safety zone between their prisoner and themselves in case he decided to attack. They'd seen how quick he was, and they kept eight feet away to ensure they could empty their Berettas into him before he reached them. On the stairwell they'd encountered a squad of eight HS, and he was promptly taken to the first floor and confined in a chamber located east of the Command Center. The room was 20 feet by 20 and contained one item of furniture, a six-foot metal table. On the west wall, virtually invisible unless someone knew they were there, were four sets of recessed metal rings. A trooper had opened one of the drawers ringing the underside of the table and produced a pair of steel manacles with chains 12 inches in length. Nine of the soldiers had covered the mutant while the tenth applied the manacles to his wrists, then led him to the west wall and secured the ends of the chains to a set of metal rings, using a viselike oval lock designed specifically for such a purpose.

And here he was, strung up like a lamb awaiting slaughter.

Grizzly smiled and gazed at the four guards standing near the door.

"What's so damn funny, ugly?" one of them demanded.

"Your face."

The guard pointed his Beretta at the mutant.

"Don't even think it!" admonished another. "Goldmane will have you executed if you shoot him."

"He's a freak. He should be destroyed," opined the trigger-happy trooper.

"We don't touch him," directed the first guard.

"Thanks," Grizzly interjected.

"For what?" inquired the soldier.

"For not touching me. I don't want your cooties."

The trigger-happy trooper waved his Beretta. "Let me slug him. Just once. Please."

"Grow up," snapped the fourth soldier.

The door opened abruptly, and in walked Athena Morris,

her left wrist in a bandage.

"Athena!" Grizzly exclaimed, straining against his manacles.

"Grizzly!" she declared, taking several strides toward him.

"Isn't this touching?" quipped the trigger-happy trooper.

Three more HS entered the chamber, the third with thin gold bars attached to his parka at the shoulders.

The quartet snapped to attention.

"What's so touching, Private?" the man sporting the insignia demanded.

"Nothing, Captain," Trigger-happy replied nervously. "We were just having some fun with the prisoner, sir."

"Your responsibility is to guard him, not have fun with him," the officer remarked.

"Yes, sir."

The captain glanced at Athena. "Wait over there," he stated gruffly, pointing at the metal table.

Athena complied, her eyes on Grizzly every step of the way. She bumped into the table and halted, eight feet from the hybrid.

"What happened to you?" he asked.

"A German shepherd," she said simply.

"Show me which one later," Grizzly told her.

Athena scanned him from head to toe. "Are you okay?"

"No complaints."

"Have you seen Blade or Boone?"

"They took the afternoon off to go fishing."

Despite their predicament, Athena smiled. She looked at the HS men, who were all standing at attention near the open door—except for the officer, and he was staring into the corridor. Then she walked over to Grizzly. "I'm so sorry," she said softly.

"For what? I'm the one who's been acting like a jerk."

"I have something I want to say to you."

"There's no need," he said.

"Yes, there is. I must get this off my chest before it's too late."

Grizzly gazed into her eyes. "Athena, I wa . . ."

She held up her right hand, cutting him off. "Let me have my say first. If I don't tell you the truth now, I never will." Pausing, she took a deep breath and plunged ahead. "We've both been behaving terribly. We've both been afraid to admit our feelings."

"I'm not afraid of anything," Grizzly said.

"Then why haven't you admitted that you love me?"

The blunt question caught Grizzly unawares. He blinked a few times, stunned by her unexpected frankness, and opened his mouth to speak, but closed it again.

"Well?" Athena prodded him.

"You don't know what you're talking about."

She reached out and touched his chest. "Please, Grizzly, no more games. This might be our last chance to talk. Everyone knows we care for each other—"

"Sure. We're friends," he said, interrupting.

"We're more than friends," Athena corrected. "You started treating everyone like dirt after I began dating Captain Slater."

"Coincidence."

"Was it? I want the truth."

Grizzly averted his gaze.

"I want the truth," Athena persisted. "Everybody believes we're in love, and I need to—"

"Who says we're in love?" Grizzly snapped.

"Everybody."

"Who?"

"Bear, for one."

Grizzly made a hissing noise. "I'll teach that bozo to stick his big nose in where it doesn't belong."

"Havoc and Thunder feel the same way, and I suspect Blade does too."

"They shouldn't butt in."

Athena placed her right hand on his left shoulder. "Are they right?"

"This is a hell of a time to bring the subject up."

"Answer me," she said, goading him. "Please. Do you

love me?''

Grizzly stared at the floor for 30 seconds, his features reflecting an ineffable sadness. He lifted his head and looked at her, about to respond.

''What have we here?'' inquired a new voice, a female voice laced with acidic contempt.

Athena and Grizzly glanced at the doorway.

Lalita Pruty was sauntering into the chamber, her hands on her hips, a smirk creasing her red lips. ''Have I interrupted something?''

Athena stepped backwards, her hands dropping to her sides. ''No,'' she said sheepishly.

Lalita snickered and moved to the right, motioning at the door with her left hand. ''I've brought one of your playmates.''

Kan Tang materialized in the doorway, effortlessly bearing Blade in his arms.

Athena gasped and took a stride toward them. ''Blade!''

''He's alive, my dear,'' Lalita said. ''For the moment.'' She looked at the Thai and nodded.

Tang walked to the west wall and deposited the Warrior on the floor within a yard of Grizzly.

''What have you done to him?'' Athena queried.

''Tang gave him a demonstration of muay thai,'' Lalita replied, and laughed.

Eric Holtmeyer strolled into the room and folded his arms across his chest. ''Three down and four to go.''

''Holtmeyer!'' Athena declared. ''You must realize the gravity of the mistake you're committing. If you release us now, unharmed, the Federation still might be receptive to your deal.''

''Surely you jest,'' Holtmeyer said disdainfully.

''If you kill us, the Federation will never accept your offer,'' Athena mentioned.

''The matter is out of my hands.''

''Be reasonable. Slaying us will ruin any chance you have.''

Holtmeyer sighed. "When I said the matter is out of my hands, I meant it."

"I don't understand," Athena stated.

"Of course you don't, simpleton," Lalita Pruty snapped. "Would you like a clue?"

"A clue?" Athena repeated, confused.

"A demonstration," Lalita clarified. "Watch." She looked at Eric Holtmeyer. "On your knees."

To Athena's utter astonishment, Holtmeyer promptly sank to his knees.

"Kiss my boots," Lalita commanded.

Holtmeyer shuffled to her on his knees, then leaned down and kissed her white boots.

"What?" Athena blurted out, confounded.

Lalita Pruty cackled.

Athena's eyes narrowed. "Holtmeyer isn't in charge. *You* are."

"You're not as dumb as you look," Pruty said, then glanced at Holtmeyer. "Get up."

Eric obeyed and moved to the right.

"You've been playing a game with us," Athena commented.

"Not at all," Lalita replied. "I've simply taken certain precautions to ensure my true identity remained a secret. But now it doesn't matter."

"Your true identity?"

Lalita walked to within a yard of Athena. "My name isn't Lalita Pruty."

"It isn't? Why would you give us a fictitious name?"

"Because I've acquired a degree of notoriety in my line of work, a fame commensurate with my accomplishments. In Asia my name is well known. My masters were concerned that someone in the Federation might have heard of me, so they decided I should use a fictitious name on this assignment."

"Your masters?"

"The Lords of Kismet."

"Who are they? What is their connection to Prudhoe Bay?"

The woman who had called herself Lalita Pruty smirked. "The Lords of Kismet want the Freedom Federation destroyed, and who better to oversee the Federation's destruction than their Exalted Executioner?"

Athena pressed her right palm to her forehead. "This is all part of a plot to destroy the Federation?"

"You're beginning to comprehend."

"But why? Who are the Lords of Kismet? Why do they want the Federation wiped out?"

"The Lords of Kismet govern Asia, and they have plans to extend their domination into North America. Naturally they would need to eradicate all groups capable of opposing their will, and the Freedom Federation is uppermost on their list. Your Federation is the single greatest threat to the execution of their goal."

"But what about the Russians, the Technics, and the Superiors? There are a dozen groups trying to gain control of North America."

"True. But the groups you mention are atheistic or humanistic in their social orientation. The Federation adheres to traditional values, particularly the Family. The people in the Home believe in faith in a supreme Spirit, and in the ultimate value of love and wisdom."

Athena's forehead furrowed in confusion. "What difference do their beliefs make?"

"Their beliefs make all the difference in the world," Pruty said. "I don't expect a liberal journalist like yourself to comprehend my meaning, but Blade would. If he was awake, he could explain the reason fully. Blade, by the way, is number one on my hit list."

Athena glanced at the unconscious Warrior, then at the platinum-haired woman with the blonde streak running through the center of her tresses. "What did Blade do to deserve such an honor?"

"Blade stands for everything my masters despise."

"In what way?"

The Exalted Executioner sighed. "I'm not here to conduct a course in Fundamental Truths, or to enlighten you on the ways of the world. I have business to attend to, commencing right now." She glanced at Kan Tang. "Chain Blade to the wall."

The Thai nodded.

"And remove his weapons," the real commander of Prudhoe Bay directed. Then she turned to the captain. "Secure Ms. Morris to the table."

"Right away," the officer responded.

Smiling sweetly, the Executioner faced Athena. "Oh. Before I forget, I should introduce myself. Janus Goldmane, at your service."

Athena saw the captain and two troopers walking toward her, and she inadvertently shivered as a ripple of stark fear undulated up and down her spine.

CHAPTER FIFTEEN

Think fast!

"Down here!" Boone shouted. "One of the shrews is in the hall!"

The column of HS was led by a beefy sergeant. He hastened down the stairs to the Cavalryman's side. "You say one of the damn things is in the main corridor?"

"It was a minute ago," Boone assured him. "I was lucky to get out with my life."

"We'll take care of the lousy freak," the sergeant assured the gunman, and looked over his left shoulder at the ten men behind him. "Let's go! One of the shrews is on the other side of this door." He yanked on the doorknob and dashed into the hallway.

Their faces set in grim lines, the rest of the squad followed their noncom.

Boone took off up the stairwell. His ruse had worked, had bought him a few precious seconds, perhaps a minute at the most. The sergeant would discover the truth as soon as he examined the bodies in the corridor and realized the troopers had died from gunshot wounds and not teeth or claw marks.

So where should he go?

He knew Blade and Grizzly were on the upper floors. His

best bet was to find them. At the second-floor landing he opened the door and scanned the hall.

Where was Grizzly?

Boone jogged along the hallway until he came to an intersection. Frustrated, he looked to the left and the right. Which way would Grizzly have taken? He opted for the right, and sprinted 15 yards to another junction. Without hesitating he took another right, and shortly thereafter he found himself opening the door to another stairwell.

The place was like a maze. Footsteps sounded from above.

Boone descended the stairs rapidly to find a pair of doors at the bottom. A door on the right afforded access to one more corridor. He opened the door on the left and blinked as brilliant sunlight and a chill wind engulfed him.

Should he stay inside or venture outdoors?

He heard the loud thumping of boots overhead, drawing nearer, and decided on the spur of the moment to step outside and swiftly close the door. He calculated he was on the east side of the headquarters building, and he could hear gunfire arising from the south. Havoc and the others must be in serious trouble. He took several strides to the south, and then glimpsed a group of soldiers and three dogs near the southern perimeter of the fence. They were making a beeline for the south side of the building.

Boone hesitated. He doubted that the soldiers to the south had spied him yet, but they would if he remained in the open. If he tried to rejoin Havoc and the rest, he might find himself caught between the troopers coming down the stairwell and the group on the south side. His best bet was to evade capture, then find his friends. He turned and ran to the north, past the stairwell door, and covered ten yards.

Another door! This one next to a section of corrugated metal wall.

Elated, he tugged on the knob, jerking the door wide and slipping inside. His right hand on his Hombre, he pulled the door closed, leaving a crack to peer through. He saw the stairwell door open and a trooper stepped outside. The soldier looked both ways, then went back in.

Boone breathed a sigh of relief. The jackass hadn't bothered to check the snow for tracks. He could try and help his companions, but first he took 30 seconds to reload his Hombre.

Voices sounded to his rear.

The gunman spun, taking in his surroundings. He was in a dark, gloomy chamber, the exact size of which was difficult to gauge, but he judged the room to be quite large. Unfamiliar shapes loomed in the darkness. He recognized a row of stacked crates and darted behind them.

In the nick of time.

Overhead lights abruptly flicked on, illuminating a spacious concrete floor and a vaulted, corrugated metal ceiling. On the west side was a workbench crammed with various tools. Parked between the crates and the workbench were eight strange vehicles.

Boone crouched low, listening.

"—see some action at last!"

"You're a fool, Billy."

"I am not."

"Only a fool would want to see action," the second speaker said to the man called Billy.

"But we're HS. We're trained to kick ass. It's what we're paid for, Pat."

"I know. But you're young. You have a lot to learn."

"Such as?"

"Such as not being so gung ho. You need to learn to kick back and relax. Don't be in such a hurry to get yourself killed. Put in your time, and that's it. The important thing is to stay alive."

Billy snickered. "You're getting senile, Pat. All you want to do is play it safe."

"I've lived this long because I do play it safe," Pat replied. "I never volunteer for a hazardous assignment."

"I don't care what you say. I still hope we see some action soon."

"Kids," Pat muttered. "Let's check the snowmobiles, like

the lieutenant told us to do.''

Snowmobiles? Was that the name for those short, squat, sledlike vehicles? Boone heard the clatter of tools being used, and he risked a peek around the left side of the crate screening him. Two men in white uniforms were engaged in inspecting the two rows of snowmobiles.

"This one can use some oil,'' the younger of the pair announced.

"You know where it is,'' responded the older man.

Boone ducked from sight. Should he plug those bozos and head out the door, or wait and . . .

More voices arose, drawing nearer.

The gunman peered past the crate.

HS were filling into the chamber. Ten. Twelve. Thirteen in all. Half of them carried Berettas slung over their shoulders.

Were they after him?

The soldiers congregated near the workbench.

"Did you hear about the shrews?'' one of them asked.

"Shrews, hell. Did you hear about those clowns from the Force?'' responded another.

"What about them?'' queried a third.

"I heard they took out some of our guys a few minutes ago,'' the second trooper elaborated.

"Why would they do that? I thought they were here on a peaceful mission.''

"How the hell should I know why they did it? I'm only relaying the word I got from Freddie in the Command Center. He gave me a buzz—''

"Your friend Freddie?'' said yet a different soldier, interrupting. "Fat Freddie, the tech?''

"Yeah.''

"And you expect us to believe a story Freddie told you?''

"Why wouldn't you?''

"Because Freddie is known for playing practical jokes. He likes to feed gullible jerks like you a line of bull.''

"No, man. He was telling the truth. He said there was

a fight in the main corridor, and that the Force chumps were being chased by our security forces outside.''

The skeptical trooper laughed. ''You'd believe anything, you know that?''

''Then why was the alarm sounded?''

''Because a bunch of damn snow shrews breached the perimeter fence, you dope.''

''Don't call me a dope, you son of a bitch.''

''How would you like this Beretta shoved up your ass?''

''By you and what army?''

''Children, please!'' snapped a burly soldier. ''We were told to wait here for the lieutenant. If he comes in and finds us fighting, he'll be pissed off. And you know what happens when the lieutenant is pissed off at us.''

''We get extra duty,'' remarked another.

''Right,'' said the burly trooper. ''So don't start going at it until you're off duty.''

Boone listened impatiently as the HS men began discussing their respective sexual prowess in obviously exaggerated terms. The minutes passed. He chafed at the delay, wanting to be with his companions instead of cooped up in the dank garage. The door was 15 feet away, and it might as well be at the North Pole for all the good it did him. There was no way he could reach the exit unnoticed.

He was trapped.

More time elapsed, and the Cavalryman shifted uncomfortably on his haunches, crouching in the shelter of the wooden crates. How much longer would he be pinned down, of no use to anyone? He was on the verge of making a dash to the door in a desperate gambit to reach his friends, when a newcomer arrived in the garage.

The lieutenant. He was a youthful officer, radiating an aura of self-importance and authority. ''Listen up, men!'' he barked as he hustled into the garage through a door situated to the left of the workbench.

With drilled military precision, the troopers quickly formed into a straight line, standing at attention.

"Three members of the Force are fleeing, on foot, to the east. We've been ordered to overtake them and return them to headquarters. Colonel Varney is going with us, and we'll pick him up at the southeast corner. He'll ride with me. Any questions?" the lieutenant related briskly.

"Then it's true, sir?" the skeptical soldier asked. "The Force wasted some of our guys?"

"It's true, Tompkins. I don't have all the details, but Goldmane wants the Force captured. Pronto," the lieutenant stated. "To your units."

Boone watched as the HS men moved to the snowmobiles, two to a machine, except for Pat and Billy, who walked to a pair of heavy chains dangling on the far side of the section of corrugated metal wall. They started tugging on one of the chains, and to the Cavalryman's amazement the *wall* clanked upward. He realized the corrugated metal section was actually a huge door. Once the door was flush with the ceiling, Pat and Billy stepped to the nearest snowmobile and looked at the officer.

The lieutenant and one trooper took hold of the handlebars on a snowmobile. They slid the machine onto the snow, to the right.

A second pair of HS did the same, and in short order all of the snowmobiles were lined up to the left of the officer's. Two troopers were apparently assigned to each unit, one to serve as the driver, while the second would ride behind the driver and carry a Beretta.

Boone saw a solitary trooper standing near the crates, and he noticed that the lieutenant did not have a passenger. Of course not. The officer had mentioned he was picking up Colonel Varney, which meant one of the troopers would need to stay behind.

The drivers of each snowmobile were settling on their machines while the gunners stood at the rear of the unit, waiting.

And at that moment, as he observed the HS men about to turn their engines over, inspiration struck the gunman.

He wanted to aid his friends, and here was a golden opportunity.

But could it be done?

None of the HS men were paying any attention to the interior of the garage. The drivers were concentrating on their machines, and the gunners were watching the drivers. Standing two feet from the crates was the excess trooper.

He could succeed if his timing was right.

Boone tensed, his eyes on the drivers. One after the other, the snowmobiles roared to life, their engines generating a strident clamor. He placed his M-16 on the cement floor, drew his right Hombre, and eased around the crates. If any of the soldiers spotted him now, he was as good as dead.

The spare trooper was calmly regarding his comrades.

Boone stepped behind the trooper, swung his left arm up and around and clamped his forearm on the man's throat, and pulled the startled soldier backwards. The trooper grabbed at Boone's arm and tried to cry out, but his inarticulate cry could not be heard above the din of the snowmobile engines. Boone hauled the man behind the crates, then rammed his Hombre into the base of the soldier's skull. "Unsling your Beretta," he said into the trooper's right ear.

The HS man let his automatic rifle slide to the floor.

"If you try to warn the others, I'll kill you," Boone warned, releasing his hold. "Don't turn around. Just take off your parka."

Eager to obey and to avoid being shot, the trooper unzipped his white parka and wriggled out of the coat. The garment dropped at his feet.

"Thank you," Boone stated, and slugged the soldier across the right temple with the Hombre barrel.

Staggered by the blow, the soldier tottered forward into the crates.

Boone bashed the man again, then once more. On the third blow the trooper sagged at his knees, then slumped over.

There wasn't time to waste.

The Cavalryman holstered his Hombre, stripped off his

green parka, and swiftly donned the white one. He zipped up the front and glanced at his buckskin leggings and moccasins. They stood out like the proverbial sore thumb, but there was no time to put on the trooper's pants. He aligned the lower edge of the white parka to permit him to draw readily, then sauntered around the crates.

All of the machines were running noisily. The drivers were revving the engines and checking gauges. Three of the gunners were already on board. Several drivers and gunners wore goggles.

Boone walked boldly to the rear of the lieutenant's snowmobile. He raised his left leg and eased down behind the officer.

"What the—?" the lieutenant blurted out, looking over his right shoulder. "What are you doing, Private? No one is supposed to ride with me." He had donned yellow goggles.

Boone glanced at the row of snowmobiles to his left. Only two of the gunners were eying him quizzically; the rest of the soldiers were concentrating on their machines or taking a seat. He smiled and nodded at the two watching him, then faced front, drew his right Hombre, and jammed the barrel into the officer's ribs.

The lieutenant's eyes widened.

Boone leaned forward. "Do as I say or you die."

"Who the hell are you?" the officer demanded, and then did a double take. "You're one of—"

"That's right," Boone said coldly, cutting him short. "And if you open your mouth again without my say-so, I'll plug you in the head." He paused for emphasis. "I have nothing to lose."

The lieutenant digested this news, his gaze on the revolver pressed to his chest.

"Do you understand me?"

"Yes," the officer said.

"Good. Then let's head out."

"Where are we going?"

"You were hell-bent for leather to go find my buddies,"

Boone noted, "so let's go find them. And don't bother stopping for Colonel Varney."

The lieutenant frowned and stared to the east. He revved his machine, looked at his men, and nodded.

Boone settled back as the snowmobile surged forward. His strategy had worked! He was on his way! Now all he had to figure out was what to do when they got there.

CHAPTER SIXTEEN

"I count eight snowmobiles," Thunder said. "Two men apiece."

"We're outnumbered, outgunned, and we've nowhere to take cover," Sergeant Havoc declared in frustration, surveying the essentially flat ocean of snow encompassing them.

"I say we kick ass," Bear stated.

"You're in no condition to take them on," Havoc responded.

"I ain't givin' up," Bear said.

"You need medical attention, my brother," Thunder commented. "Your wound is our primary concern."

"Kickin' ass is our primary concern," Bear disagreed. "Look, fellas. We can't let these chumps take us. They've already bagged Athena, and for all we know they may have Blade and the others too. If we don't snuff these dirtballs, the Force is history."

"We should take a vote," Thunder proposed.

Bear, gritting his teeth because of the pain in his right shoulder, stared at the snowmobiles. He guessed they were still a quarter of a mile distant. "This ain't no democracy," he said angrily. "I say we waste the chumps, and that's that."

"I vote we surrender and try to escape later," Thunder

recommended.

Sergeant Havoc glanced from one to the other.

"What about you, Macho Man?" Bear inquired. "You get to decide for us."

Havoc gazed at the Clansman's right shoulder. The entry point was a neat, circular hole in Bear's green parka, but the 5.56-mm round had blown a hole two inches in diameter as it exited between the right shoulder blade and the armpit. A crimson rivulet had frozen in the process of flowing down Bear's broad back.

"What's it going to be?" Bear demanded. "I say we waste 'em."

Havoc shook his head. "I must go along with Thunder. You need medical attention."

Bear frowned, placed his left hand on the Colt Stainless Steel Officers Model 45 on his left hip, and stalked toward the approaching machines.

"Where do you think you're going?" Havoc asked.

"I'm going to fight."

"Don't be stupid," Havoc chided him.

Bear glowered at the noncom. "Watch your mouth, Macho Man." He continued to walk forward grimly.

Sergeant Havoc and Thunder exchanged glances, then moved to catch up with him.

"Bear, please be reasonable," Thunder said. "The Spirit-in-All-Things does not want you to die needlessly."

"How would you know? Do you have a private line to God?"

"No, of course not," Thunder responded.

"Then don't go talkin' for the Spirit unless the Spirit gives you the green light," Bear said.

"Use your head," Havoc suggested.

"I'd like to pop yours one," Bear muttered.

"Are you blaming yourself for Athena's capture?" Thunder queried. "For ours also?"

Bear halted, his chin drooping. "Athena was nailed tryin'

to buy us time. If I hadn't been hit, she'd still be with us.''

''And if you allow yourself to be killed now, her sacrifice will have been in vain,'' Thunder noted. ''How will she feel when she learns what happened?''

The Clansman sighed and looked at the Flathead. ''Don't you get tired of being right all the time?''

''I'm not right *all* the time.''

''You come closer than anybody I know, except for Blade.''

''Hey. What about me?'' Havoc asked. ''I'm not exactly a slouch in the smarts department.''

Bear snickered. ''Who're you kiddin'? You're as dumb as the rest of us. You make as many mistakes as we do.''

''Blade makes mistakes,'' Havoc said.

''Sometimes,'' Bear admitted. ''But in case you ain't noticed, he doesn't make many. And even when he does, he's the first to admit it.''

''Sounds to me like you've put Blade on a pedestal,'' Sergeant Havoc remarked. ''No one deserves such an honor. No one *living* anyway.''

''Blade's my friend,'' Bear said simply.

The snowmobiles were now less than 200 yards off.

''We have all agreed then?'' Thunder asked. ''We will surrender?''

Sergeant Havoc tossed his M-16 onto the snow. ''We don't have any choice.''

''I guess you're right,'' Bear stated. He pulled his left 45 and dropped the handgun.

Thunder placed his M-16 on the ground and straightened. ''This is the wisest course of action,'' he assured them. ''You'll see.''

''I hope you're right,'' Bear said morosely. ''If you're not, we're as good as dead.''

What in tarnation were those dummies doing?

Until a moment ago, Boone had been elated at the success

of his scheme. There hadn't been one hitch until now. The snowmobiles had departed the garage in single file, and the lieutenant had angled toward a shattered stretch of fence, crossing the east field at 40 miles per hour. With consummate skill, the officer had weaved his machine among the pieces of chain-link fencing and curled strands of barbed wire, then opened the engine up once they were free and clear.

En route to the fence, Boone had looked at the southeast corner of the headquarters and spied Colonel Varney and another soldier. Varney had appeared stupified. He'd flapped his arms and shouted, but the roar of the machines drowned out his words. Boone had smiled and waved his left arm, his right holding the Hombre tight against the lieutenant.

The ride across the Arctic tundra was an experience Boone would never forget. The frigid wind whipped his parka hood, stinging his exposed cheeks and chin. He was forced to squint, wishing he had a pair of goggles. Belying their squat contours and relatively small engines, the snowmobiles attained speeds of 70 miles per hour. The landscape seemed to sweep past in a blur. He gripped the lieutenant's left shoulder and held on for dear life. The sensation was similar to the thrill he felt when galloping across the Dakota plains on his favorite stallion.

Boone paid careful attention to the snowmobile controls, noting the precise manner in which the officer operated the machine. He was surprised to discover the speed was increased or decreased with a mere flick of the right handlebar. He was amazed at the ease of maneuverability, and enjoyed the snowy spray spewing from underneath the snowmobile. Not only did the spray add to the excitement of the ride, but the snow partially obscured his buckskin leggings and boots.

Trailing the three Force members was a simplistic task. Their tracks were imprinted clearly in the snow, bearing due east.

Boone glanced to the rear several times, checking on the rest of the snowmobile squad. The drivers maintained a 20-foot safety gap between each unit, and they followed the lieutenant's path exactly. They were well-trained, a credit to their profession. Boone wondered if any of them had been mystified by the failure to pick up Colonel Varney. If so, and given their extensive training, they would have stayed on the lieutenant's tail and assumed there was a logical reason for not taking the colonel along.

In any event, here they were, within 100 yards of the three Force teammates.

And what the dickens were Havoc, Thunder, and Bear doing? Discarding their weapons, of course!

Boone couldn't believe the testimony of his eyes. He'd gone to all this trouble, put his life on the line, and those ding-a-lings were preparing to surrender!

Now what should he do?

The lieutenant looked at the gunman. "What do you want me to do?"

"Whatever is standard procedure," Boone said. He didn't want to alert the 14 troopers to the fact that things were not as they seemed. When he made his move, he hoped to take them completely off guard.

Sergeant Havoc, Thunder, and Bear were standing with their arms upraised, although the Clansman was holding only his left arm aloft while tucking his right into his side.

The snowmobiles closed to within 20 feet of the Force members. With a deft wave of his left hand, the lieutenant motioned for the drivers to fan out. Alternately swinging to the right or the left, the drivers stopped their machines at five-foot intervals. In 15 seconds Havoc, Thunder, and Bear were surrounded. The seven gunners stood, training their Berettas on the trio.

Boone rested his left hand on his other Hombre. The moment of truth was upon him.

The drivers were turning off their engines.

Boone leaned forward. "Tell your men to drop their guns."

"They'll never do it," the officer said, killing the machine.

"Tell them," Boone insisted.

Sighing, the lieutenant surveyed his men. He opened his mouth to speak.

Expecting the officer to comply, Boone looked at Havoc and realized the noncom had not recognized him.

"Men," the lieutenant said nonchalantly, then unexpectedly dived to the right. "He's one of them! Nail the bastard!"

Boone threw himself backwards and to the left, drawing his left Hombre as he fell onto his back in the snow beside the snowmobile. The nearest gunner, evidently flabbergasted by the turn of events, was gaping at the frontiersman in bewilderment. Boone swiveled both revolvers at the trooper's chest and fired.

The twin booming of the 44 Magnums galvanized everyone as the first gunner was catapulted to the rear by the impact of the heavy slugs.

Boone rolled to the left, toward the next snowmobile, winding up on his back within two feet of the machine, his arms extended, his thumbs tugging on the hammers of the single-action revolvers. He fired twice at separate targets. His left-hand gun sent the snowmobile's driver, who was clutching at a semi-automatic on his hip, into eternity. His right-hand Hombre blasted and bucked, and on the far side of Havoc, Thunder, and Bear, a gunner was felled with a slug through his head.

Sergeant Havoc took several seconds to react to the sudden gunplay. For a fleeting moment he thought the soldiers were fighting amongst themselves, until he spotted Boone's buckskin leggings and perceived the Cavalryman had switched parkas. He was dropping to scoop up his M-16 when the frontiersman sent a round between Thunder and himself, and as his fingers closed on the automatic rifle he flattened and squeezed off a burst at a pair of gunners to the south.

Both gunners were stitched by patterns of crimson dots, and both were flung to the ground, convulsing.

Havoc flipped onto his back and shot one of the gunners to his rear.

Six of the soldiers had died in twice as many seconds, but the lieutenant, two gunners, and six drivers remained.

Havoc twisted on his back and fired at the closest driver, and he saw the man's head snap back as the shot took the HS between the eyes. All of the drivers were drawing semi-automatic pistols. Havoc rolled up against the snowmobile nearest him to provide minimal cover for his body. At such close range, with so many professionals firing at once, he knew the Force members would not come out of the scrape unscathed.

But he never anticipated the tragedy that resulted.

Boone glimpsed the lieutenant rising over the snowmobile they had used, and he snapped a shot at the officer's head. A spray of blood and brains erupted from the lieutenant's cranium, and he sprawled over the machine, a useless pistol in his left hand.

Thunder shoved Bear to the snow and crouched to retrieve his M-16. He pivoted toward a pair of soldiers on a snow-mobile to the south, and he managed to fire at the same millisecond the gunner did. Both went down.

Bear scrambled to the Flathead's side, totally forgetting his own safety, and as he gripped Thunder's right hand a driver fired twice into his body.

Boone and Sergeant Havoc both saw their friends hit; they both were swept by an uncontrollable rage at the same instant; and they both surged to their knees and began firing like men possessed.

Havoc killed the last of the gunners, his rounds perforating the HS man from the crotch to the sternum. The M-16 abruptly went empty, and Havoc felt goose bumps break out on his flesh as the five drivers swung their pistols toward him.

He needn't have worried.

At that moment, as Havoc's life hung in the balance, Boone came to the noncom's rescue, exhibiting the speed and marksmanship for which he was rightfully a legend in the postwar Dakota Territory. His 44 Magnums seemed to fire with the rapidity of a machine gun—*Bam-Bam-Bam-Bam-Bam*—and with each booming of the big revolvers a driver died.

The sudden silence was eerie.

Sergeant Havoc rose. The battle had taken less than 60 seconds, and left in its wake bloody bodies sprawled in attitudes of death on the frigid tundra. Among the motionless were Bear and Thunder.

Boone stood, his eyes on their companions. ''Are they—'' he blurted out, unable to complete the sentence.

Havoc didn't know. He took a deep breath and hurried toward them to find out.

CHAPTER SEVENTEEN

"**Y**ou keep your filthy hands off her!"

"My! How touching. I wonder. . . ."

The acrimonious words filtered into Blade's consciousness through a haze of throbbing agony. Slowly, almost grudgingly, the pain waned. He sensed the presence of many others nearby, and he knew his wrists were shackled. Three guesses by whom.

"You suck-egg bitch!" snapped a familiar raspy tone. "When I'm done with you, you'll wish you'd never been born!"

"Your infantile threats do not concern me in the least," declared the voice of Lalita Pruty. "And if you don't cease your annoying prattle, I'll have Tang shut you up."

"I'd like to see him try!" Grizzly responded belligerently.

Blade opened his gray eyes and scrutinized his vicinity. To his left, also chained to the wall, was the hybrid. Farther to the left, in the center of another wall, was a closed door near which stood six HS troopers and an officer. Athena Morris, her left wrist all bandaged, had been strapped with leather strips to a metal table in the middle of the floor. Her head was positioned in the direction of the door. Near Athena's head hovered the malignant Ms. Pruty. On the far side of the table was Eric Holtmeyer, and on the near side, gazing silently at the Warrior, was Kan Tang. Blade's eyes narrowed as he spotted his backpack and weapons piled on the floor a yard from the Thai.

"Ahhh. You're finally with us again," Lalita stated, looking at the giant.

"I needed to catch up on my beauty sleep," Blade quipped.

"You've rejoined us just in time for the interrogation, beginning with the journalist," Lalita said.

"Don't touch her, Goldmane!" Grizzly warned.

"Goldmane?" Blade repeated.

"That's right. You've missed so much," Pruty said, and walked over to the Warrior. "He's referring to me, to my true name. I'm Janus Goldmane, the Exalted Executioner for the Lords of Kismet."

"The head of this operation," Blade deduced, based on the conversation in the corridor he had overheard.

Goldmane grinned and bowed. "I can't claim all the credit. True, I planned the scope of this operation, but I did so in bedience to my masters. The Lords of Kismet want the Freedom Federation destroyed."

Blade glanced at the Thai, and then recalled the map of Asia and those puzzling red pins. There had also been a red pin at Prudhoe Bay. "Let me guess," he ventured. "These Lords of Kismet control Asia, and they plan to expand their control, to rule every continent on the planet."

Janus Goldmane's mouth slackened. She blinked twice, her forehead creasing, then smiled. "I'm impressed. I'm beginning to understand the reason my masters have placed you at the top of my hit list. How did you know?"

"I was always fond of the old jigsaw puzzles we have at the Home," Blade replied.

Goldmane nodded appreciatively. "You have a brain the equal of your brawn. Most exceptional."

"And you?"

"Me?"

"What qualified you for the post of Exalted Executioner?

Certainly not your good looks.''

Goldmane looked at Holtmeyer, and they both laughed.

"You're priceless," Goldmane said. "And you're right. My elevation to the post was predicated on my previous experience.''

"Do the Lord of Kismet have other executioners working for them?'' Blade asked.

"Hundreds," Goldmane disclosed.

"And you worked your way up through the ranks?"

"I began my career in a Cell in Sofiya, where I was born.''

"A cell?'' Blade said quizzically.

"The Lords of Kismet have established Divisional Cells in eighteen European cities and twelve in Africa. Each Cell is comprised of seven assassins who foment unrest and eradicate the Lords' enemies,'' Goldmane divulged, then paused. "If you're competent, and if you always make your monthly quotas, you can advance through the ranks rather quickly. The Lords are always looking for new talent.''

"You had a quota?'' Blade remarked.

"Novices must kill three designated marks a month.''

"You must have dispatched more than your fair share,'' Blade noted. "Your title means you're the best of the best. And you admitted that the stratagem to reactivate Prudhoe Bay as a means to destroying the Federation was essentially your idea.''

Goldmane smirked. "You'll never guess how the plan works.''

"You plan to mix TX-9 with the crude.''

Goldmane's body appeared to go rigid for a moment, her eyes widening. She expelled a long breath, then shook her head. "Unbelievable. So you know about the TX-9?''

"I don't know everything," Blade said. "How does the TX-9 work?''

"TX-9 is a chemical-warfare toxin initially produced prior to the war. Unlike most chemical weapons, TX-9 doesn't kill those who breathe its vapors. Instead, it deranges their minds,'' Goldmane disclosed. She draped her hands behind her back and strolled toward the head of the metal table. "TX-9 is a brilliant weapon. Entire populations can be subjugated. Countries can be destroyed from within."

"How?" Blade prompted.

"Here's the way it works. TX-9, in its dormant state, can be added at any pont in the refining process. It does not alter the normal chemical properties of oil or gasoline, and is virtually undetectable. The beauty of TX-9 lies in its activation stage. The toxin become active in an internal combustion engine, and it's released into the atmosphere through the exhaust systems of gasoline or diesel-powered cars and trucks."

"Which means," Blade said, "that if California and the Civilized Zone buy your crude and use the oil and gas they refine in their thousands of vehicles, their atmosphere will become polluted with the active TX-9 agent."

"Precisely. TX-9 works on the brain and the central nervous system as a long-term, degenerative poison. It eventually turns those who have inhaled it for any length of time into slobbering idiots or crazed killers. Their brains revert to bestial levels, and their intelligence deteriorates. TX-9 is the ultimate biological weapon."

"Does it pollute the atmosphere permanently?" Athena inquired.

"No," Goldmane answered. "The critical infectious stage lasts approximately twenty-four hours from the moment the active agent is unleashed into the atmosphere. After twenty-four hours, the agent loses its potency." She paused. "Who would want to pollute the atmosphere permanently? What good would a polluted environment do us? This way is better. The active agents in the air are constantly replenished by the emissions from the cars and trucks. Within a year, the internal strife caused by the TX-9 will render California or any other Federation faction incapable of resisting a takeover by my masters."

"I can imagine," Blade said. "There would be mass confusion. The people would be killing one another by the thousands. Panic would keep those unaffected off the streets. The government would find its own troops affected, and the leaders would have no way of maintaining order. The result would be total anarchy.''

Goldmane grinned. ''Then you can appreciate the deviousness of our plan. Once our contaminated crude is being used by the Federation factions, all we'll have to do is sit back and wait for the collapse. Then the Army of the Lords of Kismet can move in and take control.''

''Won't your Army succumb to the TX-9?'' Athena queried.

''No. Our Army personnel will wear gas masks until the atmosphere is cleansed of the active agent, which won't take long once usage of the tainted fuel ceases.''

''What's to stop the California Armed Forces from using gas masks?'' Athena asked.

''Be serious. The government won't have the slightest idea as to the cause of the widespread pandemonium. Their scientists will look everywhere, but the odds of the TX-9 agent being discovered are astronomical.''

''They'll put two and two together,'' Athena said. ''If the mass insanity begins shortly after the tainted fuel is first used, they'll trace the problem to its source.''

''Didn't you hear me earlier? TX-9 is a long-term poison, accumulating in the human body over a period of months until the degenerative process is triggered. California will have been using our crude for over a year before the first outbreaks are reported. No one will suspect our fuel.''

''You've thought of everything,'' Blade said, complimenting the Exalted Executioner.

Goldmane smiled. ''Thank you.''

''But your plan hinges on the Federation making a deal for the Pipeline product,'' Athena noted. ''And Governor Melnick and the rest of the Federation leaders will never agree if something happens to us.''

Goldmane was within a foot of the head of the table. She stepped closer, studying Athena. ''Therein lies the crux of my dilemma. I must arrange a fitting demise for the Force, a death the Federation chiefs will swallow.''

"No way," Athena said.

"Where there's a will, there's always a way," Goldmane asserted. "Your deaths will delay the completion of the deal, but eventually we'll achieve our goal. Eventually the Federation will buy our crude because they can't obtain it anywhere else. They'll be suspicious after we report your deaths, but your mutilated, partially eaten corpses will go a long way towards convincing them that we weren't responsible. They'll postpone accepting our offer for a while. In the end, though, we *will* triumph."

"What reason will you give for our deaths?" Blade inquired.

"A pack of mutated polar bears will finish off the famous Force.''

"Polar bears?"

"We have a dump located two miles west of here, for all of our trash and our garbage. The polar bears hunt for scraps all the time. We'll stake you out and wait for the bears to get done eating," Goldmane divulged.

"If you plan to kill us, why are we in this room?" Athena asked.

Janus Goldmane reached out and stroked Athena's forehead. "Surely a bright journalist like yourself can ascertain our motives? Why do you think I went to all the trouble of having the medics bandage your arm? I didn't want you to bleed to death before the interrogation."

"I won't talk," Athena vowed.

"Oh, really?" Goldmane responded, and snickered. "My dear Ms. Morris, I'm an expert at my craft. I can guarantee you'll talk. You'll gladly reveal everything you know about California's government and military. You'll beg me to ask you questions."

"Never," Athena declared.

"You pathethic, ignorant wretch," Goldmane said. "Your conception of reality is so immature." She opened a drawer and withdrew a narrow, brown plastic case.

"What can we tell you that you don't already know?" Blade interjected.

"Probably nothing," Goldmane admitted, lifting a flap on the plastic case.

"Then why go to all this trouble?" Blade asked.

Goldmane looked at the Warrior and smirked. "What trouble? I *like* conducting torture sessions."

"Torture?" Athena said, aghast.

"What were you expecting? A round of patty-cake?" Goldmane quipped. She slid a six-inch silver lancet from the case.

"No!" Grizzly snarled. "Don't touch her."

Goldmane hefted the thin, two-edged instrument. "These are normally employed during surgery for opening abesses and making fine cuts," she detailed. "But they have other uses."

"Don't!" Grizzly declared.

"One more word out of you, and Tang sends you to dreamland," Goldmane said. She smiled down at Athena. "Where should I begin?"

There was the sound of a commotion in the hall, and a moment later Colonel Varney burst into the chamber. "I don't believe it!" he bellowed.

Goldmane looked at the officer, her features creased by annoyance. "I trust you have a good reason for this intrusion?"

"They didn't take me."

"Who didn't?"

Varney walked toward the Exalted Executioner. "The Snowmobile Unit. I ordered Lieutenant Erdrich to pick me up at the southeast corner of the lodge so I could personally lead the pursuit of Bear and the two other Force members."

"And?" Goldmane prodded.

"And the son of a bitch took off without me," Varney said angrily. "I couldn't believe it. I saw one of his men wave."

"Erdich is usually efficient," Goldmane remarked. "Why would he fail to carry out a direct order?"

"Beats the hell out of me. They drove from the garage to the east fence without bothering to pick me up," Varney stated. "I've tried to raise them on the radio, but they haven't replied."

Goldmane tapped the flat lancet on the table. "I don't like this. One of the Force members is still unaccounted for."

"So? What can one man do?" Varney responded.

"Plenty," Goldmane said. "I want you to check out the Snowmobile garage."

"May I ask why?"

"Just a hunch. Attend to it personally and report back here."

Colonel Varney saluted. "As you command, Executioner." He pivoted and hastened out, slamming the door after him.

Goldmane peered at the Warrior. "What are you up to?"

"Us?" Blade said innocently.

"Don't insult my intelligence," Goldmane replied. "The Force was sent here for just this purpose, wasn't it?"

"What purpose?"

Goldmane's voice hardened. "To create discord at Prudhoe Bay. To commit an act that would draw us out, make us reveal our true colors."

"We came here on a peaceful mission," Blade said.

"Is that why Bear shot one of my men without provocation?" Goldmane demanded.

"He had provocation," Athena informed the Executioner.

"What?" Goldmane queried skeptically.

"Your men insulted him," Athena said.

Goldmane scowled. "A lousy insult started all of this?"

"Yes."

"I don't believe you," Goldmane stated, and leaned over the table. "Which finger?"

"Which finger?"

"Which finger should I start with?" Goldmane asked.

''Leave her alone!'' Grizzly interjected, straining against his chains.

Goldmane looked at the Thai. ''I've had about enough of that fool. You know what to do.''

Tang nodded and strolled to within a yard of the mutant.

Grizzly's lips curled over his teeth. ''If I could get a hold of you—''

The Thai never uttered a word. His right foot swept up and in, striking Grizzly's cheek with a distinct thud. Twice more he flicked his calloused foot, connecting on the mutant's chin. He stepped back when Grizzly slumped down, barely sentient, eyelids fluttering.

''Now for some fun,'' Goldmane said, the lancet gleaming in the light. She moved to Athena's right side and gripped the journalist's middle finger. ''This should do nicely.''

''No!'' Athena cried, bucking and pitching, unable to move more than an inch due to the leather restraints. ''No!''

Goldmane touched the tip of the lancet to the end of Athena's finger, just under the nail. ''Pay attention, my dear. You're about to discover the true meaning of pain.''

CHAPTER EIGHTEEN

Blade saw the cruel grin on Janus Goldmane's wicked countenance, he saw the blood flowing from under Athena's nail as Goldmane inserted the razor tip, and he saw Kan Tang turn toward the table to view the torture. All eyes were on Athena Morris as she opened her mouth to scream.

No one was looking at him.

He tensed and extended his arms as far as they would reach, as far as the chains would allow, pitting his bulging muscles against the steel manacles. His triceps, biceps, and torso rippled and solidified in stark relief, every sinew seemingly chiseled from stone. Gritting his teeth, he felt sweat break out on his forehead and arms. The exertion was tremendous, but he couldn't afford to slack off for a second.

Athena vented her anguish in a shriek.

Goldmane laughed.

Blade lowered his head and strained for all he was worth. One of the troopers was staring at him, but he didn't care. He applied every iota of his prodigious strength to the task at hand. His shoulders and upper arms began to hurt, but he disregarded the discomfort.

"You're not as tough as you thought you were," Goldmane taunted Athena, easing the lancet from under the fingernail.

"You monster!" Athena exclaimed.

"That's what my mother always claimed," Goldmane stated calmly. "She was the first person I ever killed."

Athena's right hand pulsated with agony. She tried to wrench her arms loose, but the leather held her fast.

Goldmane playfully jabbed the lancet into Athena's palm. "Have you ever seen the skin peeled from a human hand?"

Blade observed Athena go chalk white, and he renewed his silent struggle. He closed his eyes, his abdominal muscles tightening, his arms quivering. You can do it! he told himself. You've broken chains before. A chain was only as sturdy as its weakest link, and every chain contained a weak link. Sooner or later, something had to give.

Had to.

And did.

The sweat was streaming from his pores, his face was a beet red, his veins protruding, when there came two loud snapping noises, and suddenly he was stumbling toward the metal table, off-balance, but free! His elation lasted a fraction of a second as he realized Kan Tang was five feet to his left and already rotating.

Janus Goldmane had glanced up at the sounds. "I want him taken alive!" she directed.

Blade checked his momentum within two yards of the table and crouched. The troopers were hurrying toward him from near the door. Eric Holtmeyer was coming around the far side of the table. Tang had adopted the cat stance. And Goldmane was eyeing him disdainfully, as if he was no more than a minor nuisance to be summarily squashed underfoot. Six feet away, at the base of the table, were his weapons and backpack, with his Bowies resting on the very top of the pile.

The Exalted Executioner abruptly stepped between the Warrior and the weapons. "What are you waiting for, Tang? Take him!" she snapped impatiently.

The Thai closed on his adversary.

Blade straightened and backpedaled. He knew the power in Tang's kicks, and he wasn't about to let another one land. The manacles were still attached to his wrists. Six inches of chain dangled from his right forearm, eight from his left.

With astonishing swiftness, Kan Tang moved toward the Warrior in an odd, shuffling gait, his naked, malletlike feet never leaving the floor.

Blade swung his left arm in an arc, the chain whipping out and narrowly missing the Oriental's face.

Tang halted, focusing on the chains.

Beyond the Thai, Grizzly was stirring, shaking his head to clear the cobwebs and clenching his fists.

"Take him!" Goldmane reiterated.

Blade's eyes flicked around the room, noting positions. The seven soldiers were five yards from the door, waiting with keen anticipation for the Thai to obey. Eric Holtmeyer was at the far corner of the table. Goldmane blocked the weapons.

No doubt about it.

He needed to even the odds.

With the thought came action, and Blade unexpectedly charged forward, whipping his arms from right to left, flailing away with the chains.

Tang attempted to block a blow. There was a sharp crack as the steel connected with one of his knuckles, and he wisely retreated, giving ground rapidly, effortlessly.

Blade pressed his advantage, lashing the chains back and forth, intending to drive the Thai past the head of the table. He came abreast of Janus Goldmane, who was standing smugly near the backpack and his weapons, and he took a stride in her direction and arced his right arm to the right.

The tactic caught Goldmane napping. She fell backwards as the chain clipped her on the mouth, landing on her side on the table, on top of Athena's legs. Her left hand reflexively pressed to her mouth and came away bloody. Both her lips were split, her upper gum was torn, and one of her top teeth was loose. Enraged, she straightened, spitting more blood.

Blade saw Kan Tang's eyes dart toward Goldmane, and the Thai's features visibly hardened. Why? The Warrior kept swinging, mulling the implications. Tang was one of the top martial artists in the world, trained to suppress all emotion during the heat of combat. So why would the Thai become furious over Goldmane's injury? Surely they—

Wait a minute!

Holtmeyer wasn't the head of this operation. Goldmane was. Eric Holtmeyer had pretended to be the brains of the outfit, as part of Goldmane's cover. Was it possible, then, that everything Holtmeyer had said about himself actually applied to Goldmane? If so, then Goldmane had discovered the Thai in Kamphaeng Phet, not Holtmeyer. If so, Tang was Goldmane's personal bodyguard, not Holtmeyer's. And if so, then there might be more to their relationship than that of employer and employee. Perhaps they were lovers.

Which gave him the opening he needed.

Janus Goldmane was leaning on the metal table, her left hand over her mouth, crimson trickling from her chin.

Blade deliberately halted and turned toward her, taking a step, pretending to be about to attack her again, hoping Kan Tang would take the bait.

The Thai reacted instantly, gliding to the right, skirting the Warrior and darting to Goldmane, positioning himself in front of her to serve as her defender, to ward off Blade's anticipated assault.

But Blade was already springing toward his real goal: Grizzly. In two mighty bounds he reached Grizzly's side, his eyes on the mutant's as he gripped the chain securing Grizzly's right arm. No words were necessary. Grizzly perceived his intention intuitively. Blade braced his left foot on the wall and wrenched on the chain, both of his brawny arms swelling as his muscles expanded.

"Stop them!" Eric Holtmeyer shouted.

In response the troopers started forward.

The chain Blade was holding quivered as Grizzly threw his weight and strength into the struggle. The manacles were designed to restrain an average man; the steel chains could easily withstand the strength of a normal prisoner. But neither Blade nor Grizzly were normal. The Warrior was a seven-foot giant, a titan with a corresponding physique. Grizzly was a genetically created hybrid endowed with the vitality of his namesake. Singly they were formidable. Together they were devastating. With a brittle crack the chain parted.

Grizzly spun toward the wall, gripped the chain binding his left arm with both hands, and heaved.

"Damn it! Stop them!" Holtmeyer yelled.

The soldiers were closing rapidly, unslinging their Berettas as they ran.

Kan Tang, realizing he had been duped, charged.

Blade moved to meet the Thai, adopting the horse stance, his arms bent at the elbows and protecting his stomach and chest, his fingers formed into tiger claws.

Tang never slowed down. He tore into the Warrior with the fury of a hurricane, his legs spinning, raining a series of kicks on the giant, seeking to overwhelm Blade quickly. Each kick was blocked, every sweep was countered.

Although he was holding his own, temporarily at least, Blade knew he was no match for the Thai in the mastery of the martial arts. Never before, in all his years as a Warrior and during his association with the Force, had he met anyone as supremely skilled as the Thai kick boxer. Two men came close to matching Tang; one was a Warrior by the name of Rikki-Tikki-Tavi and the other was Sergeant Havoc. But even those two did not possess hands and feet seemingly composed of solid bone. The Thai's blows were brutal, jarring Blade every time.

Tang redoubled his onslaught, mixing hand strikes with his kicks.

Blade sidestepped a heel aimed at his right knee, then used a circular block to deflect a fist flashing at his neck. The Thai executed a left roundhouse punch at the Warrior's temple, and Blade blocked with his right forearm. Tang pivoted and tried to deliver a leopard paw blow to Blade's solar plexus, but the Warrior used a cutting forearm chop to deflect the Thai.

A feral roar rent the chamber.

Blade skipped back several feet and looked around.

The seven HS troopers had reached Grizzly just as the last chain broke, and the mutant was tearing into them with unbridled ferocity. His claws fully extended, Grizzly had dispatched two of the soldiers and was gutting a third. The troopers were foolishly endeavoring to pin the mutant's arms.

"I've changed my mind!" Janus Goldmane declared, wiping the back of her right hand across her mouth. "I want them dead! Both of them!"

Eric Holtmeyer smiled and pulled an Uzi from under his coat.

"What are we looking for, sir?" the private asked.

"Just search the garage," Colonel Varney snapped, gesturing impatiently.

The officer and four HS stood outside the open corrugated metal door to the Snowmobile Unit garage. Obeying promptly, the quartet fanned out and walked inside.

Colonel Varney turned and surveyed the east field and the fence beyond. He experienced a nagging feeling that he had overlooked something important, but what?

"Colonel! Over here!"

Varney rotated and saw a trooper near a cluster of crates. "What is it?" he demanded.

"You need to see for yourself, sir."

Colonel Varney sighed and walked to the crates. His eyes narrowed at the sight of an HS slumped on the floor. How had this happened? Nearby were three clues; a Beretta, an M-16, and *a green parka*.

"The damn Force," Varney muttered.

"Sir?" the trooper queried.

Varney knelt and felt for the man's pulse. "He's still alive."

The other three soldiers were approaching.

"I want two of you to take this man to the infirmary right away," Varney announced, rising.

A pair of troopers immediately hoisted their unconscious comrade and departed.

"Colonel!" declared the trooper who had found the man.

"What?"

"Snowmobiles, sir," the trooper said, nodding to the east.

Colonel Varney spun, his ears registering the distinctive growl of the specialized machines as he did. Speeding toward the headquarters building were two snowmobiles.

"Where are the rest, sir?" the trooper asked.

"I don't know," Varney replied, putting his hands on his hips. Had the three Force members wiped out the remainder of the Snowmobile Unit? He was beginning to believe that Goldmane had seriously underestimated the Force. The bitch always was cocky and overconfident.

The snowmobiles sped through the gap in the fence and raced toward the garage. Both drivers wore white uniforms and white parkas, but behind each driver sat slumped a figure in a green parka.

"They've bagged two of the Force," Colonel Varney declared happily.

Their engines whining, the snowmobiles were swiftly nearing their destination. The drivers were bundled in their parkas to ward off the brisk, chill wind.

"Help them with the prisoners," Varney directed his men.

The lead driver, now within 50 feet of the garage entrance, stared at the officer and the two soldiers for a moment, then angled his snowmobile to the right slightly. He braked abruptly, slewing the machine the last ten feet and sliding to a grating halt on the garage floor with the rear of the snowmobile pointing at Varney and the privates.

Seconds later the second machine coasted to a stop just inside the entranceway.

"Well done, men," Colonel Varney said, complimenting them, starting toward the nearest snowmobile.

The driver was rising and turning, and as he faced the three

HS he exposed the Colt Officers Model 45's he held, one clasped in each hand.

Varney drew up short, recognizing the features framed by the parka hood. "Havoc!"

Sergeant Havoc wagged the 45's at the privates. "Lower the Berettas to the floor slowly."

They hesitated.

"Do it now!" commanded a new voice, and Boone walked toward them from the snowmobile, his Hombres cocked, his fingers on the triggers.

The soldiers were holding their Berettas at waist height. They looked from Havoc to Boone, then eased their weapons down.

"Smart move," Havoc said. "Now lie on the floor with your nose to the cement."

They complied.

"Now you," Boone said, stepping over to the colonel.

"You'll never get away with this," Varney asserted confidently.

"Watch us," Boone stated, and slugged the officer on the chin.

Varney reeled and tottered backwards.

The Cavalryman, his lips a thin line, stalked up to the colonel and slammed his right Hombre across Varney's mouth. Teeth crunched, blood gushed, and the officer dropped like the proverbial rock. Boone glanced at Sergeant Havoc. "Get going."

"Why don't you go? More of these HS creeps might show up here."

"This isn't the time to argue," Boone snapped. "Thunder and Bear are barely alive. I've told you where to find the Communications Room, and we both know that you're better with electronic equipment than I am. Get there, use our frequency, and send out an SOS. General Gallagher will be monitoring the transmission. Tell him to send in the VTOLs pronto."

Havoc nodded and hurried toward the inner door to the

corridor. "Okay. But I advise you to lower the garage door. I'll send the SOS, then hunt for Blade, Grizzly, and Athena. Hold the fort until I return."

"No problem."

Sergeant Havoc disappeared into the hall.

"If either of you buzzards move, you're dead," Boone promised the privates, then dashed to the chains suspended on the left side of the corrugated metal. Holstering his left Hombre, he used his left hand to tug on both chains, testing to determine which chain would allow the door to descend. Rattling and clanking, the door settled rapidly.

The privates were imitating bumps on a log.

Boone walked to the snowmobile he'd driven and gazed at Thunder. The Flathead was barely breathing. He grimaced and looked at Bear. Both of them required prompt, expert medical attention, the kind only a hospital in California could provide. Havoc would radio for a pair of medics to be sent with the VTOLs, and a lot would depend on the ability of those medics to keep Thunder and Bear alive until the Hurricane reached California.

If they . . .

He couldn't bring himself to finish the thought. Instead, he scrutinized the HS uniform he was wearing. Havoc had advocated both of them donning complete uniforms, not just the parka. Boone had reluctantly agreed, but he felt uncomfortable in the white outfit. A woman in Dakota, a lady he admired highly, had constructed his buckskins from scratch, and he would have a dickens of a time explaining their loss.

Which, all things considered, certainly qualified as the very least of his worries.

Kan Tang arrowed toward Blade and launched a terrific sweep kick with his right leg.

Distracted by the sight of Eric Holtmeyer unlimbering the Uzi, Blade failed to counter the kick. A lancing spasm racked his left thigh and he tottered backwards. The Thai had gone for his leg! He tried to lower his arms to deflect a second kick.

Too late.

The calloused ball of Tang's left foot struck the Warrior on the left leg, inches above the knee.

Blade crumpled, falling onto his right knee, his left leg momentarily paralyzed. He realized incapacitating his leg was part of the Thai's strategy; Tang wanted him incapable of evading those potentially lethal kicks and hand blows. Blade assumed a defensive posture, his hands in the Crane Style.

Tang shifted into the Bow and Arrow stance.

Janus Goldmane was laughing, expecting her bodyguard to end the fray swiftly.

Eric Holtmeyer was standing within a foot of the pile of Blade's gear, the Uzi barrel lowered, watching intently.

Grizzly and the troopers were a whirling jumble of claws, survival knives, and Berettas.

Blade sensed the moment of truth was at hand. With his left leg out of commission, the Thai would easily break through his defenses and kill him. Tang, Goldmane, and Holtmeyer all believed he was trapped, on the verge of annihilation, unable to move, pinned to the spot by his injured leg. They undoubtedly believed he would make his last stand where he was, but they were doomed to be disillusioned. Blade's lips compressed as he girded the muscles in his right leg.

Every Warrior was subjected to intensive training in preparation for his or her career: firearms training, martial-arts training, explosives training, and training in the psychology of a Warrior. Fundamental principles were inculcated rigorously. Foremost among them was the most basic of adages related to the art of war: The best defense is *always* a good offense. Consequently, at the very moment when his enemies considered him relatively helpless, at the moment when they thought the battle was all over except for the trifling technicality of his demise, Blade took them completely unawares by doing the totally unexpected.

He attacked.

Blade threw his body toward the metal table, toward his

gear, rolling rapidly, spinning as fast as he could, hoping Tang would take a split second to react and come after him, confident he would present a difficult target. His eyes were locked on his weapons. Instead of slowing as he neared the pile, he rolled into it and over, grabbing his Bowies as he revolved, and in the next instant he was flat on his back, his knives in his hands, staring up at an astounded Eric Holtmeyer.

Holtmeyer's amazement was short-lived, replaced an instant later by horrified agony as the Warrior speared both Bowies into his groin.

"Nooooo!" Janus Goldmane wailed.

Kan Tang was hurtling toward the Warrior.

Blade's arms rippled as he jerked them down and out, using the Bowies for leverage as he literally tossed Holtmeyer into the Thai's path. He held tight to the hilts, wrenching the big knives out as Holtmeyer sailed from him, then surged erect as Tang and Holtmeyer tumbled to the floor. Sensation was returning slowly to his left leg.

Goldmane suddenly whirled and pressed the lancet to Athena's throat.

Blade froze.

"Stop right there!" Goldmane warned. "I'll cut her! You know I will!"

Athena looked at the Warrior in vulnerable desperation.

"Drop your Bowies!" Goldmane ordered.

Blade hesitated.

"Drop them, damn you!"

Frowning, Blade tilted his arms and started to loosen his grip.

Goldmane smiled wickedly. "That's a good boy," she said, baiting him.

Kan Tang was rising four feet away. Holtmeyer was lying on his left side, doubled over, clutching his genitals, crimson spurting between his fingers, his features conveying sheer torment.

Blade was about to let go. He saw the razor edge of the

lancet gouging Athena's flesh, and he choked back a swelling rage, wishing he could vent his frustration by pounding Janus Goldmane to a pulp.

Someone else beat him to the punch.

A furry, blood-spattered form flashed into view from the left, pouncing on Goldmane from behind and seizing her forearms. Before Janus could finish off Athena, she was lifted bodily into the air and flung to the floor, landing hard within a yard of the Thai. Grizzly took a stride toward them, his gory claws extended, his lips curling back from his tapered teeth.

Goldmane scrambled to her feet. She reached into the folds of her fur coat and extracted a large, double-edged knife that gleamed in the light.

"I was hoping you'd put up a fight," Grizzly hissed.

"I wasn't appointed as the Exalted Executioner simply because of my wits," Goldmane stated harshly, lowering her body into a back stance, the knife in her right hand, her left in a leopard paw.

Grizzly glanced at Blade. "She's all mine. You can have the ballet dancer." So saying, he rushed at the executioner, his claws spearing at her face.

Goldmane adroitly blocked the mutant's initial swings.

Blade closed on Kan Tang, but the Thai unexpectedly turned toward the battling pair and performed a vaulting kick, his left foot connecting with Grizzly's shoulder and knocking the hybrid aside. The Thai came down in front of Janus Goldmane, facing the giant and the mutant, then glanced once at the Exalted Executioner.

Janus nodded, and bolted for the door. Tang backpedaled beside her, never dropping his guard, protecting her retreat.

Blade and Grizzly headed in pursuit.

"Don't let her escape!" Athena cried.

They tried. Both the Warrior and the hybrid attempted to force their way past the Thai and reach Goldmane, but Tang checked them every time. The Oriental's hand and feet battered Blade's Bowies and Grizzly's claws away with graceful, deceptive ease. Six feet from the door Tang halted, holding his ground, compelling them to swing around him if they wanted to catch Goldmane.

Blade darted to the right, and he was drawing his right arm back to throw the Bowie when Janus Goldmane snatched the doorknob, flung the door open, and raced into the corridor, drawing the door shut after her.

Damn!

"She'll bring reinforcements!" Grizzly snapped, crouching and glaring at the Thai.

Tang made no move to try and flee.

"Free Athena!" Blade ordered, swiveling toward Tang.

"But—" Grizzly began to object.

"Do it!" Blade directed. "We've got to get out of here. Leave Tang for me."

Grizzly turned and sprinted toward the metal table.

The Thai gazed at the Warrior fearlessly. His hands dropped to his sides and he bowed.

Surprised by the compliment, Blade returned the honor, then slid his Bowies into their sheaths.

Tang's eyes narrowed slightly.

"It's just us now," Blade said, and raised his hands.

In a rare break in his inscrutable expression, Kan Tang smiled, squatted, and waded into the Warrior.

Blade refused to be budged, and he refused to limit himself to his martial-arts skills as he countered the Thai's first strikes. He was also an accomplished boxer and adept at wrestling. His reflexes were honed to a preternatural degree, and there were only a handful of people on the entire planet with more combat experience. If anyone should be able to hold their own against Kan Tang, he should. He was determined to finish the fight by relying on his proficiency and his instincts.

Man to man.

No holds barred.

With no more interruptions.

And there were only two witnesses to the colossal clash.

At the metal table, Grizzly sliced the last of the leather restraints, relaxed his fingers to allow his claws to retract, and scooped Athena into his arms. For a moment they regarded one another tenderly, and then he pivoted toward the doorway. "I've got to help the Big Guy," he said, and began to lower her legs to the floor.

"No," Athena said, watching the fight.

"No?"

"Didn't you see Blade's face a minute ago?"

"I was too busy cutting you loose."

"Trust me. He wants to take care of Tang himself," Athena stated.

"Are you sure?"

"Would I lie to the one I love?"

Engrossed in the struggle near the door, Grizzly merely mumbled a careless "No." He was trying to follow the ebb and flow of the battle, concerned for Blade's safety. He could see the Warrior and the Thai trading countless blows, each one delivering a veritable rain of punches, chops, and kicks. Some of their movements were too quick for the eye to follow. Grizzly marveled at the contest. Even he would be hard pressed to match the silent ferocity the two men displayed. He saw Tang land a kick to Blade's right shin, and the Warrior retaliated by ramming his massive left fist against the Thai's chin.

Tang rocked backwards.

Blade drove his right fist into the Thai's stomach, doubling his foe in half. Before Tang could straighten, Blade kneed him in the face.

Kan Tang went flying, landing on his back and immediately surging erect, blood trickling from his nostrils.

The Warrior and the Thai circled one another.

"I still think I should help . . ." Grizzly said, then stopped. His eyes widened and he looked at Athena. "What did you just say?"

"Who, me?"

"Yeah. What did you say a second ago?"

"I don't remember," she said, grinning impishly. Then she sobered, her eyes roving his features. "God help me. I said that I love you."

Grizzly's lips moved, but no words issued forth. He closed his eyes and hugged her. "Athena," he said huskily.

"You pick a hell of a time to become romantic," she quipped.

"I don't . . ." Grizzly blurted out, opening his eyes again and staring at her. "The torture must have warped your brain."

Athena abruptly glanced at the combatants.

Kan Tang and Blade were tangling once more. The Thai feinted with his left foot, then arced his right at the giant's head. Blade endeavored to step backwards, but the ball of Tang's foot slammed into his chin. He tottered, and Tang pressed his advantage by flicking a kick at the Warrior's left hip.

Blade fell to his knees.

"No!" Athena cried.

Grizzly lowered her feet to the floor. "Stay here," he said, and took a pace toward the fighters.

Kan Tang was raising his right arm for a sword-hand chop to the Warrior's throat.

Grizzly knew he couldn't reach them in time, and his gut tightened in dread at the thought of Blade's jugular being crushed. He needed a distraction, something to divert the Thai's attention, and he got one from an unexpected source.

A series of muffled explosions rocked the headquarters building. The walls shook and the floor wobbled violently.

Kang Tang looked up for an instant.

Which was all the opening Blade required. He came off his knees, his powerful thighs propelling him up and in, his right arm lashing in a tight curve from left to right, his hand flat and his fingers rigid. The outer edge of his hand slashed into the Thai's neck.

Kan Tang's head snapped back, then lolled forward, his chin touching his chest. With a monumental effort he lifted his head and stared at the Warrior in stark astonishment. He grunted, gasped, and pitched forward.

Blade stepped aside. He was breathing heavily, sweat caking his brow.

Grizzly and Athena hastened toward him.

"Are you okay?" Athena asked.

Blade took a deep breath and nodded. "What was that blast?" he queried raggedly.

"Beats me," Grizzly said.

"We'd better get out of here," Blade said. "Grab some weapons."

But the door was hurled open before any of them could move.

CHAPTER NINETEEN

Boone heard the pounding of approaching footsteps and leveled his Hombres at the corridor door. Bear and Thunder were still on the snowmobiles. The pair of privates and Colonel Varney were lying on the floor near the workbench, bound tightly with black tape.

"Don't shoot!" called out a familiar voice as the door was opened, and in walked Sergeant Havoc. "We're the good guys." Blade, Athena, and Grizzly, all wearing ill-fitting white parkas, followed.

"How are Thunder and Bear?" the Warrior demanded, crossing to the snowmobiles. His parka appeared to be two sizes too small.

"They're still out," Boone answered. "Bear's been hit three times, once in the right shoulder, twice in the chest. He's lost a lot of blood, but he's breathing."

"And Thunder?" Blade asked.

"He took two shots below the left shoulder. Neither are close to the heart, and he hasn't bled as badly as Bear."

Blade frowned and pounded his right fist against his left palm.

"You can't blame yourself," Athena said.

"I can if I want to," Blade responded testily, then glanced at each of them. "All right. Here's the way we stand. Sergeant Havoc contacted General Gallagher, and the Hurricanes are on their way, but they won't arrive for a few hours. We're to rendezvous with the VTOLs a quarter of a mile to the east of this building. Havoc and Boone will drive the snowmobiles. Grizzly, Athena, and I will follow on foot."

"The HS troopers will be on our tail," Boone predicted.

"Maybe not," Blade said.

"Oh?"

Sergeant Havoc cleared his throat. "When I got to the Communications Room, I found two HS there. They must have found the one you shot. So I took the clowns out and radioed General Gallagher, then went looking for these three. Along the way I lobbed a couple of grenades into the Command Center." He paused and chuckled. "That should keep the troopers busy for a while."

"So let's head out," Blade directed.

Boone and Havoc opened the corrugated metal door, then combined to push their snowmobiles onto the snow.

Blade surveyed the east field, surprised there wasn't an HS in sight.

"It's cold out there," Athena remarked. "Can't we stay in the garage for an hour or so."

"No," Blade stated.

"Think of how the weather will affect Thunder and Bear," she mentioned.

"Would you prefer a squad or two of HS soldiers?" Blade responded. "If the troopers find us here, we won't be able to hold them off *and* safeguard Bear and Thunder adequately." He pointed eastward. "We head out and wait for the Hurricanes."

"Whatever you say, Big Guy," Grizzly said.

The snowmobiles sputtered to life.

Blade waved his arm to the east.

Sergeant Havoc accelerated slowly with Boone right

behind. They started across the field at under five miles an hour.

Trudging wearily, Blade, Athena, and Grizzly followed.

"I'm surprised we haven't seen Goldmane," Athena commented. "I was certain she'd be back with reinforcements."

"Maybe she's reorganizing the HS," Blade speculated. "If she's smart, she's on her way to Deadhorse Airfield to catch a flight out of here."

"Do you think we've seen the last of her?" Athena inquired.

"I doubt it," Blade said.

"I want to run into her again," Grizzly interjected. "I owe her."

"The Lords of Kismet will undoubtedly launch another attack on the Federation," Blade predicted. "When they do, Goldmane will be involved."

"One good thing came out of this mess," Athena said, and smiled at the mutant.

Grizzly reached out, then caught himself. Her left wrist was bandaged from the dog assault, and her right was held close to her waist, her middle finger swollen and coated in crimson.

"I won't break," Athena said.

"We need to get you to a hospital," Grizzly declared.

"Me? Thunder and Bear require medical attention as soon as possible, but I can hold out longer."

"You need medical attention too," Blade stated. "Your finger and wrist could become infected if we don't have them taken care of."

"Listen to the man," Grizzly said. "He makes sense."

"Which is why I'm sending Bear, Thunder, and you back before the rest of us," Blade informed them.

"What?" Athena responded.

"Havoc radioed for medics," Blade explained. "They'll be on board one of the Hurricanes. Bear, Thunder, and you will immediately return with them to California while the rest of us take care of business at this end.''

"I want to stay with Grizzly," Athena protested.

"Does she have to?" Grizzly asked plaintively.

"Sorry, Blade said, and mustered a smile. "I know the two of you are hot to trot at the moment, but you'll have to cool your hormones for a spell."

"Hot to trot?" Athena repeated, and snorted.

"It's just like I've always said," Grizzly declared. "This guy never makes any sense."

EPILOGUE

The Hurricane banked and thundered higher into the azure sky, while to its rear the headquarters building exploded, sending a monumental fireball thousands of feet skyward.

"Beautiful!" Captain Peter Laslo shouted. "Just beautiful."

Prudhoe Bay was in flames. Every major building, the Operations Centers, and Central Power Supply, and more were in ruins. A section of pipleine was a twisted wreck. Black smoke billowed above the tundra.

"Those cluster bombs do the trick every time," Laslo gloated.

"So much for the Lords of Kismet and their plan to conquer us," Boone commented. "Right, Blade?"

The Warrior, sitting across from the frontiersman in one of the two seats behind the pilot's, did not respond. He was staring thoughtfully out his side of the canopy.

"Blade?" Boone said.

"What?" Blade replied, looking at the Cavalryman.

"Are you all right?"

"Fine," Blade responded.

"What were you thinking about?"

"What else? Bear and Thunder."

"They're tough," Sergeant Havoc chimed in from the seat to the rear of Boone's. "They'll pull through. The medics were optimistic."

"Their vital signs were stable," Grizzly added. He was sitting behind the Warrior.

"I don't want to lose them," Blade stated.

"None of us do," Boone concurred.

"I just hope Athena is okay," Grizzly mentioned.

"What's the story with the two of you?" Havoc asked.

Grizzly glanced at the noncom. "How do you mean?"

"I couldn't help but notice that the two of you were sort of . . . friendly," Havoc remarked.

"So?" Grizzly growled.

Sergeant Havoc shrugged. "No skin off my nose."

"It'll be more than your skin if you don't watch yourself," Grizzly warned.

"Here we go again," Boone said happily, then came to the noncom's rescue. "Say, what's with those?" he asked, and jerked his left thumb toward the pile of camouflage uniforms and green parkas stacked on the rear seat.

"General Gallagher probably sent them," Sergeant Havoc guessed. "I told him that some of us would be wearing HS uniforms when the Hurricanes arrived. I didn't want one of the pilots to get trigger happy. Gallagher must have decided to send replacement duds along. He's always been a stickler for wearing a proper uniform."

"We can change on the way home," Boone said.

"Forget it," Grizzly declared, removing his confiscated white parka. "I've learned my lesson. I'm never wearing clothes again."

Captain Laslo's voice crackled on the intercom. "Blade?"

The Warrior raised his head. "Yes?"

"I've used the last of my bombs and all of my rockets," Laslo disclosed. "I still have two Sidewinders left, but we might need those on the way back. So what do you say? Do we head for home?"

Blade looked at the eager faces of his men. "Take us home, Peter."

The Hurricane arced to the south.

"Can I ask you guys a question?" Grizzly inquired politely.

Boone twisted in his seat. "Sure. What is it?"

"Have you ever been on a date?"

Boone glanced at Havoc, then at the mutant. "A date?"

"Yeah. You know. A date with a woman," Grizzly stated, sounding annoyed at having to elaborate.

"I've been on a few," Boone admitted.

"And I've been on my share," Sergeant Havoc said. "Why?"

"How'd you ask the woman?"

"What do you mean?" Havoc responded.

"Did you take flowers? Sweets? Write a poem for the occasion? What?"

"Write a poem?" Sergeant Havoc declared, and laughed. "You've got to be kidding. Only ninnies like poetry."

Grizzly's eyes narrowed. "*I* like poetry."

"You do?" Havoc asked in disbelief, and laughed even harder.

Boone could see Grizzly's hands clenching and unclenching. He opted to intervene and prevent a flare-up of the mutant's temper. "If you want to ask a woman on a date," he advised, "just walk up to her and do it. It's as simple as that."

"That easy, huh?"

Sergeant Havoc was snickering and shaking his head.

Grizzly turned toward the noncom. "Do you mind if I ask you another question?"

Havoc grinned. "Be my guest."

"Do you think you could survive a fall from seven thousand feet?"